P9-DWH-158

Advance Praise for *The Thread Collectors*

"*The Thread Collectors* is a gift—not only for lovers of historical fiction, but for readers everywhere who search for hidden truths behind the facts we think we know. Like the fearless, sensitive, and resourceful women they write about, Edwards and Richman have stitched together a glorious tapestry of resilience, survival, friendship, and love. This is a Civil War story unlike any other—a story readers will treasure from the very first page."

—Lynda Cohen Loigman, *USA TODAY* bestselling author of *The Two-Family House*

"In their transfixing novel, Edwards and Richman offer a vibrant tapestry of characters whose lives have been shattered by slavery and civil war, yet find a tenuous connection in scraps of fabric that symbolize hope, love, even escape. Both heartbreaking and thrilling… I dare you to put this novel down as it hurtles toward its riveting conclusion."

—Fiona Davis, *New York Times* bestselling author of *The Magnolia Palace*

"*The Thread Collectors* is a brilliant story brimming with unexpected friendships and family ties that fed my soul. Historically sound and beautifully stitched, it is a story that will stay with you long after the last page is turned."

—Sadeqa Johnson, internationally bestselling author of *Yellow Wife*

"*The Thread Collectors* is the original story of a Black woman in New Orleans and a Jewish woman in New York, both of whom are fighting for the cause of freedom and Union victory through their needlework during the Civil War. Their lives converge in unexpected ways in an unforgettable story of female strength, hope and friendship. This collaborative work is magnificent—a true revelation!"

—Pam Jenoff, *New York Times* bestselling author of *The Woman with the Blue Star*

Also by Alyson Richman

The Mask Carver's Son
The Rhythm of Memory
The Last Van Gogh
The Lost Wife
The Garden of Letters
The Velvet Hours
The Secret of Clouds

THREAD COLLECTORS

a novel

SHAUNNA J. EDWARDS
and ALYSON RICHMAN

GRAYDON
HOUSE

If you purchased this book without a cover you should be aware that this book is stolen property. It was reported as "unsold and destroyed" to the publisher, and neither the author nor the publisher has received any payment for this "stripped book."

GRAYDON
HOUSE®

Recycling programs
for this product may
not exist in your area.

ISBN-13: 978-1-525-89978-2

The Thread Collectors

Copyright © 2022 by Shaunna Jones and Alyson Richman

All rights reserved. No part of this book may be used or reproduced in any manner whatsoever without written permission except in the case of brief quotations embodied in critical articles and reviews.

This is a work of fiction. Names, characters, places and incidents are either the product of the author's imagination or are used fictitiously. Any resemblance to actual persons, living or dead, businesses, companies, events or locales is entirely coincidental.

Graydon House
22 Adelaide St. West, 41st Floor
Toronto, Ontario M5H 4E3, Canada
www.GraydonHouseBooks.com
www.BookClubbish.com

Printed in U.S.A.

For my original Stella and my future Wade.
—Shaunna J. Edwards

To my family, who fill me with love and stories.
—Alyson Richman

THE

THREAD
COLLECTORS

"If you don't know where you're going, you should know where you come from."

—Gullah Geechee proverb

PART ONE

1

New Orleans, Louisiana
March 1863

She opens the door to the Creole cottage just wide enough to ensure it is truly him. Outside, the pale moon is high in the sky, illuminating only half of William's face. Stella reaches for his sleeve and pulls him inside.

He is dressed to run. He wears his good clothes, but has chosen his attire thoughtfully, ensuring the colors will camouflage in the wilderness that immediately surrounds the city. In his hand, he clasps a brown canvas case. They have only spoken in whispers during their clandestine meetings about his desire to fight. To flee. The city of New Orleans teeters on the precipice of chaos, barely contained by the Union forces occupying the streets. Homes abandoned. Businesses boarded up. Stella's master comes back from the front every six weeks, each time seeming more battered, bitter and restless than the last.

William sets down his bag and draws Stella close into his chest, his heartbeat accelerating. He lifts a single, slim finger, slowly tracing the contours of her face, trying to memorize her one last time.

"You stay here, no matter what..." he murmurs into her ear. "You must keep safe. And for a woman like you, better to hide and stay unseen than venture out there."

In the shadows, he sees her eyes shimmer. But she balances the tears from falling, an art she had been taught long ago—when she learned that survival, not happiness, was the real prize.

Stella slips momentarily from William's arms. She tiptoes toward a small wooden chest. From the top drawer, she retrieves a delicate handkerchief with a single violet embroidered in its center. With materials in the city now so scarce, she has had to use the dark blue thread from her skirt's hem to stitch the tiny flower on a swatch of white cotton cut from her petticoat.

"So you know you're never alone out there," she says as she closes William's fingers around the kerchief.

He has brought something for her, too. A small speckled cowrie shell that he slips from a worn indigo-colored pouch. The shell and its cotton purse are his two most sacred possessions in the world. He puts the pouch, now empty, back into his pocket.

"I'll be coming back for that, Stella." William smiles as he looks down at the talisman in his beloved's hand. "And for you, too... Everything will be different soon."

She nods, takes the shell and feels its smooth lip against her palm. There was a time such cowries were used as a form of currency for their people, shells threaded on pieces of string exchanged for precious goods. Now this shell is both worthless and priceless as it's exchanged for safekeeping between the lovers.

There is no clock in her small home. William, too, wears

no watch. Yet both of them know they have already tarried too long. He must set out before there is even a trace of sunlight and, even then, his journey will be fraught with danger.

"Go, William," she says, pushing him out the door. Her heart breaks, knowing the only protection she can offer him is a simple handkerchief. Her love stitched into it by her hand.

He leaves as stealthily as he arrived, a whisper in the night. Stella falls back into the shadows of her cottage. She treads silently toward her bedroom, hoping to wrap herself tightly in the folds of the quilt that brings her so much comfort.

"You alright?" A soft sound emerges in the dark.

"Ammanee?" Stella's voice breaks as she says the woman's name.

"Yes, I'm here." Ammanee enters the room, her face brightened by a small wax candle in her grip.

In the golden light, she sits down on the bed and reaches for Stella's hand still clutching the tiny shell, which leaves a deep imprint in her palm.

"Willie strong," Ammanee says over and over again. "He gon' make it. I know."

Stella doesn't answer. A flicker of pain stabs her from the inside, and she finally allows her tears to run.

2

Camp Parapet
Jefferson, Louisiana

The ten miles' journey from New Orleans to the army camp that was perched between Lake Pontchartrain and the river had been treacherous and lengthy. William avoided all roads at any cost, regardless of whether they were dirt or paved. He didn't know when his mas' would discover that he had fled—but he was all too aware of the slave catchers camped right outside the city.

Any man they captured would suffer greatly. Lashings that ripped the skin off their back, fleur-de-lis brands marking the bearer as untrustworthy. And for those with particularly brutal masters—with enough slaves to spare—bodies doused with kerosene and lit on fire, their burning flesh a reminder to the others on the plantation that it was never worth it to run.

He took the route that Stella had advised, first through the swampland, then hugging the bayous and creeping through boggy marshes and wetlands that had to be navigated to reach higher ground. The roots of bald cypress trees and tupelo gums intertwined beneath the murky water of the ravines, causing William to stumble countless times.

He had nearly been caught three times since he'd left Stella, but he kept running, hearing her voice in his head urging him on. He was driven by his mother's spirit, too, each stretch toward freedom defying those who'd robbed her of her song. In the hour right before dawn, the sound of barking dogs was dangerously close. He threw himself into the fetid water, hoping to evade the bloodhounds, shivering until the patrollers finally moved away.

He reached the enlistment camp by daybreak, where he found hundreds of men already in line eager to join the Union cause. Some had traveled for days, through back alleys or the more dangerous open fields. Like William, all of them had to evade mercenaries eager to beat and shackle them before returning them to their masters for a rich reward.

The man in front of William stood barefoot, the cuffs of his pants reduced to a ragged edge of fringe. Fingers balled at his sides, he inched up the snaking line to the medical surgeon's tent, leaving a stamp of blood with each step. The dry earth, greedy for every ounce of moisture, drank the man's dark footprint almost instantly, only to have it replaced with another.

"Next!" Outside the mouth of the tent's entrance, one of the Union soldiers waved another man inside.

William looked down at his own narrow feet. The pair of waterlogged and sweat-stained calfskin oxfords he had on were not the typical shoes of a "contraband" man running from slavery. His herringbone trousers had a gash down the side. His tweed jacket was ripped at the elbow, and somewhere between New Orleans and Jefferson County he had lost his hat. Yet, despite his harrowing journey, his shoes remained miraculously intact.

Inside his jacket, tucked within the pocket of his waistcoat, he located the handkerchief Stella had embroidered. He surreptitiously ran his fingers over the small flower she'd stitched carefully with blue thread. Even now, with the stench of rot and death heavy in the air, the buzzing of flies, and the intense hunger in his belly, thoughts of Stella were his constant companions. He brought the white cotton cloth to his nose and inhaled it, desperately searching for the last traces of her distinct scent. William knew breath was not something that always came from the lungs, but could break forth from the heart and mind as well, filling a body with life when it needed it most.

In the corner of the tent where William was told to undress, Jacob Kling sat bent over a thick ledger. Dark curls sprouted from beneath his navy cap, and a smudge of black ink stained his index finger as he recorded the medical surgeon's clinical observations about the prior recruit. *Twenty-two years old. Negro. 5'9". Weight 175 pounds. Despite superficial wound to left foot, a solid build and determined spirit. Qualified for military duty.*

The medical surgeon chose his words carefully when Jacob first arrived at the examination tent to assist with the note-taking. "It's a sorry situation. We can't accept every man who wants to join up, despite the lengths they may have taken to get here," he explained as he opened his black leather physician's bag and arranged his tools on a side table. "The army asks me to separate out the strong from the weak. I have given up trying to determine whether a man is a fugitive," the doctor remarked, noting the futility of dividing the recently emancipated from those who had fled from bondage. "Remember, these men will not be lifting muskets, but rather wielding shovels, pickaxes and hoes. We can only take the ones who are free from both bodily defects and have sufficient sense to follow orders." He cleared his throat and pulled at his ash-colored beard. "In other words, Private Kling, my job is rather straightforward. *It is not to choose who is in every way good, but to reject who is positively unfit.*"

The doctor always began his examinations with each candidate's head, ears and eyes, and then continued on to inspect their teeth, neck and chest. He also checked their hands and feet over carefully. Earlier that morning, a young man had taken off his shirt, and both Jacob and the doctor had found it impossible to keep their composure when they saw a thick blanket of scar tissue covering the man's back. The man tried to bring his hands above his head, but the painful scars limited his range of motion. His arms only lifted halfway, his hands barely reaching the level of his ears.

Now, as William entered the tent, the doctor readjusted his focus. His eyes fell on William's shoes and his once-elegant but now-damaged clothes.

"Don't just stand there… Get undressed so I can examine you."

William placed down his satchel, removed his jacket, and slowly began to unbutton his vest and shirt. He knew he was far slighter than nearly every other man in line that afternoon. Having never worked a field, his body had not obtained the thick ropes of muscles his fellow slaves had developed. Instead, when he had been six years old, he had been plucked from his mama's pallet and delivered to the big house to amuse the master's wife with his nascent talent.

The doctor placed a stethoscope upon William's chest.

"Heart and lungs clear," the doctor said. "Slight build, fit for service."

He turned over William's palms. "How oddly free of calluses," he muttered underneath his breath. "Any skills?"

"Musician, sir," William answered quietly. But the doctor was no longer listening.

3

Upon hearing the word *musician*, the young private's ears perked up. Jacob Kling looked up from his ledger and put down his pen. He knew he wasn't supposed to speak during these examinations, but the words escaped his mouth before he could stop them.

"What instrument?"

William's eyes flickered. "I play the flute, sir."

Jacob suddenly felt the haze of the last three days dissipate. For a moment, he was not just a lowly helper assisting the medical surgeon with his intake of new Black recruits, but a musician transported back with his fellow bandmates, his cornet between his fingers, filling the air with music as he ignited the spirits of the infantrymen marching into battle. And that moment brought him even further back, to his early days with Lily, his beloved wife, finding passion through a shared love of melody.

Jacob Kling bought his sheet music at only one place in New York, the Kahn Music Store on lower Fifth Avenue. It wasn't just because it was the largest shop of its kind. Or that Arthur Kahn, a German Jewish immigrant, had launched a dazzling empire from his Brooklyn warehouse by printing thousands of pages of music that were then shipped up and down the Eastern seaboard. It was because Jacob knew that if he orchestrated his timing just right, a quality that as a musician he possessed in great measure, he would see the beautiful Lily Kahn exiting from the back office and catch a glimpse of her copper hair and radiant smile.

The first time he saw her, he assumed she was visiting her father. He had no idea about the secret meetings she held there. The ones behind the black velvet curtain, down the narrow staircase, in a dimly lit storage cellar. That revelation would come later, after he had finally managed to capture her attention one afternoon when he positioned himself near the back of the store.

On that day, Jacob devised a plan. An armful of musical scores in hand, he allowed a single page to escape to the ground as Lily stepped into the main room. The printed sheet fell only inches from her hem.

"You've dropped something," she intoned, as a catlike smile curled at her lips. She bent down to pick up the paper. "'Gentle Annie'?" she remarked. "I see you're a bit of a romantic..."

Her words were bold; her focus did not waver. Jacob saw a spark within her green irises that flashed like lightning.

"How could I not be?" he answered. As he reached to take the sheet from her, the edge of his finger grazed the soft skin of her hand. "Without the fingerprint of the heart, it would only be sound...not music."

Lily tilted her head back to appraise him. "What instrument do you play?" she asked with a pointed curiosity. "Are you a brass man?"

"Yes." Jacob nodded proudly. "The trumpet and the cornet."

"I have played the harp since I was a little girl. My father thought it might soften my difficult temperament."

"The instrument of the angels," he added.

"But I play like a devil," she laughed. "And that's a good thing. The world isn't in need of angels right now. We must raise a bit of hell if we're to build a better nation."

"A better nation?" inquired Jacob, feeling slightly out of his depth.

"We must rid the country of the foul system that profits from human bondage—slavery," she said fervently.

Jacob looked toward the curtain as two more women exited from the back room. He had never noticed anyone else there before because he had been focused only on Lily. But now he realized the women emerging were likely fellow abolitionists.

"I gather you weren't taking harp lessons behind that curtain…"

"The only person I take lessons from these days is Mrs. Ernestine Rose."

Jacob's face went blank.

"You don't know her, then?" Her eyebrows knitted together, as if she couldn't imagine someone not immediately recognizing the name.

"An abolitionist, suffragette and a Jewess like me. A heroine like no other." Lily pulled out her fan from her purse and opened it. A painted scene of white birds against a turquoise sky spread out over the silk panels.

"I'm glad I could make your acquaintance, Mr.…."

"Jacob Kling," he blurted out. "And you?" he asked, despite knowing full well her name.

"Lillian Kahn," she answered. As she lowered the edge of her fan, another smile returned to her lips. "A pleasure to meet you."

As the sound of her voice faded away, it was replaced in Jacob's head with music, despite not a single note having been played.

"Get yourself dressed, young man." The doctor's voice abruptly snapped Jacob out of his reverie. The older man had no interest in hearing about William's musical talents. "Next," he called out to the men in line.

As William pulled his clothes back on, Jacob realized he had no way of knowing how skilled a musician the man was, or even how he'd come to play the flute. But he felt compelled to offer the young man some advice.

"Outside, when they give you a uniform, mention you can play the fife."

4

Camp Parapet
Jefferson, Louisiana
March 1863

"Well, it looks like we're done for today, Private Kling," the doctor announced as he removed his spectacles and wiped them clean. Both men were exhausted, having spent nearly six hours in the tent together. "I appreciate your help. Without extra hands, we couldn't hope to examine all of the Negroes streaming in. I don't know if this experiment will be a success, but we'll need more men if we hope to prevail."

Jacob doubted that the doctor was asking for a mere musician's opinion on military strategy, so he responded noncommittally with a small "Of course, sir." A few weeks ago, he had been commanded to spend his days in the medical tent when the camp had been designated as the recruiting and training spot for the new Louisiana Native Guard, the ranks of which would be filled by Black soldiers. Already the White soldiers that had been assigned to Camp Parapet had begun to grumble loudly about becoming "outnumbered" on the base.

The doctor began to pack his surgical case. "Well, I imagine your lieutenant will need you back for evening drills. Hope your hands aren't too tired to play your cornet," he said as he dismissed Jacob.

A wave of relief washed over him at the thought of escaping the stifling tent. "Never too tired to play, sir."

Outside, the makeshift camp spread before him with its canvas tents and roughly constructed timber huts. Metal shovels and hoes were propped against the sides of wooden wagons. From the corner of his eye, amidst the din of men lining up for food, uniforms and a place to sleep, Jacob spotted the man with the torn coat, a fife now clasped in his hand. Following closely behind was a little Black drummer boy, underfed and perhaps no more than ten years old, tapping out a steady beat.

Dressed in a dark navy coat that was far too large for him, his tattered Union cap slightly askew, to Jacob, the sight seemed almost like a scene between a father and son. The drummer, with his dirt-smudged face and the snare's leather straps hanging low from his tiny frame, smiled as he played in unison with the man.

As the notes and rhythm melded between them, Jacob was at once soothed by the duet, yet also deeply saddened by their playing, for it brought on an unexpected nostalgia for those distant afternoons long ago, when he had played with his brother in the family's cramped living room in Yorkville. The apartment's single window carrying a breeze from the East River, and their harmonies filling the air.

His father had emigrated from Germany with nothing but two suitcases, a violin, and a nineteen-year-old bride, Kati, who shared his love of music. For as long as Jacob could remember, their crowded tenement was always rich with song.

His mother had taught him and his brother, Samuel, to read music before she herself had learned more than a few words of English. Music was a balm for her in this new country, where her accent and foreignness embarrassed her and the city's streets were filled with unknowns. For Kati, the violin was a refuge, a place of beauty to return to when her days felt enveloped by shadow.

With only one actual instrument between the four of them, the first gift Jacob's father gave to his young family when his import business began to expand was the opportunity for his sons to choose secondhand ones of their own.

He brought the boys to a small, ground-floor shop on the corner of Eighty-Third Street and Lexington Avenue, where the windows flashed with the brassy light of trumpets and French horns and enticed with the elegant shapes of the strings. Inside, a tiny man with delicate hands lit up the dark interior by showing the brothers how each instrument possessed its own richness and tone.

Jacob had opted for the cornet, lovingly buffed by the prior owner. He loved the brilliance of its sound, the joy that came out of its silver bell. His brother, on the other hand, had stayed faithful to what he had always known, the violin.

Looking back on it now, his brother's selection had enabled Samuel to remain closer with their mother. She enjoyed gently correcting Samuel's intonation and reminding him to maintain his posture. But while these little cajolings could seem pesty at first glance, Jacob knew it created a stronger bond between them, another layer of love.

Now in the gauzy Louisiana twilight, as he headed over the dusty path toward his unit's campsite, Jacob wrestled with homesickness. He missed the touch of his wife, the scent of her freshly washed hair. The peacefulness of hearing Lily practice her harp in their living room. The sight of her fingertips rippling over the strings as she leaned forward, her legs slightly apart, was a vision he always returned to when he needed comfort.

He reached into his breast pocket and pulled out the last correspondence from Lily. The thin paper had been folded and unfolded more than a dozen times over the past few days. He read the words under candlelight before he went to sleep, and then again when he woke and sat down to eat his rations. He had nearly memorized each sentence.

My dearest husband,
I hope this letter travels true and reaches you safely. It has been challenging not having you here by my side. I miss so much of you. Your warmth and your smile. Your tender words and your music. Today, the only comfort I could find was in my harp. There, within Bach's beautiful Sarabande, I discovered you again. I hope if you close your eyes, my notes will float through the sky, above the heavens, and land in your ears, softening the peals of war.

While I do miss you terribly, I have tried to keep myself focused on my work and to support the movement in any way I can. Ernestine reminded me at our last meeting that I must embrace a feeling of pride and confidence for the noble choice you have made. She, too, is so impressed that you are using your musical skills in leading our brave Union troops and contributing to the fight to end the evils of slavery. When she learned that your brother, Samuel, had joined the Rebel forces in Mississippi, she lauded your courage and conviction even more.

I have not received any news of his fate since our last letters. While I abhor his position, I will keep Samuel in my prayers because he is of your blood, though it remains unfathomable to me that he and his wife continue to defend slavery.

But I choose not to waste any more space in this letter about things I cannot change with your family, but rather to tell you again how proud I am of you. Today, I will join some women from the

Sanitary Commission who are trying to find ways to help support
the Union wounded, raising funds and sending necessary supplies.
Although it is a small contribution in this war compared to men
like you risking your lives, it bolsters my spirits knowing I'm con-
tributing, however small.
Your devoted wife,
Lily

Jacob breathed in the dusky air, the letter from Lily still clasped between his fingers. He scanned the sentences, the careful scrolling of her penmanship that he adored. She knew how much it pained him to know his brother had joined the Rebel forces. He often wondered, had their father not sent Samuel down South to expand the trading roots of the family business, would their paths be as profoundly different as they now were? No one, certainly not their father, would have predicted Samuel would find a Jewish bride in the depths of Satartia, Mississippi. But leave it to his elder brother, with his violet eyes and thick brown lashes, to accept Irving Baum's offer to play his violin in his family parlor, after their business dealings wrapped up for the night. His nineteen-year-old daughter, Eliza Baum, he insisted, was such a fan of the strings.

Jacob thought back to the image of the little drummer boy and the Black musician playing his newly furnished fife. And it struck him to the core, as he reflected on his own personal experience, that sometimes talent—and an instrument to use it—could alter a man's destiny forever.

5

Stella held the cowrie shell in her palm and closed her eyes. It had now been three days since William had fled, and worry for him consumed her. Her appetite had all but vanished and she kept the shutters closed most of the day because her eyes hurt from crying.

"Best get busy doin' something...instead of moping around like this." Ammanee stood at the threshold. "What would Janie do if she saw you letting yourself get all tear-streaked?" For many reasons, including their long separation during Ammanee's childhood, she sometimes refused to call their mother "Mama" and referred to her by her given name. Especially when she wanted to invoke her power to her little sister. "Frye come back from the front and find you laid up with a puffy face? He gonna suspect something real bad. Can't afford to look homely at a time like this."

Stella groaned and flipped over in the bed.

"Give me that," Ammanee said, demanding the shell. "I'll keep it safe. Can't have nothin' that connects you to Willie, you hear me? Frye ain't stupid—just ugly. He mighta seen that shell before." She tucked it safely into the back of one of Stella's drawers. "Now let's put something else in those hands of yours."

Ammanee sat down beside her and reached for the embroidered pillow Stella had created years ago, when thread wasn't as precious as gold like it was now with the war raging on. She took a needle from her apron and began pulling out the stitches to repurpose it into something new.

"Come on now," she said tenderly, as she twisted some green fiber around her forefinger. "Just like we used to do at Mama's…"

The house where Stella had spent her childhood was painted sky blue, its long shutters a deep shade of ocean. Inside, the walls were covered in a pale saffron. The furniture, castaways from a much finer house, was cracked and glued together, the black walnut wood repeatedly scuffed and polished. How many times had Janie set her young daughter to burnishing their few possessions, to remind the child that beauty did not come without a cost? It required maintenance and constant mending. Far too often, beauty also demanded camouflage. Stella's mother had learned to embroider not as a mere pastime, but out of necessity. And Stella was taught from the moment she could clasp a needle and thread to use tiny neat stitches to cover what had become embarrassingly bare.

Stella knew her mother had moved from the slave shack of Mas' Percy's plantation out to Rampart Street before she was born. Its rows of Creole cottages, that bordered the city line, were filled with light-skinned women, the so-called favorites of wealthy White men, coveted like exotic fruits they hoarded for themselves.

Her mother had pleaded with Mr. Percy to bring Ammanee, then four years old, with her, but he wanted Janie all to himself, and there was no space in the three-room house for another man's child, especially one born into bondage.

The arrival of Stella marked a turning point in all the women's fortunes. Percy, in a rare act of mercy, had granted Janie manumission, handing over her "freedom papers." As he handed Janie a new life, he also made clear that she was still on his leash. *Law says you have to leave Louisiana now that you're free, but you and your girls stay right here on Rampart Street, ya hear? I'll make sure you stay safe*, he had demanded.

But his magnanimity did not include freedom for either daughter. Only when Percy looked down at his Stella—a lighter version of her mother, a darker version of himself—did he finally break down and assure Janie that she would be able to choose the ultimate master for her. And he would allow the now seven-year-old half sister of his child to be Stella's nursemaid. A suitable transition for Ammanee who had already spent a year working full-time in the kitchen of the big house, not yet hardened but already understanding her lot in life.

Under the gabled roof and wooden rafters and within the rooms of pale lemon, the three women had grown up together. But the night Stella was "sent to Market" would change everything. That evening, she sat in front of the cottage's only mirror while Janie pulled and arranged her hair with a wooden brush. Beside her stood Ammanee, hairpins clasped in her slender, dark hand. Within the mirror's frame, their varying skin tones shone in contrast from a deep nutmeg brown to the color of wild honey. But their kinship was unmistakable in their shared high foreheads and almond eyes.

Dressed in one of her mother's refurbished dresses, Stella teetered between excitement and fear.

"Don't be thinking 'going to the Market' means just gettin' ribbons and lace." Janie ran her hands over her daughter's scalp somewhat brusquely. Stella's hair was soft, like finely spun cotton on top, but thicker wool in the back.

Janie's fingers tugged at the tighter twists at Stella's nape, and she let out a frustrated sigh. Ammanee stepped closer to retrieve a tin of homemade pomade from the vanity, and then offered it to her mother.

"This should help, Mama..."

Janie dipped her fingers into the buttery mixture and applied it to the stubborn coils, arranging them into waves.

"You have to look right. The Market will be filled with girls just like you...daughters of women like me." The words swirled inside her mouth. A bitter mixture of shame and defiance.

"This house didn't come from love, like I had with Ammanee's daddy," she gestured toward the high ceilings and tall narrow windows. "It came from sacrifice." She took a deep breath. Janie was just a whit over forty, but she felt she had gained enough wisdom to last a lifetime. "But it gave me more freedom than I'd have elsewhere, so I shouldered the cost."

As Janie now appraised her daughter's hair, smoothed into round soft curls, she felt relief at one less task that needed to be done. And Ammanee swelled proudly that Stella was wearing the slip she had embroidered for the evening, the one with violets at the hem. The deep-blue-colored flowers were her own private touch; she wanted her baby sister to be sent off with as much luck as possible. While she might not find the true love that violets signified, Ammanee hoped that her sister would at least find kindness.

"When you get there, Stella," Janie cautioned her, "you must look neither bold nor weak. Do not lock eyes with any of 'em too long, girl. Mind the old geezers, who won't pro vide 'nuf security…and avoid those who look so brash they'll trade ya in after a few years' time."

She rubbed her hands and massaged her daughter's shoulders. "Time to get dressed." She glanced at the minutes ticking away on the wall clock. "Nothing good comes from a girl that's late. Making an entrance is one thing, but uppity doesn't sell at the Market."

Janie continued to smooth the fuzz at Stella's hairline, while she repeated softly—almost to herself, "Have to look right… Betta' than right… Gals der' gonna be light 'nuf to pass… Taught you all I know… What I know?… Plucked from the fields and dumped here." In her anxiety, Janie unconsciously slipped back into the vernacular of her youth, before she was brought to Rampart Street. She hadn't had the benefit of etiquette lessons at the knees of grandmothers who would have been navigating the unspoken rules of plaçage since before New Orleans became "American." Janie had had to learn the hard way the rules of being controlled by the desires of White men. Not chained, but certainly not free.

Stella slipped on the cornflower blue dress that Janie and Ammanee had worked on together, refurbishing it to look fresh and taking in the waistline and bust so it fit Stella's slender frame.

"You sewed more violets on the bodice, sister."

"You can never have enough blue to protect you," Ammanee said as she helped with Stella's buttons and Janie fluffed the skirt.

"Got ol' Percy to give me some money to buy you this for tonight." Janie revealed a small cloth purse.

The purse was hardly anything special, just a small satchel with a garland of multicolored flowers embroidered in the center, but Stella admired it as she held it in her hands. It had never been worn before and felt blissfully new. She traced her fingertip over the flowers, noting the fineness of the stitches, but also thinking of how she would replicate the pattern later on a stray piece of cloth.

Before she left, her mother appraised her daughter one last time. "I wish I didn't have to send you out like this, but I'm not sure how long I have Percy's protection. At least he had me wait until you passed eighteen." Janie thrust her head back. "Over forty and not a youngin' anymore…and I held you back as long as I could to shield you from this life."

"Yes, Mama."

"Now remember, this ain't a ball you goin' to. It's an auction." Janie winced at her own words, as she had been only a child when she herself was sold. She was flooded with memories of the overseers stripping her own mother half-bare and pinching her breasts to show she'd be a good breeder. She and the other small children had watched from a cage. "The most important auction, Stella, you'll ever go through in your life. And God willing, the only."

Janie pushed Stella out into the hot night sky, surrendering her to the safekeeping of a chaperone who would shepherd numerous young ladies to the Market, in a poor mockery of all the niceties the young White debutantes from St. Charles Avenue were afforded. She closed the door, forcing back the emotion that welled within her, and told Ammanee to put the kettle on.

The two women spent the night pulling threads and repairing torn cloth, not passing a single word between them. Scattered around the room, a dozen broken things had been refitted together. Janie looked at her house and knew there was nothing safe or permanent or whole surrounding her, not even Ammanee—perhaps least of all her oldest daughter, the child born between her and a slave named Lewis. She still thought of him, even all these years later. It was a terrible pain she wished to spare her daughters. Love.

6

Later that same evening, in a small dance hall on Orleans Street, William opened up his flute case and joined the other five Black musicians who had been "loaned out" by their masters as the evening's entertainment.

"You're coming with me to the Market," Mason Frye, his master for nearly a dozen years, slapped William on the back earlier that day. "Pack your instrument, boy. Whistlin' Willie's gonna make me shine tonight." In the years since Frye had bought the young boy from Sapelo Island, he had come to publicly prize William as a valuable accessory.

With his wife and family away for the month, Frye hadn't bothered hiding his pleasure in getting himself ready for one of the most anticipated evenings of his year—from Willie or any of the other slaves in the house. Willie had overheard Frye telling his friends that the Market had taken a bit of planning, with more secrecy needed given all the growing unrest. How tiresome Northerners had become with their abolitionist rhetoric, their irritating interference with the centuries-old Southern way of life.

"I myself have never treated one of my slaves cruelly," Frye continued to extol to his rapt audience. "We all know men who have raised their whip when the occasion called for it, but should we interfere in what other people do with their property?" he asked rhetorically. He stood up and leaned against the mantel of his fireplace. "Indeed, I was heartily disappointed to learn that Clinton Righter had ordered a particularly harsh punishment to Willie's mother when he was just a child." At this mention, Willie's eyes quickly snapped up. Even the slightest reference to the brutality Righter had inflicted on his mother brought a flood of emotions through him.

"But I don't have to resort to such measures. They are children—gifted at times though they may be. You must simply be firm with them. Do as you're told, keep your complaints to yourself, and we will coexist without hardship."

After giving his dissertation on how best to navigate a master's obligations, Mason Frye began to gather his guests to leave for the Market.

"Hurry up and grab your flute for tonight," he demanded of Willie as they all headed out the door.

The wind quintet set up quietly, with each musician taking out his instruments and gazing into a room set with candlelit chandeliers. The strong perfume of lily of the valley emerged from the fistfuls of freshly cut flowers arranged in tall ormolu and cloisonné vases around the hall. Willie glanced over at the heavyset bassoonist whose left eyelid drooped, making him look deflated before the night even began.

The oboe player stuck a reed in his mouthpiece and warmed

up his fingers and his lips with a two-octave scale. When he finished, he turned to Willie and Scipio, the French horn player. "First time playin' the Market, boys? Who earnin' to-night?"

Scipio replied, "Not me. Sometimes I make good coin if I come alone, but wit' Massa here, I'm jus' his gift to da ladies…"

Willie was quiet. In his nineteen years, he'd only earned his own money on a single occasion, and that had been promptly confiscated by Frye to "pay off his instrument." And, as for the Market, he couldn't pretend he knew what any of this evening was all about.

The oboist's eyes narrowed more intensely on Willie. "You dat showboat living over on Prytania? Da *pro-di-gy* Mas' Frye bought off a Gullah?" queried the musician, his tongue forming the unfamiliar word thickly and mockingly.

Willie nodded.

Little wisps of white hair curled at the man's sideburns. He shook his head in disbelief. "They say you don't just play tunes for dese here dances and such. You know da real stuff."

"Not really," Willie responded quietly, ducking his head as he examined his instrument. "I just have a knack for playin' what I hear…" William didn't tell the other men how he'd first learned to play Mozart and Brahms, back in Eleanor Righter's parlor, the notes floating from her piano into his ears then to his flute. Nor did he share how she had arranged for him to secretly learn to read music with her teacher's assistance.

"Well, tonight, we keepin' it simple," the oboist instructed. "Not all of us play fancy like you. No call for it noways. Dem White bucks ain't here fuh the music."

"Mas' Frye asked us to begin with me showin' off a bit," Willie informed them. The two horn players gazed at him blankly. "Would you mind providing me with a little accompaniment?" William asked the piano player. "Nothing complicated, mind you. Just a bit of improvisin' with some chords in F major, then a few scales, arpeggio. I'll do the rest." He began to play a few notes so the musician understood the rhythm.

"Who dat by?" the oboe player asked.

The bassoonist responded before William had a chance to. He looked up from cleaning his instrument and answered quite dryly: "Mozart."

William was playing when Stella entered the room. He noticed she was one of the few women who did not hide her face coyly behind a fan. Her focus remained straight ahead, as if she was being pulled in by an invisible thread.

The notes coming off his flute were soft and airy. Behind the gilt rims of sherry glasses, men with bloated faces smiled as girls in varying shades of brown sauntered past them. Darker mulattos swirled next to quadroons and even the occasional octoroon, though that rare treasure usually secured a more private arrangement. A mixture of beauty and opportunity for the men's picking founded on desperation and fear.

Stella heard her mother's voice in her head, reminding her not to catch the attention of a man too old, nor a dandy dripping in vivid wealth. She felt the eyes of many men hard upon her and her shyness overcame her. She stepped back, almost falling into the group of musicians.

As the music came to an end, Stella felt a hand reach out to steady her, then quietly retract back in the shadows. When she glanced back, the handsome young flutist locked eyes with her and smiled. Then he lifted his instrument to his mouth, pursed his lips and began to play again. As the other musicians joined in, Frye approached Stella, pulling her into a dance for which she hardly knew the steps.

"You like the music?" Frye asked as he led her into the

circle of dancers on the floor. "That flute player is Whistlin' Willie, and he's been *mine* for years."

She felt her voice shrink inside her. She had no words to offer, despite Janie's urging that she use all her charms at the right time.

"I have a gift for recognizing talent," he added. "And beauty, too."

Stella felt the intention of his gaze, and it made her feel like a mouse cornered by a hungry cat.

Her eyes fell to the ground as his fingers clasped hers tighter. With no chance to free herself, she focused on the little flowers Ammanee had embroidered on her skirt.

The man was neither fat nor old. He wasn't particularly short or excessively tall. Aside from the gold pocket watch dangling from his vest, he made no effort to display his wealth like so many of the other men who filled the room. On the contrary, his biggest boast was that he owned a slave who played the sweetest music she had ever heard.

"I enjoy the music very much." She finally forced herself to say something in return.

"Well, Miss…" He raised an eyebrow searching for her name. "Looks like we have at least one thing in common." His eyes lit up. "I knew my boy Willie would help me get the most delicious fruit at the Market."

Stella cringed. She caught sight of his reflection in the tall gilded mirror. His wheat-colored hair, his sunless skin. She wished she could fade from sight and transform into a sprinkle of notes coming from the mouthpiece of the other thing of beauty that this man claimed to own.

Frye continued to insist for her hand for dances throughout the night, his unabashed stares dissuading any other man from approaching Stella. After all, in a room with such abundance, there was no need to compete. "I'll see you soon," he reminded her during their last dance.

"Yes, sir," she answered. Her voice was so quiet that the words were nearly lost in the din of the room, as she faced the direction of the band.

From the podium, as Willie and his fellow musicians languidly played the last song of the night, he looked down at the sight of his master's hand around the young woman, her head tilted up toward the stage, her expression filled with yearning, her eyes shiny with tears.

"Did you see the new beauty I got myself?" Frye pressed Willie later that night as the younger man climbed to the top of the coach to sit with the footman, his flute case knocking against his knee.

"You brought me some luck tonight, boy. I think she liked those pretty tunes of yours, real good."

Willie hadn't answered, but the driver's whip cracking extra loud against the horse's back sounded his inner reply.

In the days that passed, Frye began to arrange the logistics for setting up young Stella, the woman who would soon be bound to him. Her mother, through a more literate intermediary, had already communicated a list of requests for her daughter. Keeping his promise from years ago, Percy informed Frye that he wouldn't sign Stella over until Janie approved the deal.

Four bolts of fabric for dressmaking, ten spools of brightly colored thread, three cotton slips and bloomers, two cast-iron pots, a copper kettle, a wooden desk, a chair and one oval mirror... Her most ardent and expensive request that he purchase a young woman named Ammanee to service Stella as her maid.

He had resisted the prospect of taking on the care and feeding of yet another servant. But Janie had insisted and Frye had reluctantly agreed.

While having Stella in close proximity to her mother was hardly ideal, there were only a few blocks within the city where he could avoid gossip or judgment. After some careful searching, Frye found a vacant cottage on Burgundy Street with three dark rooms, one wide enough for a double bed. The widowed landlord, with a well-practiced ease and an unctuous charm, avoided any mention of the previous tenant: a cinnamon-skinned woman named Léotine, who three weeks earlier, just as her forty-fifth birthday approached, steeped herself a strong tincture of ginkgo seeds and went to sleep for the last time.

Instead, she promised Frye that if he was willing to sign the lease that afternoon, "I'd make a very good deal at a most competitive price. And you can even have the furnishings— they're practically new." As in most affairs in New Orleans, it always came down to numbers.

Outside, three tall sunflowers grew beside the porch steps, their yellow petals scattered across the front of the shabby door.

"Had to do a bit of hunting to find you the right place," Frye stated proudly as he led Stella inside the cottage.

She scanned the room and took notice of the wooden furniture her mother had requested. It looked surprisingly fresh to her, in stark contrast to the furnishings Percy had provided her mother long ago. There were no cracked table legs, and the copper pot on the small stove was polished to a high shine.

"Everything's here, as I promised," Frye announced. His pleasure with himself was immense.

Stella fidgeted. He had missed her one, most crucial request.

"When will Ammanee be arriving?" she pushed herself to ask.

"Tomorrow..." Frye answered coolly. "Tonight you're

alone. Other than the few hours when you have the privilege of my company."

In the carved oak mirror, Stella caught sight of their two reflections trapped within the glass.

"Come," he added, gesturing with his hand. He urged her to move along to the last room, his steps striking against the floor with a metronome-like precision.

"Now look over here... Never heard 'bout a girl wanting so much thread." He pointed to a split-cane basket perched on the bedside. There within the woven vessel she spotted even more colors than she had asked for. Spindles of blue, green and violet. Crimson, and even gold.

"I was feeling mighty generous," he boasted. "And someone has even delivered us a little welcoming gift." Frye pointed toward the mattress nestled within the sloping metal frame. On top of the linen and cotton blanket, lay a quilt of dozens of colorful squares.

Stella's gaze, however, had already discovered it. Her eyes were transfixed, as she fought back her tears.

Square by square, she saw the gift that Janie and Ammanee had sewn together, keeping their secret endeavor far from her prying eyes. She realized how hard they must have worked, toiling late into the midnight hours as she slept in order to finish it in time for her impending move. At first glance, Stella noticed the obvious, the red cotton from her mother's favorite dress she wore when Percy came to visit, and the pine green from Ammanee's apron. But on further inspection, she recognized that each of Janie's friends and neighbors from Rampart Street had also contributed a cutting from their clothing. Stitched into the quilt was the flash of pink from Miss Delphine's summer skirt, the dusky blue from Miss Hyacinth's well-loved robe, and the daffodil-yellow frock that Emilienne wore every Sunday to church. They wanted to protect Stella in the only way they could, by providing a little bit of their heart and their history to blanket her each night.

"You like it?" Frye interrupted.

Stella's stomach tightened as he stepped closer. She realized he wasn't asking about the quilt, but rather her new home he'd taken time, funds and energy to secure.

"Now I know the outside needs some fresh paint. I'll leave some coins so you can get the color you like...maybe a bright blue like your mama chose for hers." He smiled at his own indulgence.

"Thank you," Stella managed to answer, but her mind was still focused on the quilt.

"But otherwise, it's a pretty fine place, don't you think?"

He began to unbutton his shirt, then pulled his belt out from his buckle.

Stella remained standing inches away from him, her breath rising within her chest.

Darkness swallowed her whole as Frye shut the door and it softly clicked behind them.

7

Camp Parapet
Jefferson, Louisiana

The tent was a black hole. Lonely and dark, except for a small lantern Jacob had lit for reading, the rough shelter provided little comfort beyond protection from the rain and a place to rest. And it was quickly becoming too dark for him to even draft a reply to Lily's latest letter.

Beside his makeshift bed, next to his cornet case, he kept a rucksack of food and supplies. Having missed dinner with the rest of his infantry, Jacob removed a tin of stewed beef and headed out toward the campfire.

Hunched over the mound of burning embers, he found a soldier with straw-colored hair and a patchy goatee mopping up his plate with a hard biscuit.

"Had to pick the mold and maggots from mine," the young man muttered between bites. "Those weevils get into everything."

Jacob looked up at the soldier whose blue eyes were as weary and diluted as dishwater, and sympathized. The man was tired, restless. Like so many of the White infantry at Camp Parapet, his expectations of getting some action against the Rebs had yet to be realized. The Black men, both fugitive slaves and free men of color, who had come to join the newly established Negro regiments, were still enthralled by the excitement of the war. But for the others, anticipation had already given way to boredom, hunger and illness.

"Pulled four out of my cornmeal just this morning," Jacob grumbled. "I've told myself it's fortifying..." Jacob forced a smile and shoveled another spoonful of stew into his mouth. During the few months since his enlistment, he'd grown accustomed to not eating for taste or pleasure, but only for sustenance. Lily's most recent care package had arrived only the day before, and its contents were a godsend: coffee, sugar cubes, strips of jerky, and a warm blanket she had quilted with blue and white stars woven into the pattern. He stood up and went to his tent to search out its comfort.

While the coverlet would keep out the unpredictable wind, it was far more valuable than a cloth to keep him warm. Jacob knew just by looking at it how many hours his wife must have spent stitching the pieces of waste-cloth together to create its intricate design. His desire for her weighed deeply on him. He spent his nights thinking of all he missed about her. The sensation of her fingers stroking his cheek. The glint in her eye whenever she returned home from one of her abolitionist meetings. He looked down at the folded blanket, and his yearning to return to his former life became painful.

He did not want to hear the groans from hungry and restless men. As much as he longed to hear his wife's music floating in the air of their Manhattan parlor, he wanted to experience something even more pure. Something belonging only to her. Her laughter.

He'd lifted the quilt to his face searching for a trace of his wife's perfume. But instead of finding the scent of orange flower and neroli, Jacob discovered that Lily had hidden a more tangible surprise within the folds. She had tucked sweetly in the center several new pieces of sheet music from her father's warehouse. They tumbled to the earthen floor of his tent, like floating leaves.

After dinner, he played the new tunes that Lily had sent to bolster morale—"Home Sweet Home" and "Yankee Doodle"—as the campfire grew busy with men from his regiment. Jacob saw little of them during the day, as he spent most of the time with the army surgeon at the Negro end of Camp Parapet.

As some indulged in swigs of contraband whiskey, he borrowed one of the young captain's banjos for a crowd favorite. Letting his fingers strum over the chords, he began to sing. *"I'm in love with a girl with a heart of fire, she whom I adore…"* The men, their Union blue coats unbuttoned and their shirt tails untucked, began to sing along, their voices climbing over the flames. *"With her copper hair and white, bright smile. A fan she lowers just for me…"* They all already knew the lyrics so well.

"Girl of Fire" was a love song he had written for Lily during their early courtship. The memory still brought a smile to his lips. He had sat at the desk of his one-bedroom apartment on East Eighty-Third Street, tossing sheet after sheet of paper into the waste bin until his lyrics captured her just right. All the time and struggle he had spent on it had been worth it though. For when he finally had the chance to serenade her, Lily wrapped her long arms around his neck and garnished him with what she later described in her correspondence as, "her first deep and unbridled kiss." Jacob sang "Girl of Fire" at least weekly for the infantry, willing his lyrics to bring him closer to Lily. He always sang it a cappella or on a borrowed guitar or banjo, and never just played the tune on his cornet.

With his hand tapping on the banjo's side, Jacob threw his head back and sang out the last chorus:

"A woman who burns as bright as a candle, wanting all who love and breathe to be free…" The men walloped and struck their knees with the back of their caps, bellowing out the words.

One soldier, who had been taking deep swallows of moonshine from his mug all night, lifted his cup and cheered. He stumbled so close to Jacob that he could smell the vapor on his breath.

"Not bad singing for a Shoddy," he laughed as he gave Jacob a little shove, his mouth twisting through the thicket of his red beard. Jacob despised the new slur making its way around Union army camps. Soldiers had begun blaming Jewish textile merchants for the poor quality of their uniforms and equipment, and officers were doing little to stop the rumors. Jacob understood why—the only other scapegoat would be the federal government itself, which would not exactly inspire loyalty in the ill-used soldiers.

"I was in General Grant's camp back when he said he wouldn't trust a Jew in his army, sending all you folk out of his command. Shame ol' Lincoln had to step in and change it back…"

Jacob's skin grew cold. The events back in December were still raw in his mind. Jacob had yet to shake his wariness of the army, despite Grant having eventually revoked that order that expelled all Jews from his military district. The pretense had been that Grant suspected they were tampering with cotton and gold prices for their own economic gain. The real reason was that they were an easy, universal target in a war in which there was so little to agree upon.

Jacob put the banjo on the ground and stood up. "Not sure what you're getting at, Private. My loyalties are to my country. And I'm not a merchant. I am a musician."

"Riordan, settle down," the blond-haired soldier ordered, pulling the inebriated man back to the fireside.

"Kling will be up in a few hours sounding reveille. You don't stop this nonsense, he'll be blowing his horn right into your ear."

Riordan narrowed his eyes and stuffed his cap in his pocket, muttering underneath his breath as he turned back toward his tent. The others, realizing that the evening's entertainment had come to an end, began to follow him.

Rattled from the exchange, Jacob held the borrowed banjo out to the young, dark-haired captain from Saratoga Springs, who had lent it to him hours earlier.

"Thank you," Jacob said. "It felt good to have my fingers working in a direction other than just pressing my cornet valves all day."

"I suppose I should really just give it to you, Kling, being that you play it better than I do," the captain answered. "You have real talent. Your song took me away from my troubles, made me remember my girl Lucy back home."

Jacob's face softened. "Is she a girl of fire?"

The captain laughed. "Yes, dare I say it, she sure is."

After the men had cleared out, Jacob was still feeling unsettled. Although he knew any soldier with sense relished the chance of a good night's rest, Jacob suspected sleep would not come to him easily this evening.

In the distance, over the stretch of canvas tents and horses secured for the night, Jacob heard more music being played. It traveled over the low brush from the Negro camp, just beyond the borderline of his regiment's quarters. The notes floated through the hazy moonlight, and he went off in search of it.

With each step toward the border of his camp, the music grew louder, a flute pitched high over the sound of crackling fire and soulful voices united in song. Standing near the flames, with his instrument perched to his lips, was the unusual man Jacob had witnessed the doctor examining earlier that afternoon.

The campground for the new Black recruits did not look at all like the one Jacob had just left. He had thought the conditions in his camp were bad, but the desolation here was far worse. The tarp tents were ripped in places. The men slept on their jackets and their shirts bunched beneath their heads; they didn't even have the gum blankets or haversack pillows that Jacob and his men used for their makeshift beds. Most were just stretched outside on the damp earth, the sole canopy above them the dark sky and bright stars. But despite the inferior conditions, the music coming from the campfire was as glorious to Jacob's ears as any he had ever heard.

The fresh recruit from this afternoon stood proud. A tattered Union jacket with missing buttons now replaced the torn waistcoat, covering his white shirt. The ripped trousers had been switched out with a pair of army pants.

But at his lips he held a beautiful flute, its reflective metal polished to a high shine. Jacob realized right away that the instrument was far superior to the ones typically owned by military musicians, and for a Black man to possess it was particularly surprising. But what was even more incredible to him was the man's ability to perform such complex melodies—Jacob recognized works composed by Mozart and Beethoven—without gazing at a single piece of sheet music. In all of his time in New York City, where he had attended countless performances at Manhattan's premier venues, Jacob had never once seen those musicians play such complicated pieces without a score.

It dawned on Jacob that he was listening to a master flutist worthy of playing at any concert hall in New York. He listened hungrily to each note. And then something unexpected happened. One of the men around the campfire cried out to the flutist. "Play us sumthin' real, Willie," he complained. "Sumthin' make us 'member who we dun' left…" They did not want Mozart or Beethoven. They wanted something familiar that lifted their weary bodies and battered spirits.

8

As William picked up the flute, the words the man spoke reverberated in his brain. *Sumthin' make us 'member who we dun' left.*

William had first come to learn to play on a hand-carved fife, whittled by one of the slave elders.

Ol' Abraham had been spared the rod and the work in the fields because he had once fished the master's son out from the pond near the big house. After that, the master's wife, Eleanor Righter, forbade any harm to ever come to him.

The elderly man believed it wasn't just Eleanor's intervention, but his golden oak staff that protected him. At its top sat a serpent's head. Ol' Abraham spoke of its magical powers, the knowledge it gave off that helped him prepare herbal remedies for the sick. But even he had been unable to help cure William's mother from what she suffered at mas's hands, so when he saw William whistling with a piece of grass between his lips, helping his mama pull the indigo leaves from the stalk, he decided to whittle down a piece of tulipwood and make the boy a fife. If his oak staff could protect him, perhaps the tulipwood fife would protect the child.

Mus tek cyere de root fa heal de tree, Ol' Abraham told William, as he patted the boy on the back and gifted him the wooden flute. *Take care of the roots in order to heal the tree.*

William took to the rough-hewn instrument instantly, channeling his emotions with every breath. Soon, he began teaching himself to play by experimenting with the many sounds his breath and fingers could muster. He played as his mother nodded along to the rhythm, her entire body yearning to join him in song. By the time he mastered his wooden flute, it had become known amongst those on the plantation that the young William had been born with a rare gift.

Meanwhile, Eleanor Righter had grown increasingly frustrated with the privileged young master Ol' Abraham had saved. Her son grew into a rambunctious devil, one who sneered at her treasured Brazilian rosewood piano, the one prized possession she had brought to her home when she married. When she heard William playing his hand-carved fife as she walked down the willow path beside the slave quarters, she insisted on bringing him to the big house for music lessons. Her husband had been skeptical at first, but eventually agreed. It was unclear whether his acquiescence stemmed more from the regret he may have had for the vicious punishment he'd once given William's mother, or the desire to get his wife to stop pestering him.

Within a few short months, William's talent had impressed even his biggest skeptic: Eleanor's private music instructor, Henry Peabody, who traveled each week from the main island to maintain her musical studies.

"I've never seen anything quite like it," he admitted one afternoon, ignoring the boy as he spoke only to Eleanor. "The boy can play nearly anything just by ear alone…" Peabody shook his head. "Of course, it's just a primitive talent…"

"Well, Clinton always refers to him as my little circus monkey." Eleanor smiled, lifting a teacup to pursed lips.

"Might I ask you if you're open to teaching him to read music?" Peabody asked hesitantly, as he waded into uncharted territory.

Eleanor poured more tea for the teacher while William stood by, his throat parched. "I am not sure if Clinton would approve of your teaching him to read anything, even if it's only notes on a page… And then there's the cost."

"Yet, his natural ability could be even strengthened if William were to learn. Who knows what more he might be able to accomplish should he possess that skill…"

Eleanor considered it before she spoke. "Perhaps it can be a secret just between us. What really is the harm?"

After that, William cemented his growing reputation as a prodigy. Eleanor dressed him in a velvet sailor suit to play in the parlor for their dinner guests. "Why, I couldn't possibly have him in that ragged muslin shirtdress," she informed Clinton. "The thought of him playing in a coarse linen sack is inconceivable. The music—and our guests—demand a certain amount of respect after all."

But eventually, Eleanor's obsession with the boy began to wear on her husband. "Putting a slave in velvet just doesn't sit right with me…" Clinton complained when William approached his twelfth year. "And he's getting too old to be in those ridiculous outfits anyway…" He shook his head before downing another glass of claret. "Soon you'll be dressing him in our son's silk vest and breeches," he growled. "And what's next, Eleanor? Having a nigger sleeping in our son's bed? He should have been in the fields years ago."

What William did not know, of course, was how his growing resemblance to his mother ate at his master. Despite the fact that the boy spoke only when something was asked directly of him, his master heard his mother's voice in the notes he played. While Eleanor perceived the sweetest sound, her husband only heard revenge.

Three months later, a wealthy businessman by the name of Mason Frye showed up and offered to invest in Righter's declining indigo plantation—but only if Willie was thrown in as part of the bargain. With that, William's fate was decided. The last memory he had of his mother was of her silently taking apart her cherished cowrie bracelet. She separated out a single seashell, placing it in the indigo pouch that had once been his father's, and tucked it into his bag with a mother's prayer that it would protect him. On that terrible journey from Sapelo Island to Frye's New Orleans home, William had no idea then that his new owner—who had just ripped him from his mother's arms—would one day become a separating force between him and Stella.

It was one of many of life's cruelties he'd endured, each one a driving force forward through what often felt like an unbearable life. He had learned how to cling to small comforts when he could. The spirituals his mother took him to hear at the praise house always returned to him when he needed them most, just like they did now as he tried to adjust to this new army life.

"This one from my childhood by way of the Gullah Islands," he informed the men. "Maybe y'all know it...don't need my instrument for this one." It was the first time that he had mentioned Sapelo in as long as he could remember, and he didn't know what had moved him to mention it now amongst these strangers.

He closed his eyes and began to sing: "*Oh day yander coming day/oh ho/oh he/day yander coming/come in rope my soul come yander/freedom is a comin...*" The familiar words returned to him, taking over his whole body, voice and mind. His foot began tapping out a beat and his hands intuitively started to clap. The melody was the most natural rhythm in the world to William, springing from the blood in his veins and the mother's milk he had suckled.

He was no longer standing amidst the desolation of the campsite. His mind instead returned to that of a little boy curled next to his mother's body, the warm touch of her hand. As William sang, he let go of being a mere musician performing to an audience. He was singing toward the ghosts of his childhood, a boy singing as his mother's son.

Soon after he finished, a fellow Black recruit heard the sudden rustling of leaves and alerted him to someone listening from the bushes.

"Who dere?" He cut off his song abruptly and advanced warily toward the undergrowth. The soldiers were constantly on edge from the daily harassment of White soldiers increasingly displeased at the prospect of living—and fighting—side by side with colored soldiers.

"I'm sorry I didn't make myself known... I heard the music and couldn't help but come listen," Jacob admitted shyly, as he brushed off his trousers and stepped closer to the fire. "I... play with the 163rd Infantry Regiment of New York and..."

A large man joined his skeptical brethren, and then stepped closer. "Don't know you... No right—jes come sneakin' up." Based on the grumbling around the fire, others agreed. By the light of the fire, they could see the man did not wear the dreaded uniform of the Zouaves, a unit of the Union troops rumored to be particularly sinister in their interactions with the Black soldiers. However, it still felt like yet another violation. Even as they expressed their displeasure, they were careful not to be too loud, for their unexpected visitor was not one of them; he was White.

"I know ya," William interrupted him. "You the man who was with the doctor today…"

Jacob nodded. "Yes, that was me. Though I now see your talents would be quite wasted on a fife."

9

Camp Parapet
Jefferson, Louisiana

The men slept soundly in their tents as Jacob pulled himself up from his bed and reached for the bugle that would awaken the camp. He had slept only a few hours, with most of the night having been spent listening to music and exchanging melody after melody with William. After a while, one of the men had retrieved an old fiddle. Its varnish patchy, the scrolled neck scratched and worn, the instrument found itself in Jacob's hand. He hadn't played a violin for many years, since his brother had claimed it for his own, but through Jacob's nimble knowing fingers, the notes of his childhood returned to him.

The dark night fell away from him as the violin's body rested against his shoulder and his bow slid across the strings. He played melodies his mother had taught him and Samuel back when they were boys. Bavarian *lieder* and folk tunes that had their roots in Bohemia. Jacob would never have dared to play those compositions for his own infantry, who would have sneered and thought them too foreign and unfamiliar for their taste.

But the newness of the music exhilarated William. He reached again for his flute and instantly began creating an accompanying harmony. Soon not only were the other Black soldiers clapping and singing along, but the little drummer boy Jacob had spotted earlier that afternoon had taken out his snare and also joined in. He kept up ably—his focus was singular and intense and defied his young age.

As Jacob pulled his bugle to his lips to sound that morning's reveille, he felt newly energized. He heard Lily's voice in his head—*Every man, every woman and child deserves to be free*—and he pushed more air through his horn than he ever did before.

Later that day, Jacob sat down to write a letter to Lily. "I fear we're moving closer to Vicksburg," he wrote. His infantry had been ensconced at Camp Parapet for nearly a month and had yet to experience any significant bloodshed. In the six months he'd been in the army, there had been small skirmishes, though nothing compared to the deadly battles of Bull Run and Shiloh. But the closer they moved toward Mississippi, the more Jacob became full of dread. The energy in the infantry was palpable, fearful but also primed to engage their traitorous countrymen.

Ever since his regiment had settled in Louisiana, Jacob realized that while he was hundreds of miles away from his beloved, he was only one state away from his brother's home.

Samuel's house in Satartia, Mississippi, stood alongside the green-glass water of the Miss-Lou River. Built by slaves from one of the nearby plantations he had borrowed in exchange for commodities from his bustling emporium, Samuel Kling had managed to construct one of the most elegant residences around. Surrounded by fruit trees and gardens, air heavy with the scent of freshly cut grass and sweet olive plants that burst forth with tiny white flowers. The house was designed to impress with a perfect symmetrical facade, two large pillars in the front and gentle eaves to either side. Inside, moss-colored silk curtains hung from brass rods, and love seats were upholstered in thick luxurious velvet.

Jacob's brother had grown rich in Mississippi. The fertile land and those who reaped its bounty were the perfect patrons for Samuel's business expansion. He grew his venture from a modest storefront into a sprawling department store with a clothing house, a supply depot, a hardware house, harness shop and a well-stocked pharmacy. Whereas their father had struggled to keep competitive with the throngs of other traders and merchants in New York City, in the small Southern town, Samuel had found a niche he alone could profit from. His brother's new business was founded on one fundamental tenet: the essential needs and wants of his customers. He took their father's trade of selling knives and tools and expanded on it. If a man needed a saddle, he could purchase it at Kling's Emporium. If his wife needed cloth to make a dress, Kling's offered dozens of bolts to choose from. He had an amazing memory for names and remembered not only those of his customers, but the ones of their children and grandchildren, as well.

Samuel returned to New York City with less and less frequency, venturing home only for the burials of each of his parents under the shade of an old linden tree in Beth Olam Cemetery. The last time Jacob had seen his brother was that uncomfortable Passover when he had brought Lily down to Mississippi to meet Samuel and his young family. That was the year before the war began. He could hardly believe that the man across the dining room table had been the same boy he'd slept next to in a crowded bedroom. Showing off a gold watch chain draped across his silk-brocade vest, Samuel was no longer the scrappy older brother Jacob had seen off at the rail station eager to develop the family's trading ventures, but rather a confident gentleman well aware of his own accomplishments.

"My little brother," Samuel had said as his eyes swept over the decadent Seder meal his wife had prepared for the evening. An enormous roasted lamb rested on a sterling silver platter. Porcelain tureens were filled with roasted potatoes and glistening braised greens. One of Samuel's young daughters sat quietly nibbling on some matzoh, while the other amused herself dipping parsley in the glass of salt water.

"Tonight is about the traditions our ancestors have passed on for generations," he continued. "Times have become especially fraught, but we must remind ourselves of the importance of family bonds."

At ease, Jacob smiled and returned the toast. "Thank you for welcoming us into your beautiful home. Life here has been good to you."

"It is all Eliza's doing," he said, glancing over at his wife. "She has made it such a peaceful place for the girls and me. I only hope your Mr. Lincoln will keep his nose out of *our* economy. With seven states having already seceded and Jefferson Davis firmly at the helm, he cannot ignore the interests of our confederacy any longer. They are never going to agree to his terms." Samuel staked his political position, while taking slow sips of claret from a cut-crystal glass. Jacob cringed at his brother's use of the word *our* in referring to the Rebel nation.

Eliza was even less subtle in her contempt for President Lincoln.

"Samuel's learned quickly how things are done around here...he knows that our money comes from cotton. And cotton doesn't pick itself... Our customers must have slaves if we are to survive. What does Lincoln want...all of the South to starve?"

Jacob could still remember the look on Lily's face as she heard her new family's words. Her complexion reddened. Her eyes grew fierce.

"Do you have no decency? There is no logical reason why a man cannot be employed for a fair wage, allowing him to have both economic independence and a sense of dignity," Lily retorted. She gazed down at the prayer book by Jacob's plate. "Tonight we celebrate family, but we also pay respect to the Israelites' escape from bondage in Egypt, and yet you fail to see the irony of your words, in support of Southern slavery, dear sister."

"I see you've married an abolitionist, Jacob." Eliza's saccharine tone could hardly disguise her annoyance. She raised a disapproving glance in his direction and then exhaled an audible huff.

The painful silence that followed an abrupt end to dinner had ruined the brothers' long-awaited reunion almost as soon as it began. One could feel the air in the room turn icy, despite the warm spring weather.

The only delight Lily seemed to take away from that awkward trip had been the experience of walking in Eliza's newly planted garden, where pale pink and marble-white crushed seashells lined the paths.

The mix of scented blooms with the sun-bleached shells beneath their soles remained the one beautiful, parting memory of Samuel's abode. Now, in his diary, Jacob kept the last letter he had received from his brother. Samuel had written it two years earlier, just a month prior to the postal service stopping delivery of all correspondence between the North and the South. Keeping it brought some risk, for the other men might question his loyalty if they knew he had family fighting on the Confederate side. But Jacob felt the need to have close Samuel's last words to him. Partly out of brotherly love, partly as a reminder of their conflicting views. He kept it secretly tucked within his diary's pages.

This will be a most wretched war, Samuel wrote. *And I hope you understand that I have little choice but to support the Confederate Cause. I am not fighting to protect slavery. I am fighting to protect my enterprise, for which I have worked for many years to build and make a success. If it were to fail, my family would be without any means of financial support. I do not think we are the only two brothers in the nation to be confronted with this terrible reality that we could find ourselves fighting against each other on the battlefield. It is a thought I want to banish from my mind for my conscience is heavy with the idea of it. Please know that despite the different lives we now live, I continue to keep you in my heart, dear brother.*

The Satartia house and garden would be empty of his brother's presence now. Just Eliza and their two girls. Jacob knew there was real reason to worry about them, now that he and hundreds of Union men would be moving closer toward the lower Baton Rouge line, right in the direction of Samuel's family's homestead.

10

They handed William a shovel barely an hour after he and the little drummer boy had sounded the reveille. The child had spoken little since he'd attached himself to Willie's side. "Think that fella's not quite right in the head," one of the soldiers remarked to another recruit. "Hasn't said more than one or two words since I lay eyes on him, but he sure does a good drumroll."

"Can't be too thick," one man insisted. "Plays too well and always does what we ask of him…"

"Even if he don't talk much, he too young to be diggin' graves," another voice sounded off. "It ain't right."

William put his hand out to intercept the large, heavy tool being thrust into the boy's grip. "I'll dig enough for two men," he volunteered. He whispered instructions into the youngster's ear, then nudged him toward the makeshift shelter of branches and leaves where the child had been sleeping.

The captain in Union blues, his face a pale moon beneath his cap, shrugged. "Just get the job done." He pointed in the direction of the field just behind the hospital tent. Eight men had died during the night. None from battle wounds, but from disease. The week before six men had fallen ill from malaria. The week before that, ten from bilious fever.

William took his shovel and followed several other men to the stretch of tall grass. He had risked everything to run away and fight. He'd left his snug room in Frye's attic. He had abandoned the comfort of two meals a day. But what caused him the most anguish was not the missing food or sleeping on the hard ground, it was that he had abandoned Stella to fend for herself.

"Dig deep, boys," the captain reminded them. "Don't want any animals—four legs or two—getting to the bones."

The men grunted and thrust their shovels into the earth. They were fortunate that the weeks of rain had momentarily stopped. The mud had plagued both armies for most of the fighting in the Louisiana marshland, making any advancement toward enemy troops impossible.

"Ran here to fight crackers—not dig graves," a thick-shouldered man complained.

"Ran here to put my hate to some good," another chimed in, grunting as he threw soil behind him. "But dis—dis ain't no good…"

William paused and looked down at the growing ditch. Hate. He had a lot in him, that much he was certain. But there were different gradations of his rage.

Was the hate he had for Clinton Righter, who'd done what he done to his mama, the same he'd had for Mason Frye, who'd taken him away from his mother and brought him to

New Orleans, purchased new clothes and a shiny new flute for him? Certainly not in the very beginning. He wasn't even sure how he felt about Frye when he first came to live with him. He was heartsick to have been torn away from his mama. But the venom that would grow later—that inner fury that threatened to consume him and prompted him to run—came over William after the Market, once Frye had decided on Stella. It took hold of him most powerfully that first time his master took William in his carriage over to Burgundy Street, knocked on the blue door with its three arching sunflower plants and instructed William to walk inside with him.

"Gotta present for you, Stella," Frye intoned as he stepped through the threshold. He unbuttoned the last two buttons of his waistcoat and made himself comfortable as he sat down in one of the two secondhand chairs he'd bought months earlier to furnish the place.

William stood in the central room gazing upon the small embroidered cushions. The delicate flourishes that had clearly been done by a woman's hand—perhaps even Stella's.

"Look what I brought," Frye announced. It was nearly impossible for him to contain his tremendous pleasure with himself for bequeathing upon Stella her own private concert.

William's posture stiffened as he watched Stella walk into the house from the small kitchen garden. Immediately re-entranced by her warm, bourbon-colored eyes, her long neck emerging from the scalloped collar of her dress. He had been told to dress in his performance outfit, a billowy white blouse, silk vest and velvet knee breeches. William's face flamed with embarrassment. He was the toy performer, brought in to amuse Frye and impress another one of his playthings.

"I remember how you liked his playing…" His thick fingers plucked at the fibers of his pant legs. "So, Willie, play us a tune!"

William hesitated. In one brief, rage-filled moment, he scanned the room to see if there were any fireplace tools, any brass candlesticks, anything that might be heavier than the lightweight flute between his hands. William often recalled that afternoon, arising unbidden from the recesses of his memory. For that was the first time he realized that there were humiliations deep enough to inspire you to kill.

New Orleans, Louisiana
April 1863

It had been a month since William had fled, yet they'd received no word whether he had reached Camp Parapet safely. Stella had anticipated this dreadful vacuum of silence. William, like nearly every slave, couldn't read or write, and even if he could find a Union officer to pen something for him, it would be far too dangerous for her to receive any message from him.

Frye had recently slipped back into the Union-controlled city, and his temper was now worse than Stella could ever remember. He had always been relatively mild mannered and, if not easy to manipulate, at least easy to placate. But no more. It wasn't only the heavy weight of New Orleans being under occupation and the toll it was taking on his livelihood and his family. It was also Willie's terrible betrayal, an act that enraged him beyond measure. How many times had he ranted to Stella that he'd put a several-hundred-dollar bounty on his prized slave's head? Each time, her body shook with fear, but she forced herself to see the bright side that William had not yet been captured.

He never knew she listened to every word he muttered. On a few occasions over the past year, when Frye lay in bed with Stella, he had carelessly let slip information regarding the locations of the few remaining Rebel strongholds outside the city walls. Frye spoke surprisingly freely as he pulled out his pipe, musing aloud about the situation. He openly doubted her mental faculty to even understand, let alone ever use, the secrets he was now revealing. Stella knew he would never suspect that she had been making mental notes to use in designing William's escape route. He'd always found her docility to be her main virtue; he believed her to be as compliant as a small child and unflappingly loyal as a dog.

So unthreatened by her, he'd even taught her the alphabet and some rudimentary reading when he first brought her to the cottage. He could not resist her sense of awe when he pulled a book from his satchel and placed the leather-bound cover with its gilded pages between her two delicate hands.

But despite the comfort and ease Frye clearly felt with her, Stella possessed absolutely no loyalty to the man. How could she? Theirs was an arrangement not of love, or even personal choice. She remained insufferably yoked to him. And his most intolerable power over her was that he could deny her the freedom to love whom her heart had chosen.

Stella did not hesitate for an instant when she sensed the information that Frye had offhandedly noted could potentially assist William. Before learning of Camp Parapet, her beloved William had been considering making the far longer—and more dangerous—trek to Port Hudson. Unknowingly, Frye had saved Williams dozens of miles in his journey and virtually assured his escape.

Never once had she questioned the risk she'd undertaken to abet Willie's escape. She knew it was worth the consequences because it was done out of love.

So it had taken her by great surprise when Ammanee returned home the following week, her eyes ablaze and her spirit fiercer than Stella had ever experienced.

"Miss Hyacinth need yo' help, Stella," she pleaded as she entered the cottage and quickly shut the door.

Janie was sitting there on one of the low stools, unraveling a piece of old crochet work she hoped to repurpose into a pair of new gloves.

"Her boy, Jonah, gonna be taken to the battlefront with his mas'. They leavin' the plantation in a week or so, and she sure he's gonna be killed."

Stella's face softened. It was terrible news, but not surprising. She had heard heart-aching rumors of countless young Black men throughout the South being forced to accompany their masters to the front and extend their servitude to them there. Sometimes it was merely doing their laundry and cooking, but others had been forced to take their owner's place in the fighting.

"That is terrible, Ammanee, but what can *I* do?"

"He wants to escape…to join up with the Union just like Willie. I know the journey ain't far, but there still Rebs and paddy rollers round the city."

Stella stared at her blankly, still not quite sure what Ammanee was beseeching from her.

"You could listen real good the next time Frye come to visit. Put an ear out if he sayin' anything where his men are hiding. Jonah's gonna have enough against him when he make for freedom. Putting a little knowledge in his ear about the best way out, it's the least you can do for one of our own."

Stella looked down at her feet. She noticed a hole in her

stocking that needed mending. Gone were the days when she could have asked Frye for a new pair for the season. The whole city was hungry now, and the shelves were bare.

"Hyacinth just want me to say if I hear anything helpful?" She suddenly felt so tired, and she had felt a sour pit in her stomach all day. She knew her lack of appetite had to be from all the worrying over William.

Ammanee paused. "I told her you'd make a map for him."

Stella's eyes widened. "A map?"

"Yes. That you'd stitch something into some cloth...so Miss Hyacinth don't mess up the instructions and Jonah don't forget 'em when he's on the trail."

A terrible silence swept through the room. Janie put down her crochet work as Stella looked aghast at the dangerous suggestion.

"That don't seem like a good idea..."

Ammanee grew distraught. "You got a real chance to help, Stella."

"I don't see it that way," Stella answered. She swallowed hard, stunned.

"You could even rifle through his bag while he's sleeping..." Ammanee pressed. "And now wit' you knowin' your letters..."

With that, their mother stood up quickly from her chair, dropping her sewing to the floor. "Hush now!" Janie sharply warned Ammanee.

Even when alone, the women never openly discussed or even alluded to the fact that Frye had taught Stella basic reading. It brought with it grave danger for all of them. Even before the war, reading was a punishable offense—and now that Frye was a captain in the Confederate forces, it could mean immediate punishment for him as a Southern man who had broken their unwritten code. Even worse, angry mobs who had grown increasingly violent and hostile toward their Union occupiers might want Stella killed for the transgression.

Ammanee moved across the room and grasped Stella's wrist tightly. "You *say* you can't help, but with Willie out there, risking his life every day...every night...how could you choose *not* to help?"

With that, Ammanee released her grip, knowing full well that she had wielded the most effective tool in her arsenal— her sister's love for William.

Stella felt her sister's words like a stabbing pain in her belly. She had always harbored a deep affection for Miss Hyacinth. Only a couple of years older than Janie, she'd been a fixture on Rampart Street for as long as Stella could remember. Tall and voluptuous with eau de Nil–colored eyes. An unspoken competition always existed as to which of the two women, Hyacinth or Janie, was considered the most beautiful.

But middle age had since softened the two women's rivalry, evidenced by Hyacinth having corralled the other women on the street to offer a swatch of their clothing to make Stella a welcoming quilt when she moved into the cottage. The gesture still gave Stella a tremendous sense of comfort, and on the many nights she'd wrapped herself in that coverlet, she could feel the embrace of her neighbors who also knew the hardship of her suffering.

That evening, Ammanee slipped into Stella's bedroom and lay down beside her.

"I'm sorry I got short with you. I know you not feelin' like yourself. I can tell you missing William something awful, and your stomach is all in knots. But we gotta help whenever and whoever we can these days. All those men fightin' for freedom. We gotta be brave, too."

Tears filled Stella's eyes. "You've always been brave. You've always been the stronger of us two."

Ammanee reached for her sister's hand and squeezed it. "All of us born into someplace unfair. Some just got it harder than others I s'pose."

But Stella knew that it was Ammanee who had given her the courage to love William, even if it had to be in secret. She had been the one who helped navigate their clandestine meetings. She kept guard when the bedroom door was closed. She made sure no gossip spread about the young man who found a way to sneak in and out through the blue-painted door.

And now Ammanee was right. How could she not help?

12

Stella was confident that Frye would be stopping by the cottage any day now. She knew he wasn't one to stay away from her for too long, if he could help it. He enjoyed reminding her and Ammanee that he was one of the few men in the city who had not abandoned his "fancy girl" to fend on her own, despite how much he had to keep paying "out of his own pocket" to maintain their household on the side. One certainly didn't need to look far to see that many of the women on Rampart Street had fallen on even harder times since their masters had either gone off to war or had their incomes slashed by the devastating inflation that had struck the South.

As a recently promoted quartermaster in the Confederate army, Frye was responsible for organizing supplies, lodgings and transportation throughout the Miss-Lou border. This new job required much travel on his part, and while he couldn't risk being seen strolling down Magazine Street to check in at his mercantile warehouse that the Union forces had commandeered, he could still sneak into the city every now and then and see Stella. And even for those who knew him, his relationship with her provided a plausible cover for his other endeavors in town.

In the small backyard behind the cottage, a withered fig tree grew. In her spare time, Ammanee had begun brewing a fig brandy she knew was strong, but palatable.

"Offer him a drink," Ammanee whispered as she helped Stella in the kitchen during Frye's next visit. She lifted a dark blue jug filled with the liquid in Stella's direction. "Might help loosen his tongue…"

"I think he prefers the expensive stuff." Stella smiled. "Not sure he's going to want our homemade moonshine."

"Still, it can't hurt to try and soften him up a bit."

Stella nodded and poured some of the liquor into a pitcher, arranging two glasses beside it.

"Maybe I will take a taste of your tipple." Frye spread himself out over a chair as Stella handed him a glass. "If you only knew the lengths I'd gone to make it here to see you today," he mused aloud, and then took a deep swallow. Almost instantly, his face deepened in color. Ammanee had made her latest batch extra potent, but Frye would never admit it was too much for him. He took another gulp and downed the glass completely.

Stella had a clear objective that afternoon. Somehow, she would guide the conversation to ask if he was headed near St. John's Parish, where the sugarcane plantation that Jonah would be running from was located. If she could steer his mind there, he might disclose his next movements and deliveries. Or at least a tidbit or two about what else was happening in the area that could help Jonah.

Stella poured a glass of the brandy for herself, too, so he'd think that her sudden curiosity in his work was just her tipsily filling the air.

Hours later, after he sat up from the bed and began pulling on his clothes, she had already designed the map inside her head. She always searched for a distraction whenever she lay on her back and was forced to surrender to him. It felt like a betrayal to imagine William during these wretched moments. But now the white ceiling above was her canvas, and stitch by stitch she could imagine the path she was going to embroider for Hyacinth's only son.

As soon as Frye left, she approached her sister.

"Tell Hyacinth to give me the cloth, and whatever thread she has. You know we don't ever have enough…"

Ammanee returned with a piece of thin white cotton that had probably come from one of her own undergarments.

"She only had a little bit of green thread," she indicated, offering Stella the half-used spool.

Stella took the materials back into her room, holding them in her lap while replaying in her head the information Frye had drunkenly blathered.

Stella felt keenly aware of the profound responsibility. This wasn't a child's plaything, a map for hide-and-go-seek. It was a man's life in her hands. She would need to create a simplified code for the map, and the color thread she selected would have to convey a precise and definitive meaning. A green running stitch could be used to show a safe route through most of the forty-mile stretch from St. John through St. Charles Parish to the contraband camp. A red lantern stitch would be the most important, for it would be the one that highlighted the possible presence of Rebel guerillas. A feather stitch of blue thread could signify the Mississippi River, an essential reference point for Jonah as he traveled.

Stella struggled to think of how to harvest the necessary thread. The little bit that Miss Hyacinth had provided wasn't enough to create the map, and Stella's own sewing basket was now empty. She leaned her head back, then scanned the surfaces of her bedroom, contemplating all the sources of colored fibers she might be able to find. On the top of her chest of drawers sat the embroidered purse from Percy that Stella had worn on that fateful night when she first went to Market. She picked up the bag. It was hard not to admire the handiwork of its creator, who had stitched the garland of multicolored flowers with such skill.

As Stella's finger caressed the rainbow of delicate rows, she knew she had found the perfect source for her materials, and she smiled. There was satisfaction knowing that the finery last worn on that dreaded night could now be repurposed. There was justice knowing that those threads just might help a man on his journey to freedom.

Stella spent most of the night working on the map, her fingers looping and retying thread until her handiwork was as precise as she knew it needed to be for Hyacinth's son. She handed the finished product over to Ammanee the following morning.

"I don't know if it will help Jonah, but I've done the best I could. I decided to use green thread to show what I think will be the safest route based on what Frye said...the red lantern stitches show the areas to avoid..."

Ammanee smiled softly. "Reminds me of when you were just a li'l thing and I taught you there was meanin' behind the colors..."

"That's why I used green to show the best path...wanted to make sure the map was full of hope." Stella lowered her eyes. Those afternoons seemed so far away to her now, when

Mr. Percy's carriage pulled in front of the cottage, the then-teenage Ammanee took her hand and led her outside to the small patch of backyard, in the hope of shielding Stella from having to hear the heavy sounds of Mr. Percy's grunting coming from behind their mother's bedroom door.

"Let me show you something," Ammanee had said gently as she drew Janie's sewing box between them. She unraveled a length of red floss with an exaggerated flourish that was meant to distract Stella. "We can make what's old new again," she announced, her round nut-brown face flashing with a smile.

But while Stella's nimble hands and long fingers took naturally to the rhythmic simple stitches and quickly learned how to sew a button or mend a hole, what she loved most was how Ammanee connected meaning to each colored spool in their mother's collection.

"Red is the color of love," she informed Stella as she quietly repaired a tear in their mother's dress. "Green is the shade of hope." One afternoon, when she was twelve, Stella discovered that Ammanee had taken one of her worn pillowcases and embroidered tendrils of ivy at its border and a golden crown.

For years, she had slept on that pillowcase with the green tendrils and golden crown until it became so worn, the threads nearly fell apart in her hands. She believed the hope embroidered into the cotton would rub off on her.

Perhaps the newly created map and the old pillowcase contained a similar essence. Stella had no idea if the work she'd done would be able to aid Jonah. The journey was so full of risk, even a man with a strong sense of navigation would be in constant danger. But he would certainly feel the presence of love when he tucked it inside his breast pocket, knowing his mother had taken every step in her power to help him. And wasn't that the reason she had created the handkerchief for William, so her beloved could feel her spirit guiding him as he fled? Stella knew it was the only thing she could do to not feel completely powerless.

Ammanee took the map and folded it into thirds and tucked it into the corner of her basket. "You sure you want me to give it to Hyacinth, not you?"

"My stomach's still not quite right," Stella admitted. "Gotta grind some gingerroot and make a tea to settle my nerves."

"Well, I best get this to her quick. She gotta find a way to get it to him before he leaves, but she been schemin' while you been sewin'. We did our part. Rest is in God's hands."

Long fingers of sunlight reached into the main room of the cottage and Stella was content to stay inside and rest. Since William left, she no longer felt the strength or interest to do much, and the subterfuge of embroidering the map had left her particularly drained. Ammanee, however, seemed more restless than ever. Her sister always enjoyed going on a daily walk, haggling for what few provisions they could afford at the grocers who set up shop near the grand St. Louis Cathedral. Prices were so high now, a sack of flour had reached two hundred dollars, so their shopping consisted of only a bag of cornmeal or a small tin of Borden's Milk previously traded by a Union soldier for something more substantial.

Since General Banks's Union army had taken over the city, all of the beauty and vitality seemed to be enveloped in shadow and unrest.

Over the past few months, every time Stella walked down Rampart Street toward St. Claude Avenue, she saw cracks of neglect and need starting to press through. Once upon a time, each home was coated in bright colored hues, and flower boxes were tended to with great care. But now there was neither the money for maintenance nor any patience for such delicate flourishes. The women behind each door were devoting every ounce of their energy just to survive.

13

Stella believed she was giving Ammanee a gift by asking her to deliver the map to Hyacinth. For years, she'd assumed the reason Ammanee seemed to relish every opportunity to do the family errands was because her sister was the more sociable of the two of them. But Stella had recently discovered the real reason her sister ventured out every chance she could. Ammanee didn't run off to the market because she loved picking out the ingredients for their supper; it was because there she could meet a sweetheart of her own. A man named Benjamin, whom she'd grown up with on Percy's plantation.

A few weeks before, when Janie and Ammanee believed she was napping, Stella had overheard the two women talking in the main room. It was then she learned that her sister was not only in love with Benjamin, she also yearned to marry him.

"Mama, I'm turning twenty-seven next month and I'm gettin' so old…" Ammanee pleaded.

Janie touched the edge of her turban. "You're getting old? What about me?" She laughed. "I just made another poultice out of walnut powder and black tea to cover my gray… Why you think I'm wearing this tignon on my head, chile? We're all getting older."

Ammanee forced a smile. "Yes, Mama, but I mean to start pushin' for something more in this life. Times are changin'. Men are fightin' for what's right…"

Janie was silent.

"I'm just thinking the next time Percy pay you a visit, you might ask him to be the go-between for getting me and Benjamin permission to marry. He could put in a good word to Mas' Frye."

Janie's face changed. "Why you wanna do that now? Not goin' mean anything with the law… And you won't be together," she reminded her daughter. "Unless you looking to go back to live at the plantation and he buys you back from Frye."

Ammanee's expression melted. "I got a heart, too, Mama. You know Benjamin and I loved each other since we was little…but there's lots of other things about him you don't know." Her voice escalated. "Like that he took the strap for me when I broke some of missus's china. He'd take the blame for my shortcomin's. Said he had been carrying it and tripped. Helped me out many times like that."

Stella's heart broke as she listened to her sister share all that Benjamin had done for her when she was just a little girl.

"He made sure I got an ashcake for breakfast when all the others were cutting the line." She took a deep breath and stared deeply into their mother's eyes. "He was the one lookin' out for me when you were gone, Mama. More like a big brother then…but still."

"When you even see him now, anyway?"

"He's doin' blacksmith work now on the farm, they took 'im from the fields 'cause he was good at fixin' things... And Mas' trusts him. He comes into town every week to get supplies. We try and meet up each time he comes...even if it's just for a short bit of time."

Janie shook her head. "That's not what I wanna hear." Her voice was laced with disapproval. "Ol' Percy see him doing that, chatting with you when he's supposed to be working for him, you make it bad for all of us. He'll come down hard on me and Lord knows I'm already scared he's gonna throw me out of my house and onto the street. He may not put much food on the table, but at least I still have a roof 'cause of him."

"But, Mama—"

"Don't Mama me... You know full well askin' something like that from him is just plain foolish. Better save favors for something that mean something in the world. Marrying don't mean nothin' for a slave. Law still gives Percy all the power. He can sell Benjamin anytime he want...tomorrow if he feels like it. If he buys you from Frye, he can sell you to his friend in Tennessee or even to Mississippi." She touched her hand to her forehead. "What you *want*, Ammanee, *don't mean a thing*. You better off just jumpin' the broom and be thankful you met someone who made your heart feel alive for a minute or two in this life..." Janie sighed. "How many times do I have to tell you? We don't own our lives, none of us free. You still a slave, but you think Stella or me really free havin' to lay down with these stinkin' men whenever they want?"

Stella cringed listening, though she knew every word her mother spoke was the truth. Still, her heart sank for her sister. "Jumpin' the broom" was the only ceremony slaves had to show their commitment to each other, but it meant nothing to men like Percy or Frye.

"Guess I was hoping he might show me some kindness, if you asked him to, Mama."

Janie's eyes softened. "Let me tell you somethin' about yo' daddy, chile." She looked like she was about to cry. "He asked me to jump the broom with him, but when Percy heard 'bout it he got ragin' mad. Two weeks later, like clockwork, he sold yo' daddy to some mas' outside Mobile, Alabama. And, after that, I never heard from him again." Her voice broke. "And only time I ever saw him again is when his expression come over yo' face or you look up at me and give me one of yo' rare smiles. Every time I look at those big dark brown eyes of yours, I'm reminded of him." Janie covered her mouth for a moment to stifle her emotions. "Don't you see? We asked for too much and then they went and ripped us apart." Her words suddenly grew cold again. "Percy took me harder after that. Made sure to show me who was in charge."

From behind the threshold, Stella closed her eyes and winced. She thought of herself, Ammanee and her mother. Their innocence—their entire being—held in the merciless grip of a White man. Was that the blindfold worn by the young and enraptured? A childlike belief that everyone was entitled to the most basic freedom—the ability to make a life with the person you loved.

14

My darling Jacob,

I hope my last care package reached you safely and that you are now wrapped by a blanket of stars each night, one that will protect you and envelop you in my loving embrace. It gave me great comfort to work on a coverlet that would not just provide you with warmth, but also contained my whole heart stitched into every seam. Sewing does not come easy for me. But the other women helped ensure the blanket was something you'd be proud of when it arrived.

Keeping busy has been a balm. My hands feel empty when I'm not working. I long to feel your fingers between mine. I miss our promenades down Fifth Avenue and the gentle way you hummed a waltz into my ear, so we could dance in our living room, even when there was no one around to serenade us.

I must tell myself not to be selfish in wanting you here be-

*side me. I try to remind myself that despite my longing for you,
you are fighting for what we both know is an essential right of
all men, regardless of their color or creed. I often think back to
that last visit to Samuel's home, when I pushed you to tell me
what you truly felt about this wretched war. Jacob, you did not
pull me into your arms and whisper fake beliefs into my ears, as
would have been the easiest thing to do! You remained silent for
two days, pondering in solitude, until you had considered deeply
your honest position.*

*Please know that, in your absence, I am trying to do my own
part. Miss Rose has been so busy with her Abolitionist Newsletter and writing her column for "The Liberator," she's asked me
to start using my social network to corral other young women to
create our own quilting bee. We'll be donating our proceeds to the
Sanitary Commission to bring more hospital supplies to you and
your fellow Union men. I pray you will never need such bandages
or medicine, but with each push of my needle and thread, I will be
thinking of you and your fellow men fighting for freedom.*
Your loving wife,
Lily

Jacob folded the envelope that had arrived that morning and
placed it with the others in his pack. His wife's letters were
frequent and always full of news from her life back in New
York. A unique and infectious energy radiated off the pages.
Before Lily, he'd never met anyone who was so intent on abol-
ishing the injustices of the world, particularly slavery. After
their uncomfortable and unsettling trip to visit Samuel, Lily
had pressed him to choose a side in this war, believing that
apathy was as malignant as condoning the system of bondage.

"Who are you?" She'd pushed him to answer on the train

back north. "Are you the man that says nothing or the man that acts upon his beliefs?"

The locomotive wheels jostled them from side to side, Lily's green eyes peering out from beneath the brim of her hat, looking straight through him.

"You pursued me with such passion, you were relentless, never letting up for a moment." Her gloved fingers twisted in her lap. "And yet there at your brother's home...you let me do all the protesting at that dining room table, not once even backing me up."

"I'm sorry," he apologized. "It had been two years since I'd seen Samuel and I didn't want to ruin such a short visit."

Lily let out a short sigh that showed her disgust. "Many are saying there might be a war brewing between North and South. At some point, you're going to have to plant a stake on which side you believe..."

The rest of their journey was spent in silence, with Jacob replaying his wife's strong words in his head. She was right. The opposite of apathy was conviction. Anything less would make him a weak man and he hated to imagine Lily thinking him a coward. He had courted her with such assuredness, despite her financial and social standing being above his own. He fought hard to show her father that he was a fine salesman, not just a dilettante musician, with a fierce work ethic and a desire to succeed. Both he and Lily had eschewed the old-world traditions of their parents and grandparents, who had used rabbis and matchmakers to forge marital unions grounded in economy and familial ties. Instead, they saw their union as an extension of the modern age, the American dream, where marriages were made by choice, by love.

In the carriage back to their apartment, he gave his answer. "I wrote 'Girl of Fire' when I closed my eyes and thought of you, but I also believe each lyric to be true. Without freedom a man has nothing… I wouldn't even have you." He clasped her hand. "My feelings just come through more easily in my music, darling."

She had taken him in her arms, her brocade shawl falling from her shoulders. He still remembered the look in her eyes when he pulled back from her lips and began humming the song.

Lily was so alive, so full of purpose, and he loved her even more deeply because of it. Among a thousand dim lanterns, he had chosen the brightest candle for his bride.

Now, as Jacob walked in the direction of William's tent, he thought for a moment that his imagination might be getting the best of him. In the distance, the lyrics of Lily's song floated through the air, but this time the rhythm was slightly adjusted and the tone was deeper, with the tenor even more soulful.

A strong sense of camaraderie came over him, one that he hadn't experienced in the six months since he had enlisted. Even though he didn't know them, he felt an unexpected bond forming between him and these new recruits who had taken it upon themselves to reinvent his music. That was the exhilaration of creating one's own compositions, that one's personal melodies could be reborn in the voices and spirits of others. The men in his infantry had always kept him at arm's distance. They were mostly polite and cordial, but the feeling of being an outsider was still hard to shake. Many in his company had never met someone Jewish before. He knew he wore his background quietly, never fully revealing himself, but his sense of vulnerability and foreignness was always with him, a trait born into him from his first breath.

It felt strangely wonderful to hear his lyrics reinvented by a group of new soldiers.

"Private Kling? You're always sneaking up on us," William uttered, slightly bemused. "Sir," he added quietly.

Jacob smiled. "Got a message that Colonel Abbott and a few other high-ranking officers are visiting the camp tonight and I told him there was a musical prodigy over here…convinced him he needed to get you to perform with us."

"So they want a little tune from the Black maestro?" William leaned on his shovel. He'd heard the request so many times in his life, and he was surprised how after digging ditches all morning, the invitation tired him more than the heavy labor.

"It's not an order…" Jacob clarified. "Well, not at this point yet. I didn't think you'd be bothered by playing for them… that's why I suggested it. But you did put down on your papers you were a musician, and that comes with a certain amount of responsibility besides playing reveille and battle call."

"I didn't say I wouldn't…" William knew he was lucky to have the privileges of a musician within the ranks. He wanted to fight for his freedom, but he also wanted to get back to Stella.

"They askin' for the classical stuff?" Memories of having to perform Bach and Beethoven for Frye's guests at a moment's notice returned to him. He loathed to think he had traveled this far and risked so much to fight for an unshackled life with his beloved, only to become an officer's pet performer again.

Jacob paused. "I'm probably going to perform the usual repertoire, some ballads, maybe a few waltzes… We have five players between us in our camp…" he began to think aloud "…me on cornet, a couple trumpet players, a fifer who's not as good as you…and a pretty good bassist."

"Gonna bring someone with me, as well," William added,

his voice rising to be heard over the grunts of the men digging beside him. "Got a drummer by the name of Teddy." He nodded, the sound of the moniker bringing a smile to his face. "He'll be coming, too."

15

When Ammanee returned, Stella searched her expression for traces of happiness from seeing Benjamin, but she could find none.

"She told me to tell you how thankful she was," Ammanee reported. "She said Jonah's leavin' tomorrow night. So we should keep him in our prayers."

"Of course we will," Stella assured her. Benjamin, William, Jonah...the list for the Lord to shield got longer each day, filled with more and more young Black men who needed every bit of added protection they could gather. "I only hope the map helps Jonah." She pulled herself up from the sofa where she'd been napping most of the day.

Ammanee nodded, but Stella sensed her sister was now distracted by the mess in the house. Her eyes scanned the cottage's small living room, which was in disarray. Stella had left her teacup on the side table, and the pot of cornmeal Ammanee made for lunch was still on the stove. But the mixture had since turned into a hard mush making it that much more difficult to form into ashcakes for tonight's supper.

"The place needs a proper cleanin'," Ammanee snipped as she went toward the back door to fetch her broom. "We don't want no rats, though I know some people now so hungry they cookin' 'em. And I don't wanna make a fight, but that pot of cornmeal done dried up and ruined. What we gonna eat for dinner?"

Stella smoothed her skirt, then placed a hand on her stomach. She hated Ammanee being angry at her or, even worse, thinking she had to play maid.

"I'm sorry, sister. I'm just not feeling quite right. I think sewing that map musta upset my insides. Made me think too much about what could've happened to Willie..." Stella kneaded her abdomen through her waistband. "Just got so many butterflies worrying about him.

"Let me help you clean that pot. I shoulda put the cornmeal away hours ago."

"You know you can't scrub no pots or pans. It will ruin those dainty hands of yours, and Mas' Frye will think I'm not doing my job."

Stella's eyes fell. "I realize I've made things harder for you these past weeks. I feel real bad about it."

Ammanee looked up from scrubbing the pot. For the first time, she noticed something strange about Stella's complexion. Her skin, which was typically a smooth shade of sandalwood, now looked sallow, almost green.

"You feelin' more than worried, Stella. You sick, aren't you?"

Stella tried to straighten herself up. "No, just feelin' low."

Ammanee shook off her wet hands, dried them on a dishrag and then put a palm to Stella's forehead. "You don't got a fever. But you still don't look right to me..."

"I'm sure it's nothing. I felt better when I drank some of that gingerroot tea."

"How much ginger tea you been drinking?"

"I've been making a small tincture every few hours. Why?"

Ammanee's face blanched. "Sister." She lowered her voice. "You don't think you're with child, do you?"

An almost primordial instinct took hold of Ammanee—just like her own mama when she first learned she was pregnant.

"Sit down. I don't want you fainting on me..."

Stella reached for the kitchen stool and settled into it.

"You had your monthlies?" prodded Ammanee.

Stella shook her head. "With the stress of Willie leaving... and the worry of pressing Frye for information, I hadn't really been keeping track."

"How many times you missed?"

Stella's shoulders fell inward. "Only one, I think..."

"But you're tired. You sick..."

Both women knew this could really only mean the obvious.

"Do you know who he daddy is—if that baby William's or Frye's?"

A deep wave of nausea washed over Stella. Either way, it was a terrible hardship. If she were carrying the baby of the man she loved, Frye would know she had betrayed him and, at best, would sell her and Ammanee. But even she knew that it was unlikely she would escape more dire consequences if she were to birth a baby any darker than café au lait. And if her child were to be born a quadroon, she feared she would lose him eventually. For the only real way for him to ascend in this world would be to get as far away from his dusky mother as possible.

It was supposed to be joyous news to imagine a life growing inside one's womb. But now, as her mind darted between the possibilities, she saw the heartache that would inevitably result in either outcome.

"We don't know if it's anythin' to be worrying 'bout just yet," Ammanee reassured her.

"If there is a tiny seed inside me, I so want it to be Willie's..." Stella's voice cracked. She had always known how little she controlled in her situation with Frye, but the anguish had been manageable until now.

"We gotta have a plan no matter what," Ammanee stated as calmly as she could. "Isn't that what Janie always told us? Only fools don't prepare for a storm."

Stella nodded. "I'm not getting rid of it, if that's what you're going to tell me to do. If it's Willie's, it might be the only thing I have bindin' him to me." She placed two hands on her belly. "His love growing inside me..."

"I wasn't gonna say that." The truth was Ammanee didn't know what she was going to suggest. But one thing was certain: her own life was once like that baby growing inside her sister. Janie could have taken a tincture of black cohosh to get rid of her when she got pregnant. Her mama couldn't have known then if the baby was Percy's or her enslaved beloved's. Of course, it had been different then; Janie had still been in the slave cabins and for most masters, another slave child was an economic windfall—no matter the father. But Janie had chosen to endure any future hardship rather than terminate something that might have linked her forever to the man she loved.

"We gotta think about how you gonna hide this from Mas' Frye for now. You one month along...with you being so slim, you still got a few months before you start showing..."

Stella's eyes lifted and she reached for her sister's fingers, holding them tight. The strength between their interlocked hands defied the necessity of any words.

"And eight months until we know who the daddy is…"

Ammanee knew to be grateful that they had some time on their hands, especially since the Union occupation made Frye's covert visits far less frequent.

She looked at Stella, so scared and uncertain. All she wanted to do was fold her into her arms and hold her. Ammanee had often wondered back to the moment of her birth, when she arrived a dark chestnut brown rather than a milkier one, putting all questions of her paternity to rest. Had Janie cradled her to her breast and felt relief that she had conceived a child made in love? Or had Ammanee's birth sent her into despair? For no matter the outcome, Percy would own the one thing that, for Janie, personified love.

16

William withdrew his flute from its case and rubbed it clean with a cloth. It was the only tangible object in his possession, besides the clothes in his pack, that still connected him to Frye.

He held the mouthpiece to his lips and produced a few notes, the lightness of the melody momentarily softening the fatigue in his bones.

He'd been digging ditches all day. His usually well-kept hands were cracked and bloody, and he winced as his fingers pressed the holes on his instrument. But William ignored the pain and allowed the music to envelop him.

Despite his visceral hatred of having to play at Frye's command, Willie understood that his survival had always been tethered to his talents. If he were smart in his choice of songs tonight and performed to the best of his abilities, he'd no longer be a nameless Black man in a sea of other recruits. Instead, the officers in charge would remember him. If he played his notes right and they requested for Whistlin' Willie to play more often, maybe he'd get a little more food, or even some medicine if necessary down the road. Perhaps he'd be more likely to survive and find his way back to Stella.

Survival was a skill William had learned from his mother— from watching her quiet actions, not by her words. Ever since William was a young boy, older folks on the plantation whispered that William had inherited his musical gift from his mother, Tilly. Her voice was her instrument. She sang in the indigo fields whenever she collected the blue-green leaves. She sang while she wove the seagrass baskets they used for the harvest. She sang low, murmuring almost to herself, when the overseer walked behind her with his cane raised high, and as loud as she could on Sundays when she joined her fellow slaves in desperate prayers for deliverance.

Tilly was a tiny thing, but her voice was far stronger than others who eclipsed her in size. It came from a place deep within her, a bottomless well of grief and hope in equal parts. She sang to keep her body and mind from breaking, the spirituals lifting her up when she wanted to fall down. When the basket on her head became too heavy, or when her fingertips bled from ripping the indigo leaves from their sturdy, verdant stalks.

She loved the tambourine, too. For the rhythm it sounded, for the ancestral call it ignited in her bones. It was the ringing of a chime that transported her to a place where she was momentarily free.

Many were enamored by her natural musicality, but William's father, Isaiah, was the first to interest Tilly enough to break her cadence.

"You got a lovely singing voice," he complimented her one afternoon as he took her basket of green leaves from her.

Shaded by a thatched roof, Isaiah toiled over the processing vats, where they converted the indigo plants into the coveted dye.

She smiled, her unusual slate-gray eyes softening for a moment.

Isaiah emptied her bounty into the water-soaking barrel. The bottle green blades floated on the surface before sinking. Hours later, he would remove the wilted leaves and transfer them into another vat, where he would beat them with a wooden paddle until the water transformed from green to blue.

"Heard you singing last week, and I still got your voice inside my head," he whispered.

She didn't answer him in words, but began humming something soft, as she took her leave.

The spring William was born, an onslaught of devastating floods afflicted Sapelo Island, destroying the flowering season of the rice and indigo. Master Righter grew increasingly unpredictable, his rages became more frequent. The more his anger flared at his overseer and his own debts, the more the beatings at the plantation escalated. Isaiah, robbed of enjoying any moment as a new father, was the frequent target of ire and arbitrary punishments. Fearing for his job if the plantation failed, the overseer sought to bend Isaiah, a natural leader, to his will to make the other slaves fall in line.

All the while, Tilly sang even louder. She sang when she was forced to try to salvage what she could of the crop. Working all morning and into the night, under a full moon, with William swaddled on her back.

"Talk'um dey gone'way frum here. Mek fuh freedum," Isaiah confided one night, when they lay together on their straw pallet. "We need to run," he whispered. Even within the relative safety of their squalid cabin, he barely vocalized the dangerous idea of escaping to the North. And even then, adding another layer of secrecy, he uttered them in the Gullah language, created by the slaves from a mixture of West African, English and Creole. He laid his lips right against her ear, so she more felt than heard the words.

Tilly knew there was no way to flee with a child, and no way she could ever leave her son behind. She pulled William to her breast.

"Heard that debts are so bad, they may have to sell some of us. I know they'd sell me. Then you and Willie lost to me forever."

Tilly gently sighed in response. She recognized things were getting much worse for Isaiah. His natural pride—the quality that she loved most in him—was what made him a target of the master's and overseer's unbridled wrath.

"Way I figure, we can die either here or out there, but either way we'd be free from this…" Isaiah ventured against her silence. He knew that it would be a struggle to convince her.

She didn't answer him. Her breath stopped as she clutched her infant even tighter to her side. Isaiah listened to her quiet inhalations and knew she wouldn't ever go.

"We wouldn't get far with him." Her finger laced around William's and she brought it to her mouth. There was nothing normal about mothering when you were a slave. She had heard of women who smothered their babes when they decided to flee, forced to extinguish their lives rather than risking their child's fate being dictated by a White man.

"I heard there's a woman in Savannah who can help us get North…"

Tilly mutely shook her head. The tabby shack was constructed from mud walls made from shale and oyster shells. The damp and dark enveloped them. The minutes that passed felt excruciatingly long. She could not go with him.

"Sunday at dusk," she whispered. "When we're all still in the praise house, I'll sing louder than I ever have…they won't hear you run."

Isaiah kissed William goodbye that morning, pulling out a pouch made from indigo print cotton from his pocket. Inside was a seashell bracelet that had belonged to his mother. It had been worn on her mother's wrist all the way from Africa, a reminder of a place where she had once been free.

Tilly sang as loudly as her lungs would allow. She shook her tambourine with as much vigor as her body possessed. And when the tears streamed down her face, everyone believed it was because the spirit had gone deep inside her and her chanting was the sound of its release. None of the others knew about Isaiah's escape that afternoon. No one even suspected it, except Ol' Abraham, who possessed a preternatural wisdom that made him almost holy. He walked with the aid of a carved staff he had whittled from one of the golden oak trees that grew outside the slave quarters, a wood that was meant to protect, and he was known to experience visions that predicted the fates of men. He looked over to Tilly as she sang to the rafters, her hips swaying, her body shaking with song. In an effort to contribute to her shield of safety, Abraham banged his staff extra loudly against the pine floorboards and joined her in her intonations. Together, those in the praise house yelled out, "Lord, I done done what you told me fo' do."

When the dogs barked, the overseer turned in his hammock, cursing the Negroes with their especially noisy Sunday afternoon service. He turned a blind eye to their carrying-on in the praise house—just as long as come Sunday morning they all turned out to listen to master's carefully chosen Bible passages exalting the virtues of obedience and servitude. He heard Tilly's voice ringing in his ears, and he vowed he'd use the cane on her the next time he saw her for ruining his rest. He thought about getting up and meting out punishment right away, but the lure of sleep kept him from rousing.

Hours later, right after dawn, when it was discovered that Isaiah had fled, chaos and calls from the big house for retribution ensued.

"It's that damn Tilly, with her voice," the overseer baited his boss. "That's how he got away."

A nod from the master was all that was needed to signal her fate. Tilly's wrists and ankles were then clamped and chained.

With her arms wrapped behind her, they tied her to a stake. One man forced her mouth open as the other reached for an iron poker searing hot from a fire of stoking coal. As William cried in the arms of one of the female elders, the sky grew dark. The other slaves muffled their gasps. Other than her stifled screams, no other sounds could be heard as they burned out Tilly's tongue.

Robbed of her voice, Tilly held on to the only thing she had, baby William. She could no longer speak, she could no longer sing. Yet on the nights when William refused to slumber, she forced herself to murmur a broken tune to coax her infant son toward sleep.

Later, when her nightmares wouldn't subside, when her mind raced with thoughts of Isaiah's being caught, she did the only thing she knew that could help her find peace. Tilly found a bucket of white paint and began mixing it with indigo sediment and lime. She vowed her growing son would not grow up with evil spirits floating around him. So she mixed an indigo dye and stained the ceiling where William slept in haint blue, using another indigo-sodden rag to leave behind the tinge of turquoise on the rafters. Dragged upon foreign shores, early enslaved Africans believed the hue would trap the evil spirits that tried to do harm, tricking them to believe that the vibrant pigment was the sky or water, ensuring they remained at bay. Without her tongue to protect him, Tilly needed to believe her son's life and suffering would be somehow lessened if she shielded him with the color of blue.

As he grew from a toddler to a little boy, she rejoiced at her son's talent revealed by a wooden flute carved just for him. Every night, as she watched William sleep in the pallet beside her, she reached into the indigo pouch for one of the cowrie shells from Isaiah, silently praying her son would have not one voice, but two.

17

William couldn't help but see a bit of his younger self when he saw Teddy. The child stirred a sense of protectiveness inside him, as he remembered how elders like Ol' Abraham had sheltered him.

"Hey, Teddy," he called out as he approached the little drummer boy's bed, a mere blanket folded over damp leaves. "You an' me, we gonna play together tonight and show 'em we're more than just a couple of ditchdiggers. Go get your drum on." He extended his hand to the child and pulled him up.

As Teddy stood, he reached for his snare, lowering the barrel to his waist and adjusting the straps.

"You got your sticks?"

A smile emerged on the boy's lips as he withdrew two wooden rods from his pocket. "Yes, suh," he said and straightened out his shoulders.

William ran his free hand over the top of the boy's cap, adding a slight downward tug to ensure it was on securely. He had resolved to protect this young man who had so quickly taken root inside him. Whatever reason he spoke only the barest amount of words, William knew it must have come from a place of terrible pain. William had grown up with a mother robbed of her voice. But theirs was a language that transcended words, and as he did with his instrument, she, too, had used rhythms to communicate. When she wanted Willie to come to her, she'd tap on her knee. And when she wanted to express happiness, she used both her hands to beat out a small drumroll of excitement on the closest surface she could find. William would do everything in his power to make sure Teddy could use his drum to channel his emotions.

"Come." William beckoned the young musician to join him in venturing over the hill to the officers' camp. "We're going to show 'em how to really play a song."

William and Teddy walked through the sucking mud of their campsite, away from the swampy earth hugging the lake. As they ambled toward the main fortification, where the White campsites lay, the ground became firmer and some patches of grass even appeared. By the time they reached the officers' quarters, dusk had already descended. While some unfortunate soldiers sometimes found their campsite ruined by standing water after a heavy rain, the officers had claimed the highest, driest area.

William saw Jacob setting up a small performance area with five other White musicians.

"Who we playing for tonight?" Willie asked, looking around. He couldn't spot a single audience member anywhere.

Jacob pointed at a canvas shelter. "Inside, there's a bunch of officers. They've been in there all day, but I'm guessing they're

coming out soon. The mess cook has been fixing them dinner." He gestured toward a small fire with pots hanging over it.

The smell of bacon fat floated through the air and worsened Willie's hunger. He'd hardly eaten anything all day, only
a hard biscuit and some watered-down barley coffee. "Mind
if I practice a bit with my new friend over here?" he asked,
eager to distract himself from his empty stomach.

"Of course not," Jacob answered. "How old are you?" He
knelt down near the young drummer. "You don't look a day
older than ten. Maybe even nine, up close…"

The boy looked down at his snare.

But before William could cover for his silence, Teddy picked
up his sticks and began sounding out a beat that both musicians sensed was his own rhythmic code.

The men in their uniforms emerged from the canvas tent flap
with tired eyes and grumbling stomachs. After filling their
plates with cornmeal and a rough meat stew, they pulled their
chairs around the makeshift stage that Jacob had helped arrange. Bottles of whiskey were passed around, and the men
soon relaxed beneath the canopy of stars.

"Well, play already!" one of the men barked in Jacob's direction.

Jacob signaled for his fellow band members to pick up their
instruments and start.

The brilliant sound of the cornet and trumpets soon brightened the night. An able trombone player and a clarinetist had
been discovered in Company B, who each added another har-
monic layer to the performance.

In her last package, Lily had included three new songs just
printed at her father's warehouse—"The Young Volunteer,"
"Aura Lea" and the emotional "Weeping, Sad and Lonely."

The latter's lyrics had been especially moving for Jacob when he read them for the first time.

Dearest love, do you remember, when we last did meet,
How you told me that you loved me, kneeling at my feet?
Oh! how proud you stood before me in your suit of blue,
When you vow'd to me and country ever to be true.

He felt that Lily had sent a personal message with her choice of songs, and that thought invigorated him as he belted out the words to the officers. The freshness of hearing new melodies was appreciated by everyone. Even Willie, who sat under a tree waiting his turn to play with Teddy, was impressed.

After performing for over an hour, Jacob, tired and dripping in perspiration, announced they had a special guest to play next for the officers.

"I think you're going to be amazed. We have a master musician in our ranks this evening," he announced over the chatter. "I felt like I could have been in one of New York's great concert halls when I first heard him play. Gentlemen..." He motioned in the direction of William and Teddy. The two Black musicians slowly emerged and readied themselves to play.

Willie made a slight wave with his left hand and Teddy began to produce a soft, undulating beat. At first, it sounded like the patter of light rain, but then promptly strengthened in volume and speed. Willie put his flute to his lips and introduced a beautiful melody, as high and as bright as sunshine.

Jacob realized right away that the composition was neither classical nor modern, but instead something purely of William's imagination. It filled the space with such ease, the improvised notes had to belong to the fifth element, above the mere fire, water, earth or air.

The officers fell silent, then became entranced. Teddy's

steady beating continued as Willie's flute rose and then dipped in dizzying arabesques.

"More! More!" the men clamored once Willie withdrew his instrument from his lips, and Teddy allowed his arms to fall to his sides.

And the two soon did as they were commanded, playing several more sets.

Afterward, as the night came to an end, Jacob pulled William to the side and affirmed what he had known all along. "They're going to be asking for you from now on," he said. "You did what we all dream of...they didn't see you or Teddy up there. They only heard the music."

Such a moment only happened to Jacob once in his life, and it was a memory that he kept buried in his heart. It was only before an audience of one. And the woman he played for was not his beloved Lily, but rather his mother as she lay dying.

Her last weeks had been excruciatingly difficult. The cough that had lingered for months soon worsened and made it nearly impossible for her to breathe. Jacob had written to Samuel urging him to come home to visit her before it was too late, as the doctor had said it was only a matter of time before she joined their father in death.

Kati had never quite flourished in Manhattan, the way that many of her fellow female immigrants had once their husband's businesses became more lucrative. She had always preferred the safety and security of her parlor, rarely venturing into the bustle outside. With her boys now grown, Kati yearned for the days when they performed music for her in the living room, particularly Samuel, who was as strong on the violin as Jacob was on the cornet. A quiet woman, she was more drawn to the sounds of a stringed instrument rather than a brass one. The violin was a conduit for unleashing her homesickness and longing for the familiarity she had left behind, emotions she struggled to express in words. And nothing brought more happiness to his mother's face than the times she picked up her own instrument to join her eldest in a duet.

Now, in her morphine-induced delirium, she begged her son to serenade her on the violin one last time.

"Samuel, darling, play me a *lieder*," she implored, her voice so weak her words became trapped in her gasps of breath. *"Samuel..."*

"Mother, it's me, Jacob," he tried to clarify. He leaned in closer and then sat at the edge of her bed, clasping her pale hand.

"Samuel, just one more song," she pleaded as her eyes looked through Jacob's countenance and only saw her other son, who in reality was hundreds of miles away, with his new life in Mississippi.

Jacob gently lifted her palm to his cheek, hoping perhaps she might recognize his touch.

"My violin is just over there, my darling..." She pointed toward the corner of the room. *"Please take it and play..."*

How could Jacob not oblige her? He stood up and went over to retrieve his mother's instrument, pulling the burgundy violin from its dark leather case. It had been one of the few things his mother had brought with her from Germany and he admired the elegant patina and shape.

Quietly, Jacob tuned it until it sounded perfect. He placed the instrument beneath his chin and began to play, despite not having done so for nearly a decade.

His mother's face softened to the music. Her eyes closed, her lips turned into the faintest smile, and most importantly, Jacob heard her breathing relax as the notes filled the air.

He played the music of Samuel and his childhood. The Bavarian waltzes and the slow, haunting Romani music that was easy enough to improvise.

But he put something else into his playing because it was all he had to give her at this moment. He put into each note the only true thing a son could offer to his mother: his heart.

And when he put down the bow and came closer to Kati's bedside one last time, he folded his hand on top of hers.

She did not say either Samuel's name or his. Her eyes were closed, her lips curled into a peaceful smile. She simply whispered, her last few words: *"Ich liebe dich, mein Sohn."*

"I love you, my son."

18

Several weeks had passed since Stella first suspected she might be with child. Now, after missing her second monthly in a row, she and Ammanee both knew her pregnancy was almost a certainty.

When Miss Hyacinth rapped on Stella's door and asked to speak with her privately, Stella was still bleary-eyed from a midday nap. The weather had become particularly muggy for early spring, and despite her sincere intentions of helping Ammanee with some of the housework, she had fallen asleep yet again.

"How can I help you?" Stella asked as she stood up and tried to arrange herself.

"It's not me," Hyacinth whispered as she pushed herself inside. "It's Emilienne's brother..." She entered the threshold with her head held high, the sound of her skirt recalling a bird's rustling feathers. "We're wonderin' if you might do the same sort of stitching for him that you did for my Jonah."

Stella stood quiet as she took in the sight of Hyacinth. The woman, now close to fifty, was tall like an empress. Her cinnamon complexion, celadon eyes, and long neck all created an aura that evoked another time, another place, one better than Rampart Street in the middle of a war. Stella now understood why some of the other women had coined the nickname Queenie for Hyacinth, and why her own mother had never adopted that moniker for herself. As lovely as Janie was, she certainly didn't have the same regal quality.

"Emilienne's brother, he's going to run, too..."

Stella clasped her hands in front of her, ringing her fingers together. Frye had visited just two days prior and he had been as loose-lipped as ever, prattling on about where he was shifting supplies to next. But she hadn't been listening as intently as the last time. Instead, she'd been preoccupied with concerns that he might notice the swelling of her breasts, or the darkening of her nipples. Stella had prayed he would be oblivious to the signs of pregnancy that another woman would know so well.

"I'm just not as sure about the information as I was the last time. I wasn't listening for the sake of remembering," she cautioned. "I wouldn't want to be the one responsible for bringing harm to the man."

Hyacinth's gaze was intense, her voice calm and measured. "No one would ever think that, child. We only askin' because anythin' you can remember might aid her brother. I gotta believe the one you gave my Jonah musta helped him."

Stella's eyes lowered. It all came down to faith. As was the case with Willie, they would likely receive no letters or messages ever letting them know if their beloveds had indeed reached safety.

"We've had our own ways, always…you know that, Stella."
Hyacinth stepped closer and reached for her hands. The warmth
of her touch radiated through Stella. "Why you think we paint
our doors blue, or hang bottles from our trees? Or put a broom
by the back door? We gotta trap those haints, and protect who
we love." Hyacinth sucked in her breath. "Us sistas of Rampart believe your needle and thread can protect our boys…"

Her words sounded like a proclamation in Stella's ears. She
still was full of worry that her stitches could lead one of their
own down the wrong path. But Ammanee's initial urgings
rang true in her ears. Stella had the ability to help.

"I'm going to need to find some mo' thread," she finally
said. "I used an old purse the last time, but there's hardly anything left to it now."

Hyacinth considered the request. "I'm not sure if it'll work,
but I got a small shawl. Woven real loose…with a lot of different colors in it. Maybe you could use that."

Stella had one herself, but it was only in a natural shade of
oatmeal. It had once belonged to Janie, and now she often
wrapped it around her shoulders on cool days.

"That will do just fine," Stella replied, as she imagined how
she'd untangle the fibers and thread her needle.

"We gotta use everything we have," Hyacinth reminded
her. "Help the boys get their freedom. Then maybe, God willing, they come back to get us so we can get ours."

Stitch by stitch, Stella pulled the last threads from her old
purse. She wanted to make sure to take every last bit from it
before moving on to Miss Hyacinth's shawl.

In her hand, the large scarf felt almost weightless, the cotton weave as light as gossamer. She loosened the grid-like pattern that made up the loomed cloth, and then slowly began
removing one thread at a time. First the green, then the blue,

and lastly the red. The scarf consisted of hundreds of fibers, so Stella didn't need to use all the colors there. After she had finished, the yellow, black and lavender threads remained, bountiful and in place, and Stella was happy to have something to return to if another map was ever needed.

She hadn't used her own cotton cloth for the backdrop, and instead took an old burlap flour sack. Its coarse fabric was in sharp contrast to the delicateness of the shawl. But it was easy to use and cost nothing, and while Emilienne would have surely offered up a swatch of material from one of her petticoats, Stella had thought the brown burlap would work just as well.

With the job completed, she folded the map like a napkin and placed it in the pocket of her skirt.

"I'm finished now," Stella informed Ammanee when she found her up the next day sweeping the kitchen floor. She did not speak aloud of the map, but her sister still understood the meaning of her words. "I'm going to stop by Emilienne's cottage and give it to her. I don't want to delay."

Ammanee set down her broom. Her hair was wrapped in a kerchief, and her wide brown eyes looked over her sister, appraising her health. She didn't want Stella venturing out if she was feeling weak again.

"You've been up most of the night. Maybe I should take it..."

Stella shook her head. "The walk will do me good." She cupped her hand to the small of her back.

"I could come with you..."

"Don't worry, sister," Stella insisted. "And it's been days since I saw Mama. I'll visit her afterward."

The morning sun warmed Stella's face, and she soaked it up like a thirsty sponge. Days of rain had brought forth the budding of fruit trees and birdsong. Despite the paucity of the cupboards and the stresses of a city under occupation, nature was still pushing forth.

Emilienne's cottage was close to Janie's, on the far end of Rampart Street, just steps from the church of St. Anthony of Padua. Next to its wrought iron gate, an enormous magnolia tree grew with large, globe-like pink flowers. Stella smiled, remembering how she used to gather the fallen petals in her basket when she was a little girl and her mother would pickle them or make them into tea.

Her sister had always loved the church, with its three symmetrical arches, a tall steeple with a clock in its center. Ammanee still volunteered to sweep the choir hall and bring flowers for the altar. Stella was baffled that her sister still kept her allegiance to the place, for its once beloved chaplain, a Frenchman by the name of Turgis, who had spent his early days at the church preaching against the evils of keeping men and women in bondage, had turned his back on the enslaved. In the past few years, he'd spent his time ministering to the Confederate army. But in spite of all this, and how fiercely she condemned the Rebs, Ammanee continued to visit and do her weekly chores there.

Stella could hardly contain her contempt when Frye mentioned that he and some officers were going to meet at the old church after his recent visit with her.

They're gonna start using the place to have Rebel meetings, can you believe that? she'd told her sister, dismayed to think of a holy place being defiled in such a way.

But Ammanee hadn't answered. She just raised an eyebrow and a strange, almost cunning smile emerged on her lips.

The exterior walls of Emilienne's place were a deep shade of carnelian red. Stella knocked on the black door, noting that much of the dark pigment had faded during the war.

"Who's there?" a low voice emerged through the cracked window.

"It's Stella, ma'am." She patted her pocket, warming the map with her hand. "I've brought you something..."

The door opened and Emilienne ushered her inside. Short and plump with an enormous bosom, Emilienne was the complete opposite of her friend Hyacinth. Her tiny hands reached to grip Stella's. "Thank you, *chère*, for doing this for me."

Stella pulled the folded burlap from her pocket. "As I told Miss Hyacinth, I'm not sure it will help your brother, but I've stitched it with what I know..."

Emilienne touched the material, her palm covering it like it was something holy. "Give 'em some knowledge. Give 'em some protection. That's all we can do, right?"

Stella nodded. She still felt the butterflies in her stomach, the nausea afflicting her worse in the mornings. But working on the latest map had offered solace from her own troubles, her own constant worrying. Stitch by stitch, she felt she was channeling the maternal love that was growing inside her. There was so much she could not control, but sewing a path through the darkness, how could that not be good?

19

At first, Lily had turned her nose up at Ernestine's suggestion that she corral the young women of her social set to stitch coverlets for Union hospitals or charity auction events.

"I realize that kind of work is important, but I think my skills would be better suited to helping you with the *Liberator* newspaper," Lily said. "I'm a far better writer than seamstress, Ernestine."

"I know you'd rather use your pen than a needle and thread, but there's more than one way to fight a war, Lily," Ernestine countered. "Think of how you'll be aiding the soldiers who are laying down their lives to rid the country of slavery. It is abolitionist work at its core, my dear child."

Lily wasn't completely convinced, but she forced herself to find deeper meaning in the challenge. "Perhaps I can embroider in a line or two from Frederick Douglass," she mused aloud. "'What to the Slave Is the Fourth of July'?"

"Now, that's my girl." Ernestine's face brightened. "Your efforts will inspire our men and give them even more courage. In the meantime, round up as many women as you can find and get to work. I've promised the Sanitary Commission twenty quilts by Christmas!"

"Will you be joining, too?" Lily asked.

Ernestine lifted her swollen hands. "My arthritis makes it impossible, so I'm handing the torch to the young."

Sixteen ladies now sat in a large circle in the parlor of Lily's apartment, with colorful patchwork blankets spread over their laps. Baskets of raw materials rested at their sides. Nearly all of their husbands were away fighting, and each of them was eager to contribute something to the war effort.

"Thank you for organizing this," Adeline Levi said as she worked on her stitches. She was the quickest and most accomplished sewer in the group, and within a matter of days was already on to her second quilt.

Lily's first effort had not come out as seamlessly as she'd hoped. She had created a simple pattern of crimson and white squares, but soon discovered that she was short of the amount of red material she'd require. Around her ankles, scraps of fabric carelessly cut collected like fallen leaves.

"You need to sketch out your design before you start working on the actual quilt," one of the women reminded her. "Didn't your mother teach you that when you were little?"

A hard lump formed in Lily's throat. "No, she didn't, unfortunately," she replied softly as she plucked out the threads to start anew, this time adding a third color into the design to make up for the missing red. She looked up and saw Jenny Roth place a palm on her belly and smile with maternal beneficence, as if to suggest that her babe was learning to sew right there in the room along with them.

A terrible, unspeakable ache suddenly seized Lily, one of the many painful longings she'd endured throughout her life as a motherless child. Had her mother lived, would she be as skilled as all of the other women in the room, who seemed to be able to quilt with their eyes closed? Each row of stitches took her three times as long, and she lacked the confidence they had. This was exactly the reason she had not wanted to organize the sewing circle in the first place. Why hadn't Ernestine let her just contribute to the newsletter or help with her speech writing? She was clumsy wielding a needle, but her pen had always felt like a sword in her hands.

The soft-spoken Henrietta Byrd noticed Lily's frustration, and quietly set out to aid her.

"Switch seats with me," she told the woman sitting next to Lily.

Henrietta sat down and took Lily's quilt into her lap. "Think of it as a grid," she instructed kindly, "and all you need to do is secure one square to the next. Use the running stitch—it's the easiest one. Just rock your needle in and out, then up and down."

Lily watched Henrietta's slow, methodical sewing while rubbing her sore thumb.

"Do you have a thimble?" she asked Lily. She reached into the pocket of her skirt. "Here, I have an extra."

Lily took the thimble and Henrietta then handed the quilt back to her. "You're going to get the hang of it, I promise."

Henrietta was right. With further practice, Lily's stitches became more even and soon her confidence grew. On the back of her first quilt, she painstakingly embroidered the words of Frederick Douglass, not knowing if the recipient would ever notice the poignant message sewn near the border. But she did it anyway, as a reminder to herself of the broader work that needed to be done. A quiet satisfaction came over her as her finger traced the letters.

She turned next to the quilt she made for Jacob, which would always be different from the ones she made with the sewing group. Lily had carefully selected the fabric, with each piece of cloth specifically connected to her and her husband's history. From the linen closet of her father's home, she pilfered the navy cotton tablecloth she and Jacob had used for their first Shabbat dinner together. She immediately imagined it cut into squares for the blanket's midnight-colored background. From her own armoire, she took the cherished white bedsheet from their wedding night, knowing she could use it to create the myriad of stars in the design.

As the women in the sewing circle had taught her, she sketched out the pattern first. Studying the rough drawing, she realized she wanted to add yet another layer of love, so Lily planned on stitching a heart-shaped amulet made from the hem of her nightgown, to be placed beneath the quilt's center panel.

She did not expect Jacob to recognize the source of the materials she used, particularly since she hardly ever showed him her more sentimental side, preferring to hide behind a veneer of practicality and strength. She knew he would only see constellations atop the interlocking of dark blue squares that made up the night sky. But since the war began, she knew the importance of putting her entire spirit into every endeavor. So as she fashioned the only protection she could now give him, she sewed her soul into every stitch.

20

The next day, as the officers relaxed within their tents, William pondered what music he would perform for them that evening. His mind traveled backward to a time when he was still under the yoke of Mas' Frye. When he had his Sundays off and he'd secretly meet Stella in Congo Square, just across Rampart Street north of the French Quarter.

It was the perfect venue for their rendezvous, as the square bustled with crowds, music and dance. For almost a half century, Congo Square was the only place the slaves of New Orleans could congregate on Sundays, their single day of reprieve as written into the law. From the moment William arrived in the city, he was drawn to the square. He savored the active marketplace, the scents of spices and the joyful chatter.

But William particularly relished the sounds of the instruments that filled the air. Men pounded on drums of all shapes and sizes, dried gourd rattles shook and calloused fingers strummed banjos. Most poignant to William was the melody coming from the reed pipes, filling him with a nostalgia for the hand-carved flute that Abraham had made for him back on Sapelo Island. Those afternoons when he waited there for Stella were his life's sustenance. Not only because he was finally able to see his girl, but also because he relished the rhythms that floated through the square. The music of his African ancestors breathed a new vitality into him and brought him close to the memory of his mother.

It was still so easy to imagine Stella arriving on the arm of her sister, each with a basket on her wrist, his beloved's smile a ray of sunshine. He'd follow Ammanee's lead as she wandered through the crowd and led them to a place she knew her sister could remain undetected for an hour or two. Their transient shelter was often a deserted warehouse or cellar, places that were almost always damp and unsightly. But neither he nor Stella cared about the shabbiness of the conditions. All they yearned for was the warmth of the other's embrace.

William closed his eyes and tried to pull inspiration from those memories and sounds.

"Let me see your drum," he instructed Teddy. The boy lifted the snare straps from his neck and offered his instrument to William.

When he went to hand him the sticks, William shook his head. "No." He smiled. "I won't be needing those."

The boy watched as William began tapping out a beat on the snare skin with his bare hands. The rhythm was not a traditional drumroll, but rather one that mimicked those he'd heard back in Congo Square. As William played, the boy's eyes lit up.

"Now let's see if you can do it…"

He handed the drum back to Teddy, who began replaying the beat he'd heard a few moments earlier.

"Yes, just like that," William said, grinning. He reached for his flute and began playing a melody that quickly rose and then dipped in pitch.

Jacob looked over and felt his body come alive. Any man would have felt moved listening to William play, but with the accompaniment of this unique drumbeat, it was particularly thrilling.

"Don't worry," William assured him. "I'm not gonna start with that tonight. I'll play 'em some Mozart first. Then maybe some folk tunes. But once they got a little whiskey in them, I'll play a li'l music from Congo Square."

Jacob surveyed the two canvas tents. He almost wished he and his men weren't performing for the officers this evening, so that he could just relax and listen to William. These rhythms were so new to his ear. He yearned to pick up his cornet and add another layer to their music.

"Who's gonna want to listen to my old 'Yankee Doodle' after hearing you play?" Jacob teased.

William shrugged. "Got the feelin' any music does the same for most folk. It takes their thoughts to another place."

Jacob knew that was true. Aside from his military duties as musician, his talents best served his fellow soldiers during their times of recreation, when his playing transported the weary men's minds back to their warm homes or the arms of their beloveds, and eased the longing in their hearts.

Teddy sat crouched by his snare, softly tapping out the new beats he had just learned.

"The boy doesn't talk much, does he?" Jacob observed. "Barely heard a word from him..."

William glanced at Teddy, compassion in his gaze. "He's talking, Private Kling. He's just speakin' with his drum."

My darling Lily,

I am writing to you at daybreak, after a long night of entertaining a handful of officers. Sleep has been impossible after the sheer exhilaration of last evening! I, along with a few other musicians from my regiment, played more of the music that you had included in your last care package, and it delighted everyone to hear something new. I dare say we are all becoming tired of the same Union songbook that we've been playing over and over again!

But the most extraordinary event of last night's performance was by a Negro flutist. This fellow, William, is a musical prodigy like I've not witnessed before. He can play all the classical composers from Mozart to Beethoven by memory and yesterday evening, after he played several familiar tunes, he enthralled us with melodies that must have originated in his African roots.

I cannot begin to describe, dear Lily, how his music changed the energy in the air. At first, the officers twisted their faces. Most disappointingly, I heard one even say something disparaging about "monkey music." But as William continued on and his accompanist, a little drummer boy, complemented the performance with a particularly engaging beat, the men's reactions transformed to nothing short of veritable elation! Their boots began tapping against the damp earth, their mugs lifted high, and their faces beamed with a delight I haven't seen since we heard of Rosencrans's boys' defeat of the Rebel forces at Stones River.

I hope you know how much I miss you. You continue to be my torch whenever I feel lonely or approach despair. But when I'm alone inside my tent, I imagine you with a new quilt over your lap, a needle and thread in your hand. I know you are working hard to keep other men like me warm, and men like William free.

I continue to sleep under your coverlet of stars, my darling.
Your faithful,
Jacob

21

Ammanee opened the back door of the old church and walked inside. The familiar scent of incense and damp plaster welcomed her as she headed toward the broom closet to fetch her pail and sponge.

The place was almost a second home to her by now. She knew each room, each chamber, like the back of her hand. Years earlier, Janie had first suggested she and Stella go across the street to St. Anthony of Padua to keep themselves busy. Most often it was during those afternoons when ol' Percy came to visit, and the girls' presence was not wanted in the small Creole cottage. Sometimes they ventured just outside the house and Ammanee showed Stella how to perfect her embroidery skills. But other times, she just took hold of her sister's hand and pulled her in the direction of the church. Even before Father Turgis had arrived, there had been priests and deacons there who had been willing to extend scraps of kindness to the young slave girl.

Deacon Dupont give me biscuits to change the water in dem urns, Ammanee proudly informed a young Stella. *He don't like the smell of mildew water when the priest preachin'.*

She delighted in letting her sister know that they treated her special at the church and shared with Stella some of the stories Deacon Dupont had told her, like how the old church had been founded as a mortuary chapel for those who'd perished during the yellow fever plague that had swept the city decades before.

As Ammanee grew older, she offered to do more chores to help with the parish. She scrubbed the floors and wiped down the pews. She polished the outside banister and swept clean the steps. But Ammanee never let Stella help with this work, for she knew that the girl's hands had to be protected. Her palms needed to remain soft and devoid of calluses for when the time eventually came for her to go "to Market." Still, the place became a sanctuary to them both on those summer afternoons when the Louisiana heat was insufferable but the chapel was cool and quiet.

As Ammanee entered the church, she missed those afternoons Father Turgis had first shown her special attention. He'd once spoken of God's love for all his children, Black or White. He came from a different place, not Africa like her people, but a country called France. But the war had changed his priorities; he no longer preached in favor of the Black man's freedom, but rather ministered to the soldiers who he claimed needed him as a chaplain on the battlefield. She sensed by the way he lowered his eyes that he didn't also include Black men like Willie or Jonah who had run away to join up.

Every couple of weeks, the church was used as a secret meeting place by the local men still loyal to the Confederacy.

Though many of them had taken the oath of allegiance required by General "Beast" Butler, they knew that if the Union were to prevail, it would take away their entire way of life with it. Far away from Union headquarters, St. Anthony was a place where men like Mason Frye believed they could gather to discuss strategy undetected. Quite a few also had mistresses they kept on Rampart, so this location was even more attractive. None of them had gotten this far by wasting time.

Ammanee got down on her knees and took her scrub brush to the floors. It soothed her restlessness when she could transform something dirty to clean. She scoured the dirty footprints from the White men's elegant boots, swept up the ash that had fallen from their pipes. But it was harder to get rid of the feeling that they'd defiled such a holy place. She thought of all those Black men, women and children who for years had beseeched God for deliverance and freedom. This latest blasphemy by the Rebs was yet another violation that made her arms work harder, her breath more labored. She wanted every one of them erased.

22

New York, New York
April 1863

Lily awakened and pulled off her blanket as the first rays of sunshine entered the bedroom. All night long she'd dreamt of Jacob. He'd been away for nearly seven months now and those blissful memories of their early days of marriage were growing more distant with each passing day.

She missed so much about Jacob. Their morning ritual of reading the paper together over cups of steaming coffee and warm buttered toast. The twilight hours when he returned from work clutching a bouquet of yellow roses. The smile on his lips when she read aloud a speech she was working on for her next abolitionist meeting.

Now their marital bed felt lonely and far too big for her, and she longed for that comforting sensation of waking up to her husband's warmth. She hated thinking about how much danger he was in, or that one day she might learn he was wounded, or even worse, dead. But Lily forced herself to believe that once the nation was no longer divided by this terrible war, Jacob would return to her safely.

Her own life of comfort was almost an embarrassment to her, far too grand for a woman of only twenty-three. The couple's apartment on Twelfth Street off lower Fifth Avenue in Manhattan had been a wedding gift from Lily's father. A beautiful space with alabaster ceilings, French doors and buttermilk-colored walls. On the days following their nuptials, her father had walked through the space, his chest puffed out and a grin of satisfaction on his face, delighted that his financial success meant his daughter's married life could begin at a smart and stylish address.

Lily knew her father wanted his progeny to move forward, and far away from the overcrowded row houses where he had brought her mother as a young bride when they first arrived in New York. He intended his gesture to be a generous one, but also to serve as a reminder to his new son-in-law that Lily was not the daughter of a simple peddler, but a man who had created a formidable enterprise from hard work and entrepreneurship.

It was well-known Arthur Kahn had taken risks that would have scared off most men. Renting a large warehouse space in Brooklyn. Negotiating extensive bank loans to invest in the necessary printing equipment. Hiring a dozen artists to design the title pages and even more skilled typesetters. While he had told Lily he appreciated that Jacob had helped his late father steer their own family's business beyond tinkering, he didn't believe the two enterprises could ever truly be compared.

Still, despite having initially been skeptical of the young man who'd asked for her hand, he'd since come around to accepting Jacob. He saw how he supported Lily's abolitionist beliefs, and how he was not frightened away by her tempestuous nature like other suitors had been in the past. Most importantly, thoughtful and sensitive Jacob would know how to fill the painful void left by the death of her mother, Elsa.

Be brave, Arthur Kahn had always whispered into his daughter's ear. It was his motto, uttered every time Lily awoke frightened. Especially now, with Jacob away and the fear of losing him freshly stinging her each morning, no different or less so than the day before, Lily repeated those words to herself again and again. She knew that on the outside, she gave an aura of someone teeming with courage, except at the sewing circle when her shortcomings seemed in high relief. But inside, that scared child—who knew so little about her mother—still remained. All Lily knew about Elsa was that she had died struggling to give birth to her, and that they both shared the same red hair.

While her father spent his hours toiling and building his empire, Lily spent much of her childhood lost in the carved oak shelves of his library. There amongst the rows of leather-bound books and old maps, she fell into another world and tried to shed the timidness that plagued her. She searched for stories of women she could admire, soaking up tales of Joan of Arc and Isabella of Castile. Women who girded their beliefs deep within their bellies, and were not afraid to pick up a sword to defend them.

Years later, when she clasped Ernestine Rose's newsletter to her breast and walked into the theater to hear her speak, Lily discovered a female figure who was brimming with courage and conviction. Behind the stage's podium, a round, matronly woman wearing a black dress and stiff white collar stared fiercely into the crowd and announced quite matter-of-factly, to Lily's sheer delight: *"Good afternoon, ladies and gentlemen. Let me begin by sharing my roots. I was born a Jewess from Piotrków, Poland. And I have been a rebel since the age of five..."*

The crowd stirred. Some men in the audience jeered. Another man stood up and demanded she get off the stage and go home. But Ernestine remained undeterred. Her voice grew louder to ensure it could be heard over the restless crowd. *"I will not be silenced,"* she insisted. *"I have come here to speak about the evils of keeping men, women and children enslaved, and I will remain steadfast."*

Lily's heart pounded as she saw how swiftly Ernestine took down her opponents with her intelligence and wit. She had always hated injustice of any kind. But slavery had always struck Lily as particularly abhorrent and she could not understand how any person could dare to justify keeping others in bondage for their own economic gain. Hearing Ernestine speak with such eloquence and passion had motivated her to help in any way she could. A few days later, Lily walked into the office of the *Liberator* newspaper and volunteered the Kahns' printing presses free of charge. Her father was not yet aware of the offer, but that didn't deter her. Lily was confident after hearing Miss Rose triumph over far more challenging protestors, Arthur Kahn would be swayed to help the cause.

When Ernestine suggested she create a sewing circle Lily thought Ernestine would find another volunteer to help her with her newsletter or coordinate with the printing presses. But to her relief, Miss Rose didn't believe one of Lily's responsibilities had to be exchanged for another. "A smart woman doesn't prevent a sister in arms from her aspirations," she reminded Lily. "She supports her, she encourages her to keep reaching for more."

23

"I've been informed that our military hospitals have a desperate need for clean bandages," Lily told the women during their weekly sewing circle.

Adeline folded her hands over her most recent exquisite creation. "It's true. I've heard from various members of the Sanitary Commission there is grave concern that our men are dying from infections because the nurses are being forced to reuse bandages. Any help we could give would undoubtedly be appreciated."

"Very well, then," Lily said, resolutely. "I suggest we put down our quilting needles for the time being and concentrate on more urgent matters." This was the sort of call to arms that energized her. "Let us gather all the materials we can. Bed skirts, chemises, your old nightgowns... We can put them to far better use than just lying around untouched in our armoires."

"I have my mother-in-law's entire linen set from her house in Harrisburg. Since her passing, it's just been sitting in a trunk," Henrietta volunteered. "They can all be cut up and used to help our men."

"I can offer my father's home to store everything, but make sure everything is laundered first," Lily reminded them. "We don't want to send off anything unclean that could harm our soldiers."

"Lily's right," Adeline chimed in. "Have your maids wash all the clothing."

"Let's not waste any time," Lily added. She sat back with satisfaction as the women continued to chatter about this new project. This was the first instance since the sewing circle began when she felt like she could put her truest self to good use.

Over the next several days, wagons arrived intermittently at her childhood home, bringing cartons of donated material.

Arthur Kahn had tried to make the best of his daughter's most recent endeavor, despite the fact that the contributions now took over the entire parlor.

"No place for me to sit here now," he chided as he went to his humidor to retrieve a cigar. "Glad the neighbors can't see this deeply into the house. They'd think our maids were waging a protest against doing the laundry."

"Oh, Papa." She smiled, while trying to organize all of the cloth into piles. Lily had spent the better part of the day stacking and folding undergarments and placing them on the sofa. The coffee table was overwhelmed by several towers of bedsheets.

"Every single one of these donations will help our soldiers once they're repurposed. Who would have ever thought mere curtains and petticoats could aid Union men like Jacob?"

Her father pinched the papery skin of his cigar, though he knew better than to light it and contaminate the mounds of precious cotton his daughter had amassed.

"Your determination is applaudable, daughter," he commended. "Have Annie bring you a few of my undershirts. It wouldn't be right for me to not contribute something, too."

In a few hours the other women would be arriving to help Lily sort through the mass of shirts, sheets and petticoats that filled the living room. A mountain of laundered white fabric to be torn into strips and rolled for bandages.

The first on the scene was Henrietta. "How should we begin, Lily?"

Lily stepped over to a tall stack of petticoats resting on one of the upholstered chairs. She touched the first layer gingerly with her fingers. The sheer cotton would be the easiest to tear. "We've been told to rip them into long ribbons, and then roll them up into small wheels," she said, lifting one off the stack.

"Like this…"

She brought the thin, gauzy material to her chin, smiling as she emphatically tore it with her hands down the middle.

24

Camp Parapet
Jefferson, Louisiana
April 1863

"Get up, Teddy. Get on up now!" William shook the boy as he lay asleep on a bed of leaves. Wrapped around him was a flimsy sheet, the cotton smudged with soil. "You missed calling reveille!"

The child's eyes darted open. He'd fallen into an unusually deep slumber and his dream about his mama and papa had been so vivid, they had seemed close enough for him to touch.

"Teddy!" William's voice was urgent. "We're heading out today. Pack up your things and get your drum ready. We're all moving on to Port Hudson in an hour."

But the boy didn't get up as quickly as he should have.

"C'mon," William said, giving him a gentle tap with his boot. "Couldn't sleep in when you were on the plantation, could ya?"

The boy looked up from his folded arms. He'd said only a

handful of words since William had befriended him, but this time his voice rang out crystal clear. "Wasn't ever no slave, suh."

Teddy. The young musician who played his drum with such energy and determination, but who was as quiet as a church mouse for the first two weeks he'd been in Camp Parapet. No one seemed to mind that Teddy arrived with his tongue so tied up in knots he could hardly speak. William had learned it was well-known within the ranks that General Phelps would not send back any slave who had made it this far. They'd given Teddy a drum, not knowing what else to do with one more runaway slave, as he appeared to be, and a child no less.

"I'm sorry, didn't realize yo' was free," William said.

Teddy stood up and wiped the sleep from his eyes.

"Suppose there's lotta things we all keep inside," he said as he lifted his pack, then reached for his drum.

"Gonna be marching all day." William handed Teddy a canteen full of fresh water. "I'm up for listenin' if there's anythin' you wanna tell me."

Over muddy roads and humid swampland, Teddy's story poured out of him. A dam lifting from his months of silence. He was born Theodore Bennett, the son of James and Phebe Bennett, and only a few months before, he'd had a warm bed and parents who loved him.

They lived in a pale blue shotgun with pink trim on Dauphine Street in New Orleans, a street lined with gas lamplights and blooming flower boxes adorning the freshly painted homes. The families there—all free people of color—took pride in the houses they owned. On Sundays, they all prayed together at St. Augustine Church on St. Claude Avenue before the men ambled to the Bennetts' shop on Hospital Street, where the smell of tobacco leaves and rolling paper filled the smoky air. Even now, as the boy walked alongside Willie, the smell of damp oak leaves clinging on his uniform reminded him of the woodsy scent from his father's store.

His daddy was not a big man. Slender and elegant, with Haitian blue eyes, as his mama used to say. He slept in linen pajamas and rubbed his hands with a scented shea butter at the end of each day because he spent his afternoons rolling dried brown leaves into their wrapper. James Bennett caressed his beautiful wife only with soft hands that smelled of sage, not tobacco.

They had come at night. Under the cloak of darkness, five White men with bloodshot eyes, who brought coils of coarse brown rope with them. Teddy heard the sound of their boots on the porch steps even before they kicked in the front door.

His daddy leaped from his bed and ran to the front door to beseech the intruders to leave his family alone.

The men instead whooped and spat. One of them thrust his foot into a low rattan stool, and another smashed a table to the ground. Before his father could reach the kitchen to grab a knife, he was pulled down to the ground, a knee pressed into his neck as the men howled and tied his wrists behind his back.

"You think ya better than us, nigga?" The White man seethed between gritted teeth. His accent marked him as a likely inhabitant of the Channel, populated by hard-drinking Irish immigrants who were relegated to taking on the most dangerous and poorly paying jobs. He pulled more rope off from his shoulder and began grunting and tugging, binding James's ankles so he could no longer move.

Teddy's mother crawled deeper into the bedroom, her eyes alight in a fear like the boy had never seen before. She lifted her hand and pinched her son's lips shut tight, and then mouthed for him to quickly get beneath the bed, pulling a white sheet off the mattress and wrapping it around him.

Her husband must have forgotten that he had a shaving knife sitting on the edge of the bathroom sink. Before she met the eyes of the men coming down the hallway, she held the silver blade in front of her, her hand trembling as she raised it in the air.

"You get out of my house," Phebe demanded. She pulled her voice deep from inside her, rising above her fear. From his refuge beneath the bed, Teddy could see her bare feet beneath her nightgown as she moved away from the bed, instinctively luring the men farther away from her only child.

One of the men cackled viciously.

Another looked at his friend and commanded: "Get this uppity Black bitch."

The third man didn't waste his words. He leaped upon her and then wrestled the razor from her grip.

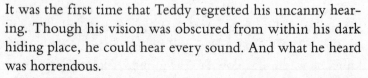

It was the first time that Teddy regretted his uncanny hearing. Though his vision was obscured from within his dark hiding place, he could hear every sound. And what he heard was horrendous.

His daddy continued to buck on the ground, his thrashings reverberating across the wooden floor, his gagged mouth stifling his roar. Before he shut his eyes tightly, Teddy glimpsed Phebe—her arms now held down and her face ground into the floorboard by the dirty hand of one of the intruders. For a moment, she snatched a final look at her son, her terrified eyes imploring him to move deeper into the shadows. She then turned her head away from him and began to pray aloud. "Holy Mary, Mother of God, pray for us sinners now, and at the hour of death." For a moment, her assailant's rutting stilled, startled at hearing invocations of their shared Catholicism. But a moment later, he continued his violent exertions before beckoning his fellow accomplice over.

After a seemingly interminable time, Teddy heard a new, awful sound. It was Phebe's gasping and gurgling for breath as the largest of the men wrapped his hands around her graceful neck and squeezed the life out from his mother.

The other men then moved out of the bedroom back to where James remained hog-tied. He lay there motionless, physically exhausted and emotionally bereft. He had failed to protect his wife, but he would still fight to protect his son.

"Cowardly crackers," James managed to spit out. "Coming at night to rape a woman. Still got the stink of the Channel on you," James taunted. The men surrounded him and began to kick him. "Bet you don't dare to touch me where others can see. Gotta do it in the dark," he continued.

The leader of the crew leered into James's face, showing rotten teeth and spewing fetid breath. "Oh—we happy to show the rest of these darkeys on your street what we gonna do to you." With that, he took hold of one of the knotted ropes and started to drag James to the door. As he slid on the floor, his linen pajamas snagging at the few splinters it met, James searched his mind for a reason why his family had been targeted. Was it the envy of a White competitor or the ire of a White laborer whom he had denied credit at his store? Or was it the most insidious reason of all—the random savagery of men.

The marauding crew dragged James out to the street, bellowing and daring the neighbors to call out for the authorities. But none of them dared. One window quickly closed and the lace curtains of another were drawn tight. The people on Dauphine longed silently to help the Bennetts, but fear overtook them. So they shut their doors and hastened to their darkened bedrooms, praying their own families would be spared.

Teddy came out much later—after his father's terrified yelps had faded away and he no longer heard the boisterous laughter of the White men. With great caution, he crawled from under the bed and ventured to the front door. His hand shook as he moved to open it farther. He did not need to turn the knob, as the assailants had not bothered to close the door behind them earlier. Teddy moved out into the street, his eyes finally resting on the ground beneath the lamppost down the block. Slowly, he allowed his vision to travel upward until it met his father's swinging feet. While James's hands had always been soft, he had never paid the same attention to his calloused feet, which had borne the brunt of his standing for hours on end at his counter.

Teddy stood there as the wind swept down the street, setting the knotted rope to creaking. He listened for a while, his eyes never straying from the sight of his daddy's feet. And he kept listening until he realized he had only one option now that he was completely alone in the world. He ran.

PART TWO

25

May rolled into New Orleans with its warm humid air and rain. As the flowers on the fruit trees ripened from the moisture and heat, Stella's breasts continued to swell and her stomach and hips became rounder. Just two days before, she had finally let out the waistband of one of her skirts and adjusted the row of buttons on her blouse.

"You gonna have to tell Mas' Frye soon," Ammanee stated the obvious as she shucked a bowl of peas for dinner.

Stella sighed. She'd managed to keep her pregnancy a secret every time Frye had slipped into town, distracting him with liquor and drawing him to bed fully clothed. But as her third month approached, Stella knew it was only a few weeks at most before her body's transformation would become impossible to conceal.

"Why weren't you more careful, chile? Didn't you wash

with lemon juice afterward, like I told you?" Janie demanded when Stella finally broke the news to her.

"'Course I did, Mama. I cleaned myself every time, like you taught me. Just didn't seem to work...that's all."

Janie shook her head. "I ain't gonna shame you too much. Lord knows dat lemon didn't work for me." She stared off into the distance. "Nuthin' we can do now but wait. But that baby come out dark, you know what you gotta do..."

"Mama!" Ammanee's shocked voice broke in. "You gotta stop right now!"

Janie nodded and swallowed hard. "I'm just bein' practical," she quipped back. "You girls think the pain of being a mama ends with childbirth." She shook her head. "But you wrong. It starts the second dat cord gets cut." She fixed her gaze on Stella. "I'm not goin' sit here idle when we gotta talk 'bout the hard stuff," she continued to press. "When Frye comin' here next?"

Stella shrugged. Frye never told her when he'd be visiting, and she doubted he even knew himself. One lesson from Janie had sunk in, and that was to focus only on the things that were within her control. Her eyes fell to her lap. While her mother was admonishing her, she'd been quietly unraveling more threads from Miss Hyacinth's shawl, winding each color into separate skeins. To her amazement, word had started to spread that her maps were lucky. Week after week, a new request came in. A knock at her door. A whisper. A trusted confidence between her and someone whose loved one was running to join up. *Might do no more good than a rabbit foot or a good luck charm*, she always reminded these new women (for it was invariably women who made the request on behalf of a man). But the requests kept coming.

"Mama, do we have to talk about Mas' Frye now?"

"Mas'," Janie snorted. "*Now* you actin' all respectful?"

Stella ducked her head further. She didn't want to even think about him. She just wanted to keep her fingers occupied with something that could possibly help. Other expectant women might have spent their hours weaving a blanket for their new babe, but here she was unraveling one for other people's children, brothers, husbands and lovers. With every stitch she made, Stella felt herself drawing nearer to William.

"Put that sewin' down now, girl!" Janie's voice rose. "Stop riskin' yo'self for strangers. You gotta think 'bout yourself now and what yo' gonna do."

She struck the arm of the wooden chair, and Stella winced.

"It's time you told Frye you're having his baby," Janie insisted. "Best you tell him now so he think you're not hiding anything…"

Stella gripped the edge of the shawl to steady her nerves. "I'm not ready to tell him just yet, Mama."

"You can't stretch this out much longer," Janie stressed. "And if you're *not* gonna get rid of it, only one thing you *can* do." She sucked in her breath. "Gotta make him think there's no chance this baby's anyone's but his… But if you spring it on him when you got a melon-size belly beneath your nightdress, he goin' know you were trying to run something past him."

"I agree," Ammanee murmured. "Tell him all sweet that you've missed two monthlies now. He don't need to know it's really three…you still look small enough."

Stella's body twitched. She had never for a moment imagined that the child growing inside of her might be Frye's. She willed herself to believe only that the baby was William's, never letting the other possibility be more than a fleeting thought in her mind.

"And when the baby come out darker than me, what's he goin' say then, Mama?"

Janie's eyes lifted toward her daughter. "What yo' sister hear at that meeting in St. Anthony's? Yanks are movin' in thousands toward Port Hudson."

Janie clicked her tongue. Ammanee had been specific in what she'd overheard in her eavesdropping at the church. Though she didn't understand all the military language the men had used, she did grasp that Confederate losses were mounting and that every Southern man would need to grab his musket or risk the Union taking control of the Miss-Lou River. Janie's steeliness took over once again.

"We goin' hafta hope somethin' bad happens to that man," she said through gritted teeth. "That in six months' time, Frye don't come back."

That night, Stella lay in bed unable to sleep. Port Hudson was only one hundred miles from New Orleans. High above the cliffs that overlooked a bend on the Mississippi, it was a stronghold of the Reb army. She hadn't said anything to her mother or sister, but Frye had offhandedly mentioned its importance to her on his last visit, confirming Ammanee had heard correctly.

"Wish I could stay longer," he'd mused aloud to himself as he lay in bed, lazy and sated. His pale body, clammy next to hers, stretched out over the white linen.

"But we gotta protect the river from those damn Yanks."

Under Ammanee's watchful gaze, Stella had practiced the doe-eyed expression she would adopt whenever he talked about military affairs, the one that looked soft and vacant. Gentle, pretty and ignorant—that was the way he always liked her. The emptier she seemed, the more information he'd reveal, free in his belief that nothing would ever take root in that untutored mind of hers.

He'd even taken a map out of his rucksack and unrolled it on his naked belly, indicating where he'd be moving army supplies next. As his finger traced the snaking curves of the Miss-Lou, past the stretches of bayous and marshland between the point where William had joined up and where the next big battle to control the port would likely occur, her heart escalated with fear.

"What's the matter?" Frye prodded as a small whimper escaped Stella's lips.

She shook her head and forced a smile.

"Don't worry 'bout me being in any danger out there," he murmured, patting her arm absentmindedly. "I'm going to be just fine."

26

Port Hudson, Louisiana
May 1863

The trek to Port Hudson had left the men exhausted and weary before they'd even reached the treacherous bluffs of the Mississippi River. William and the rest of the Third Louisiana Native Guard had marched for five days straight, through stretches of mosquito-laced swampland, deep forest and dangerous bends, carrying much of the weight for the Union army.

"We no different than a damn mule," one of William's Black compatriots complained. Thick coarse rope had bled tunnels in the center of the man's palms from dragging a cart of heavy artillery for miles in the thickest, wettest heat.

William's hands were also raw and ragged. *"I don't ever want to push another wagon out of the mud!"* he said, expelling the words like a field holler, a call to channel their collective misery into song.

Another man joined in: *"Gotta get me a rifle, gotta get me fightin'…*" Then a new, deeper voice entered, adding a rich bass line.

William's eyes blazed as he scanned the faces of his regiment around him. Teddy, who had a rucksack on his back loaded with tin plates and mugs, took out his sticks and began pounding out a beat on his drum.

"Gonna win this war, gonna go back to my girl and have her be mine… Gonna buy my own patch of land… Gonna be free!"

The music raised itself above the grunting and panting of the men as they dragged the White troops' supplies through the terrain. William's spirit bolstered. He could feel the energy between them all shift.

But when one of the men belted out, *"I'm in love with a girl with da' heart of fire. She da' girl I adore…"* a shiver ran down William's spine as Jacob's lyrics danced through the air like a kite's tail, full of color and passion. While the men in William's unit had added their own flourishes to the song—layering in different harmonies through the varying ranges of their voices—the words would always belong to Jacob.

A baritone chimed in, *"A woman who burns bright as a candle, wantin' all who love…all who breathe to be free…"* William looked over at Teddy beating his drum, still too shy to join in the singing. But the boy was smiling for the first time.

William hadn't seen Jacob in several days and wondered where he was amongst the several thousand Union men pushing toward Port Hudson. Was he ahead of their regiment, or behind them? He had no idea. He only wished Jacob could be here so he could thank him for giving his regiment a new fight song.

Days later, when William and the Third Louisiana Native Guard finally reached Port Hudson, more grunt work awaited them. Within a few hours of setting up camp, the line officer informed them they'd be put on "fatigue duty," building bridges in support of General Banks's efforts to take control of the Rebel-held port.

"Get your shovels!" their lieutenant ordered. But the men wanted to fight, not sling mud or lay down timber.

"Rebs camped down below these parts, and we outnumber 'em by the thousands," someone muttered within the crowd.

William took out his fife and wiped it clean. If they ever let the Louisiana Native Guard fight, it would be he and Teddy leading the men into battle.

Over the next few days, William leaped eagerly at any chance to incorporate music into his daily routine. He roused Teddy at the crack of dawn and pulled him out of his grass-and-leaf-filled bed to sound reveille with him. He found the boy again at midafternoon, when they were required to play for drills.

In between these duties, William helped collect wood for the new bridges, while Teddy busied himself cleaning the White officers' campsite and quarters, emptying and refilling pails of water, discarding trash and delivering food.

"I never hear a complaint from that little one," William overheard a lieutenant remark, unaware that one was not likely to hear much of anything from Teddy.

"Wish all them Negroes were more like him," he sniffed to his colleague. "They don't seem too eager to dig them trenches, but can they really fight?"

His friend laughed. "Guess we'll find out if Banks ever decides to throw them into the fire."

"The general wants to give the men a little respite tonight," William was informed three days later. "Get your flute…and bring the drummer boy along, too, if you like."

He scrambled to his feet, his heart pounding at the opportunity to finally breathe some life into his weary lungs. William now almost never thought about his early tutelage under Master Peabody back in Sapelo, but as the serious man had once enlightened him, *The flute is just a lifeless piece of metal unless you breathe life into it*... He longed to play. He missed the invigoration of performing, the time and place he always felt most alive.

"It'll be mostly White regimental bands playing tonight," the lieutenant added. "But you and some horn players from the First Guard are invited along...so make us proud."

"Yes, sir!" He saluted. He would need to find Teddy. He wished he could find Jacob, too. He hadn't seen him in over two weeks. Every time his regiment sang "Girl of Fire," he wondered if their paths would overlap again.

From his breast pocket, William removed the embroidered handkerchief Stella had made for him and studied its stitching. His beloved wasn't fiery the way Jacob rhapsodized about his girl back home. Stella was quiet and soft. So reserved at times that when she allowed you into her confidences it felt like the most precious gift in the world. It pained him that he now had no way to communicate with her, and he worried if she was still safe. He brought the cloth to his nose, but Stella's perfume had vanished long ago. Still, her spirit enveloped him as he went in search of another quiet soul, Teddy with the drum.

Within a long stretch of green and yellow grass, the musicians from a dozen Union regiments were setting up. William had just helped Teddy adjust his snare straps when he looked over the crowd of troops and saw the outline of someone familiar. The head of thick black curls. The slightly bent posture, the unmistakable cornet being lifted from its case.

It was Jacob. William tried to wave to him, but the distance between them was too vast for Jacob to notice, and already a throng of men were starting to assemble in the middle ground for the concert.

"Hey, look!" William nudged Teddy, showing him that the private who had shown up at their nightly performances back in Camp Parapet was now also setting up in the bordering field.

"I'm gonna let him know we're here, too," William said, smiling. He lifted his instrument to his lips and began to play a long and beautiful thread from his imagination.

The melody, as light as a bird's wings, dipped and rose in the air, like an invitation beckoning to a distant partner. It fluttered in trills and rose above the sea of tired and dirty men who had collected there in the fields to find a brief musical interlude from the war. While some of them immediately turned their heads to better hear William's rapturous music, he wasn't playing for their ears. He breathed his entire spirit into his instrument so the sound would, most importantly, reach his friend.

Jacob lifted his head and knew almost instantly the airy melody could come from no musician but William. He put down his cornet and followed the arc of the notes.

William lowered his flute, and from across the sea of navy uniforms that separated them, he raised his hand and waved.

27

Since sundown, Stella had been nervously awaiting Frye.

"He's gonna be there tonight with the rest of 'em," Ammanee insisted. "I just know it...got a feeling in my bones." She clasped her broom and swept the parlor clean one last time. "Heard nearly twenty men comin', and the priest looked damn scared."

Stella's heart raced. "I was hoping for a couple more weeks..." She placed a palm over her belly.

"Best just to get it over and done with." Ammanee shook her head and appraised the neatness of the room. "And Mama's hopin' he do right by you...gives you a little more coin from his purse, when he learns you're with his chile. Mas' Percy hasn't given Mama nothin' for couple months now, and she's sufferin' bad."

Stella's stomach growled. She and Ammanee didn't have

much, either. They'd eaten nothing but dandelion leaves and a little bit of boiled potato for supper. The nausea she'd experienced in the beginning had long since vanished, and now she found herself constantly dreaming about food. Buttered corn bread. The molasses candies that William would offer up from his pocket, or even her mama's sweet yams. But the larder was near bare, and the opportunities for bartering amongst the women of Rampart had grown sparser with each passing week. Everyone, it seemed, had less to offer than before.

"S'pose he wants to throw me out?"

"All the more reason you need to make sure he thinks the babe's his, Stella." This time Ammanee's voice was strong. "You can't be 'fraid. You don't *get* to be 'fraid," she emphasized. "Think 'bout William out there, doing what he's got to do to survive. You gotta protect who ya love. Why you think those women want all those maps of yours? Nobody want no harm comin' if they can prevent it."

Stella stood in the center of the foyer, hands folded in front of her belly, hair pulled tightly behind her ears. She was shivering, despite the warmth of the summer night. She'd heard Frye's heavy boots on the porch outside and steadied herself to greet him. She knew he never knocked. He just turned the knob and pushed inside. It was his right.

Frye stepped into the parlor, and his already weary face seemed to grow even more agitated when he took her in. Before she could tell him in her own words, Frye's eyes fell to just below her waistband. The small swelling there was no longer a question. "What you got in there, Stella?" His eyes narrowed, his voice palpably annoyed.

She immediately sensed the Reb meeting had left him in a foul mood and impatient. Long gone was the rather placid man who had first brought her to this cottage. War had left its scars on Frye.

At first she said nothing. Her hands moved upward to fan over the small, hard mound of flesh. Somewhere beneath she felt a tiny heartbeat flutter.

"I'm pregnant, Mas' Frye." She took a deep breath. "I'm gonna have a baby..." The sentence tripped out of her mouth. "*We gonna have a baby...*"

The words felt like poison to her. How many times had she imagined saying the exact phrase to William? In her daydreams, she imagined his face transforming in happiness once he heard the news.

But Frye only stared back at her with empty eyes. She saw no flicker of joy spreading over his face. No delight in his gray irises.

Stella watched as his expression drained. An exhausted sigh escaped his lips.

"What did you go and do that for?" He shook his head. "What a damn bother."

Frye pulled his watch from his breast pocket and Stella could see him calculating his options. Was he going to exhaust his breath discussing something he had no interest in, or was he merely going to satisfy himself with what he'd come for at considerable risk?

"Well, you still look able," he replied dispassionately as he slid his eyes toward the bedroom. "And whatever situation you got yourself into now, I won't be able to increase your allowance." He looked around the carefully maintained cottage and appraised his generosity. "Remember your place, Stella. Even with a war goin' on, I've kept up my side of our arrangement, and you'll need to keep up yours," he said, reinforcing that she'd always be a transaction for him.

He began unbuckling his belt.

"Stella," he said coolly. "This will always be *all* you get."

An hour later, the cottage still smelled of Frye. Stella could detect his scent on the sheets, in the air that permeated every room. She stripped the bed and brought the linen out to the garden and pumped water into the pail.

She wasn't sure if she hated him for not caring or hated herself more for lying, but either way she was filled with disgust.

Stella began pounding the bundle of cloth, swishing it with a wooden paddle. Making the sheets clean again soothed her.

"Let me do that for you." Ammanee gently touched Stella's wrist. Stella was always amazed at the way she quietly spirited away during Frye's visits and seemed to sense the exact moment to return. "I know you're hurtin', but you're done with the hard part now."

Stella's face crumpled. "I miss 'im," she whispered as she pulled William's memory back to her. "I don't know what I'd do if I didn't believe there was a bit of him growin' inside me. I think I'd just wither and die, sister."

"You wouldn't die—either way," Ammanee corrected her as her hands took tighter hold of the paddle. "Look how strong you becomin'. You're doing your part for him and others," she said, alluding to the maps that Stella continued to create clandestinely.

Stella nodded. "But Frye told me somethin' troublin' when he was gettin' ready to leave. I'm not even sure I heard him right… He said I should consider myself lucky I'm here 'cause they're planning somethin' on the Yanks here in the city…the way he was speakin', it sounded like revenge."

Ammanee stopped paddling the sheets. "I think they're plannin' some sort of sabotage near Banks's headquarters. I heard the same at the church during the Reb meeting."

Stella's flesh grew cold. "We gotta warn somebody," she

said, her voice strained. "It's not something I can figure out how to tell in thread…we got to tell a Union man."

Ammanee grew quiet. "I know." They both fell silent, each aware of the risk they were contemplating.

Neither Stella nor Ammanee liked to talk gossip, but their mother took no issue with it. If anything, she relished a juicy tidbit.

"Got a sense Claudette is takin' in some Yankee boys on the side," Janie shared with her girls. "I've seen a couple blue-coated men going in and out of her door at late hours."

"I don't think that could be true, Mama," Stella protested. The women of Rampart Street may not have held the same sentiments of the Confederate-supporting women who had snubbed Yankee men severely during the first months of occupation, but they were astute enough not to flaunt any allegiance to the Northerners.

"She hungry, we all hungry." Janie shrugged. "I'm not judgin'. We all gotta find a way to survive. And she's putting meat on her bones, while we're eatin' like rabbits."

"She might have a better cupboard than us, but ain't she 'fraid her mas' might find out?" Stella's voice lowered to a hush. "He discover she layin' with Yanks, he might kill her." She feared the same punishment if Frye ever discovered that she'd lain with William.

"Yes, he certainly might…" Janie agreed as she ran a finger over the rim of her teacup. "I sure hope it don't come to that, but I'm just sayin' if we ever need to barter for some butter or flour, Claudette might be the one to ask."

As soon as Janie left, Stella pulled her sister aside.

"Ammanee, remember what we were talking about?" Stella instinctively looked over her shoulder. The revelation of a possible attack near Union headquarters had left her mind racing ever since. "What if we told Claudette?" she suggested. "If what Mama said is true, maybe she could pass on the information to one of her Yankee visitors? Maybe warn 'em?"

Ammanee made a face. "I don't know if we can trust her... she's always been a bit of a lone wolf."

"Lemme go pay her a visit. I'll feel her out. Maybe bring her somethin' pretty." Stella still had half of the shawl left. Her hands had gotten so nimble at pulling out the threads, and there was enough to spare to make a small gift. "I'll embroider a little lavender sachet for her. Won't need much cloth for that. And I have some dried flowers from last year sitting in a jar. Miss Claudette will like that, make her feel good. I'm bringing a little something French for her."

"You be careful, now," Ammanee admonished. "Miss Claudette only looks out for herself. She might bite yo' head off you come askin' her for favors..." She hesitated for a moment. "Maybe I should go instead, Stella."

"You're the one tellin' me to be brave all the time. Tellin' me I got choices, that I gotta make a difference. No, let me do this," Stella insisted. "Besides, I don't want the Yanks thinkin' we were ever involved in any treason against 'em. Remember how they hung Mumford just for tearing down a flag? Best we let them know."

Ammanee slowly nodded. "You right. Who knows if they already suspectin' something with those meetings in the church."

Stella took her sister's hand and squeezed it tight. The dirty sheets had fallen to the bottom of the barrel, and she could see their two reflections staring back at them on the glassy surface. They no longer looked so different; something had shifted, and one woman's gaze was no longer stronger than the other. They were beginning to become one and the same.

28

Miss Claudette's cottage was the only one on Rampart Street with a fresh coat of paint. Even the flowers in her window boxes looked more buoyant: the petals freshly watered, the pink and white flowers almost jubilant as they sprang forth. Stella stepped onto the porch and rapped on the bright green door.

"Who's callin' me now?" a holler came from inside. "Don't ya'll know a gal needs her beauty sleep!" She didn't bother with the dulcet tones she normally used for her gentlemen callers.

"I'm sorry," Stella apologized. "Do ya have a moment to talk…? It's me, Janie's girl, Stella."

Seconds later, the door flew open and Miss Claudette stood there with her hair wrapped in a cotton turban and the sash of her silk robe tied tightly around her waist. Stella had never seen someone wearing so much purple.

"Well, ain't you gone bloomin' when no one was lookin'," she exclaimed as her eyes fell to Stella's belly. "Seems like just yesterday you and yo' sister were playin' under that ol' magnolia tree by St. Anthony's."

Stella blushed. "Yes… I got myself all grown now." She withdrew the small sachet from her pocket and offered it to Claudette. "Brought you a little somethin' pretty today."

Claudette took it and a smile emerged on her face. "Been a long while since someone gave me somethin' that smells as lovely as this." She brought the pouch of dried lavender to her nose and inhaled. "Thank you," she said as she waved Stella inside.

On the table sat a loaf of warm bread. Stella's stomach ached just looking at it.

"S'pose you hungry like the rest of 'em," Claudette said knowingly. "Don't normally like to share with those dried-up birds that like to gossip 'bout me." At this, Claudette hesitated, glancing again at Stella. "But you clearly with child and I hate to think you goin' hungry." Walking over to the table, Claudette cut a slice of bread for Stella and told her to sit down.

Stella took the bread and tore off a small piece, letting the warmth flood through her mouth. It tasted better than anything she'd had in months.

"So what has you comin' by, Miss Stella?"

"It's a bit delicate," she started slowly, not knowing how much to tell Claudette at first.

"I heard you been stitchin' some good-luck maps for some of the ladies round here…but I don't need that from you. I got no children, no sweetheart. Just my mas', but he hasn't shown his face in two years. I don't think he's comin' back."

Stella lowered her eyes. Janie was right. Miss Claudette was just like the rest of them, merely trying to survive.

"I've got some knowledge…somethin' I don't know what to do with. But my sister always tellin' me we gotta be strong and help the Union when we can. Otherwise someone's always gonna be ownin' us…"

Miss Claudette's gaze softened. "That's right, chile. Tell me what you got, and I'll tell ya plainly if I can help."

Stella paused and tried to gather the right words. She didn't have anything concrete, only the offhand remarks from Frye and what Ammanee had overheard at the church. She had no date, no time or even what kind of revenge the Reb men were planning.

"I think my mas' is plannin' some kinda sabotage with other Reb men. Think he might be plannin' an attack near Magnolia Street…"

Claudette's eyebrows perked up. "That's quite a tidbit for a gal in your situation to be carrying about."

"Yes," Stella agreed. "And it's not just what I know, but something my sister overheard, too. We're plenty scared and think maybe you might be able to give a warnin'…let some of the Union boys know?"

Miss Claudette's expression tightened. "So now you gonna be judgin' me." She crossed her arms across her ample chest and leaned back in her chair.

"I'm not judgin'," Stella responded softly. "Not at all. I'm just hopin' to make sure nothing wrong get done, just tryin to do what my sweetheart is off doin', tryin' to help."

"Lemme think about it," Claudette said. "Only way I've been able to survive is to mind my own. I stay outta politics— no matter who wins this damn war, I aim to make it through."

"I'd think they'd appreciate the information," Stella pushed.

"Now look at you." An unexpected smile flourished on Miss Claudette's face. "Wasn't too long ago, Emilienne knockin' on my door for a contribution for your welcome quilt. Now you comin' here trying to help win the war. Certainly never thought you'd grow to be so bold."

"I didn't think much of myself before. But as my sis always tells me, being scared is a choice. And so is being brave."

May 30, 1863
Port Hudson, Louisiana

Dearest Lily,

I am sorry it has been so many days since my last letter to you,
but it has been impossible to find the calm I need to write. Even
as I clasp my pen, trying to find the right words to relay to you,
my dearest love, I must reach for the blanket you sent me and find
comfort in those white stars you stitched to pull me out from this
darkness. I have seen so much bloodshed in the past few weeks,
and it has left me badly shaken.

I fear that I have not known the horrors of war until now. Camp
Parapet was a lazy haven compared to the inferno of Port Hudson.
Just three days ago, the stretches of green grass were covered in
more blood, more limbs than one could have ever conjured in their
worst nightmare. The fields that stretch beyond my campsite, toward the mouth of the river, are still filled with the dead.

We were not expecting the Rebs—who we outnumbered by the thousands—to have put up such a fight! And for the first time, General Banks agreed to give rifles to all the valiant Black soldiers in the Louisiana Native Guard, to see just how committed they were to fighting for their freedom.

I don't believe any of us could have anticipated the bravery that ensued, my dearest love. As my own regiment lay waiting in the outer banks, they sent the Native Guard in first, led by one of their own. This brave lieutenant, André Cailloux, I'm told, steered the charge, calling out to his men, both in English and French, "Let us go forward!" He continued to battle forth, even after he was struck by a mini-cannonball that tore through his flesh. And even then he would not be silenced in his urgent call to drive his comrades, until he received one final blow.

I weep as I write this, for the fields are still littered with the corpses of hundreds of Black men along the north front of the Mississippi River, Cailloux's and countless others. But the parties have still made no call for a truce, and who knows how long these brave soldiers must lay there without the cover of earth and a proper burial befitting such noble men. I fear it was a needless sacrifice, ordered by men who had not taken the time to understand the enemy's superior position, and careless with the lives of men they do not consider their equal.

I am heartbroken and worried for my musician friend, William, and the little drummer boy who is always at his side, for they are part of the Third Guard. Do pray for them, as I know your prayers continue to keep me safe.

Your loving husband,

Jacob

29

The June heat was stifling and the stench of death permeated the air.

William rubbed his bloodshot eyes. It had been over two weeks since the deadly battle began, and several hundred Black soldiers now lay dead in the ravine below the bluff. Their swollen bodies rotting in the heat, their corpses haunting the surviving members of their regiments.

"I've seen dead stray dogs treated better," a young man, barely twenty years old, muttered as he sat down beside William. "We fought hard, and now they won't even let us go bury 'em right."

William sighed. His body was battered from the harrowing assault that had left over five hundred Black men dead. The White general had told them they should consider themselves honored that they were to be armed and deployed. *The country will be looking to see how hard you fought*, he'd declared. But no one had informed them that they were being sent on a suicide mission, charging into an exposed ravine in which they'd be fired upon by the Rebs from both sides. Of course they'd spared most of their White soldiers this fate, instead sending out the men whose blood they didn't mind being spilled. The commanders had barely bothered to send a scout along to survey the Confederates' defenses once they'd settled on sending the Black soldiers in.

William still had nightmares of dragging Teddy out of the line of fire after the two of them had led the battle call. Somehow, he'd managed to pull the boy into a ditch as rifle-musket bullets whizzed overhead from all directions and the earth exploded from the heavy artillery the Rebs fired on the enemy below.

For nearly two days, they huddled there with not a morsel of food between them. Only after the Confederates declared victory did they manage to claw out to safety.

Teddy had lost his snare in the chaos, the straps giving way when William dragged him out of harm's way. For a second, Teddy had seemed as if he would turn back to search for his drum, until Willie shook his head, indicating a grief-filled "no." Without a word, Teddy had put his hand in William's and turned away from the battlefield.

William was grateful when Jacob had found their campsite days later.

"I was so worried," his friend stated, bringing with him a handkerchief of food. Not much. A few pieces of stale bread. A tin of navy beans. While the Union soldiers were far better off than the Rebs, who were rumored to already be starving under siege, the Black soldiers were the last to partake of the Union's depleted rations. William shared what he could, giving most of it to Teddy, who looked so malnourished and never asked for anything.

"I'm just so glad you both made it out. I was sick to my stomach when I heard," Jacob said.

William could hardly speak. The campsite was filled with the men who remained from the Louisiana Native Guard. It was bad enough that so much life had been lost, but the fact that the dead still remained down there, exposed to the buzzards and the elements, was impossible to bear.

"For the first time, I'm not sure I'm ever gonna make it outta here," William confided. He was exhausted. He still had the smell of death in his nostrils and the sound of the men's screams in his ears. "I signed up because I didn't care about my own life. I have a girl back home. She's not free to love me, and I'm not free to protect her." He shook his head. "We fightin' for what's right…but leading us into an ambush, then not givin' a damn as we lay there and rot? What's the difference, then? We just slaves either way? We just bodies to shield you and yo' men?"

Jacob crouched down next to him. "I don't know if it means anything to you, but I couldn't rest till I found out if you and Teddy made it out."

"That boy might be even braver than me." William looked over at Teddy. "He kept on playin', even with the bullets buzzin' over his head. Now he's heartsick he lost his drum."

Jacob's eyes widened. "His parents gotta know they did a fine job raisin' him. Wherever they are, they must be proud."

William shook his head at Jacob's naiveté. Teddy had shared his story with him and it had gutted William to his core.

"Jacob, it's like you didn't hear me before," William said as he took a stick and drew into the mud. "Nobody thinkin' of whether a Black man got a wife, or got parents who love 'em." He closed his eyes trying to block out the sight of all the

Black corpses that lay in piles on the ground. "We just nigger bodies to these damn generals. Hell, no one even wants to believe we got a soul."

Jacob winced. "That's not true. I do."

Then, underneath his breath, Jacob began chanting a string of words in a language that William didn't understand.

Yitgadal v'yitkadash sh'mei raba b'alma di-v'ra chirutei, v'yamlich malchutei b'chayeichon uvyomeichon uvchayei d'chol beit yisrael, ba'agala uvizman kariv, v'im'ru: "amen."

Against the backdrop of the destruction and despair, Jacob's voice sang sad and low. His eyes closed. His hands tightly clasped. His body swayed back and forth.

At first, William had held himself rigid, needing to hang on to his growing anger as a relief from the despair. But the rhythm and the intention of Jacob's intonations stirred something inside him. The exoticness reminded William of the mystical words back on Gullah.

Another few verses followed, before he murmured one more time, "Amen."

"What was that?" William asked. The ache in his heart had strangely softened. The melody had penetrated deep within his bones.

Jacob looked at him, real tears filling his eyes. "I'm not a religious man, William. I haven't said those words since my mother passed. But that was the Jewish prayer for the dead.

"Everyone deserves to be remembered," he intoned solemnly. "No death is in vain."

Forty-seven days later, General Banks finally let the Louisiana Native Guard recover the bodies of their dead. But by now the corpses had all but putrefied. Mounds and mounds of Black men lay shriveled beneath their blood-soaked Union blue coats. For years, William had believed that color evoked protection. But no more. The trust was broken.

William covered his face with his sleeve to shield himself from the smell, but the sight was too ghastly for words. They could identify the elegant Lieutenant Cailloux only by the signet ring on his now gray, decayed finger.

He hated that Teddy was asked to distribute water to the men as they carried the carcasses of the dead away on stretchers. But the boy did so without betraying his nerves.

When they returned to camp that evening, neither could have expected what was waiting for them. Beside Teddy's makeshift bed, Jacob had left a used, but well-cared for, drum.

July 18, 1863
New York City

My darling Jacob,

I am not sure if news of what happened here in New York will have reached you by the time you receive this letter. Even now, as I write to you, my heart is heavy beyond measure. In your last letter, you shared how deeply affected you were by witnessing the horror of what your friend William and his regiment endured. And now I find myself, like you, bearing witness to a horrendous torrent of cruelty against innocent men, women and children.

For five days, Manhattan has been on fire, with angry mobs rioting and causing terrible wreckage and chaos. The unrest was sparked by the new conscription laws; men were irate that their names could be pulled from a barrel to meet our noble president's call for 300,000 more able bodies to join the fight. But never could I have imagined the hatred that teemed beneath the architecture of our great city, the festering evil of men who were enraged by the possibility of being forced to fight in what they called "a nigger war."

The self-proclaimed "protesters" began their destruction on Monday, just two days after the marshal drew out the first batch of names. They stormed the draft headquarters on 46th Street and Third Avenue, throwing rocks and bricks through windows and beating any policemen who stood in their way. They smashed the draft barrel, scattered the name cards throughout the floor and then set the building on fire.

But the worst was still to come, dearest husband. They then unleashed their wrath onto nearby colored families and businesses. Jacob, they pulled men from their homes, beating them relentlessly, and eleven men were lynched.

And then, as if the nightmares would never cease, these rioters committed even more unspeakable acts! They attacked the venerable Colored Orphan Asylum on Fifth Avenue, which houses dozens of orphans. I've been informed by ladies of the Sanitary Commission sewing circle that the children there are the sons and daughters of Negro soldiers who are either off fighting, or had been killed when they joined the Union ranks.

These poor orphans were sitting quietly at their desks when hundreds of men, women and even youngsters, stormed the building armed with bricks, clubs and bats. Miss Rose told me she heard from someone who witnessed the attack that the men were crying "Burn the niggers' nest!"

I am sorry that I am detailing all of this horror to you in a letter. Perhaps it would have been better served remaining within the pages of a journal. But the only solace I can find after learning of such wickedness and heinous prejudice is to take comfort that I am married to a man who fights on the side of justice and equality. Know that you are not alone. The rioters might have defaced our newspaper headquarters with the words, "Death to the Lincolnites!", but we women will not be dissuaded from joining the fight in any way we can.

Please write and reassure me you are safe and without injury. The mail has been frightfully slow, and I continue to worry about your health.

You must come home to me, my darling man. I miss you. To-morrow I will join some of the women from the Sanitary Commission. With the summer heat now in full swing, we've decided to postpone our quilting activities (it's far too warm to send you all blankets!) but, instead, we will continue to spend our hours pre-paring and rolling bandages. I hope these pieces of gauzy white are never used to wrap any of your limbs, and that only my quilt should keep you in a tight embrace when it becomes cool again.

I adore you and pray for better times.

Your devoted and loving wife,

Lily

30

Stella returned to visit Miss Claudette, only to discover that the woman had decided to maintain her stance against mixing business and politics.

"Now, listen, it's not because I don't wanna help—I jus' don't like bein' no spy. Too much danger for a woman in my situation…"

"I understand, Miss Claudette," Stella sympathized. "I wake up every mornin' scared somethin' gonna happen to me and my baby. Things are not good here in the city, but they sure not good outside New Orleans, either," she sighed. "But the more we help try to make things right in this war, the sooner we can start livin' truly free."

"Free?" Miss Claudette's eyes softened on Stella. "You so young. You still have all that hope growin' inside you." She shook her head. "But me and your mama, we know what life's truly like. We know what it's like to have gone through the auction block."

Stella quivered.

"Now don't start to cry. I know you went off to Market, that you basically got sold, too, but that's different from seein' your daddy whipped until his back like a rawhide, or seein' your mama's wrists torn up by manacles." Miss Claudette rose and wiped her hands on a dishrag. "I've been lookin' out for myself for a long time, and one thing I learned is that the only thing worth trying to save in this world is yourself. Besides, you don't have any *real* information anyway about what they're plannin'. Nothin' that will get any Union man to listen, anyhow."

Stella's brow knotted in frustration. "If I can get more, will you at least consider it? Isn't there at least one soldier you could trust?"

"*Trust* is a heavy word in times like these, girl. Only thing I can really trust right now is a couple of banknotes in my hands."

"She's not goin' say anythin'," Stella informed Ammanee as they peeled a few potatoes in the garden. "And maybe Frye's just blowin' smoke about doin' something crazy. Who knows if they even got any real plans?"

Ammanee clicked her tongue. "Deacon Dupont actin' mighty strange lately though. I saw him arguin' with some old geezer 'bout not using the church anymore. Afterward, he was white as a sheet."

Stella shook her head vigorously as if to ward off Ammanee's words. "I have to focus on things that are real, like Mama says." Stella didn't mention to her sister that it was really Claudette who had reminded her of this. She looked down at her belly. Approaching her sixth month, she was rounder than she had expected. Stella was relieved Frye hadn't visited in a while, as she had yet to devise a way to hide how much bigger she had become.

Her fingers hadn't been as busy recently as she'd have liked. Most of the men who'd run using her maps to guide them had done so months ago, and those who had stayed back, like Benjamin, were either working for men too old to fight, toiling the land while their mas' was away and the mistress took charge, or were too old to do much good as soldiers.

"I haven't had cause to do a map for a while... I'm thinkin' maybe I could use the last bit of the shawl to make something for the baby. Something that will let this babe know the love that is in my heart—for him and for his daddy. I need to put all that love somewhere and I can't put it in a letter. And he can't write to me neither." She bit the quick of her nail.

"You always lookin' for a place to put that heart of yours." Ammanee smiled at her sister. "Let me finish the potatoes, and you go and rest. Then you take that shawl and pull whatever thread you need and make something special for your child."

Stella had many stories inside her that ached for a place to go. The memory of the first time she went to Market and her eyes locked with William's. The feeling in her chest when he brought his flute to his lips and breathed life into her soul. The moment he felt safe enough to tell her a little bit about his childhood back in Sapelo, where the color blue stained his parents' fingers and drove away the island's haints.

Stella reached for what was left of Miss Hyacinth's shawl, and some of the leftover blue thread she saved earlier. The idea for an embroidered swaddling cloth had come to Stella naturally. Carefully, her fingers began stitching a garland of azure flowers and tiny cowrie shells for its border.

Each stitch soothed her, and over the next few days, Stella found herself returning to the fabric and needling her longing into its stretch of white cotton. *Green is the color of hope*, she heard her sister's voice reminding her again of the language of color. She yearned for a time in the future when her child could play in a field of sweet grass and wild blooms, running with a smile as radiant as the sun. She withdrew a handful of emerald threads. Her arm moved like a dancer, pushing the needle through the muslin and returning it out the other side. Deeper from the edge, Stella sewed tall blades of feathery grass. The following day, she created a small, yellow butterfly nestled within the verdant meadow.

She would never be able to control the war raging outside the city borders, but Stella fell into a peaceful world of needlework where she could fashion a more hopeful landscape in which to wrap her unborn child.

When it was close to being finished, the swaddling cloth looked like a work of art and by far the finest thing she had ever made. Stella wanted to seal it somehow with a symbol of the spirit in which it was made.

She reached for the color that embodied love, warming a nest of red thread in her hand.

The final effort was the letters *S* and *W* hidden in the swirls of stitches within the heart.

31

"We're heading out tomorrow," Jacob's field officer announced. The Union had finally emerged victorious following its nearly two-month-long siege at Port Hudson and the recent battle of Vicksburg. Despite the heavy losses his troops had suffered, the death toll devastating to the Black soldiers of the Louisiana Guard, General Banks had achieved his goal of taking control of the Mississippi River and cutting off all outside trade to the Confederacy. "It should take us a couple days to get to Port Gibson, but we're needed as reinforcements there," he added. "So best get a good night's rest."

A shudder rippled through Jacob at the news. It was just over three years since he'd visited Samuel down in Satartia, but the proximity of his brother's abode to Port Gibson—and the devastation he knew the Federal army would leave in its wake—filled him with dread.

The last letters between the two men had been cordial enough, but their philosophical divide remained palpable. With all communication halted between the North and South, Jacob had no idea if his brother had enlisted in the Confederate army, or if he'd paid a substitute to stand in his place so that he could personally steer his emporium through the war and inflation.

But one thing was certain: Jacob hoped he would never come face-to-face with Samuel on the battlefield.

The following morning, as his regiment lifted their packs to their shoulders and began marching north, fear consumed him. As a musician, he wouldn't be wielding a rifle, only sounding the battle march and later helping with stretcher duty for the injured and the dead. But the idea that Samuel could be on the other side of the gunfire nearly paralyzed him.

When the men eventually made camp for the night, Jacob heard a flute off in the distance. Unmistakably, he knew it had to belong to William.

He looked up at the stars and breathed in the night air and, after a moment, began walking in its direction.

William stood outside a small tent, his flute to his lips. Teddy sat cross-legged with a stick in his hand, drawing in the dirt.

The two of them were among the few survivors remaining from the Louisiana Native Guard. Several hundred had perished on the battlefield, with General Banks unafraid to sacrifice them in his path to victory. Many of the surviving soldiers had thrown in their caps after they witnessed the army's callous and indifferent treatment of their fallen comrades.

Jacob waited until William had finished his passage before approaching.

"I was rereading a letter of mine and it was weighing heavy on my heart." Jacob tapped his breast pocket. "Then I heard you playing..."

"At least you get letters," William said as he lowered his instrument. "Me and Teddy, we got no paper comin' from the ones we love." He shook his head. "And even if we did, we couldn't read 'em. My first mistress back on Sapelo Island, she risked herself to have me learn to read music, but wasn't no need to share the alphabet with me."

A pit fell in Jacob's stomach. He'd never considered that most men in William's regiment had probably never received a letter, let alone written one. He had treasured every word Lily had sent him. He couldn't imagine how William had managed to keep going without any words of support or affection from the woman he loved.

"My Stella, she knows her letters, but can't write me 'cause it's too dangerous. And I can't even put a sentence down to tell her how much I love her." His voice cracked with emotion. "Jacob, you're lucky. If somethin' ever happens to you, your Lily got a bit of your voice down on paper." William took a deep breath. "Won't be no record of me when I'm gone. Just an ol' flute that coulda belonged to anyone."

Jacob paused. He'd followed the trail of William's melody, hoping to make himself feel better, to banish all thoughts of his brother from his mind. But now his heart ached for a completely different reason. He couldn't believe William had never been given the chance to write down his emotions.

"I could get a pen and some paper. You could dictate a letter to Stella…"

"What's the good if I can't send it?" William asked.

"Do you play your flute for an audience of strangers, or do you play for yourself?"

"I play it for myself…"

"Well, consider it the same thing. A letter—a letter to your beloved—is your heart and soul on paper," Jacob explained. "And if anything were ever to happen to you, I'd make sure the letter got to Stella. Even if I had to move heaven and earth to find her, I'd do that for you."

"Why would ya do that for me...it's an awful lot to ask."

"Why?" Jacob repeated. "Because you and I are more than just fellow musicians. You and I are friends."

Jacob soon returned with writing paper and a pen.

"Close your eyes and just tell me what you want Stella to know."

William sat down as Teddy huddled beside him, the little boy's head resting on his shoulder. His words floated in the air like a story.

"Stella,

Where are you on this dark night? Have you gone into the garden to look at the stars, the white moon? We're separated now, but we both are beneath the same tarp.

My heart beats hard when I think of you. I wanna fall into your dark eyes and find comfort there. I wanna believe that when I left you on your own, I did the right thing and that no harm will come your way.

I want you to know I'm alive. That I'm not hurt. That I even got the chance to play my flute and even a fife for my troop. I'm putting my skill to good use every day I can and I'm hoping we win this war soon and I can get back to you and make you my wife.

You'd be happy to know I keep your handkerchief against my breast. Most of the White soldiers here keep letters from their beloveds next to their heart, but I keep something you stitched and it's got a whole lotta love. It protects me, Stella. I know that.

Wait for me, girl. I'm coming home to you. I promise.
William."

There was one other thing he wished he could also convey in the letter, his desire to send Stella the monthly wage he received from the army. He'd kept every cent of the seven dollars. William never complained like some of the other men in his regiment about how the White soldiers received thirteen, while the Black Union men not only made less, but also had money withdrawn for their food and clothes. He had over fifty dollars now rolled inside his breast pocket. Every night he dreamt of Stella, he imagined how he'd spend those hard-earned bills. But for now the words he'd shared with Jacob were enough.

32

New Orleans, Louisiana
August 1863

The explosion near Union headquarters set New Orleans on edge. The Union forces swept through the city trying to track down the culprits who'd planted the pipe bomb beneath the steps of the office building. Whispers began to circulate that several Confederate wives had played a key role in the plot. Even after signing the required oath of allegiance to the Union, these women had seen their comfortable lives disappear and be replaced with starvation and financial ruin. But Stella and Ammanee suspected that it wasn't these women who had done the damage, but rather Frye and his compatriots.

"Two dead," Stella repeated to her sister as she cut the stems off a few figs to share between them.

"It coulda been worse, I imagine," Ammanee mused. "Still, Miss Claudette mighta said something. She could've warned them that something was brewin'." A small huff escaped her.

"I'm gettin' more restless," Stella admitted as she handed a segment of fig to her sister. "And scared," she added a moment later. "Reckon, by the end of August, I'll be six months along, and I was hopin' this war be done before this baby come out. Can't believe still no end in sight…"

"Nothin' great won without a fight, sis." Ammanee took a bite and let the sweet juice flood her mouth. "No one ever said it was gonna be easy."

Stella felt the baby kick inside her. "Think this little one agrees with you." She put a palm on her belly and smiled.

"You use up all Miss Hyacinth's shawl on that swaddling cloth?"

Stella nodded. "Nearly. Not much for me to do now except pray William's safe and Frye leaves me alone…" She wiggled her fingers, wishing there was something to keep them busy.

"Don't pray too hard for that," her sister cautioned. "The jar's down to the last few notes, Stella, and the priest only payin' me a few coins each week for my chores. We still need Frye to put food on the table."

Stella scanned the room to see what they might be able to sell should they need the money. Janie had already sold her oak furniture for a fraction of its worth when Percy stopped visiting and her allowance evaporated, even the mirror with the leaves she'd always been so proud of.

"We got the sofa, the table, the chairs…" She counted each item. "We could still get by if we sold them."

"Used to be you could tell which houses on Rampart were hurtin' by the missin' paint outside. Now you can tell if people sitting on the floor inside." Ammanee rose from her seat, wiping her hands clean on her apron. "We're not sellin' anything just yet, sister. I'm meetin' Benjamin this afternoon, and he promised he'd bring me a little cornmeal from the plantation.

Percy's missus not watchin' the place too carefully now that he gone. Supposedly she stays in the big house all day, just cryin'."

Stella's mouth watered. It had been so long since she'd tasted one of Ammanee's ashcakes. "Tell Benjamin thank you." She looked over at her sister, who had a particularly hopeful glimmer in her eyes, and recognized the expression she herself once wore every time she'd meet William in Congo Square.

When Ammanee returned, she was flushed. She put a small sack of meal from her basket on the table.

"Thought maybe I'd be comin' home today and askin' you for a map, but Benjamin still sayin' he got no plans to run."

At least she knew where he was, Stella thought to herself as she looked forlornly out the window. She'd taken a walk while Ammanee had been out and run into Miss Hyacinth.

"Rips my heart out not knowin' where Jonah is," the elegant woman had confessed. "Don't know if he made it out safe. Don't know if he hurt with all the fightin' goin' on. Especially now that they letting the Corps d'Afrique take up guns." She shook her head. "Guess we just gotta keep hopin' the Lord keep 'em all safe."

"Yes," Stella had agreed. It was exactly how she felt. Her worry for William's safety was her constant companion.

But Stella wanted to share a bit of her sister's joy. "Still you must be happy you got some time with Benjamin."

Ammanee didn't answer. She washed her hands and then sprinkled some of the meal onto the counter, adding water to make the mush.

The silence that followed filled the nooks and crevices of the cottage, a reminder to Stella that as close as she felt to her sister, there were parts of Ammanee that would always remain a secret to her. Even after several months, Ammanee had never shared the conversation she'd had with Janie about wanting to get married. She never spoke to Stella of her own desire to have a child, even as she watched Stella's stomach grow with each passing week.

"You always proppin' me up, sis," Stella pressed gently. "Pushing me to do somethin' 'stead of just thinkin' 'bout myself." She stood up, went over to the counter, and reached for a small mound of dough to roll. "But I'm here for you if you ever want to talk 'bout your dreams and your hurt."

Ammanee took two of the patties and added them to the coal fire. "My job always been to care for you, protect you. Mama told me that when I first came to live with y'all and you just a baby yo'self."

"But I'm grown now, sister."

Ammanee stiffened. "It's still my job and Frye still own me." She reached down to flip the ashcakes, avoiding Stella's gaze. "You gotta remember—we different, you and me."

That evening, Stella went to her room. The small white chamber never provided any sort of refuge for her, merely serving as the place where she slept or had to lay with Frye. She preferred to spend her hours either in the parlor of the cottage or in its tiny patch of garden outside.

But the conversation with Ammanee had left her distressed. While she recognized the system had forced them into different paths of bondage, she wanted to believe that as sisters, they'd managed to transcend those constraints. She hated that she had to submit to Frye's demands to keep a roof over their heads, but she also knew her mother had made the same sacrifice for them with Percy. And she knew it wasn't fair that Frye forced Ammanee to sleep on straw in the kitchen, or that no matter how much love she might hold for Stella, she was still a slave in her own sister's house.

Stella felt the baby stretch and kick inside her. The movements seemed to give life to her own restlessness, her desire to break free.

She placed her hands on her abdomen and slowly began to hum a melody that William used to murmur into her ear. Back then, the music had soothed her instantly, and she felt the same calm come over their unborn child.

Folded at the bed's edge was the quilt made by the women of Rampart Street. Squares stitched from something each woman had worn, the cloth passing from house to house, neighbor to neighbor.

Despite the heat, she pulled it up to her chin, protecting herself and her baby in the blanket like a shield.

33

Port Gibson, Mississippi
September 1863

The early autumn nights were still sweltering and uncomfortable. Jacob had spread out the quilt from Lily on the floor of his tent, rather than sleeping directly on the ant-infested grass that had left small, angry red bites on so many of the men's limbs.

The blanket had grown quite worn over the past few months. The white stars were now a soft brown from their constant exposure to the earth. The dark blue squares were becoming threadbare in places, but the fabric still brought him closer to her.

He pulled out Lily's most recent letter. It had taken over a month to reach him, and he read her words greedily.

August 3, 1863

My dearest Jacob,

I continue to pray that you are safe and well. It is still hard for me to believe that next month will mark the one-year anniversary since you joined your regiment. I remember so vividly the week you de-parted, coming as it did near Rosh Hashanah. Do you recall how I tried to make you an apple and honey cake before you went off, but I burned the top? As the Jewish New Year approaches again this year, I must hone my baking skills so I can be far more masterful when you return. I will bake so many cakes for you, darling. Cin-namon spice, lemon drizzle and a dark chocolate one with vanilla icing. We will have such a celebration when you come home to me!

I have some frustrating news to share with you. Papa came to visit last night, and he is pressing me to live with him while you're away. He doesn't feel it's safe for me to now stay in our apartment all alone. I think the violence of last month's riots has shaken him deeply, and he was furious at me for going into the streets to see if I could help any victims of the vile mobs.

He has asked me to move back in with him sometime next week. Of course, he assured me that he will make the payments required to maintain our home while I'm staying with him. Though reluc-tant, I have agreed. I'm terribly put out to be leaving the sanctu-ary of our apartment, where I could otherwise continue to sleep in our marital bed. My only comfort will be that I will once again have my childhood harp there to play upon.

I send you my warmest embrace and love,

Lily

Jacob folded the paper and slipped it in with the bundle of Lily's other letters. It distressed him to think that New York had become so volatile over the past couple of months, and that his wife's safety could be jeopardized. Although he knew his father-in-law would take good care of her, he felt strongly that it was his place to protect Lily. That he could not do so saddened him.

He smiled as he remembered that charred honey cake she'd made him before he'd enlisted. Another Jewish New Year had just come and gone, but he'd had no one else in his regiment to mark it with him. In a modest act of celebration, he had managed to find a tart apple, which he ate happily, savoring the sweetness as it washed over his tongue.

Yom Kippur, the Jewish Day of Atonement, was approaching in a little over a week. Even though he didn't keep kosher or attend weekly services, Jacob was still planning to honor the tradition of fasting on that day. Both the Kahns and the Klings had always believed that these holidays should be observed out of respect to their forefathers.

He was grateful that when Wednesday came, it did not bring with it too much manual labor, for he had not eaten since sundown the night before. He worked slowly as he helped unload the medical supplies from the latest wagon delivery, the heat and lack of food making him grow faint.

"You alright?" William asked. He had been ordered to clear some of the detritus from the field hospital. A wheelbarrow of soiled bandages needed to be burned.

Jacob wiped his brow. "Haven't eaten since sundown last night. Today's the holiday we Jews fast for our sins."

William laughed. "You don't strike me as much of a sinner, my friend. Don't never see you gettin' into any trouble."

"Well, I keep my vices to myself," Jacob joked. "But in all seriousness, it's considered our most solemn day of the year when we repent for our trespasses and hope that God will inscribe our names into the Book of Life." He put down a crate of iodine bottles and gathered his breath. "I guess it seems more important than ever to have God list me in that book, since there's so much death all around us." He motioned toward the tent where the cots were filled with countless dying or severely wounded soldiers.

"Yeah." William nodded solemnly. "Sure does look like

God's book's lost a few pages of names this year. My regiment must have buried at least seventy-five men yesterday."

The few days prior had been difficult ones for Jacob, as well. His infantry was involved in clearing out the carnage the Vicksburg siege had left in its wake, and under military protocol, the musicians were also pressed into service at the field hospitals. The stink of dying men, many of them with their limbs cut off, the stumps wrapped in bloody bandages, was a horror that Jacob couldn't shake. Nor could he forget the sounds of their desperate wailing and pleas for more morphine.

Nurses kept vigil beside the wounded, their white aprons stained crimson, their hands gripping those of the soldiers who had—at most—only hours left to live.

That evening, Jacob had sought out William to unburden his thoughts. "I can't get any of it from my mind," he confided. "Seeing those doctors sawing off limbs of boys not yet bearded. Their cries are still ringing in my ears." He was supposed to be hungry after a day of fasting, but he could now manage to eat only a few bites of his gruel. "What's left of a man if he's all cut up like that?" Jacob asked as he cradled his head in his hands. The campfire danced and jumped in sparks. He could never imagine returning to Lily with parts of him gone.

"It's hard," William agreed. After a long breath, he continued, "But guess I'm just more used to it. Spent most of my life not feelin' my body was my own, not whole. And back in Sapelo, they did something to my mama that no boy should ever see." He looked over at Teddy. "Ever wonder why I take this boy under my wing? Speaks so little. Just plays his drum and does whatever's asked of 'im?"

Jacob remained quiet.

"'Cause he reminds me of myself after they burned out my mama's tongue." He wiped his forehead with a rag. "Guess me gettin' cut up by some doctor don't scare me too much after that. Men like me cut up all the time, with parts of us stuck in our mouth after they tie us up swingin' from a tree. So havin' a leg sawed off by a surgeon…" William shrugged and then turned away from Jacob.

Nausea tore through Jacob, roiling the little food in his stomach. This was the first time William had ever spoken so candidly with him about his past.

One of the other men in William's unit came out of his tent and immediately noted Jacob sitting by the fireside. "What you always hangin' out in our camp for? I've seen yo' face more times than I care to since Port Hudson. Don't you know we s'pose to keep 'way from you all?" The man shook his head in admonishment. "You ain't got no friends beside our Willie here?"

"Leave him alone," William said. "This man made sure I got a fife when I joined up. Known him since I got my blue threads in Camp Parapet."

"Still," the man insisted. "It's damn strange he don't wanna hang out with his own. Gon' jes' lead to trouble."

Jacob looked over at Teddy, who was polishing William's flute. He did not dislike the other men in his unit. Most of them, except for Riordan who was prone to hurtling slurs, were good and decent. But he always felt like an outsider. He hardly ever drank, and he was never the type to enjoy the kind of mischief the others engaged in once the moonshine had taken over.

"Actually, Private, when I'm here with William and Teddy, I feel like I am with my 'own.'"

That night, Jacob returned to his faded blanket of stars. His body stretched over the fabric, he imagined himself stretching out beside Lily. His limbs fell away, and the memory of the first time he lay with his wife returned to him.

"What's your favorite part of me?" she'd asked as her fingers traced the outline of his naked chest. Her figure had looked like carved marble in the moonlight as it nestled against his own, the sheets peeled away from them.

He kissed her again deeply, the answer coming to him instantly, for it was the truth. "Your face and figure are beautiful, my darling. But what is it I love about you the most? The answer is your soul."

34

Frye stormed in late that evening, fuming. With every visit, his demeanor grew more foul, his once relaxed manner eviscerated by the pressures of his job and the turning tides of the war. This time, his bad mood quickly worsened when he noticed how much bigger she'd become since his last visit.

"You makin' me sick to my stomach now you got that whelp inside you, Stella," he grunted. "How am I ever s'pose to relax in this house when you got that big belly on you? Breathing so hard just to move around." He sat up in bed and began pulling on his clothes. "Hell, no one's doin' what I want 'em to these days."

Even in his frustration, Frye did not reveal what had happened hours before.

But she didn't need to hear about it from him. The following morning, Ammanee was more than happy to share what she'd overheard those men discussing at the church.

"Frye might not be comin' back here for a while," Stella mentioned as her sister entered the kitchen. Morning light streamed into the room, highlighting Stella's growing abdomen beneath her nightgown. "Seems he don't like bein' with a pregnant woman...says it's not natural. Think I repulse him now." A satisfied smile spread across her face.

"You never looked so pretty, sister. But I guess it's good if that keeps 'im off you." In spite of her fears about their dwindling supplies, Ammanee couldn't help share her sister's relief at shaking free of Frye for a bit.

"Best news I've heard in a while," Stella laughed.

"Won't miss hearin' him stompin' his boots on the way out," Ammanee agreed. "But you shoulda seen him last night, carryin' on 'bout how the Yanks stinkin' up the city, ruining their way of life. He said he wasn't gonna die a coward, and if the others weren't man enough to show Banks they weren't willin' to live under his thumb, he would do something about it on his own." Ammanee clicked her tongue. "Man not well in the head, Stella. And it's getting worse. Even his Reb pals think he gone crazy. He talkin' about sending a care package to headquarters with some rags from a yellow fever patient, sayin' he want to make them Yanks all sick with disease. Then he started carryin' on about all sorts of madhouse stuff—like a bomb."

"All this makin' me nervous, sister. You talking like he's comin' unhinged."

"He's already unhinged, Stella. We just have to hope he don't bring any of it back here," she warned. "Only good news was that the priest says he don't want to let them meet in the church no more. He's scared, too, by the way they talkin'. And boy did Frye get spittin' mad then! Tellin' the priest that his ol' superior Father Turgis was off being chaplain to the Reb men and he should find ways to help, too," Ammanee continued. "But Deacon Dupont told him plainly that Father Turgis just helpin' tend to the sick and wounded, not plottin' to kill anyone. And he and the church won't be a part of any of that."

"Well, that's a relief." Stella touched the small of her back and went to sit down. "At least the deacon got some sense in 'im."

"If he find out I've been spyin', though, he gonna be real mad." She took two coins from her pocket and put them in the tin. "Deacon Dupont paid me this morn for scrubbin' the floors extra good. And I was happy to do it. Wanna get rid of Frye's stink."

That Sunday when Stella went to Mass with her mother and sister, she felt especially grateful that the deacon seemed to have finally drawn a line in the sand. With no more Reb meetings in the neighborhood and Frye's obvious distaste for her blooming physique, Stella didn't anticipate seeing him again for her last two months of pregnancy. That meant she could focus all her prayers on having the war come to an end and William safely returned to her.

The faces within the congregation had always belonged to a mixture of Whites, free people of color of all shades and even a few slaves. But Stella and the rest of the women of Rampart almost always sat in the back pews so as not to call attention to themselves.

"Don't need to hear no whispers from any of them uppity ladies up front." Janie would wag her finger and remind her daughters when they went to Mass, "Just sit in the back with me and the other gals. You all still get to hear the same ol' sermon. We all got the same God."

This morning, as the organ sounded, Miss Emilienne slid into the pew a few minutes late and gestured for Stella to make room for her.

"You look like you' ripenin' just right," she whispered into Stella's ear and gave her a little pat on her thigh.

From the pulpit the priest began preaching about God's will, his forefinger emphasizing every word he quoted from the Scriptures.

When the service ended and they'd each taken the Eucharist, Miss Emilienne pulled Stella aside. "Not sure if you know this, but it was my mama who delivered you when you was born."

Janie was a few steps ahead, in conversation with Ammanee.

"I might be as old as yo' mama Janie, but I was born in a Creole cottage just like you. And I learned 'bout bringin' babies from my own mama when she was alive. There's been many a babe on this street who I brought into this world with my own two hands." She touched Stella's cheek. "So don't be shy when you start havin' yo' pains. You hear me?" She smiled warmly at Stella, her hazel eyes pulling her in. "You just tell yo' sister to go fetch me, and I'll come no matter what time of night it is. Least I could do after how you helped my brother with that map."

"That's mighty kind of you, Miss Emilienne," Stella answered as she caressed her belly. "It's not easy asking for help when things just so hard for everyone."

"Yes, chile. But we can help each other. That's how we hold on for all those we love." Her voice was full of empathy. "Never had a babe of my own, but I helped my mama birth my brother, Jeremiah. Mas' took him from her early and sent him to the fields." Tears filled her eyes. "But my hands were the first to touch him. Felt like he was my own baby till he got ripped from me and Mama."

Now it became clearer to Stella why Miss Emilienne had been so desperate to get a map to her brother, to help him run. She had always thought she and Ammanee were unique, bound by blood but leading different lives side by side. But Miss Emilienne reminded her they weren't so special after all. As everyone around her knew, there were so many ways to not be free.

35

New Orleans, Louisiana
October 1863

The pains started coming that morning. Stella awakened to a terrible gripping in her abdomen.

She and Ammanee had done the counting when she'd first admitted her period was late. From their calculations, the child wasn't due until mid-November. But that was next month.

She groaned and curled herself up in a tight ball, and then called out for her sister.

"What's wrong?" Ammanee rushed in. Her eyes fell upon Stella, who was rocking from side to side, moaning.

"Somethin' ain't right. I didn't want to say anything last night. Just thought I'd had some upset from the yam we used to stretch out the porridge." She felt another constriction in her belly. "But this mornin', it feels like someone's squeezing me from the inside out."

Ammanee came closer and touched Stella's forehead. A few

cases of yellow fever had been reported recently in the district, sending ripples of fear throughout the community.

"You not hot, thank the Lord." She scanned her sister's eyes and skin for signs of jaundice, but luckily noticed none. "S'pose it could be the root that's giving you them pains," she observed softly. She placed her palm on Stella's stomach and felt the hard ball of her belly contract. "But I'm thinkin it's mo' that this baby comin' early…"

Stella groaned again. "Ammanee?"

"Yes, I'm here," she reassured.

"Somethin' leakin'!" Stella cried out. She reached toward the back of her nightgown, which had become soaked through.

Ammanee's eyes glowed in the dim room.

"Yo' waters broke, sister." She took Stella's hand. "But everything's goin' to be alright."

"It's too early for the baby." Stella's voice broke. "We can't let nothin' happen to him, Ammanee." Instinctively, Stella knew that she would bring a son into the world. She started to cry. "Nothin'."

"Hush," Ammanee comforted. "You just get ready to meet that beautiful chile of yours."

Stella's eyes glistened. "I thought I had mo' time…nothin' ready yet. Don't even got a basket to put 'im in."

"We don't need to fret 'bout none of that now." Ammanee gave the mattress a little pat. "Let's get you up so I can take off that wet sheet, and you can change into somethin' dry."

"We gotta get Miss Emilienne," Stella pleaded. "She said she would help when the time came."

"Yes, sister. Goin' go run and tell her, and I'm also gonna let Mama know."

"Please, Ammanee, can you do one more thing 'fore you go?" she asked as she struggled to get to her feet.

"Of course, sister. Anything."

"Can you take the quilt away from the bed?" Stella's eyes fell to the blanket folded at the bottom of the mattress. "It means a lot to me. Don't want anythin' to ruin it."

In the small Creole cottage with the sunflowers outside its door, four women worked in their own ways to usher a new life safely into the world.

Janie went to boil a large pot of water and to collect fresh rags.

Ammanee prepared a cool compress for her sister's head and gave her something to absorb her pain. "Take this," she instructed, pressing William's cowrie shell into her palm. "Squeeze it every time a pain comes… So now Willie be with you here in his own way."

Stella took the shell and grabbed it tight.

Miss Emilienne scrubbed her hands in a basin of hot water, and then went to peek underneath the white sheet that Ammanee had spread over Stella's lower half.

"Lookin' like you already halfway there, chile. You just gotta breathe and let yo' body do all the work."

"That's right, you strong," Ammanee comforted her. She took the now warm compress off of Stella's brow and went into the kitchen to wring it fresh again.

"Not long now till we know who the daddy is," Janie muttered as she watched over a pot of boiling water.

"I'm not worryin' now about what shade of brown he gonna be," Ammanee replied sternly. "We first gotta make sure he come out hollerin', not blue in the face."

Janie's eyes grew fierce. "Don't make me feel like a wolf, chile. No matter what Stella hopin' for, till this war over, that baby gonna belong to Frye whether it's jet-black or light as café au lait."

"I tole you we can't be thinkin' 'bout that yet, Mama." Ammanee twisted the rag tightly, the drops of water falling in the sink like tears. "Just pray the baby and Stella are safe, is all."

Janie sighed. "I'm gonna pray for what's best for my daughter," she stressed. But even she was unsure of what that might be.

Miss Emilienne tended to Stella's labor for several more hours, until daylight turned to dusk.

"You almost there now, gal," she coached. "Conserve your energy. Don't push until I tell you."

The pain was immense. Down below, Stella felt the seething burn of what Miss Emilienne called the "ring of fire." She gripped the cowrie shell now with all of her strength.

"I see the head," Emilienne announced as she looked up from between Stella's legs. "You doin' good, girl."

"Go bring Mama in," Stella pleaded to Ammanee, her eyes shiny. "I want her in here, too."

Ammanee paused. Part of her selfishly wanted to be the only kin in the room. She longed for this moment to be just between them, evidence that she was more of a real mama to her sister than Janie ever was.

"That's what you want?"

Stella grunted and groaned. "Yeah, go get her, sister. Please—I'd like all of us together when he comes out."

The room was cast in starlight and a single burning taper when Miss Emilienne finally pulled the baby from Stella. Both Ammanee and Janie could hardly believe their eyes as the child glowed with life.

"You was right," Ammanee beamed.

The infant was a boy and his skin a warm, dark shade of pecan. But even more comforting to Stella was that she could instantly see William's expression in the baby boy's searching eyes.

She missed the portentous look that passed between Janie and Ammanee as they took in the child's skin.

A hush as ancient as time came over the bedroom, as Stella took her newborn to her breast. As many times as she had imagined this moment, nothing could compare to the wonder of having that tiny finger wrap around her own. She kissed the top of his head, where the soft curls were still damp from the cloth that had wiped him clean.

The other women had left her to rest and to have a moment alone with her most perfect creation. "You gotta think of a name now," Ammanee said, smiling as she grabbed the towels Miss Emilienne had used during the birth, and then left to soak them.

But Stella had been carrying a name inside her head ever since she first realized she was pregnant. "Wade," she whispered as she traced his perfect nose and chin. She had wanted the first letter of the child's name to mirror his father's, but she especially loved the moniker, for it evoked the sensation of walking through water. Even if William had to struggle to do so, she knew he would still manage to get back to them.

"You mine," she proclaimed as her face radiated pure joy. Her heart was still beating fast from the labor, but the baby's scent and the warmth of his skin began to settle her. Stella lifted Wade's tiny arm to her lips and kissed it, and then did the same with each of his five fingers.

An hour later, Ammanee came back and took hold of Wade. "We need to get a fresh diaper round that baby's bottom," she announced. "Haven't been this busy with a baby since Percy brought me to take care of you."

When she returned again, she carried the child in a seagrass basket. Tucked around him was the embroidered swaddling cloth that Stella had created, its colorful symbols in high relief like a protective talisman.

"Miss Claudette heard the news and dropped off this pretty li'l thing." She lifted it so Stella could see her baby now resting safely in the hand-me-down Moses basket. "And now yo' little boy be in the swaddlin' cloth his mama made for him. Lots of blue thread in that." She smiled. "Baby already protected."

36

New Orleans, Louisiana
November 1863

Stella kept Wade near at all times. She memorized every curve of his features, savored every gurgle or coo. She had never had the chance to lie down and fall asleep next to William, but now the baby allowed her to feel as close to his father's heartbeat as she could. It made her feel stronger, and more hopeful, than she ever had.

Despite the fact that the war still dragged on, the women of Rampart rejoiced at the new life on their street.

Ammanee listened to Miss Hyacinth's advice that fenugreek and fennel teas encouraged a mother's milk to flow. She steeped strong brews that she delivered to Stella in bed.

Miss Claudette brought staples for their larder, a small tin of precious flour, and even a few pats of butter and eggs that felt more valuable than gold. For the first time in months, the house smelled of warm biscuits and love.

Even Janie seemed to settle into her new role as grandmother, helping to change diapers and bathe Wade.

"Never had a boy of my own," Janie mused as she dipped
her elbow in the water basin to check its temperature. She
dampened some rags with the warm water and gently began
to sponge Wade's body.

The baby wiggled as he delighted in the sensation of the
water trickling over him.

"He growin' big," she marveled. "You girls were tiny little
things. But he eatin' real good, becomin' our li'l man with
each passin' day."

Stella stood next to her and playfully pulled Wade's toes.
"Life's so easy in the beginnin'," she said softly. Her eyes began
to tear up and her emotions got the better of her. "Mama,
how am I gonna keep him safe from any pain?"

Janie briefly covered Stella's hands with her own, but didn't
venture an answer. That mystery of life, she hadn't yet unraveled.

Stella awakened to an angry pounding on the cottage's door.
Ammanee had put an extra bolt on after hearing recent re-
ports of robbery and marauding in the area. She wanted to
make sure that with the new addition to the household, they
were all extra safe.

Stella leaped up in bed, her first instinct to make sure that
Wade was secure beside her in his Moses basket. It was almost miraculous that he had not been wakened by the insis-
tent rapping.

Seconds later she heard Ammanee and Frye arguing, his
voice loud and desperate.

"Hurry up and help me now, you hear?" he roared. Stella
tiptoed out of the room, only to see Frye standing in the parlor
clutching his arm. The sleeve of his jacket was soaked in blood.

"We ain't no doctors, Mas'," Ammanee tried to reason. "You need to get that looked at by someone who knows what he's doin'." She was shaking. "We can't get no bullet out of you…"

"Bullet! There's no goddamn bullet, you dumb bitch. I got myself blown up with a pipe bomb," he seethed through gritted teeth. "Damn thing went off before it was supposed to."

He fell down onto one of the chairs and pulled off his coat, revealing a forearm of torn, mangled flesh.

"Gimme some of that fig brandy you keep in that jug," he ordered Ammanee.

"Yes, suh."

Stella had never heard so much fear in her sister's voice before. She watched as Ammanee darted off to the kitchen to fetch the fermented drink.

When she returned, Frye grabbed the glass from her and took a deep swig. "Where's Stella?" His eyes darted across the room; his white face and spittle-laced mouth made him look like a rabid dog. "You two gonna clean me up! You gotta make me right," he commanded. "I can't get home to my wife like this. The Union boys already out there, lookin' for the saboteur."

"'Course, suh."

"Where *is* that goddamn girl," he demanded. "I'm out here bleedin' on the floorboards, drowning in pain…" He grabbed Ammanee's nightshirt with his free hand and pulled her near him. "Get her now!"

But right before Ammanee could break free from his grip to do his bidding, Stella slipped through the doorway.

"Here I am," she announced.

She measured her voice to make certain it sounded as concerned as it possibly could. "What's happened? You're hurt!"

The fiery rage which he'd lashed out on Ammanee seemed to have taken the last grains of strength left in him. The loss of blood was substantial, the cloth around his arm now saturated red.

He looked up at Stella, his face drained to a porcelain white. Then he keeled over and fell to the floor.

Of all the horrors that Stella had imagined during the war, having Frye arrive at the cottage bleeding and injured had never been one of them.

"What are we gonna do now?" she beseeched Ammanee.

Her sister was standing over him, slapping his cheeks to see if he'd come to. Frye's eyes opened and wobbled from side to side, before closing again.

"He's not dead," she remarked. "Let's try and get him to the bed."

The two women went to the opposite ends of his body. "Wade alright?" Ammanee asked before she took hold of Frye's feet.

"He's in the bedroom drawer," Stella answered. "I didn't know where else to put him, but I'll move him, soon as we done."

Ammanee nodded. "Looks like Frye goin' be out awhile. His old, grubby body tired from fightin' the pain, and that tipple I gave him probably helped.

"We just gotta hope he don't bring the Yanks to our doorstep. Can't imagine what would happen if we caught helping out a criminal."

"But we also gotta hope he don't die here, either," Stella added.

Ammanee looked up at her and didn't answer.

They managed to bring him to the bed. Ammanee boiled some of the cloth they used to diaper Wade and, once the wound was cleaned, they wrapped Frye's arm in homemade bandages. All the while, he whimpered and cursed in his delirium.

The flesh had been burned off on much of his forearm. His hand had also puffed out with another layer of white skin with a blistery fluid underneath.

To keep him sleeping longer, Ammanee brewed a tincture made from wolfsbane, a deep blue flower that grew in their garden. Janie would ask for the homemade brew whenever her bones were especially hurting, as it helped numb pain and brought on drowsiness.

"What's he gonna do when he comes to and realizes I'm no longer pregnant, sister?" Stella was more frightened than when Frye had fallen over hours before. "He's gonna take one look and know right away that Wade isn't his."

Ammanee gripped her wrist. "We ain't thinkin' 'bout that now, Stella. We'll just keep Wade away from Frye's eyes. We gonna keep him safe, I promise."

37

For the next two days, as Frye dipped in and out of consciousness, the two women took turns cleaning and bandaging his arm.

Stella slept next to Ammanee in the kitchen, their bodies curled together on a mattress made from straw. At her side, Wade stayed in his seagrass basket. She tried to anticipate his cycle of hunger, bringing him to her breast before he had a chance to cry and alert Frye to his presence, though there were times she could do little to muffle him.

But on the third night, the women were awakened by the sound of glass shattering. Frye had hobbled through the darkness in search of some of Ammanee's brandy, dragging himself into the room where the women now lay.

Stella jumped up, just as the baby began to howl, and Ammanee quickly reached to light a candle. Glowing in front of them was Frye. His pink-rimmed eyes were as wild as a coyote's, his top lip quivering with rage.

"Now, here I was, all worried I'd gone crazy thinking I heard a baby cryin'," he seethed as he peered down at the basket. "Thought I was havin' some sort of fever dream. Knew my Stella's belly was still round beneath her skirt, so the baby couldn't be here yet." He hobbled nearer, gripping his bandaged arm to his chest. "But by the look of this pickaninny, seems my nigra's done a whole lot of lying to me for a long while."

"Mason." Stella's voice shot into the air like a flare, using his first name for the first time. She swiftly gathered Wade into her arms and tried to shield him from view. "It's dark now and you're badly hurt. You just be imagin' things, sir."

"I'm certainly not imagining that this here baby's as black as coal," he fumed. "Not an ounce of my blood in that mongrel there of yours." He spat at her.

Ammanee leaped up and dared to try to drag him away from Stella and the baby.

Shaking free of Ammanee, he continued, "Don't matter anyway if you're a little whore, Stella. That little monkey's still gonna fetch me a good price when I go to sell him. Maybe even enough to get out of here. That baby ain't yours. He's my property. He's mine to do with what I want, even if he ain't my son."

A terrible sound escaped Stella, a wail she couldn't control.

"Mas', I think it's the pain makin' you talk like this," Ammanee attempted to reason. "It's pitch-dark in this house now, but when the sun come up in a few hours, you'll see that sweet chile is all yours."

Frye turned to look at her for a moment, his tirade having stolen all his energy.

Seizing the opportunity, the older woman coaxed him back

to the bedroom. "What's that you come in here for anyway? You wanted some more of my fig brandy fo' the pain? Right, sir?" she placated.

He grunted as he draped himself against her. "I'm no fool," he muttered.

"That's right, Mas'," she hushed him. "You just real tired, and the pain's got to you. Gonna give you something to make you feel alright."

Ammanee left Frye in the bedroom and returned to her sister, shutting all the doors along the way. Stella had a look in her eyes of such maternal ferocity that Ammanee didn't need words to know what her sister was planning.

The women got to work. Ammanee poured the fig brandy into a glass and Stella made a strong tincture of wolfsbane, steeping two extra spoonfuls of the dark blue flowers, rather than the standard pinch.

In silence, they blended the two liquids in a larger glass than they normally used.

Stella looked over at Wade, who was now asleep in his basket, his half-moon eyelids and full mouth giving her even more reason to do what she knew needed to be done.

Stella lifted the glass, eyed the proportions and then added a generous amount of honey to ensure it still tasted sweet. She put the drink down on a tray and went to bring it to Frye.

But Ammanee's fingers reached out and gripped her wrist. "You put that down now, girl," she whispered. "You not bringin' it to him." Her face was more resolute than Stella had ever seen it before. "I am."

Stella shook her head. "No. It's my son, so this is somethin' I gotta do. Alone."

Ammanee calmly placed her hand on her sister's shoulder to stop her, then took hold of the glass. "If this ever come back to haunt us, that boy gonna need his mother." She took a deep breath. "My job my whole life was to protect you, Stella." Her voice was steady. "So that's what's gonna happen again now. I'm gonna be the one to give it to 'im," she insisted. "Not just for my sister, but for my nephew, too."

"Brought you li'l somethin' to help you get back to sleep," Ammanee said as she ventured into the room.

Frye grabbed the glass from her with an angry swoop of his hand, drinking it down in one thirsty gulp.

"Tastes different than it normally do," he remarked as he smacked his lips and put his head back on the pillow.

"Stella wanted to make sure you had a little more sweetness now, Mas', so we added some extra honey," she replied as cheerfully as she could. She watched him closely. "Now you should get yo' rest. You just not yo'self. Conjurin' up all sorts of crazy visions tonight."

He could barely answer; his eyes began to droop.

"Now you rest, Mas'," Ammanee urged him.

Stella watched from the door as Ammanee smoothed the covers over Frye. When Ammanee picked up the glass with its few remaining drops of potent liquid, Stella lifted Frye's brocade vest from the back of the chair. He'd have no need for it in the future.

Settling herself into a chair in the small parlor, Stella began to carefully pluck out the fibers of the heavy embroidery. Her deft fingers flew as they waited for him to take his last breaths. There wasn't any reason to waste such beautiful, fine threads.

38

November 20, 1863
Brooklyn, New York

My darling Jacob,

Papa left this morning's newspaper on the dining room table for me. No doubt, he, too, was profoundly moved by the front page report from the President's visit to Gettysburg. If ever a man could summon the ghosts of the hallowed dead to ensure that we not forget their sacrifice, it is our Mr. Lincoln. He is absolutely right that every death should have meaning! And I believe his remarks at the new Soldiers' National Cemetery will not be forgotten any-time soon. As a permanent reminder to myself, I have written his powerful words into the pages of my diary: "...these dead shall not have died in vain—that his nation, under God, shall have a new birth of freedom and that the government of the people, by the people, for the people, shall not perish from the earth." So many of your letters have detailed the loss of life, dear husband, but now your recollections resonate even more profoundly. I will endeavor to honor them as best as I can, even if my efforts are far humbler than what you and your fellow Union men are undertaking to win the war.

I will rejoin the women at the Sanitary Commission tomorrow. With winter on its way, we've resurrected our quilting bee again. Under Henrietta's guidance, I've finally gained confidence in my sewing and feel like my contribution is worthwhile. I found a trunk in the attic of some of Mother's old tablecloths and I've reminded myself not to be sentimental, but to put the newly discovered materials to good use! Miss Rose came to dinner last week and together we managed to convince Papa to print additional copies of the latest edition of the "The Abolitionist." So, dear husband, I'm trying my best to heed President Lincoln's words and contribute in every way I possibly can to the greater good.

I pray you are safe, that you are fed and you are warm. Please write and let me know what I can send to you as you embark into the colder months. I've pressed my love into every word of this letter, so much that the nib of my pen is nearly worn to a nub.

I sign off with all my affection.

Your devoted,

Lily

39

Frye lay rigid in the bed. His face as white as tallow, his eyelids sealed like melted wax.

Stella held Wade to her breast, the baby happily suckling now that the house had been restored to calm. There was no more shouting, no more pots banging to the ground. The wolfsbane tincture had sent Frye into a permanent sleep.

Ammanee stepped into the room and reached over to gently stroke her nephew's head. "We don't never tell no one 'bout this. Not even Mama," she instructed.

Stella's eyes grew wide. "Is it wrong, sister, that I feel nothing?"

"Not wrong, sister. Think that man ever thought about how you were feelin'?" Her voice turned hard. "Shoulda never said those things about sellin' Wade."

Stella nodded. There was a certain code all mothers had for protecting their kin. It was as clear as black-and-white.

It had been Ammanee's idea to tell Deacon Dupont about the sudden death of Mason Frye. "He knew the man," she reminded Stella. The deacon had witnessed firsthand how Frye had recently become undone by the pressures of war.

"He'll know we're tellin' the truth about how he got his injury," Ammanee said. "Heard him tellin' the other men he was plannin' on doing somethin' crazy," she reasoned.

"I sure hope so," Stella said as she clutched baby Wade even tighter to her chest.

"I ain't gonna lie," Ammanee continued. "Just goin' tell him straight up that he came here after he got hurt, that we tended to him best we could."

"You think he'll help us?" Stella wasn't so sure. She had never been as trusting in the deacon as Ammanee.

"'Course he'll help. He's a man of God. Won't want to tell the missus, either, that he died over here on Burgundy Street. Got the good sense not to share that part, I'm sure."

It was true. When Ammanee brought Deacon Dupont over to the cottage the next day, he made no suggestion that he didn't believe the circumstances of Frye's death as the women had described it. An unfortunate situation, but nothing more.

"I told him no good would come from evil," the deacon said underneath his breath. "May God have mercy." He swiftly crossed himself before making the sign of the cross over the bloating body.

"Amen," Ammanee intoned.

"I'll send word to the undertaker to have him quietly removed. This sort of incident will have to be handled with the utmost delicacy," he reminded the women. "As I'm sure you both understand." His eyes darted to Wade.

Stella adjusted Wade's swaddling cloth around him and buried her nose in his sweet skin, avoiding the priest's eyes.

"I don't want to upset the family and I don't want the Union men poking around, either," he clarified. "Just want to do what's right."

Ammanee knew the priest well enough to know he believed every Christian deserved a proper burial. She kept her thoughts to herself on what Frye deserved.

After the undertaker removed Frye's body from the cottage, Ammanee turned to Stella. "Time we burn some sage around here and cleanse the place real good," she announced.

She knew their neighbors would start talking soon. It only took one woman seeing a corpse carried out to get the gossip flowing, and Ammanee hated to think of any haints flying through their door.

"Gotta get rid of that man's energy." She looked around the parlor. "Scrub the floors with some cedar oil, too. Tell his spirit he's not welcome here ever again."

"Let me put Wade in his basket and I'll help you," she said. "Don't want any part of him coming back, sister. Not ever."

PART THREE

40

Forty-seven boxes of rolled bandages and five boxes of quilts filled the hallway of the Kahn town house on Pierrepont Street in Brooklyn. Beneath the chandelier-lit atrium, Lily moved like clockwork instructing the porter to load them all on the wagon.

"We need to get these down to the armory as soon as possible," she instructed.

The young man began lifting the lighter crates onto his hand truck. "You've sure been busy here, miss," he noticed, impressed.

"The ladies and I certainly have." She crossed her arms and smiled, appraising their collective handiwork.

Several more boxes littered the parlor. They contained more fanciful quilts that the women knew could be sold for fundraising. Adeline Levi had repurposed two pairs of old damask curtains for a blanket made in the pattern of dove-gray and sage-green clouds. It was so exquisite, the silk so fine, that Lily was thinking of purchasing it herself to welcome Jacob back to their marital bed when he finally returned home.

"You finished in here yet?" Arthur Kahn stepped into the vestibule dressed in a dark suit, newspaper tucked under his arm. "Can't seem to find my hat…"

Lily smiled. "It's over there, Papa." She pointed to his black top hat resting on the table. The two maids were out with fever, but father and daughter were managing the best they could. "Did you take your tonic before you leave?" Lily reminded him. One of the sewing ladies had recommended a new homeopathic mixture of elderberry and linden flower as a means of staving off illness and boosting his immune system. She needed to make sure that at his age, her father took every precaution.

"Yes," he grumbled as he navigated the towers of boxes in the hall. Arthur reached into his pocket and retrieved a few coins to pay the boy hustling to load his wagon as quickly as possible. "Make sure those get there safely," he directed, wagging a finger. "My girl's put a lot of work into helping our soldiers. I don't want a single package lost."

He took his duster coat off the hook, put on his hat and wiggled his hands into his gloves.

"Ask the cook to make us steak for dinner," he requested before he departed for the office. "Something with iron will be good for us."

With the boxes now en route to the Thirteenth Regiment Armory on Henry Street, where the administrators would ensure the supplies were sent to Union field hospitals and infantries in need, Lily allowed herself a breath.

There was still so much to do, and she loathed to feel idle.

She felt newly invigorated by her recent correspondence with Frances Gage, a passionate abolitionist and suffragette who was now overseeing a refuge for freed slaves on Parris Island in South Carolina. Within Lily's social circles, the conversation was now focused not only on abolition, but on women's rights, as well.

"Frances is a formidable presence," Miss Rose agreed when she joined Lily for tea later that afternoon. "I'm so glad the two of you struck up a friendship when she came north for the Sanitary Commission's Annual Fair." She stirred a spoonful of sugar into her tea. "I had the pleasure of listening to her speak in Akron years back, lobbying for women to have the same property rights as their husbands. Frances didn't succeed in that, of course, but still we must admire her for keeping the fires aflame." She lifted the dainty-flowered cup to her lips, smiling at Lily through the plumes of steam.

In the midafternoon light, Miss Rose's age revealed itself. At fifty-three her dark hair had become tarnished with threads of silver. Baggy pouches of skin settled beneath her eyes. Often Lily would look at her and imagine what her own mother might look like now, for she and Ernestine would have almost been contemporaries.

"This room is particularly lovely, isn't it?" Ernestine approved, as she scanned the Kahns' living room. So many of Lily's late mother's favorite trinkets still lined the mahogany shelves. Painted porcelain figurines and decorative ornaments made from silver filigree.

"You might not know this," the elder woman confided, "but in the years before I began public speaking, I owned a fancy shop in Brooklyn. I sold perfumes of my own creation, fragrances blended with all sorts of flowers, from orange blossom to rose. I bet you didn't know that those scented paper liners you've put in your drawer were actually my invention?

I patented it back in Berlin before I immigrated here with my husband."

Lily could hardly hide her shock. She had only known Ernestine to be the pinnacle of practicality, without the slightest weakness for any frippery. An almost masculine air surrounded her. She never wore powder or rouge. Her dresses rarely had lace or beading, and she was known to remind the ladies in her fold that in order to be taken seriously, they must strive to have their words be the focus of attention, not their countenance or their clothes.

"I know it must come as a bit of a surprise," she laughed and adjusted herself in her chair. "But it provided the financial independence I needed to pursue my nobler passions."

"I had no idea *your* papers were lining my trousseau," Lily giggled.

"Not a word of it to the others." Ernestine grinned conspiratorially. "Now tell me, what has Frances written to you of late? I'm so curious about her work down in South Carolina and her new acquaintance with this impressive nurse Clara Barton."

"It was such an inspiring letter!" Lily gushed. "She wrote of Miss Barton's heroic efforts in tending to the sick outside Charleston, and how they are so appreciative of the bandages we sent to her field hospital last month." Lily looked out toward the now-empty vestibule, where the tower of boxes had crowded the space only a few hours before. "I'm glad more are on the way to those in need."

"That's wonderful. Some good news at least. Today's headlines were quite distressing." Ernestine let out a sigh. "I honestly never thought the war would last this long."

"Each month that passes makes Jacob's absence that much harder. It's difficult for me to fathom that he's been away for well over a year now," Lily admitted. "I'm grateful for the letters between us, but still the days without him are weighing on me more and more."

She did not share with Ernestine her deepest longing, which was her increasing desire to have children. Ernestine had no progeny of her own, and Lily did not want to create any unnecessary discomfort between them by sharing emotions that Miss Rose might misinterpret as Lily's waning interest in their work.

But her yearning to become a mother was strengthening every day. She envisioned a little one in her arms, squirming happily with life. A boy with dark curls like Jacob, or a red-headed girl like herself. She imagined the patter of footsteps scampering down the staircase of her childhood home, the sound of laughter filling the halls.

It was strange how her body pulled her toward motherhood, while she was all too aware of the painful reality that the war continued to claim men like Jacob in incomprehensible numbers. She was one of thousands of women who didn't know if their husbands would ever return to them, or if their injuries might prevent them from siring children even if they survived. One of the newer women in her quilting bee had rejoiced when she learned that her husband was on his way back home to her. But when he arrived, he was missing both his arms.

"You are keeping yourself engaged in important work," Ernestine reminded her. "You've become a real leader to the other women over the past year, corralling them to put their skills to good use, and then arranging the distribution of their work so it gets into the right hands."

"Thank you, Miss Rose," Lily said. "I've learned a lot from them as well, but there's still so much work to be done."

"Yes," Ernestine agreed. "So very much, indeed."

That evening, Lily returned to her childhood bedroom. On the shelves, tucked between her favorite books, she spotted her old diaries. Running her fingers along the spines, she remembered first the year, and then the month, when she'd witnessed the horrific event that had first sparked her desire to join the abolitionist movement, sending her into that Manhattan theater where she'd first heard Miss Rose speak.

October 3, 1857

Today I witnessed such a terrible injustice that it made me vow to take action against the atrocity of slavery. How can a young woman, having miraculously made her way to safety from her enslavers in the South, suddenly be seized upon in my beloved Brooklyn by two men carrying nets and shackles? It is hard for me to comprehend that here on the streets of New York, I was the only one, in a sea of people, who tried to help.

This young Black woman, who looked not a day older than eighteen, was out doing errands just like I was, when she was taken in the most brutal manner! They clamped handcuffs on her wrists, and then muzzled her protests by tying a piece of cloth around her mouth. When I pushed through the crowd and protested loudly, I was told by a police officer that the men were acting within their rights, as they were representing a slave holder from down in Charleston who "owned" this woman. "Blame the Fugitive Slave Act," he cited. "She's still their property, even if she's now on Northern soil."

When I continued to protest, he clenched my arm tightly and told me he'd arrest me if I interfered with the enforcement of Congress's law. "Take it up with them, young lady," he patronized me.

And so I will! I will no longer merely walk past the posters the abolitionists have plastered on city walls announcing their upcoming meetings and debates. I will instead begin attending these events and help them in any way I can. The barbaric institution

of slavery should not be upheld here in New York, or in any other
part of this country, for that matter.

I pledge this today and forever, dear diary.

Over six years had passed since Lily had written those words
into her red leather journal. She traced her curled handwrit-
ing, remembering the young woman who'd written them.
Her convictions had not waned since then. If anything, under
Miss Rose's guidance, she'd grown even more committed.
But the pages that captured the ensuing months would also
describe her falling in love with Jacob. She wasn't sure she
had the heart now to read them without her tears falling. She
wanted to be that *girl of fire*, as he called her. A woman brimming with energy and love.

41

Major General Phipps had commanded William to follow alongside his unit toward Lafayette.

Phipps had become quite enchanted by William's musical skills over the past few weeks, asking William to perform for him personally whenever he allowed himself a moment of respite. Now, as they packed up to head toward the western border, Phipps had even allowed him to bring Teddy along. "I spoke to your lieutenant colonel, who's fine with it," Phipps explained. "The man has no great affection for music, and it's not like he's losing two riflemen," he laughed.

William forced a smile, trying not to remember all of the riflemen "lost" at Port Hudson. He was just grateful his music had kept Jacob, him and Teddy together for a little while longer. The thought of being separated from either of them made him feel particularly unsettled after seeing how meaningless a Black man really was in this war.

"Just remind that boy that he's got to make himself useful. I'll need him to fetch me my meals, and my pails of water to do my ablutions… There'll be all sorts of stuff I'll need him to do for me when he's not beating out roll call or drills."

"Yes, sir," William assured the commanding officer. "He won't disappoint you…neither of us will, sir." But by that point, Major General Phipps was already striding away.

Teddy had started taking on more responsibilities over the past few weeks, warming the boy up ever more to William. The two of them looked so much like father and son that when a new Black recruit joined up, he'd always ask if the two were related.

Not my daddy, Teddy would answer softly. *But he good to me.*

These moments bolstered William's heart. He had no memory of his own father, and his mother had been robbed of the ability to share her stories of him. It was Ol' Abraham who'd pulled him aside one day and said, *Hear a bit of your daddy in your playing, son.*

William would never know if his musical ability had indeed come from his father. But on some nights when he couldn't sleep, he'd bring to mind a storybook image of himself as a child standing next to parents in the praise house back on Sapelo Island. He imagined his daddy clapping out the rhythms that led the whole room in song, his mother's face shining as she swayed back and forth, her hand tightly wrapped around his own.

William chose to believe that his musical talent—the one thing that continued to save him—had its origins in love.

***

They rolled up their blankets and packed their rucksacks. William cleaned his flute and his fife, then tucked them safely inside his bag. Teddy secured his snare straps around his neck.

He'd grown a couple inches over the past few months, so his pant cuffs no longer dragged over his boots and his jacket didn't sag in the shoulders like an old man. He was filling out and becoming more confident. William could hear it in his drum playing, his beats stronger and bolder. On the nights they huddled with their own, Teddy even began to sing along. On that last night in Port Gibson, one of the men in the Native Guard began singing:

"Amazing grace, How sweet the sound.
That sav'd a wretch like me!
I once was lost, but now I'm found,
Was blind, but now I see

'Twas grace that taught my heart to fear
And grace my fears reliev'd
How precious did that grace appear
The hour I first believ'd!"

The men's voices rose and combined in harmony, and the lyrics—which they'd all sung in church or the fields at one point in their lives—floated into the brisk night air. Teddy, to William's amazement, belted out the lyrics. Whenever William heard the song, he thought of his mama. Even if Tilly could no longer sing it, that spiritual had always been one of her favorites. She'd shake her tambourine vigorously every time it filled the walls of the praise house, letting herself join in the only way she could.

"Thinkin' 'bout my mama with that one." William wrapped his arm around Teddy when the song came to an end. He dug his other hand into his pocket to clutch his indigo pouch.

Teddy nodded solemnly, his eyes wetting to a bright sheen. "My mama loved it, too."

Jacob's pack had grown even heavier since Port Gibson. It now contained the two winter sweaters Lily had sent in her most recent care package, as well as the several-inch-thick folder that held his latest sheet music.

Before they headed out, he went in search of some of the musicians from regiments he'd played with over the past few months. He handed out the new scores from Lily, knowing she would approve.

The men were appreciative, thanking him as they slipped the paper into their belongings. While new sheet music was hardly expensive, finding a place to purchase it was near impossible under the circumstances.

One of the trombone players looked down at the score of "When Johnny Comes Marching Home" and smiled. "I've been wanting to learn this one for a while now."

Jacob was known within the camp to only have more uplifting scores in his possession. Other popular tunes like "Dear Mother, I've Come Home to Die" and "Tell Mother I Die Happy," about dying, weren't the kind that Lily would send him. She preferred songs full of hope and encouragement, and now Jacob had left his fellow musicians with a little bit of her spirit.

When the infantries eventually raised their packs and began marching out together, he heard it again. "Girl of Fire" was one of the first songs both Black and White soldiers sang as they trudged onward.

For four days they walked westward. They marched through the dense Louisiana forests of longleaf pines and cypress trees, and through swampland where Spanish moss draped over the ancient oaks.

"I miss those tiny blue flowers that fragranced the night air," Jacob mused to one of his fellow infantrymen. "I remember them from the last time we moved camp. The smell was like nothing we have up North." He took a deep breath in search of the scent, but with winter on its way, the blooms were already dried on the forest floor.

"I overheard Phipps talking. The Union just took Knoxville," the young private told Jacob as he rolled out his blanket for the night. "If we take the rest of Tennessee, we're that much closer to winning this war," he said, sounding hopeful.

Jacob placed his thin, scratchy military blanket on the earth, then pulled the quilt over his legs. He made sure that the side with the threadbare stars was the one that faced him.

"Let's hope that's the case," he agreed as he put his head down on his rucksack and closed his eyes. He hoped Lily had bought the quilt with the gray and pale green clouds she mentioned in a recent letter, and thought of the two of them beneath it as he drifted off to sleep.

When they reached Lafayette four days later, the weather had grown unseasonably cold. It was nothing like the frigid temperatures of New York or Boston, but some of the Black men had never even seen frost before.

"Nevah saw a leaf like this." Teddy pulled a weed from the earth, a thin layer of pearl-like moisture encapsulating its head.

William studied it, his breath melting the veil of ice as he spoke. "We better set up our tents to keep our bodies warm," he advised, glancing over at the other men who were working extra hard to get the poles into the frozen earth. With William and Teddy's new assignment from General Phipps, they had been given a small, battered tent—an unaccountable luxury. "And check in on Phipps," he reminded the boy. "Don't forget you're supposed to make sure he has everything he needs."

Hours later, after their new camp was constructed and once they'd managed to start a campfire and warm their tins of food, William looked around the site of tired men. Some were old faces, others were new. He hadn't seen Jacob since they'd arrived, but he pulled out his flute and told Teddy to get his drum.

He roused the men to start singing "Battle Hymn of the Republic." He knew as soon as Jacob heard the music, he would come.

42

Thinking she and the baby would benefit from a little fresh air, Stella decided to take a walk down Rampart Street. Despite the brisk temperature, the sun was shining. She placed Wade in the Moses basket, covered him snugly, then headed over to Miss Claudette's to show her how handy the gift was proving to be.

"Come in!" Miss Claudette was overjoyed to see them when she opened the door, although clearly a bit fatigued from the prior evening's demands. Almost as soon as they entered, she informed Stella that one of her callers had complimented the handkerchief Stella had made to thank her for the basket. On a square of white cloth, Stella had used some of the amber-colored threads from Frye's waistcoat to stitch three dainty stars. "He admired your handiwork, Stella, and with Christmas coming up soon, he's thinking he'd like to send one home as a gift to his sweetheart." She held her arms out, eager for a cuddle from Wade. "I think I could get him to pay you half a dollar for it," Claudette calculated in her head.

Stella handed her the baby and smiled. "Well, that's certainly good news. We could really use the money," she admitted.

Miss Claudette lifted Wade to her lips and gave him a little kiss on the forehead. "Then maybe word'll spread among the other Union boys, and you'll get a few more orders. It's light enough to send in the mail and it has a lovely bit of charm."

"It would be my pleasure," Stella said. She felt a tremendous satisfaction at the thought of Frye's threads being sent up North for Yankee women to wipe their noses with.

"And if Ammanee's up to it, I hear they're looking for a new cook down at the Union barracks. There were rumors goin' round that the White women they'd hired were puttin' all sorts of nasty things in their food." She scrunched up her face. "Don't want to tell you what, or you'd wretch."

"I'll let Ammanee know… I'm thinkin' she'd be perfect for it." Stella was especially grateful for Miss Claudette's attempts to support them in any way she could. In spite of her initial standoffish manner, she had grown to be a source of comfort to Stella in particular.

"Janie helpin' you all out with things?"

Stella sat down and smoothed out her skirt. "You know Mama. She's set in her ways, but she loves the baby and she's even been doing his nappies, helping me with the washing. She tries her best, but she don't like this cold snap we've been having. It's hard on her arthritis."

"Not good for any of us," Miss Claudette agreed. "Boil her some wolfsbane if her joints are givin' her pain."

Stella tensed up. She couldn't tell Miss Claudette that they'd recently used up their entire supply of those powerful blue flowers.

"Yes," she answered quietly. "I've heard it works magic."

Over the next few weeks, Stella worked diligently on making the new handkerchiefs. She pulled the gold and green threads carefully from Frye's vest, and using her shearing scissors, she cut out neat little squares from the last of the white linen she'd used for the maps. Depending on the Union soldier's request, she embroidered gold-colored stars or tendrils of ivy. For a little more coin, she took the few remaining threads from Hyacinth's shawl and stitched on a colored flower. A red rose for a passionate love, or a purple forget-me-not for a worrier. For mothers and sisters, the yellow jonquil, a symbol of familial affection, was a favorite choice.

"Reminds me of old times," Ammanee observed, as Stella sewed and the baby napped.

"You taught me how to hold my first needle." Stella smiled up at her.

"You were always a natural, and now you're better than me." Ammanee looked tired from her day of cooking for the soldiers, but at least she was allowed to bring home a lunch pail of leftovers to share with her sister. "They liked the hoppin' John," she said as she rewarmed the food on the stove. "Don't know what those White women were cookin' for them before, but I never saw men so happy to eat rice and black-eyed peas."

Stella's eyes widened as she took a forkful. "Is that ham hock I'm tastin'?" The salty pork exploded like fireworks on her tongue.

"Little bit chopped up, yes." Ammanee smiled. "An old favorite, black-eyed peas, onions, bell pepper…"

Stella could have cried, it tasted so good. She ate half her serving and then put down her plate. "I wanna save some for Mama."

Ammanee shook her head. "No, finish it. I made her a plate before I came home. No one there seein' how much I put in my pail. It's 'nuf for us all."

43

The care packages started to arrive at the campsite in droves. Boxes from loved ones as far north as Albany and Buffalo were delivered via Adams Express. Over the past several months, the Boston-based shipping company had managed to expand their mail delivery business. As a private company that served both sides in the war, they proved capable of delivering across all Confederate and Union lines. Their business was booming.

Men who had not received a single letter all year were now rewarded with a box from their loved ones. Some included a warm sweater or a new pair of trousers, while others revealed delicacies like home-baked bread and cookies, chutneys, and jams. A few lucky devils even boasted about receiving dried fruit and candy. Some who didn't have family or sweethearts were even getting packages from young single women, with notes tucked inside a hand-knitted pair of gloves or hat asking to strike up a correspondence with someone eligible and courageous.

Despite the harshness of camp life and the war's continuation, a Christmas spirit began to permeate the air. Aside from the increase in care packages and better food, Jacob noticed that even the most surly soldiers behaved a little kinder toward each other. Their musical requests changed, too; no longer did the men shout for the wartime ballads. Instead everyone wanted to hear songs of holiday cheer.

Jacob had always looked at the holiday from an outsider's perspective. As a child, he'd delighted walking through the crowded city streets, lampposts draped in wreaths of holly and apartment windows glowing with the light of tall tapered candles. The mood was contagious, even if he knew his family would not be exchanging gifts or pretending there would be visits from Saint Nick.

But memories like these reinforced the sense that despite having spent his entire life in America, many of its fundamental traditions would never be his.

"No presents for you? Not even from that girl on fire?" one of the infantrymen ribbed him.

Jacob shrugged. "Not today." It was true: nothing had arrived for him since they'd arrived in Baton Rouge. But since his conversation with William, he realized how fortunate he was to ever get anything in the mail at all. Before William, Jacob had no idea most Black recruits had likely never received a letter, let alone a care package.

He put his cornet back in its case. He'd spent much of the morning giving his instrument a well-needed cleaning and adding some oil to lubricate its valves.

"My sweetheart sent me some treats." The soldier opened his palm and showed him two pieces of maple sugar candy wrapped in beeswax. "You're always sharing what you get... you should take one," the man said, grinning.

Jacob took it and thanked him.

The soldier popped the other one in his mouth. "Merry Christmas, Private Kling. Here's to us making it through one more year."

Not wanting the candy to warm too long in his hand and melt, Jacob dropped it into his pocket. As much as he wanted to taste its sweetness, he knew someone else who would appreciate it even more.

He wandered over toward the edge of camp and found Teddy on his hands and knees scrubbing officers' shirts with a bar of soap and a washboard. A tin pail of sudsy water sat within arm's reach.

"Got something for you," Jacob announced. He reached into his pocket and withdrew the candy. "It's not much, but I thought it would give you a little holiday cheer."

"Thank you, suh," Teddy answered. He took the tiny piece of candy, unwrapped it carefully, and placed it in his mouth. "Haven't tasted any candy in a while, suh." A smile spread across his face.

"Glad you like it," Jacob said with a warm smile. He only wished he had more to give. "Have you seen William? The major general wants a special concert for Christmas Eve, and I gotta settle on a program that'll keep everyone's spirits bright into the New Year."

"He's over there." Teddy pointed. William was standing outside his crude tent staring out toward the forest, his flute in hand, grazing his side.

Jacob recognized the faraway look in his friend's eyes. William wasn't thinking about Christmas or even music. He was thinking of Stella.

"It's strange to realize that this is my first Christmas not bein' a slave," William confided.

He thought back to his childhood on Sapelo when Eleanor Righter handed out a single orange or grapefruit to her slaves, as if the pieces of fruit were as exotic and valuable as pieces of gold. And even back then, while the other slaves were given a day's reprieve, William was always required to go up to the big house to entertain the mistress's guests. "While the others were out enjoying themselves all singin' and dancin' down at the tabby shacks, I had to play her favorites—all those Baroque pieces that she loved.

"Worst part was havin' to wear that velvet suit and lace collared shirt cast off from her damn fool son." William let out a deep sigh. "When I finally got home, Mama would have saved some roasted opossum and sweet potatoes for me from the feast, leavin' a little tin plate on my pallet, but I still always felt like I was missin' out on somethin' special."

"I'm sorry," Jacob sympathized. "I'm feeling bad now that Phipps is making you play tomorrow. For me, it doesn't matter. It's not even my holiday."

"No matter." William shrugged. "The major general don't want no Vivaldi or Bach, just some high-spirited tunes to make it feel like Christmas. At least he's letting us decide what music we're gonna play."

"True," Jacob agreed.

"But I'd really like to get Teddy somethin' special, make it feel like a holiday for him. He's just a boy, should have somethin' that lifts 'im up." William rubbed his head. "There was a man back on Sapelo we called Ol' Abraham. He was the only one of us slaves who got to cut down his own tree on Christmas Eve. Miz Eleanor owed him somethin' big after he saved her son from drownin'. And she loved that idea of the 'forest tree,' ever since that opera singer Jenny Lind had one in her hotel room for Christmas and it made such a fuss down in Charleston. Missus thought she was given Abraham somethin' real special lettin' him have one in his shack." He closed his eyes remembering the man who'd given him his first instrument.

"He used to decorate his tree with all sorts of the nice things. 'Course not with anythin' pricey like the mistress did with her tinsel and painted ornaments. Abraham's was still something special with pinecones and necklaces made from dried berries." He sucked in his breath. "I would really like to make up a tree like that for Teddy."

"Don't see why we couldn't," Jacob said. "We got a whole forest surrounding us out there. I'm sure we could go out and find a tree and bring it back to him here."

William raised an eyebrow. "Really?" he said, warming to the idea. "Maybe we could bring him out there with us, let 'im pick out the one he wants. Could also shoot a rabbit to roast, make it a feast."

Jacob nodded. "That sure sounds better than having to eat the hog my men are planning on roasting tonight. I've had so much pork this past year, my ancestors are grumbling in their graves."

"Got another surprise for you," William roused Teddy from his slumber at daybreak. The boy was sleeping on a bed of oak leaves inside his small tarp tent, his drum beside his curled hand.

While he'd hoped he, Jacob and Teddy could have gone on their outing yesterday, their Christmas Eve responsibilities for Phipps had made it impossible. Instead they'd spent the day and evening entertaining the White regiments.

But now as the morning mist stretched across the camp, the men all snoring off the effects from the previous night's revelry, he didn't think the three of them would be missed over the next few hours.

"Do I need my snare?" Teddy asked as he rubbed his eyes.

William never went anywhere without the flute Frye had bought for him because it was too valuable to be left alone in his tent. But the drum would be cumbersome if Teddy had to help carry a tree back to camp.

"No, just bring your coat. You'll need something warm."

Teddy put on his blue Union jacket and slipped his hands into a pair of threadbare socks one of the White soldiers had discarded when new ones had arrived for Christmas. Teddy used them as makeshift mittens.

The two met Jacob at the edge of the camp. Dressed in civilian clothes, a wool sweater Lily had sent to him back in Port Gibson, he was happy to be included in giving Teddy a fond Christmas memory. Rumors had begun circulating amongst the infantrymen that a new campaign would be starting in the New Year, perhaps closer to Texas, and Jacob shuddered to think of what was ahead for all of them.

William looked out toward the wilderness. "Won't go far, don't want to run into any trouble." No Rebs had been sighted in the area recently as far as he was aware, but he knew they always had to be vigilant. "Got everything we need?"

"Yes," Jacob said, and tapped his satchel. He had tucked within his pack some vittles and a small handsaw he'd borrowed from one of the other men.

"Brought you that score you wanted to look at, too." Jacob handed it to William with a pencil. "In case you wanted to make any marks on the accompaniment."

"Thanks." William grinned and slipped it into his jacket.

"Where we goin'?" Teddy cut in.

"It's a Christmas adventure," William answered and pulled him briefly to his side.

They trekked east toward the rising sun, three figures of differing heights trudging off into the distant woods.

To construct temporary shelters for hundreds of infantrymen, the campsite had been purposefully laid out in a stretch of land only a few miles outside the forest.

William felt surprisingly buoyant as they traipsed over the leaf-strewn ground. He hadn't felt this happy for some time, probably since he'd last set off to see Stella in Congo Square. It certainly wasn't last night's festivities that had left him in a good mood. Yes, he'd fulfilled Phipps's request for a holiday performance for the troops, where he'd dutifully performed familiar hymns like "Deck the Halls" and "O Come, All Ye Faithful." But the concert had left him feeling like a performer, not a fellow brother in arms. Perhaps if some of his own Native Guard buddies had been present, he would have felt a deeper sense of camaraderie. But once again, he was just playing for a group of White men, most of them more interested in their food and drink than in the music.

Today, however, he felt like he owned the day. He could almost smell the fragrance of spruce, feel the pine's sappy needles in his palms. He was grateful for his memories of Abraham because now William could do something Teddy would always remember.

William set off on their journey singing, his voice belting out the warm and familiar spirituals of his youth. With a boost of confidence, Teddy took the lead and began singing the profound and soulful lyrics:

> *"O sometimes I feel like a motherless child*
> *Sometimes I feel like a motherless child*
> *Such a long, long way from my home..."*

The pitch and tone of Teddy's voice was deeper and richer than Jacob expected, and the poignancy of the words penetrated deep inside his heart. To hear Teddy sing solo for the first time felt like the young man was sharing a new instrument he'd kept hidden until now.

When William joined in, adding his own harmony, the blending of their voices sounded like the melding of two deeply linked souls.

"I've never heard that one before," Jacob admitted when they had finished. The powerful words stirred him, and he couldn't help but think of his own mother, who he'd lost nearly a decade before.

"These songs we singin' aren't printed on any papers from up North like the ones your girl sends you in her care packages." William lifted his chin in Teddy's direction. "Right? These songs get learned in a different way, in the praise house, the cotton fields or even in the kitchen."

Teddy nodded.

"Maybe you got one like that of your own to share, Jacob?" William asked as they continued through the trail.

Jacob struggled to think of one. Almost every song he knew could be traced to a popular or classical tune that the composer had at one point written down on a score. He recalled a few German lullabies his mother had sung to him and his brother as children. But in their foreignness, they hardly seemed appropriate now in the Louisiana woods.

"Gotta think about that…"

"Well, I got a Gullah one for you in the meantime." He let out a little holler, and then began to sing.

They reached the thicket of trees around noontime, just as the morning sun had started to disappear behind the clouds.

"What we doing out here?" Teddy asked.

"We're gonna make a nice little Christmas tradition of our own," William explained. He scanned the forest. They'd need a small sapling, something easy to cut down. "First we'll make a li'l fire, cook somethin' up real tasty."

"Ya want me to go catch a rabbit?" Teddy asked. "You got some rope?"

"It don't need to be a rabbit. Squirrel taste just as good." William dug into his pack and tossed a coil to Teddy. "But be careful, now, ya hear?"

Teddy nodded and set off, his grin indicating to William that all his efforts were worth the trouble.

"Sure we coulda done all this back at the camp, but I just wanna feel free today," William announced, turning to Jacob. He inhaled the crisp air. The scent of spruce and pine was invigorating. "Fightin's called off till the New Year anyway, right?"

"Like to think everyone's hunkered down for the holiday," Jacob agreed. Realistically, they both knew the Rebs hadn't been sighted in the area for a few weeks. Most of the fighting in Baton Rouge had taken place last spring and summer, and Phipps had only brought them there now as a holding point for the next campaign.

William pointed to a chest-high sapling. Spindly branches feathered in green needles jutted from its slender trunk. "We'll cut that one down, then bring it back to put in Teddy's tent. He'll remember this afternoon real good." A smile spread across his face as he started collecting kindling for the cooking fire.

The first shot made them fall to the ground. The soil was still damp on their hands.

William's eyes flared. Without either of them speaking, they instantly knew it had to be Teddy.

In the split seconds that followed, all they thought about was getting to him. They ran toward the sound, William hurdling over fallen trees to get there faster.

Jacob reached for his pistol, not yet knowing the target. Then his eyes fell. He saw William cradling Teddy, blood running from his neck, his head drooped back.

A wave of adrenaline came over Jacob. He charged forth and spotted a shadowy figure who looked to be a mere boy himself, the rabbit ears clutched in one hand, the other holding the shotgun whose blast had sent him and William into a frenzy. Jacob kept running forward and fired a shot at Teddy's assailant, but he missed the fallen tree that lay covered up in his path and crashed to the ground as the tree twisted and tore through his ankle.

Yet Jacob didn't feel the sharp stabbing pain at first. All he heard were William's piercing wails.

"He gone. He gone and dead." William's sobs were loud and relentless. He held Teddy to his chest like a baby, the boy flopping like a rag doll.

Teddy's blood was all over William's shirt.

Jacob struggled to pull himself up from the earth, but the pain in his ankle was too great.

"You not shot, too?" William sounded delirious.

"I think I just twisted it," Jacob grunted, attempting to drag himself toward William.

"This my fault, this all my fault," William wept. "Just wanted to do somethin' nice, and I got the boy killed." He was rubbing his hand against Teddy's blue jacket, seeming to try in vain to coax him back to life. "I was the one who told him to wear his coat."

No other shots, however, had been fired. It was more likely

a random act of violence by a hunter out for the day, rather than a Reb sniper.

"This is not your fault," Jacob insisted. "But we need to get him back to camp." The incident had happened so quickly. Terrible pools of nausea and pain flooded through his body as he tried to make sense of everything that had just happened. "Maybe they can still help him."

William shook his head. "No life left in 'im. They shot 'im right through the throat," his voice cracked.

"No..." Jacob broke down. "It can't be true..."

William took two fingers and gently closed Teddy's eye-lids, erasing the expression of fear frozen on the young man's face. "Nothin' nobody can do for him now."

Blood had started pouring from Jacob's own wound. His ankle clearly was far more than just twisted, as the skin had torn open to the bone. "If you bring him back there, he can get a proper burial," Jacob said through gritted teeth.

"Proper?" William's voice rose, recalling all he'd witnessed at Port Hudson. "They're just gonna toss my boy in a ditch!"

William regained his composure and the harsh reality of their situation made him move more quickly. They were still alone in unfamiliar woods, and Teddy's murderer could be drawing a bead on them even now. He gently placed Teddy down on the ground and walked over to Jacob to examine the bloody gash just above his ankle. Around the wound, the flesh already had begun to swell and discolor.

William closed his eyes and sucked in his breath. He took off his coat, then tore off his sleeve and wrapped it around Jacob's ankle to stave off the bleeding.

"Wish we had some whiskey. I could really need some right now..." Jacob mumbled.

"Hush." William looked down at Jacob's leg, trying to decide how best to focus his efforts. "Gonna go get you some help," he decided. "Right away."

"No." Jacob's answer was a strong rebuke. "You gotta take care of Teddy first," he implored. "My ankle's bad, but it's not going to kill me."

"I can't lose you, too," William muttered.

Jacob pushed through his pain. "We're gonna bury Teddy right, the way he deserves. Like a soldier."

William opened his hands, having nothing more to give.

"You're not gonna be able to dig a grave deep enough without a shovel, William," Jacob advised. "So go find a trench to lay him down in, and then cover him up with whatever you can find. Dirt, twigs, maybe even leaves."

"Gotta do it right," William agreed. "Can't let him lay here all exposed." The flute inside his jacket was pressing hard against his heart. He reached past it, withdrew the handkerchief Stella had made for him and wiped his eyes.

William did as Jacob suggested. He found a spot where the earth had naturally eroded and placed Teddy's body down into the basin, first checking to ensure he would face eastward according to Gullah tradition. William slipped the small square of cloth, the one with the blue-colored thread he believed had brought him protection, inside Teddy's coat. As much as he hated to be without it, knowing that something from Stella's loving hands could stay behind with the child gave him comfort. He patted the boy's cold hand and drew his arms together into a final resting repose. Then, without uttering another sound, William covered him with as much earth and brush as he could find and placed the boy's drumsticks on top, marking the grave with one of Teddy's possessions, another tradition he carried from his people back on Sapelo.

As William was making the small burial mound, Jacob tried to drag himself closer.

"Bring me over," Jacob again pressed through his pain.

William went to Jacob and threw his arm over his shoulder to carry him over to the makeshift grave. "What were those words again you said back in Port Hudson?" he asked Jacob.

"Yiska gal…"

William often recalled the poignancy and rhythm of the Jewish prayer for the dead since he'd first heard Jacob utter it for the hundreds of Black men slaughtered at the bluffs of Port Hudson.

"The Kaddish?"

"Yes," he murmured, brushing away his tears. "I've already said the Lord's Prayer, so let's do that one, too."

Jacob held on to William's shoulder tightly, gripping him for support, struggling through his pain to lead his friend through the words.

> *Yitgadal v'yitkadash sh'mei raba b'alma di-v'ra*
> *chirutei, v'yamlich malchutei b'chayeichon*
> *uvyomeichon uvchayei d'chol beit yisrael, ba'agala*
> *uvizman kariv, v'im'ru: "amen."*

"We need to find two stones now and put them down on the grave," Jacob explained after. "That's another one of our traditions. We do that to show the living will always remember the dead."

William let his body soften a little. "Lemme put you down for a moment, then." He gently placed Jacob on the ground, then went to fetch two rocks. When he returned, he lay the stones on the mound and lowered himself to his knees. Pressing his two hands to the earth, William said another prayer, one too quiet and perhaps too personal to reach Jacob's ears.

44

New Orleans, Louisiana
December 1863

Christmas that year felt different to Stella. She sat in the parlor with Wade nestled at her breast, his little finger around her own. Her son's peacefulness was contagious and, as she nursed him, she felt her entire body relax. As Stella looked down, she vowed to keep him safe in spite of their uncertain future.

Janie peered over and gently caressed her grandson's head. "Chile gettin' big," she mused. "Better keep you fed and your milk flowin'."

"Don't worry, Ammanee's taking good care of us," Stella reassured her mother.

"What time's she comin' back?" Janie asked.

"She'll be done with work 'bout three o'clock, once she finishes makin' the men their holiday meal. Think they're letting her roast turkeys."

"Hope they let her bring more than just one pail home this time." Janie grinned.

Stella's stomach growled. She hadn't eaten turkey since the war began. The thought of it made her mouth water.

"Your sister done good for herself." Janie clicked her tongue. "She's like me. She'll do whatever it takes to survive."

Stella's heart twinged. She knew her mother was implying that she was weak, or at least not as strong as Ammanee.

"Guess she's had to be. Life not bein' easy for her like it's been for you," Janie added.

"Mama," Stella said softly. "I wouldn't say my life's been easy—"

"Different grades of easy, like different shades of brown," Janie muttered to herself.

Stella thought back to that night when her mother and sister prepared her to go off to Market. She knew nothing of love yet, of wanting a choice in who she lay down with. Instead she'd been sent to the slaughterhouse wearing frippery her own mother had sewn and Ammanee had embellished.

"I'm not a survivor, too?" Stella bit her tongue. It felt like her whole adult life she'd done nothing but try to survive.

A pail full of corn bread, stuffing and trimmings. A hamper with some wrapped-up turkey and pie. Ammanee brought back far more than the two women were expecting.

"We got ourselves a feast." Janie rubbed her hands together as she helped Ammanee unpack.

"Hope you all don't mind, but I knocked on Miss Emilienne's and Miss Hyacinth's doors and let 'em know we had plenty enough to share," Ammanee informed her mother and sister.

"Of course!" Stella said, as she rose from the chair. She pulled down her blouse and placed Wade over her shoulder. "They've been so kind and generous with us when we needed help…the Moses basket, all the bits of food here and there. How could we not?"

Janie reached into the hamper and took a piece of corn bread. The girls didn't need to hear their mother's answer. Her thinking was clear in every bite she took.

Ammanee and Stella set out plates of everything they had to offer. Five turkey legs. A small bowl of stuffing and cranberry relish. Three pieces of corn bread. Miss Hyacinth and Miss Emilienne helped themselves only to the smallest of servings, still elegant in navigating the limited amount of food available.

"Gotta make sure our Stella has the most," Miss Emilienne instructed. "A li'l bit of Wade is all I need for dessert."

"He sure is sweet," Miss Hyacinth agreed. Her Nile-green eyes flickered with delight as she peered at Wade wrapped in his swaddling cloth.

"Seeing such a perfect bundle gives us hope. What could be a better Christmas present?"

"War being over," Janie reminded them. "That would be a mighty fine present, too."

"Ain't that the truth," someone grumbled.

"And a ham," Janie added for good measure.

Ammanee stood up and began clearing their plates. She hadn't taken any food for herself, and Stella hoped it was because she'd already eaten before she returned home. But something in her sister's face didn't seem quite right to her.

"Somethin' wrong, I can tell." Stella gently pulled her sister away from the wash pail. The two of them had been cleaning the dishes since the others left. She had begged her sister to let her do it all herself, but Ammanee wouldn't hear of it. "What is it? You can tell me anything, sister."

Ammanee inhaled deeply and then wiped her hands on a dishrag. "Didn't want to say anythin' just yet, but I guess I can never hide nothing from you." She smiled as she dug a hand into her pocket and withdrew a small silver ring that had been fashioned from a teaspoon. Ammanee slipped it on her left finger, her eyes moistening. "Benjamin gave it to me today. Said it was a promise ring."

Stella grasped the tip of her sister's finger and tugged it nearer so she could see the ring more fully. "My Lord, Ammanee. He made that for you?"

"Yeah, from one of the spoons from the big house. Said the mistress in such a state with Percy gone, she wouldn't miss no tiny spoon."

Stella inspected it more closely. Where the two ends of the spoon conjoined, a small silver rosebud flourished. "It's beautiful."

A plum-colored flush came over Ammanee's cheeks. She folded her fingers toward her chest, then brought the ring closer to her heart. "He came to the mess hall, dressed up real nice with the best clothes he own. Pulls me aside and tells me he don't wanna wait any longer. Told me he don't care if the law don't recognize it, he just wanna jump the broom with me, wants me to be his."

It had been months since Stella had overheard Janie's conversation with Ammanee in the main room. She'd hated to admit to herself just how much it had weighed on her that her sister hadn't felt comfortable enough to share her deepest yearnings with her. A tremendous sense of relief washed over her now that Ammanee had finally taken her into her confidence.

She placed a hand on the small of Ammanee's back. "You of all people should have love, sister."

"He says the mistress promised to make him a boss. She tellin' 'im he's the only man she trusts to farm her land. He's so handy fixin' things, makin' tools, she knows she gotta treat 'im bettuh these days."

Stella fell quiet, unsure how to react. Certainly, she wanted the best for her sister, but did Benjamin envision Ammanee returning to Percy's plantation? With Frye dead, Stella thought her sister was closer to freedom than ever. After all, she highly doubted that Frye's wife knew about his double life and his related private transactions.

"Bein' with Benjamin, helpin' him farm the land, havin' his baby, it sure sounds sweet," Ammanee mused aloud. "Still, it's hard to trust any White folk to do the right thing. Know Mama would tell me I'm just bein' a fool dreamin' 'bout this kinda life, but I'm still hopin' the Lord has a plan for me."

Stella sensed no weepiness in Ammanee's tone. She sounded resolute, almost the same tenor in which Janie spoke to them. *Wasn't 'bout what you wanted, but what was the best way to avoid the ditch*, she always reminded them.

"Part of her right, Stella. Can't imagine ever goin' back to a plantation. That kinda life real hard to imagine enduring, even if it means bein' there with Benjamin. But it's supposed to be different now that the Feds winnin'.'"

Stella could see just how torn Ammanee was. Regardless of how rosy a picture Benjamin painted of the role his mistress had promised him, the world in which he envisioned their union was hardly one out of a fairy tale. Her sister could be leaving their cottage for a life fraught with far more insecurity and hardship.

But Stella always believed that any ray of light was worth reaching toward.

"I want you to have love, want you to have a baby of your

own and never gotta fear somebody gonna take it from your arms." Stella said these words as though they were a prayer. But she knew they were only wishes at best. And being raised as Janie's daughter, she knew far too well that their wishes almost never came true.

45

William hoisted Jacob up and tried to take as much weight off his ankle as possible. The shirtsleeve he'd used for the bandage was now soaked a cardinal red.

"Gotta get you back now," he said. "You losin' blood, and that bone's gotta be set right." He didn't mention to Jacob that once back on Sapelo, he'd seen a slave lose his leg because the overseer wouldn't give the man immediate care, and then an infection set in. He pulled Jacob's arm over his shoulder. "We'll do this slowly," he attempted to reassure him.

But Jacob could hardly take one step even on his good leg. The pain was too intense. "Don't think I can…" he groaned. "Willie, just leave me here." His face was a deathly white. "Only thing you gotta do is promise to mail the letter in my haversack back at camp. Didn't get to mail it to Lily before Christmas."

"I'm not leaving you, and you'll be mailin' that letter yourself." William's voice was firm.

"We're gonna try and get as far as we can." He took the canteen out of Jacob's rucksack and urged him to drink some more water. It was still early, so there was plenty of sunlight. "I'm not gonna lose you, too."

As William tried to drag the two of them toward the direction of camp, their path became diverted by the difficulty of the terrain. After nearly thirty minutes of struggling to move forward, he realized a new plan was required.

"Might need to carry you." William was already struggling to breathe.

Jacob didn't answer.

"Jacob?" William let go of his friend's arm and laid him down. Jacob was now white as a sheet, his eyes had rolled backward inside his head.

William repeated his name, but there was no response. Jacob was barely conscious, the only sound that escaped his lips an almost inaudible moan.

"You not dyin' on me," William said, as though it was an order. He began to rifle through Jacob's pack to search for his canteen. He dribbled water into Jacob's parched lips, then his own. "Yeah, I gonna carry you now." He looked down at his friend, determination setting in, quickly combined their food and water into one pack and then lifted Jacob into his own slight arms.

William had never been a man of great physical fortitude, so carrying Jacob demanded every last ounce of his strength. The forest, which only hours before unfurled as an invigorating expanse, now felt like a dizzying labyrinth. He struggled to find his bearings, and he could no longer sense how to get back to camp.

Nearly an hour later, after taking intermittent breaks to gather his breath and make sure Jacob had more water, he noticed a plume of chimney smoke rising from a gap in the woods.

He put Jacob down and walked closer. He had no memory of passing a home at any point earlier that day. But, here, within a small clearing, was a run-down shack with a small shed.

William glanced over at Jacob resting on the earth. He didn't know how much farther he could carry him, and he knew Jacob required immediate care. The wound needed to be cleaned and the ankle properly braced or else Jacob could lose his leg, or even die.

He made a quick decision. Neither of them was wearing their Union blues. William couldn't look any worse, for that matter. One of his shirtsleeves was missing, having used it as a makeshift bandage, and a significant portion of his pants and jacket were covered in blood. But he knew his only option was to knock on the door and take a chance someone might help.

William again hoisted Jacob into his arms and began walking toward the house, the danger of the unknown slowing each of his steps. He realized that the person who might greet him could even be the monster who'd just killed Teddy. But he forced himself to banish such thoughts. Perhaps because it was Christmas Day, maybe, just maybe, someone would take pity on them and help.

He made it to the rough-hewn door, braced Jacob against the shack's wall, and then rapped with his one free hand. No one answered. He tried again with more strength.

"Who's there?" a weathered voice grunted from behind the wooden divide.

"Need help," William said. "Please. Ma'am."

After several prolonged seconds, the door creaked open and an old woman's face peered out.

She opened the door wider and saw Jacob leaned against the doorjamb. Her cautious expression suddenly transformed at the sight of them. "You brought my Johnny back?" Her voice sprang to life. "I prayed he'd come back for Christmas! Oh thank you, Lord!" She knotted her hands together, and then beamed up at the sky.

"Ma'am." William immediately grasped the woman's confusion, living alone in the woods in these conditions during a war, but didn't want to correct her. He knew it might just be the saving grace they needed.

"Can I step inside and get 'im warm, clean 'im up? He twisted his ankle real good. Need to brace it," William said in a servile tone, lowering his gaze so as not to be caught looking a White woman in the eye.

"What you sayin', nigger?" Her tone now switched to the sound of a knife's blade. "You crazy? You not putterin' round no house of mine. Bring Johnny in, put him down by the fire and I'll take care of him. I'm his mama. Don't need no slave tellin' me how to treat my boy."

William sucked in his words and slowly treaded inside. The smell of bacon fat permeated the dark interior. Salty and strong, it clung to the air like an oily blanket. As he scanned the room, he saw the trappings of a woman used to living in the wilderness on her own. A cast-iron pot dangled inside the hearth. A bear-hide carpet spread out on the floor. A shotgun lay braced in the corner.

He walked toward the fireplace and gently laid Jacob down on the animal rug.

The woman stepped toward William. He nearly flinched at her long hair with ropes of gray and rough skin, catching a glimpse of eyes so pale he could almost look through them. She extended a bony arm, her hand clutching a tin bucket. "Fetch me some water to boil, boy. Pump's out in the back."

Her face twisted, and she snatched the pistol from Jacob's waistband, and William did as he was told. The weapons were a clear reminder that at any moment, the situation between them could turn deadly.

"Yes, ma'am." William lowered his gaze again and quietly took the pail. Before he left, he looked over his shoulder, in the direction of the hearth. The woman was already kneeling over Jacob, muttering things only a mother would say to a beloved son, as she gently peeled the bandage from his wound.

He brought in the water and fetched more firewood so it could be heated over the flames.

"Don't just stand there." The woman glared, her eyes narrow and feline. "Take that axe and cut me two straight planks so I can brace Johnny's leg."

"Woman damn crazy," William swallowed his words. All that mattered was putting that bone back in place for Jacob.

He grabbed the axe and went to the chopping stump. Beside it, he found a thick log he thought he could cut down to the right size.

William lifted the axe into the air and cleaved hard on the timber, splintering it down the middle with great force. He raised the tool again, this time striking the wood with even more ferocity. Every emotion—his frustration, his fear, his rage—William channeled into each and every swing. He thought of Ol' Abraham, who'd whittled a fife out of a piece of tulipwood: had all his hope and yearning for more been pressed into that piece of branch?

William grunted as he continued. He knew this timber had to set Jacob's leg right. When he finished, he took the small handsaw from his pack and cut the edges good and clean. For a moment, the strong fragrance released by the freshly cut bald cypress allowed William to forget the pain of having buried Teddy beneath a coverlet of leaves only hours before.

He brought her the wood, holding it out like an offering.

"You be off now." She grabbed the planks without thanking him. "Don't need you here no more."

William stood frozen. "Would like to stay, if I could," he stammered out. "Could help you round the grounds till the boy's better." William forced himself to be polite, despite the woman's utter unwillingness to do the same for him.

"My Johnny gonna be just fine," she huffed. "I've set more than a few bones in my time. Get, nigga." She turned away from him.

William's stomach flipped. He couldn't leave Jacob out here in the woods with this woman.

"But I could help until we at least know he's come to, could chop more wood out there for you. Fetch some fresh logs." He was desperate to show her how he could be handy.

She sneered at his offer. "You sleepin' in the shed, then. Don't go thinkin' you ever comin' in here."

He looked over at the crudely constructed shed. The roof was half caved in. The hard, earthen floor was strewn with old farm tools, most of them rusty and dull.

"Yes, ma'am. Just wanna make sure Johnny's on his way to healing." William purposefully emphasized her son's name to reinforce that Jacob would receive all the care he needed. He hated to think what would happen should she suddenly realize they were Union men.

"Don't you worry 'bout my boy," she snapped. "Once his leg's all braced, once he's eaten his mama's food."

"Sure he will," William agreed.

"Now, go chop that wood you promised me!" she ordered crudely. Just before she shut the door in William's face, she muttered one last thing. "Merry Christmas, boy. I'll pray for your nigga soul."

He gathered as many fallen tree limbs as he could find and arranged them in a pile. All the while, the chimney exhaled long feathers of blue smoke. At sundown, the woman emerged again, this time clutching her flannel robe around her thin frame with one hand and holding a shallow bowl in another.

"Brought you some supper," she grunted. She bent down and placed the food on the porch as though for a dog.

The door then closed shut. Through the flimsy curtain in the window, William saw her silhouette illuminated by the warm glow of firelight. The lack of knowledge of what was going on inside made him shudder.

For two nights, William slept under an old horse's blanket that was covered in fleas, his rucksack his pillow. Without any warm clothes, he shivered in the cold December air. His hands chapped, his belly still hungry. The flute which he'd since placed in his pack felt more useless than ever.

It had been nearly ten months since he'd run away to join the Union forces. And in that time, he'd seen countless men die, and hundreds more become maimed. He'd carted away wagons of limbs and helped carry stretchers with wailing men. But he'd never felt the futility of the war like he did now. In the middle of the Louisiana wilderness, he'd been forced to abandon a perfect child to rot beneath a flimsy veil of twigs and leaves. And now, his only other friend lay alone inside a house with an angry Reb woman, writhing in pain and possibly dying.

He pulled the blanket over him and saw the stars peering through the cracked roof. He never knew the story of why his beloved had been given the name "Stella." The only time he'd ever heard the name before was when his mistress had mentioned she was learning some new piano music called "Stella's Waltzes." *Beauty in the constellations*, she had mused aloud. While it was then his mistress told him the true meaning of the Italian word *stella*, it would take him several years to understand the true meaning of the name.

He looked into the darkness for her, his only star.

46

For three days he lived and toiled like a mule. Fetching and cutting firewood, sleeping in the freezing shed. Eating whatever gruel the old woman provided, when she remembered to. William told himself he was keeping careful guard over Jacob, but truthfully the woman wouldn't let him anywhere near him.

As he labored outside, he tried to check through the window for the faintest shadow of his friend. He had no idea if his leg was braced properly. He had no inkling if Jacob had yet been able to pull himself up and rise. If they were ever going to get out of here, Jacob would need crutches. William raised the axe again, angrily splintering more wood. He didn't know how to create something so necessary for their escape. It was one thing to cut and sand simple planks, but it was a wholly different matter to fashion and assemble crutches.

He was at a loss on how to proceed. His flute lay in his pack, unplayed since the Christmas Eve concert. He pulled it out and quietly blew air into it, softly playing some notes. The sensation of the instrument between his cracked hands gave him well-needed courage.

He looked up again at the window with its dingy lace curtain. There was still no movement inside that he could detect.

William stood and walked closer to the house. He began playing the notes of "Jacob's Ladder" on his flute, and with each chorus, the music rose in volume. The song, which he knew Jacob would recognize from when William had sung it before, would let his friend know he hadn't left his side.

"Why you makin' all this noise?" The woman hurled out of the house. "My boy runnin' a fever now!"

"Fever?" A terrible panic passed through William. His flute fell limply to his side.

"Yes! Gonna need you to go into town and get me some powder. Come here closer, don't wanna be yellin' here on my porch. And I caught you tryin' to steal my boy's flute like that?" She glared at him. "Gimme that."

"Not Johnny's flute, ma'am."

"That flute can't belong to no blackie. It's shiny as a nickel, even I can see that." She stepped closer. "Gimme it or I'm goin' inside and gettin' my gun." Her narrow eyes left little doubt in his mind that she would not hesitate to carry out her threat.

William froze, considering his options. "You'll be sure to give it to him when he wakes up, right, ma'am?" he asked.

To part with his flute would be like offering up one of his limbs. But William also realized that if Jacob regained consciousness, he'd discern immediately that the flute was a message. William would never leave the flute behind unless he was coming back for both of them.

"'Course I'll give it back to 'im," she sneered before snatching the instrument from William's grip.

He stood motionless. Empty-handed, hungry and cold.

"Now go into town and get me that fever powder, boy."

William lifted his eyes and glared back at her, suddenly empowered by having nothing left to lose.

"Town?" he asked. He didn't even know where he was. "What town, ma'am?"

"You just a dumb animal." She shook her head. "New Iberia, five miles down that way." She pointed through a path in the woods. "You head north."

At his quizzical look, she scoffed. "Don't know nothing. Follow the dirt path. At the end, there's a red barn with sheep out front. Hang a right and keep going 'bout three miles. General store just round the corner. Owner's Mr. Cross. He knows my credit's good with 'em."

William eyed the path. "Can I see Johnny before I go?"

"No nigger comin' inside my home, told you that before." She waved the flute angrily in his direction. "Now you get goin'. Anythin' happen to my son, it's gonna be you get the blame!"

She shooed William in the right direction, then slammed shut the door.

The dirt road that stretched out from the shack was long and winding. Despite the directions he'd been given, William didn't know where it might lead or how long it would take him to find the town. He was a lone Black man walking through hostile territory, his clothing splattered with blood, his hair matted in disarray, his body unwashed. From the outside, he looked far worse for wear than when he'd arrived in Camp Parapet to enlist.

But he had three clues as to where he was, and how to get

back to Jacob. The red barn, the general store and the store owner's name, "Cross." When he got to the red barn, he removed from his rucksack a piece of sheet music Jacob had gifted him for Christmas before they left camp.

As he drew symbols and images on the back of the music, William suddenly came alive. He had begun to make a map.

47

December 26, 1863
Brooklyn, New York

My dearest Jacob,

Brooklyn is covered in a thick blanket of snow tonight as I am thinking of you, cherished husband. Did you and your fellow soldiers receive any reprieve for Christmas? I read in the papers that Lincoln's youngest son, Tad, sent presents to many of the Union regiments for the holiday. He was apparently deeply moved by their plight after visiting several army hospitals with his father and wanted to show his gratitude. I found this so touching and it increased my admiration and affection for our president and his family even more.

Last night, as Papa and I sat in the comfort of our parlor, I caught a glimpse of our neighbors across the street. Through their living room window, I saw their children rapturously unwrapping boxes under the warm glow of their fireplace, and I couldn't help *but think of that little drummer boy, Teddy, you've mentioned so fondly in your recent letters. I know it's a modest gift, but in this package, in addition to a pair for you, I'm including a second pair of mittens that I bought at the latest Sanitary Commission Fundraiser. While my quilting skills have improved greatly over the past year, I'm still not much of a knitter, and these ones—crafted by Henrietta—seemed quite fetching to me in their dark blue yarn.*

The other women on the committee have been exchanging news regarding their husbands. Jenny Roth was fortunate enough to have hers come home on furlough to meet their son for the first time. The boy was born nine months after he left, and his father got to witness his first steps. How she wept when she said he will return to Virginia in three days' time! My heart broke for her, Jacob, but I also envied the brief interlude that she had with him.

I continue to hold faith that Lincoln can steer us all toward peace, and that after our nation's myriad struggles, the dead will remind us how much has been lost and how much more will need to be done after all this madness ends. It's not just about ridding the country of slavery's injustice and cruelty, but also forging all the new paths we will require to bring about greater equality.

Miss Rose continues to include suffrage in her talks, and many of the women in my circle are now almost as passionate about that issue as they are regarding abolitionism. We dream of a brighter future where race and gender are not used against any individual, and instead where opportunity unfurls before all who are willing to reach for it.

I apologize if I am sharing too much of what is in my head in this letter, but there is no one to share my thoughts with when I'm home. I feel more lonely here with Papa now spending so much of his time either shuttered in his office or down at the warehouse. He is good and kind, I know. He offers our newspapers the chance to use his printing presses, and is generous in his donations to the hospital and wounded veteran funds. But I know he does not like to hear me prattle on. While Christmas is not our holiday, I was at least grateful he spent the evening with me by the fire, reading as I worked on a new quilt.

Please take care of yourself, darling husband. I am keeping our marital hearth aflame in my heart and mind. I remain your girl of fire.

Your loving wife,

Lily

P.S. I do hope the second pair of mittens will fit Teddy! Given he's not yet grown, I chose a smaller set for him.

48

William trudged through the woods toward Iberia. On the back of the sheet music, he'd already recorded as many landmarks as he could to help lead him back to Jacob. The first rough drawing he put down was of the old woman's house and her shed. Then he outlined the path that led to its entrance from off the main road, which was flanked by two large poplar trees. When he eventually saw the red barn where she'd instructed him to turn right, he sketched that onto the paper and indicated the direction with an arrow. There were no sheep there, but he figured they were additional casualties of war.

As he continued trekking forth, he spotted a large sugar-cane plantation. The facade of the sprawling mansion, with its tall white pillars, was painted a pale yellow, stark against the grill of dark wrought iron gates. William took note of it and marked it on the page with a larger home and a sugar-cane stalk. He added a lemon inside the drawing of the home to indicate its color. After walking several more miles, he finally saw the general store in the distance. He jotted down a cross as a symbol for the store, a reference to its owner's name.

He kept himself at the forest's edge for a moment before stepping into the sunlight. It was ingrained in him never to enter an open space without first carefully considering his surroundings. While the northwestern Louisiana parishes were supposed to be under the control of General Banks, that alone hardly guaranteed William's safety. Towns like Iberia were still populated by men and women loyal to the Confederacy. To them, a Black man in blood-splattered clothes wandering toward the general store would not be a welcome sight.

Adjacent to the small white-framed shop, William noticed a crowd of men spilling out of a tavern. Liquor seemed to have been liberally imbibed. With their suspenders draped off their shoulders and their ruddy faces inflamed, he'd be walking into a mess of trouble if they caught view of him. A ripe prize for humiliation and violence.

But he needed to get Jacob the fever powder. He made a quick calculation: if he could keep out of their sight until he got to the town square, he might be able to duck into the store without drawing their attention.

William looked down at his ripped clothes. He regretted not searching for a stream or creek to clean himself up, but he hadn't dared to venture from the path, lest he get lost. He tucked his shirt into his trousers, ran a hand across his brow and gazed out toward the store. *Man's name's Cross…maybe that's a sign*, he thought to himself. *Jesus help me*. He gathered his nerves and ventured forward, hoping he wouldn't have to make a similar kind of sacrifice.

The thud of a boot, the sound of a scornful jeer. The impact of a fist into his left eye. The pulling of his Union greenbacks from his breast pocket. William didn't remember the sequence of events, only the consequences of the attack. The drunkards eventually dragged him over rough ground and dumped him in a wagon. After several minutes, they left the road and entered another set of woods. When they tossed him from the still moving wagon, he must have hit his head upon landing because he lost consciousness. *Nigger think he can stroll round here in plain sight, probably stole that money*, were the last words he remembered hearing.

He awoke to the sound of birdsong, so incongruent to his pain. With his one hand that hadn't been damaged in the fight, he touched his now swollen-shut left eye and traced his lip, which was puffy and split open with blood. His other hand was throbbing, and he could not move two of his fingers.

The men had left him for dead out there in the wilderness. The only saving grace had been when one of them asked the rest of the group who had brought the rope to string William up, and it became evident that in their drunken stupor no one had thought to do so.

William tried to get up, but his head was pounding, his wounds were raw and his body ached.

He lay on the damp earth, his one open eye struggling to focus on the single patch of blue sky that peeked through the treetops. He wondered if this would be where he would die. Would his last breaths be in the middle of some nameless wood, his lifeless body a meal for the wild animals, perhaps the same buzzards that had eaten his comrades back in Port Hudson? After fighting for freedom, for a life back home with Stella, would it all come to this humiliating end?

He had almost no strength left in him. His faith bled out of every pore. He closed his right eye and felt himself melting into the earth. But the image that greeted him as he shut his lids was not of Stella. Instead, someone else appeared.

Alternating between brief states of consciousness and sleep, William felt himself wading into azure waters. He saw a strong figure stirring indigo stalks into a vat of liquid, next to him a seagrass basket filled with blue flowers. He watched the man's eyes lift and meet his, a look of recognition bridging the two of them as the man pressed a warm, dye-stained hand against William's cheek.

When William finally came to again, it was as though he had been visited by an apparition who had come to guide him to safety. He had always felt the protective spirit of his mother over the years, but this was the first time he'd ever felt the presence of his father. He forced himself to open his one good eye and to use his one good hand to push himself to stand up. His fingers reached inside his tattered coat pocket. Miraculously, he found the piece of sheet music still folded inside. William took a deep breath and slowly put one foot in front of the other in what he hoped was the right direction. He would not give up on Jacob—or himself.

Over the next few days, he struggled to find his way, unsure of whether he was now closer to the army camp or to the old woman's house. He used the sun as his compass, studying the path for something, anything, he might recognize. He drank water from the river stream and was lucky enough to catch a fish, which he was forced to eat raw. Far from improving, his wounds grew worse from the ordeal. His damaged hand became more swollen, intensifying the pain.

But every time he was on the precipice of giving up, the vision of his father in his dream returned to him and renewed his strength. Thoughts of Tilly's fortitude and Stella's complete belief in him became an elixir to help him venture on. Each moment he felt he might surrender to despair, William felt himself being picked up by someone who loved him.

Had someone asked, he would not have been able to say how many days he wandered in the woods. Time for him had dissipated, no longer structured by the days of the week but solely by his ability to survive from sunrise to nightfall.

Eventually he found himself stumbling into the mouth of what he realized was the Union army's former campsite that he, Jacob and Teddy had departed on Christmas Day. But now the stretch of land was completely empty. He half hoped to still see Jacob's tent. That worn quilt of stars folded by his pack, his cornet case resting to its side. But none of it remained. The men must have packed up their tents and loaded the supply wagons, leaving just a barren field of crabgrass and mud. The only proof that the area had recently been occupied by Phipps and his men were the charred marks in the grass from their campfires, and a few scattered remains of military paraphernalia tumbling about in the damp winter air.

He was exhausted, and his heart sank with a sense of hopelessness as he walked through the vacant expanse. His hunger only added to his depression. He scanned the surroundings around the abandoned firepits to see if any bits of food might have been left behind. He discovered two cans of lima beans that had been tossed near a heap of litter. Grateful that he would at least have something to eat for his next meal, William sat down on the grass and pulled out his roughly drawn map.

It seemed essentially useless at his present location, for it began from the front porch of the old woman's home and its path followed out toward Iberia. He could conceivably try to retrace their footsteps from their ill-fated Christmas Day journey, but it seemed like pure folly to think he could somehow stumble upon that shack again now when he had initially only found it by chance after dragging Jacob for some time. The only sensible way to try to reach it was to find a way back to the town with Cross's General Store, and then use the map to get back to Jacob.

William put the paper back in his pocket and reached for a heavy rock. With all of his remaining strength, he smashed open both cans of lima beans. At least for now, he had supper. He savored the food and contemplated his course of action for the next day before passing out.

49

January 3, 1864
Brooklyn, New York

My darling husband,

The mail has been so poor lately, and I am uncertain whether you
and your regiment are still encamped at the same address in Louisiana to which I'm posting this letter. I have not heard otherwise
from you, so I can only hope my last care package and this latest
missive reach you, my love.

The New Year has come and gone without much fanfare. All
of us here, particularly myself, are so disheartened that the war
continues to wage on. It feels misguided to me to celebrate the New
Year with no sign of peace in sight. I have tried to maintain a sense
of purpose in this time of discord, but I worry I'm not contributing
enough, Jacob. Still, I try my best, as I know you expect me to do.

You would be pleased to learn that I recently attended a fundraising lunch connected with the Union League Club. They have

begun a formidable initiative to recruit 2,000 new Colored soldiers and outfit them with uniforms and equipment. While the horror of the July riots stained so much of New York City, I'm thankful that at least a few good men and women have come together to support those brave Negroes who yearn to take up arms for the cause. I know from your own letters that detailed the experiences of Lieutenant Cailloux and his men at the battle of Port Hudson, how much you value their valor and commitment. So you can imagine my outrage when I recently learned that our government has not given equal pay to these brave soldiers!

At our last meeting, Miss Rose read aloud a letter from a Negro corporal in the 54th Regiment of Massachusetts to President Lincoln that was published this fall in a local paper. This man, a Mr. James Henry Gooding, rightfully protested to our great leader the fact that men like him are being paid $3 a month less than their White comrades. "We have done a soldier's duty, why can't we have a soldier's pay?" he petitioned. And isn't he correct, dear husband! To think that yet another inequality is most painfully being propagated within the Union ranks is truly appalling.

Miss Rose is now working with two of our colleagues to write a manifesto in support of equal pay for every man enlisted, regardless of the color of their skin. We're hoping it will reach the ears of those in Congress, and this wrongful injustice can be rectified swiftly. In the meantime, these men in the 54th Regiment are swearing off all pay until it's the same as their White peers'. I can hardly blame them, yet to fight without any compensation only adds another layer to their tremendous struggle.

How inconsequential my gift of new mittens must have seemed. It feels like such a small gesture amidst so much hardship. It's a persistent challenge to try to express my gratitude for all the daily sacrifices you and your fellow soldiers make each day. I have never been one to go to synagogue to pray, preferring my meditations and requests to God be made in the privacy of home. But do know that I continue to keep faith that you will be returned to my loving arms and your friends will also soon feel the embrace of their beloveds.

After I fold this letter, I will play my harp and hope the notes somehow reach you.

Your faithful wife,

Lily

50

William awoke and contemplated the best way back to Iberia. He doubted he'd ever be able to find it if he ventured again into the heavily wooded forest and remembered instead that there was a small town several miles east of the camp. He started walking toward the closest main road, thinking that perhaps there would be a paved route back to the town that would eventually bring him closer to Jacob.

In the early-morning daylight, as the crows circled above, he heard the sound of an approaching wagon. High on its driver's perch sat two men in Union garb. William was ecstatic, sure he had now located part of a Union unit that would help get Jacob back safely.

William took his undamaged hand and began to wave furiously for them to slow down.

The driver pulled the horse's reins and came to a halt in front of William.

"Officer, suh, y'all gotta help me. I'm a Union man, enlisted back in March at Camp Parapet. We was just encamped with General Phipps in the 163rd New York Infantry." He was breathless and his overwhelming physical deprivation and mental desperation had nearly overtaken him. "One of our men, he injured. I had to leave him at a Reb house near Iberia. He need care, real care." By now he was speaking so fast, it was virtually impossible for the men to understand what he was trying to tell them.

"What nonsense you spewin' there, nigger?" the Union man's voice was skeptical and impatient. "You don't look like no soldier." He peered closer, inspecting William's ragged clothes, his lack of uniform or musket. There was no evidence at all that William was who he claimed. "And even if you were, you're not with your men. Not doing your duty while we fight to get you free. That means you're nothing but a loathsome deserter."

"No, suh," William insisted. "Anything but. I doing all I can to help a fellow soldier." He reached into his breast pocket. "Look, suh, I made a map!" He shook it in the man's direction. "See these are the symbols here how to find him. It's not far from Iberia. If you take me there, and someone come with me to Cross's store…" He placed his finger on the smudged sheet of paper. "See, if we follow this path, we gonna find him."

"He's damn crazy," the other Union man muttered to the driver. "No way he's one of us."

"Please," William urged. "You gotta help. You just gotta—"

"Get in the wagon. Back there, with them sacks of grain," the driver barked. "We've got orders from the quartermaster to deliver these supplies close to Algiers. When we get there, you can spin your bull to whoever will listen. That is, if they don't just string you up first for deserting."

51

Lily woke abruptly, her heartbeat escalating beneath her nightdress. She'd just suffered the most terrible nightmare. Jacob was injured and stranded in a dangerous place. His face was gaunt and pale, his eyes beseeching her for help. She could see him so clearly that she could almost touch him.

"Are you alright, ma'am?" The housemaid opened the door to check on her. "I heard you call out."

"I'm fine, thank you," she feigned, adjusting herself against her pillows. "I just had a bad dream, that's all."

The young woman shut the door and Lily tried to calm her breathing. For several days, she'd had a persistent, nagging feeling that Jacob might be hurt. Her father must have noticed her lack of appetite, the perpetual worry that lined her face.

"What's the matter, my child?" he prodded as she poked at her eggs at breakfast. "You haven't been yourself for days, and now you can hardly put a forkful in your mouth."

"It's nothing..." Lily tried to put on a brave face. "Only I haven't heard from Jacob in some time, and I'm worried."

Arthur lifted his coffee to his lips and took a long sip. "You know how terrible the mail is, Lily, particularly with the war going on."

"I'm quite aware of the war. Thus, the worry concerning my husband, who is fighting in it."

"Jacob is a strong young man. And I hardly doubt that an enlisted musician faces the same level of danger as the average soldier, my darling."

Lily's face reddened. "You have made your fortune from musicians, Papa. So these men like Jacob, who purchase your sheet music from their own pocket so they have something to inspire and console others while away at war, do you not hold them in high regard? And when the drummers—some as young as eleven or twelve years old—are the first to march into battle, are they not in as much danger as any of the other infantrymen?"

Arthur put down his cup. "Of course, I hold them in the highest esteem, daughter. I was only trying to console you, to mollify your fears."

Lily glanced at her plate. "I'm sorry. I know I'm hardly a medium, that I can't know for certain that he's injured. But my heart feels like it's breaking."

"Perhaps a letter will arrive in today's post, and you will feel better." Arthur wiped his mouth with his napkin and reached over to grasp his daughter's hand. "So let's hope by supper you will have heard from Jacob. Your suffering pains me and I hate to see you not eating."

He stood up, bent over to kiss her on the top of her head and then departed for the warehouse. Next to his plate, he had left his newspaper, the headlines folded away from Lily's view. She let it sit there. This morning, she didn't have the strength to read them.

By 6:00 p.m., no letter had arrived, and Lily asked the maid if she could have her dinner set on a tray and brought to her room. She had failed to accomplish anything all day. She'd tried to draft promotional materials for Miss Rose's upcoming debate, but the words kept getting tangled on the page. She sought solace in her harp, but even that brought her little relief.

From the moment she was old enough to understand she was motherless, Lily longed to understand what happened to the soul after death. But her father had few books about the Jewish faith in his extensive library, and he had not believed that as a female she required a Jewish education, other than knowing how to say the Shabbat prayer should her future husband be so inclined to celebrate the Sabbath. When she asked him if her mother was in heaven, her father answered only, "Olam Habah. Your mother now exists in the world to come."

Lily blinked away her tears. She didn't want to envision a life without Jacob. She wanted him to return safely to her arms. Their future life together was the only place Lily truly believed was the world to come.

52

The wagon rolled along the craggy road. William jostled back and forth, his battered body bumping against the lumpy sacks of grain.

He loathed the fact that these men did not believe him, that they had not taken him at his word, that he was merely trying to get back to one of *their* own. Even worse, they had ridiculed him. They had laughed at his map, mocked his pleas for help and even gone so far as to suggest he might be a deserter. To have his loyalty questioned enraged William. If he didn't think they'd shoot him if he jumped out of the wagon, he would make a run for it and get to Jacob another way.

The sound of the wheels rolling over the uneven terrain brought him back to all the miles he had trekked with his regiment, longing to catch a break by riding in one of the caravans. While his muscles felt fortunate to no longer have to lumber along the road, he started to get an eerie feeling down in his bones. He peered outside the covered rear, hoping to get a sense of where they were heading. From what he could discern from the sun, every hour brought them farther east and that much farther away from Jacob.

He positioned himself in the corner, attempting to keep the horizon in his line of vision. Outside, William could see the muddy terrain stretching into the distance, and after several hours, he watched the landscape become wetter, more fertile. Soybean crops and a few intermittent rice paddies emerged as they drew closer to the Mississippi River. He now could guess the direction they were moving.

While it wasn't the way toward Iberia, he nonetheless felt a new sense of hope.

The men were moving closer to New Orleans.

"The boys picked this one up near St. Martin Parish." The quartermaster snatched the cloth of William's jacket and dragged him toward the supervising officer.

William tried to straighten himself out and pulled himself from the man's clutches. "I'm a Union man, suh. Mustered in with the Corps d'Afrique back in Camp Parapet. Was recently under the command of Major General Phipps and served as a military musician."

The commanding officer appeared skeptical. "All our men are in uniform, even the colored ones, so it don't look to me like you're telling the truth."

"Suh, it was Christmas Day that I got separated," William rushed to explain. "Wasn't wearing my uniform and went out with some other men. One of 'em got shot and the other got hurt real bad. Private Jacob Kling, in the 163rd New York Regiment, a musician, too. He's out there with a real bad leg." William pulled out the sheet music and pointed to the old woman's shack drawn on the back. "I made this map to try and get back to him."

The officer looked down at the now fragile paper and sneered. "You call this a map?" He laughed, little droplets of spittle flying into the air as he hastily returned the paper, as if it would soil his hands. "How's anyone ever gonna find someone from that?"

"Suh, you get me back to Iberia where Cross got his store, I know I can retrace my steps."

"Get 'im out of here. Not even worth court-martialing. He said he was at Port Hudson, probably got deranged from all that." The man shook his head. "Call that a map…" The quartermaster turned back to his ledgers, dismissing William from the tent and his mind.

Standing alone, William felt himself fade from the other soldiers' interest. Some were busy dragging sacks of grain from the wagon, while others loaded additional supplies for further transport elsewhere. Dealing with an injured Black man on a quixotic quest to rescue some Union private with an odd-sounding name was not worth their while.

Finally a young man carrying a pail of water took pity on him. "The contraband camp's five miles west of here in Algiers," he informed William.

William was too exhausted to explain himself to yet another soldier. "West?" he confirmed, as the man motioned the correct direction to him.

"Yes. A big camp over there. Lotta runaway slaves looking to join up there or at Parapet."

William didn't answer. He'd already made that journey, which begat ten months of digging trenches, getting shot at by the Rebs and then seeing his compatriots' corpses left rotting in the heat. His reward for his efforts? Burying an innocent child and then having his loyalty questioned while trying to get back to help his friend.

No White man other than Jacob seemed to care about him. The only time he was ever really seen was when he had a flute in his hand. And even that was now gone.

He glanced in the direction of Algiers. He had passed through the area before on the way to lavish house parties with Frye, as it bordered the outskirts of New Orleans. From there, he knew he could find the place he'd longed to be every moment of the day since he'd first run off to fight.

So as the night fell, he simply started walking. No one tried to stop him.

William set out to return to Stella.

53

Nearly all the remaining curtains on Rampart Street were drawn shut. The row of once colorful houses looked weary, as though life had been sucked out of them. Dead leaves tumbled on the sidewalk, and even a few rats scampered across the road. William, embarrassed by his ragged clothes, his battered hand and face, walked as quickly as possible toward Stella's cottage on Burgundy Street.

Her place, like all the others, was in desperate need of repair. A large branch had fallen over its roof. The tall stalks that in summertime sprouted bright yellow sunflowers now resembled withered brown ropes. William's only thought, however, was that his beloved was inside, hopefully safe and unharmed.

The knock was unexpected. Stella had just picked up Wade to nurse him when she heard the rap at the door.

"Who's there?" she questioned from behind the wooden divide.

William could barely answer. The words got choked in his throat. He had traveled so far, his spirit was nearly broken and the pain in his body was immense. He had used every ounce of his strength to get back to his love, but he had succeeded.

"Stella?"

His voice was as golden as honey. She would know it anywhere.

The door flung open. Rag-torn, bruised and shining, he reached to touch her.

"Stella," he repeated her name again, to convince himself he wasn't dreaming. But he had hardly a second to take her all in. As his eyes fell on her, he realized she was not alone.

The vision of her and the baby swaddled at her breast threw him for a moment. Had that bastard Frye planted his seed in Stella's womb? He swallowed hard, as though someone had poured poison down his throat. But he forced himself to look again, this time more closely.

The infant's nutmeg skin and the expression of its eyes… the child was his. His whole heart now tore open.

"William!" His name fell out of her mouth like a cry.

She pulled him into the threshold and closed the door behind them. As she cradled their baby in one arm, she grabbed him with the other and kissed him so deeply, he knew it wasn't a mirage. He was home.

The inside of the house smelled like molasses and clove. Ammanee had brought two squares of gingerbread the night before, and the fragrance still lingered, making the place feel more alive than its worn exterior otherwise suggested.

"You hurt," Stella intoned, her voice breaking.

"But I'm here." He brought Stella's hand to his face and let his tears run across her fingers.

After a few minutes passed, she guided William to the kitchen where she helped to gently remove his clothes. She boiled a pot of water—not too hot so that the cloth she submerged in it wouldn't burn him—and gently wiped his body clean.

He stood in the narrow center of the space between the sink and the wooden counter, still not certain that he was really experiencing her touch, her tender care.

"Ma' dere," she repeated over and over again, the Gullah expression for "my dear," "my love," he'd taught her early on. Those two words off her tongue were healing notes to his ears. Stella kissed the back of his neck, his shoulders and the small of his back. When she turned him around, she gently lifted his one good arm and placed her lips on the inside of his wrist.

In the corner swaddled in the embroidered cloth, Wade gurgled and cooed. Every sound of life the baby made restored William's soul.

"You hurt so bad." Stella shuddered as she softly glided the cloth over his swollen eye. His damaged hand was too painful for her to even touch. He winced every time she tried.

"Gonna get better now that I'm here," William assured her. He wanted to savor every moment now between them. He didn't want to upset her with his pain. But there was still a word he needed to utter, a name, actually, to ensure she wasn't in danger having him back within her quarters.

"But, Stella," he asked quietly as she wrapped him in a towel. "Where's Frye?"

There are secrets that one keeps because the burden of them should never be shared. So Stella kept the story of Frye's demise hidden inside her chest.

As much as she trusted William to never disclose her and Ammanee's deed, no good would come of his knowing what they had done.

"He came here injured," she explained truthfully. "Wanted me to give him care."

She reached down to retrieve Wade and buried her nose in his warm scalp. Then she lifted her face back again to William's. "He gone and died here though. Not coming back," she assured him.

His master, his owner. The man who enslaved him and kept his beloved in a cage for himself. This knowledge that Frye was dead, William could hardly believe.

"You mean to say…" He stumbled over the next words. They seemed so unfathomable to him, but they were at the forefront of his mind. *That we can be together now?*

Stella came closer and cupped her free hand on his face. "William. That is exactly what I'm saying." She nearly broke down saying them herself. *"Yes, you are free to love me."* She looked around the house. Ammanee would be gone for the night and most of the following day, assisting in the contra-band camp, and they would only have each other and their little family. "And I you."

The sun was high in the sky the next day when he finally pulled himself away from the covers and went to his soiled jacket to retrieve the map.

"Stella, got something to show you," William told her as he brought it back to the bed.

"I gone and left behind a good man who hurt real bad." He sighed, looking at the creased and dirty sheet music. He turned it over revealing to Stella his crude drawing. "Made this, hoping it could lead me back to him." He traced his finger over the pencil-line path, the symbol of the barn, the canary-colored sugarcane plantation and lastly the dark cross that marked the store. "Doesn't look like much, but I know if I got close again, I could find him." William's hands tensed, as he recalled his thwarted journey to get his friend help.

Stella sat up, wrapping the sheets around her naked form. "Hush," she silenced him. "No use rilin' yourself up. You gotta heal."

She rubbed gently at his arm. "You rest now. That ol' map can't do anything tonight. We talk about that tomorrow."

Stella let him sleep, and when he awakened it was nearly dusk. The hazy light filtered into the room and William looked around to find her.

Stella had taken the worn indigo pouch from his trousers and laid it flat on the small side table next to the bed. The cowrie shell that he had given her before he left now rested on top. She had fulfilled her promise to keep it safe for him. William reached for the shell and brought it to his lips, in awe that this small thing had been warmed between each of Isaiah's, Tilly's and Stella's palms. He heard Wade crying in the next room and the feeling of love, of fatherhood, of this special talisman having brought him to this place, overwhelmed him.

"You probably lookin' for these." Stella stepped into the room carrying his pants. "I couldn't soak 'em 'cause then you'd have nothing to wear." She smiled. "But I scrubbed out the stains as much as I could."

He took them, pulling them on with one hand, then leaned forward and kissed her.

The swelling in his eyelid had retreated, and he reveled in his ability to take her in, in all her beauty. Her maple-colored eyes, the soft, dark braids of her hair, fuzzing at the top where her coils were looser. Motherhood had amplified the curves in her hips and the fullness of her breasts. The mere sight of her was a healing elixir to his aching bones.

"Ammanee coming home soon," she said. "Yo' shirt all torn, and that jacket will gotta go."

"How's your sister?" he asked, realizing he hadn't even thought of her once since he'd returned.

"She's the same," she answered. "Yet different," Stella added after a considered moment. "But you know Ammanee. No matter what she thinkin' or sufferin' that girl still stays so strong."

Ammanee bustled home just after sunset.

"Brought home some soup and bread," she chimed as she came through the door. "Stopped off to see Mama first, and gave her some leftovers, too."

With her happy eyes and radiant glow to her complexion, Stella knew right away her sister had been able to sneak away and see Benjamin at some point during her day.

"Looks like today was a good day for you." Stella went over and squeezed her sister's arm. She knew Ammanee was private, so she chose not to ask for any details about Benjamin if she didn't want to share them.

"I got a surprise today," Stella admitted. She could hardly contain her joy; it felt like it was spilling out of her.

Ammanee's eyes quickly darted to the Moses basket. "Did my favorite boy do something new today?"

Stella brought her hands to her chest. "No, but my other one did."

William stepped out of the kitchen, revealing himself.

"Are my eyes seein' right?" She gasped. Her fingers fluttered to cover her mouth. "Willie?"

"Yes." The white of his teeth flashed back in a smile.

Ammanee rushed over and threw her arms around him.

"See, Stella. The Lord is good. He send your Willie back home." She clapped her hands and did a little dance with her feet. "And you comin' home not to just yo' girl. You got a son!"

54

More weeks passed without word from Jacob. "Something's definitely happened to him, Papa," Lily finally broke down and wept to her father. "The mail has always been unpredictable, but I've never gone this long without a word from him. I have this terrible dread inside me, which won't leave."

Arthur took a handkerchief from his pocket and handed it to her. "Wipe your tears, daughter," he offered gently. "What's that song Jacob wrote about you, 'Girl of Fire'?"

She nodded.

"Your husband knows you're strong." He pulled her down to the soft cushioned sofa to sit beside him. He was not used to showing his emotions, but he sensed his daughter was starting to break and it was a sight he couldn't bear.

"You know, you're a lot like your mother," he said. "She had your same red hair. Your fervent temperament." It was the first time he'd let himself articulate it aloud. "She had that Hungarian spirit, passionate about everything she undertook. She was the one who insisted we have the glass conservatory added so she could read her books amidst the sound of the rain or the sight of a bird flapping its wings."

He took a deep breath. Remembering brought the anguish rushing back. Not just that he'd lost his beloved, but that his wife had never had a chance to experience and love their daughter.

"Your mother willed herself to stay alive long enough to hold you, however briefly," his voice cracked. "That was the kind of strength she had, Lily."

Lily soaked up every word. "Thank you for sharing that with me, Father. I know so little about her."

"I am a selfish old man," he sighed. "It has never been easy for me to face my grief, having lost her so abruptly and at such a poignant moment in our life. I'm used to the business of music, not emotions," Arthur admitted. He squeezed tight Lily's hand.

"But what I'm certain of is that your mother, if she were here, would counsel you to have faith. To regain your composure and to be strong. We must believe Jacob will come home."

The dead. The newspapers over the past two years estimated that tens of thousands of boys had been slaughtered. From Bull Run and Shiloh, to the more recent horrendous tolls in Chickamauga and Gettysburg. The newspapers had not detailed the atrocities of Port Hudson, but Lily knew from Jacob's detailed accounts the horror that occurred there, as well.

If Jacob were dead, how would she even be informed? The thought plagued her. Messengers did not show up at one's doorstep with a telegram bearing the news. No government office or administrative system existed that collected the information should Jacob be wounded or hastily buried in a field somewhere.

Lily was painfully aware of women in her sewing circle who had received letters from soldiers who'd recorded the last words of their fallen husbands, or from compassionate nurses who wrote to them of their dying wishes. But the most common outcome for one awaiting news from a loved one was to just suffer and wait.

"I don't know what to do," Lily confided to Ernestine Rose.

"I can only think of what I would do in your situation." Ernestine paused, measuring her words carefully, her hands knotted pensively in her lap. "For centuries, women have been groomed to stand idly by, to wait for men to be the active ones and bring them the answers. But we have started to change all that. We've begun the fight to own our own property within our marriages. We have been advocating for the vote. For every problem we face, we women have started to rise from our velvet cushions and demand answers."

She paused. "I think you should go look for him, Lily."

"But how? Where would I even begin?"

Ernestine considered the young woman in front of her. She'd known her now for years, and worked with her side by side on the abolitionist cause and in raising funds for the Sanitary Commission's efforts.

"At some point, a woman must look inward and use everything she has within her power. If I only gave you instructions, dear Lily, how would you ever learn?"

"My last letter from him was two weeks before Christmas. It's now February. I can't sit here in my childhood home like a little girl and not do something, Papa."

"You are frustrated, darling, but so is every mother, wife and daughter of a soldier."

Lily stood up from the sofa. "I am going to book a trip down to Satartia, Mississippi, and pay a visit to my sister-in-law. After the fall of Vicksburg, Jacob wrote and told me it was now under Union control. It will be safe for me to go there."

"Safe?" Arthur's cheeks puffed out with disbelief and his complexion turned a deep shade of red. "This is madness. You cannot possibly travel all the way down there."

"And why not? I could name at least five women I've known who have done that same trip already... Ella Stein went down to Virginia to tend to her husband after getting a letter from a nurse that he had been badly wounded. And what about women like Clara Barton and Frances Gage?" Lily's frustration boiled over. She struggled to catch her breath; the whale boning within her dress nearly made it impossible for her to gather the air she needed. "Papa." She now tried to bring her voice down from a fever pitch. "Do you think they ever got anything done just sitting in their parlors?"

"I don't know anything about these women," he fumed. "All I know is that you are my daughter, and I don't want you venturing across the county during these perilous times, let alone the country—and by yourself, unchaperoned." He shook his head, emphasizing that the matter was closed. "And I have a business to run, I cannot just pick up and leave."

"I am not asking you to, Father." Her mind was made up. "I love you, dearly, but I'm not undertaking this as your daughter, but as Jacob's wife. And it is my right to do what's best for him. That is my choice alone to make."

The housemaid helped make the preparations for Lily's departure. Together they laid out a single trunk in the center of

Lily's childhood bedroom and placed her most essential garments inside.

"I will only take three day dresses, aside from the one I'll wear on the morning I set out," Lily instructed. "One for dinner, as my esteemed sister-in-law will expect a certain level of decorum. Plus four extra chemises and drawers, a change of petticoat." The list unfurled inside her head. Leather gloves and a wool shawl. The barest necessities that would enable her to travel light, but still maintain an essential appearance of propriety, as she ventured into unknown waters.

"Please, reconsider," her father begged her when she was ready to leave later that day. Outside, a coach waited to take her to the station.

Lily kissed him on both cheeks, savoring the warm familiarity of his sandalwood cologne.

"How could I?" She smiled. "I wouldn't be your daughter, if I just sat back and did nothing."

55

A few days before her departure, Lily sent a small parcel of coffee and two tins of shortbread through Adams Express, hoping it would reach her sister-in-law in Satartia. She spent several hours crafting the letter she would include, realizing she'd need to temper her true feelings toward that branch of the family if she were to successfully enlist them in her search for Jacob.

My dearest Eliza,

I struggle to believe it will be nearly four years this spring since we visited you and Samuel at your beautiful home in Mississippi. As you may know, the post office has made it impossible to send letters to any Confederate states. So I am now trying to contact you through the only means I know of, which is Adams Express. I can only pray it is successful.

Though we are personally divided on the issue of slavery, I beg you now to open your heart and read the following without preju-dice. I fear something terrible has happened within our family that will require us both to transcend all such differences between us.

It is my hope that Samuel is safe and unharmed, hopefully even at home in Satartia with you. Unfortunately, I believe my Jacob has either been killed or gravely wounded, as I have not heard from him in nearly seven weeks. I plan to take the train from New York to Chicago and then if a connection on a train south proves impossible, journey by steamboat down toward New Orleans be-fore venturing farther east toward you. It is my intention to comb all of the field hospitals from Port Gibson to Baton Rouge to find any information about Jacob, or at least his regiment. Those are the last two places I know Jacob was stationed.

As you can imagine, it will not be easy for a woman to search through such devastation for her missing husband, particularly one who is not a high-ranking officer but only a military musician. I know many others, like my father, consider my impulse to ven-ture so far—and alone—to be rash and dangerous, but I cannot just sit still and do nothing. Therefore, I am beseeching you to as-sist me by allowing me to use your home as a base for my further travels to the field hospitals, or wherever else my investigation into Jacob's whereabouts may lead.

I will be leaving New York without first receiving any answer from you, as I cannot wait indefinitely and, sadly, it is unclear if this parcel will even reach you.

I know that it must be very hard for you to have Satartia and the rest of Yazoo County under Union control. But I can only hope you will not turn me away, and will instead open up your residence as a temporary refuge for me. I doubt I could find any other locale that would welcome me, a Northerner in search of her Union army husband, during these most turbulent times. I am confident I would

do the same for you, as your sister-in-law, if you had been thrust
into the same wretched circumstances I now face.
With deepest family affection,
Lily

Upon signing her name, Lily had reread the closing, wondering aloud if it was perhaps too syrupy to be believed, given the chilliness between Eliza and her. But after a moment of reflection, she sealed the envelope, resolving that no amount of flattery, cajoling or deception was too much if it helped lead her back to Jacob.

The two-day train ride was the only smooth leg of her journey. When Lily arrived in Chicago, the stationmaster confirmed that the only way to get to Mississippi was by a steamboat down to New Orleans and then by coach to her final destination.

"Sherman's done a mighty efficient job of destroying all the rails south of here," he told her bluntly. "A few boats leaving from Bridgeport, a short carriage ride from here, that will take you through the Illinois and Michigan Canal and then head down the Miss-Lou River, assuming you can find one willing to take a woman all the way down there."

He drew her a little map on a scrap of paper to show her the direction of travel. Lily watched the deft markings of his pencil, trying to get a sense of this alternative route.

The stationmaster chewed down on his pipe. "Can't say that I advise this, ma'am. February weather can bring with it all sorts of problems, and that's during the best of times, and we're in the middle of a war. Far too dangerous for a woman to undertake." He blew a puff of blue smoke through the kiosk window. "Sorry to say this, but you should really just turn yourself around and go back home to New York."

But Lily would do no such thing. She snatched the paper where the man had written down the dock's address and promptly arranged a coach to the embarkation area of the canal.

"You're risking your life, ma'am," the captain of one of the steamboats told her when she arrived. "While we are willing to take passengers—I must tell you, just last week one of our boats got a Reb cannonball shot straight through her engine right as she was sailing past Memphis. So the trip didn't turn out too well for any of the passengers."

"I've been told this is the only way I can get to where I need to go," Lily said, undeterred. "I need to go to Satartia, Mississippi. I've been assured that we can get there if we take the junction to the Yazoo River."

The man chuckled at her virtual commandeering of the boat. "Can't do that, ma'am. Supposed to be heading directly to New Orleans."

She reached into her purse and handed him a substantial bundle of money. "Is this enough to alter course?"

The crisp union note flashed in the seaman's hand. "Tell ya what. I'll get you round Grand Gulf, right near Port Gibson. Less than a day trip to Satartia."

Lily nodded her agreement to that plan.

"He must be pretty darn special," he muttered as he waved the deck boy over to help with her trunk.

"He is," she said and stepped on board.

Once on the boat, Lily avoided the gaze of the rough-looking crew. Prim in her bonnet, woolen cape and shawl, she was not just the only gentlewoman on board, she was the *only* woman on the entire boat. The captain ordered a crew hand to lead her to one of the private cabins on the lower deck. There she found herself grateful to be alone as the boat pushed off into the cold, wintry night.

That evening, one of the men left a tray of food outside her door, consisting of a dreary stew and hard piece of bread. Lily forced herself to eat a few bites. She hadn't eaten a real meal in days, having only taken sustenance from the small basket the maid had prepared for the first leg of her journey. How she wished she had taken one of the tins of that shortbread she'd instead sent to Eliza. The thought of it now made her mouth water.

She took out her diary and tried to record her journey so far, hoping one day to be able to recount it to Jacob and share with him the lengths and risks. But her pen soon loosened from her grip and her eyes became heavy with fatigue. Lily found herself pulling her woolen shawl tightly around her shoulders, as she curled into the hard bed and drifted off to sleep.

Days later when she finally arrived at Grand Gulf, she struggled to make herself presentable. Her tiny cabin contained no mirror and had only the smallest washbasin for her toilette, but Lily did her best to plait her hair and smooth out her clothes. When they eventually docked and she was able to once again walk on sturdy ground, her legs wobbled and her stomach became queasy from so many days on board.

"Need a horse and carriage, ma'am?" an eager older man asked her. Despite the strain of the boat trip, she still looked like a ripe fruit amongst the throngs of impoverished locals who had assembled to gather supplies from the boat or catch a bit of news.

"Yes," responded Lily. While there were plenty of people around her, it seemed like an unlikely place to start her search.

"Where you off to, then?"

"Satartia, Mississippi," she answered plainly. One of the

shipmates she'd tipped generously over the past days had unloaded her trunk for her.

"East?" He shook his head and bugged out his eyes. "You headin' into dangerous territory, ma'am. Sherman's been real busy round those parts. They're not safe for anyone, let alone a lady."

"Yes, I've been told, but it will not deter me." She touched her purse with her hand. "If you find me a driver—" she leaned in "—I promise to make it worth your while."

As much as the lure of taking some much-needed food and rest in Grand Gulf pulled at her, Lily spent no time in the city. She did not want to waste a moment on her mission to find Jacob.

While her coachman wanted to travel on roads he believed to be the most secure and free of danger, she begged him to take her closer to areas where previous combat had occurred, for she planned to stop at any encampments they passed. At these wretched, tented sites, Lily combed through the beds of the countless wounded men from both sides, beseeching the nurses for any news of her husband, a musician in the New York 163rd Regiment. But these stops resulted in no information on Jacob, and instead only filled her head with the horrors of the war.

Farm animals left to rot in torched fields. Homes with their windows shattered, walls charred to ruin. For stretches of time, Lily could hardly look out the side of her buggy. As evening was waning, they eventually arrived at Satartia. She was grateful, for finding a place to stay for the night would likely have brought its own set of travails. Few boardinghouses would have been willing to offer up lodging to a Northerner even with her Union banknotes. Instead of the beautiful estate she remembered from her visit years before, the version of Eliza and Samuel's house that now greeted her had also suffered from the barrage of war. The once elegant facade, with its alabaster-white Greek columns that framed the doorway, was a shadow of its former self. The large fruit trees that previously bordered the property had all been hacked down. The expansive verdant lawn that had captivated her before now looked like dry thatch. Through the broken gate that had once led to the flower-lined seashell path, Lily could see the landscape beyond was bloomless and in disarray.

She handed the payment to the driver, who brought her trunk up to the porch before quickly returning to the coach.

Eliza opened the door before Lily could even knock.

"What's going on here?" Her voice floated into the crisp, winter air in a tone that was not quite shrill, but certainly far from hospitable.

She was dressed in a somber back bodice skirt with bustle, and her dark hair only accentuated the gauntness and sharp bone structure of her face.

"Lily?" Her green eyes squinted. "Is that you?"

"Yes, it is." Lily retied the ribbons of her bonnet and then straightened her cape, stepping closer to greet her sister-in-law.

"I can hardly believe you are here on my doorstep," Eliza announced, unable to contain her confusion and visible annoyance.

Lily quickly recognized her letter hadn't made it. "It's as I feared," she apologized. "You haven't received my parcel. I sent you a letter explaining everything—"

"No, I have not," Eliza cut in. Her eyes fell upon the trunk at her doorstep, then lifted to watch the coachman already departing down the drive.

As Lily was about to clarify her presence, another voice emerged.

"Eliza? *Who is it?*"

Eliza gestured and Lily followed her into the dimly lit

house. Blasted by a disturbing smell of water damage and moldy carpets, Lily took in that the interior had fared no better than the outside of the mansion.

"Eliza?" The voice repeated its question, again without receiving an answer.

There in the middle of the vestibule, Lily's mind adjusted to the sight before her. Samuel in a wheelchair. From beneath the wool blanket that draped over his lap, she could see he only had one leg.

56

"Samuel," Lily uttered his name softly. She struggled with what to say next, her rehearsed speeches falling away.

"You're a surprise to see." He filled in the silence. "We weren't expecting you, or anyone for that matter." His eyes darted across the shadow-filled vestibule.

The wood-paneled walls that had once glimmered to a high polish were now dull and scarred with deep scratches. The framed artwork she remembered from her last visit no longer hung anywhere in view.

"As you can tell, we're not in the best condition to receive guests." Samuel tried to force a laugh. "Your Union men left our home in quite a state." He looked down at his one foot on the heel of the wheelchair. "Not to mention what they did to me."

Eliza moved behind her husband and gripped the top of

the cane chair. "You must be tired from your journey, Lily," she clipped, changing the subject.

"I can't complain. I'm grateful I've made it safely here, after a few unexpected delays."

Eliza wheeled Samuel into the parlor and positioned him by the window. The green silk curtains that Lily had once found so striking were streaked with tar and water stains.

"Samuel likes being in the corner of this room where the light filters in," Eliza explained. "I hope you don't mind staying with him while I prepare us some tea."

"Not at all," she said and settled down in one of the chairs next to him. In the thin veil of light, Lily absorbed her brother-in-law's profile. The face ravaged by lines, the salt-and-pepper stubble of his beard. "I'm sorry, Samuel. This war has brought so much loss." She reached to squeeze his hand.

He shifted his upper body slightly to turn to her. "I gather this is not a social call. Have you come bearing news about my brother?"

Lily paused and gathered her words carefully. "I have no news at all, Samuel. That's why I've come such a long way." She took a deep breath. "I haven't heard from Jacob in over two months. And while that might not alarm some wives, I'm petrified because it's so out of character for him. For nearly two years, he wrote me a steady stream of letters."

"I'm relieved to hear you've not come to say he is dead." Samuel's voice broke. "I regret that we squabbled the last we saw each other, Lily. None of us could have imagined what hell was to come." His entire body began to tremble.

"I know," she agreed. "It's unfathomable to think of so many lives lost, so much ruin…"

"You cannot mean to equate anything up North to the level of destruction we've endured here." Eliza's voice sliced through the air as she balanced a tray with a mismatched tea service. Her six-year-old daughter, Clementine, stood next to her with a sparse platter of molasses cookies. "Our neighbors had their homes and fields burned downed by the Yanks. Their animals slaughtered in their backyards," she said bitterly. "We even had General Grant take over this house for three nights. His men defiled it in the most dreadful way. And all this while I was left to fend by myself alone, with my daughters." The porcelain rattled underneath her white-knuckled grip.

"Eliza," Samuel tried to calm her. "Lily has traveled a long distance, and she has entered our house as family, not as the enemy. She is not searching for a nameless Union soldier, she is looking for Jacob, *my brother*."

Eliza set the tray down and Clementine placed the plate of cookies to its side. "I am sorry," she said, lifting her chin and straightening her shoulders. "But to have her swan in here and pretend like we've all suffered *equally*, when we so clearly have not, is just galling to me. Unlike her and the rest of her New York friends, we have lost almost everything." She dabbed her eyes with a handkerchief.

Lily looked down. "Perhaps my presence here is too uncomfortable. I don't want to upset any of you any longer." She went to stand up.

"Please." Samuel lifted his hand to stop her. "You are Jacob's wife, Lily. You *are* and will always be welcome in this house." He shot a pleading glance at Eliza. "Yes, we've lost so much during the war, but I'm not going to lose my family, also." He cleared his throat. "How brave you are to come here and search for him," Samuel affirmed. "But having experienced firsthand what it's like out there, I'm afraid it will be like looking for a needle in a haystack."

57

"I've been having nightmares," William confided to Stella. "Jacob's still out there and nobody gonna help him."

"Shhh." Stella tried to console him. She didn't want to hear any more about this White soldier he'd left behind in the woods with some shrew.

"With his ankle all busted up and twisted, he won't be able to start walking for a long time," William said as he tried to calculate when he himself would be able to try to get back to Jacob. Over the past few days, he'd opened and closed his sheet music map nearly a hundred times, and now the piece of paper was becoming almost too brittle along the folds to touch.

"You better stop doing that, William," Stella cautioned him. "It's going to fall apart."

William's eyes fell to the creased, battered paper, with its childlike depictions of symbols he hoped would lead him back to his friend. He could still hear the Union soldiers' laughter ringing in his ears when he tried to explain it to them.

Stella brought Wade over and sat down across from him at the table. "You gonna have to tell me why this man's so important to you, 'cause I know you lived a life full of loss before all this happened. Why this time any different?"

And with those words, Stella broke their unspoken agreement, to safeguard each other from the pain of their respective lives and focus on the brief, bright moments they had together.

At first, William struggled to share the terrors of his desperate journey to Camp Parapet. How to explain to Stella the fear of that ten-mile trek that seemed like ten days, the roots that had risen up to block his path like bars, and the swampy vines that had seemed like chains as he struggled to push through. And those were merely the enemies of nature he encountered, not the sounds of men and dogs he hid from, unaware if they were catchers or just working men returning home late. Then the sickening anguish he felt when he arrived at Camp Parapet, the squalor and flood of diseased and defeated men making William acutely aware just how pampered his enslaved existence had been. But as he spoke, he realized how much he had longed to unburden himself, to share everything he would have put in letters had he been able. Until the entire tale came pouring out of William.

"That first day, Jacob didn't see me as just another runaway slave. He saw me as a musician, and if he hadn't told me to let on how I could play the fife, I'm not sure I'd still be here now." He sighed. "A Negro soldier's life ain't worth a damn to the Union army. But that instrument gave me more value than most others. Or at least shielded me from the worst of it."

Wade now asleep, Stella listened intently as William described the unique friendship he experienced with Jacob.

"We had a sort of musical kinship," he explained. "Never thought much about how my flute playin' could make others actually *feel* before, ya know?" The bruises on his face had almost healed by now, and his soft, brown eyebrows lifted like two caterpillars. "I spent my whole life playin' for my massas. Didn't really think 'bout what emotions it brought out in any of them. Why would I care?"

"Yo' playin' special, William. You know that…noticed it the first time I walked into Market. Heard you playin' like it was an angel singing."

"Thank you, my love." He inhaled deeply. The vision of Stella with his son gave William a new kind of breath, one different from when playing his flute. It was hard for him to believe he no longer had possession of his instrument. He missed it, felt like an amputee without it. He wasn't even sure he could make Stella understand his bond with Jacob, for music had always been the language in which he best expressed himself. Still, William pressed on.

"But in the past year, Stella, I learned that my playin' could reach into people's souls. Got them out of their despair. Made 'em think 'bout their loved ones back home. Made 'em feel brave before they marched into battle. Made it feel safe for them to cry when they're sittin' round the campfire."

Stella placed Wade in the Moses basket and knelt at William's side, absorbing every word.

"Jacob helped me realize all that."

"He sounds like a special man, William."

"So now you see why it's killin' me that I left him alone with *that* woman. She think he's her dead son. And he in danger if she figure out who he really is—a Yankee foreigner." The flimsy paper trembled in his hand. "All I got to go by is this damn piece of paper, Stella, and now it fallin' apart."

That evening, William fell into a deep sleep, his chest rising and falling beneath the sheet. Stella got up and marveled at the sight of him in her bed. The folded map was on the night-stand, next to his indigo pouch, for safekeeping. She picked it up and went into the parlor, where she sat and lit a tapered candle to examine the paper more closely.

William had explained what he'd drawn there more times than Stella could count. The path from the old woman's house toward the red barn with the missing sheep. The right-hand turn that would take him on a road that passed by a yellow-colored residence amidst a sugarcane plantation. The general store in the town of Iberia, owned by a man named Cross.

Stella wanted to preserve this fragile piece of paper for William. At the rate William kept fixating on it, it would likely disintegrate in a matter of days. So she did what she was best at. She set out to find cloth and thread.

Stella began to pace around the house. Over Christmas, she'd used up almost all the materials she had left. Frye's vest had enabled her to make dozens of handkerchiefs to sell, but only a few frayed bits remained. She had no more embroidered cushions, no more threads from Miss Hyacinth's woven shawl. Everything had already been pulled and harvested over the past year for the sons and brothers of the other women of Rampart Street.

Her heart pattered in tune with her feet. Surely she had something she could scavenge and repurpose. She went to the kitchen and saw the four clean nappies she'd washed and hung out on the clothesline that afternoon. Could she spare one of those? It would be hard. How many times had she struggled to keep Wade clean and dry during the course of a day?

But she wanted to make this for William, to stitch into the cloth both her love for him and acknowledge what this man named Jacob meant to him. As with the other maps she'd made in the past, she didn't know if this one would work in helping anyone reach their destination, but her heart came through best when she was using her needle and thread.

It didn't take Stella too long to reflect back on a handmade gift once bestowed upon her, one where the materials had come together to communicate a sentiment that transcended words. She tiptoed back to the bedroom and collected the quilt made by the women of Rampart Street, lifting it gently off William's feet. A flood of emotions ran through her. It was a giver's quilt, a warm embrace, a coverlet and a shield.

The threads—the red, the green, the blue and the yellow— that had been used to stitch each piece of fabric together were intact. She laid out the quilt over her lap and began to un- ravel it.

58

"There are hospitals all over these parts, Lily, taking care of what must be thousands of wounded soldiers from both sides," Samuel informed her the following morning. "So as much as my heart is breaking knowing my brother is missing, I fear it will be near impossible to actually find him at one of those places."

"I know and I'm fully aware of the challenges and the low likelihood of success I'll face." She lifted the coffee to her lips. The unexpected taste of chicory surprised her.

"I'm sorry we don't have real coffee to offer you." Eliza must have noticed Lily's reaction to the steaming beverage. "We paid a premium for it down here even before the occupation, but then your Yankee brutes destroyed Samuel's store and absconded with nearly all of our inventory." Her voice was laced with bitterness, as she reached over and placed a hard biscuit on Lily's plate. "But that's obviously among the smaller inconveniences we've had to respond to. It's amazing the other skills I've been forced to pick up over the past months just to deal with them all—gardener, barterer and even driver. I never drove a horse and wagon until now."

"Mama even fixed a wheel the other day!" Clementine chimed in.

"Hush," her elder sister, Hortensia, scolded her. The girls were well-mannered, even endearing. That morning they wore matching dresses that depicted a pattern of pink roses. With the material far too flimsy for winter, Lily suspected her sister-in-law had shrewdly used bedsheets to make their frocks.

"Your mother certainly *has* undertaken a great deal." Lily looked at the girls with compassion. It broke her heart a little that she hardly knew her nieces. In the three years since she'd visited, they'd grown so much.

"Yes, she has. And I'm incredibly grateful for all of her sacrifices," Samuel added. "It's been seven months since I lost my leg, and it kills me every day that I'm incapable of being the man around here that I once was." His pale face twisted as he tried to regain his composure, but Lily could see the emotion that raged beneath the surface.

"So, Lily, if you still are intent on venturing out amongst the hospitals, please accept my apologies, but driving a horse and wagon isn't something I'll be doing anymore," Samuel acknowledged regretfully. "Instead, Eliza will have to be the one to take you."

"Perhaps I could hire someone to take me," Lily offered politely. "I'd hate to put you to any further trouble."

Eliza threw down her napkin. "That's all we need... Our neighbors finding out that we're housing a Yankee relative in our home. It's hard enough being the only Jewish family in Satartia. Now we'll be accused of being traitors." Her voice rose. "How can you just waltz into these parts and not notice what your army has done? Our town has been destroyed, everything for miles around has been torched, and the stink of the dead suffocates us every time the wind blows near. Do you think there's anyone in these parts willing to help you look for Jacob, a Union man they know's part of all this hell?" She huffed in disbelief. "For someone who thinks she's so smart, so progressive, you can be quite shortsighted."

"Eliza." Samuel's voice again grew firm. "I want to find my brother as much as she does."

"I didn't say I wouldn't take her, Samuel. I'm only reminding her that just because she has a purse full of Yankee bills, it doesn't mean she can do anything she wants!"

"I wasn't—"

"Please!" Samuel interrupted, his tired face growing pink. "So much loss, so much unbearable, unfathomable loss," he muttered. "I was at Vicksburg. I saw it with my own two eyes, lived every damnable minute. Men with bright futures, eighteen-year-old boys with sweethearts back home, some who'd never even had their first glass of whiskey. So many of them gone." His voice broke. "And I lost my leg in that terrible inferno. So not for a moment will I also now suffer a needless war in my own living room. We are family here. I will not permit another word about who has suffered the most."

A painful silence filled the room.

Eliza cleared her throat. "Very well, I will speak no more of it." She pursed her lips, then began gathering up the morning dishes. Clementine and Hortensia stood up to help.

"We'll need to leave within the hour," Eliza instructed brusquely. "It's a full day's travel to get to both Vicksburg and

Oxford. Both places have Union hospitals set up there. The military hospital in Yazoo City is only for our boys of the Confederacy, so Jacob wouldn't be there."

"And don't forget the old Baxter plantation," Samuel reminded her. "The Union took over that house and turned it into an army hospital."

"I'm well aware, husband."

Lily followed Eliza and the girls to the kitchen with the breakfast cups and plates.

At the threshold, Eliza stopped and turned to Lily. "Please understand that none of this is easy for me. It won't be the first time I've visited one of these hospitals." She sucked in her breath. "The last time I went was one of the most anguish-filled days of my life." She lowered her voice so the girls could not hear her. "A nurse wrote to me after Samuel's leg became infected with gangrene. She relayed his last sentiments to me in case he didn't survive the surgery." Eliza glanced back at her husband in his wheelchair, his head now resting on his chest, his eyes closed from all the exertion.

"'Lizzy—you and the girls have been my world...'" She recalled a portion of Samuel's words, then bit her lip, forcing back the tears. "As soon as I got that letter, I rode off. I even left the girls sleeping alone in their beds. I wasn't thinking about anything except that I needed to get to Samuel's side, before it was too late."

Lily's eyes fell. At least Eliza understood her desperation, her willingness to undertake any risk to find her husband. Perhaps this was Eliza's attempt at a truce. "How dreadful that all must have been for you." She was truly sorry now to reawaken such painful memories for her sister-in-law.

Eliza dabbed her eyes with her yellowed handkerchief and nodded.

"I so appreciate you helping me," Lily added as she gently touched Eliza's arm. "Wherever Jacob is, I just hope that now *I'm* not too late."

The two women sat perched on the driver's bench of the old wooden wagon. Eliza gripped the leather reins tightly between her bony hands, her axe-cut features reddening in the cool late-morning air.

She spoke little as she steered the two of them through the dirt roads, littered with debris. Horses shot dead in dry pastures, their massive carcasses in a state of rot. Empty and busted chicken coops and paddocks. Houses with windows shattered and barns burned to the ground.

Eventually, they pulled up to an enormous field, with dozens of white tents pitched across the yellow grass. Congregating outside were men propped up by crutches, and others with their heads bandaged or their feet wrapped in filthy strips of cotton.

"The more severely wounded ones will be inside the tents in beds," Eliza cautioned Lily. "I hope you have a steel stomach."

Lily would never forget the first row of patients she saw when she walked through the hospital tent. Men whose faces were gaunt and as translucent as ice. Pleading, watery eyes looking up from rickety cots.

Lily approached a nurse in a blood-smocked apron, and asked if they had anyone that fit Jacob's description.

"Your husband was in the 163rd New York Infantry?" the woman inquired gently.

The air was ripe with the stench of death, of blood and

festering wounds. Lily drew her fingers over her mouth. She could hardly breathe. "Yes. He's a military musician."

The nurse considered this information. "I'll check the registry, but if I recall correctly, we did have a few men from there this summer, but no battle wounds though. All of them just had dysentery or bilious fever."

"Summer?" Lily repeated, trying to mask her disappointment. The last letter she'd received from Jacob was before Christmas.

"Yes," the woman confirmed. She paused at a bed where a man was moaning for water.

"If you'll excuse me for a moment." She went to the rear of the tent and returned with a tin ladle filled with liquid. Bending over the ailing young man, she lifted his head and dripped water into his parched lips.

For months, Lily had worked on stitching quilts to fund the needs of hospitals much like the one she was now standing in. She'd rolled hundreds of bandages. She'd read letters from women like Frances Gage, who volunteered to help the sick and wounded. But seeing firsthand the pain and hopelessness in each man's face made her realize that the human suffering of this war could never truly be comprehended by someone far away in New York. She had imagined it would be terrible, but reality was so much worse.

"Water," another man begged between parched blue lips, his shivering hand reaching out from beneath a thin white sheet.

With the other nurses all engaged, Lily could not stand idly by. She went to the rear of the tent to fetch him fresh water.

"I'm sorry I couldn't come inside to help you look," Eliza apologized as Lily returned to the wagon. She'd spent the past hour huddled on the wooden perch, her cape wrapped around her.

"It's just far too upsetting for me." She touched her throat, as if she might become sick. "When I arrived at the hospital to see Samuel that night, I entered the wrong tent and was 'greeted' by an enormous barrel of amputated arms and legs." Eliza's face blanched. "It's not something I'll ever forget."

Lily winced. She, too, hadn't been prepared for what she'd just witnessed inside. "So many men maimed, like your Samuel." She lowered her eyes and tugged at her gloves. "When this war eventually ends, so few of us will remain unscarred."

She thought not just of all the soldiers, but also of the country divided, cut so crudely in two.

Eliza looked up toward the sun peeking through the gray clouds. "I'd say we can get to the Vicksburg hospital on the route back, but after that I'm afraid we must head home. This is the first time I've left Samuel alone for so long. I'm concerned he might need help with his more, um, delicate needs."

"Of course," Lily answered. Her stomach gripped, thinking of a grown man dependent for such intimate care.

Eliza turned to Lily, her expression softening. "I honestly hope you find Jacob. And I pray that you'll both be spared such hardship afterward."

It was the first time in Lily's memory that she and Eliza had ever wished for the same thing.

59

William awoke and came into the parlor holding Wade.

"Li'l man slept through the night," he announced as he cradled his son tenderly in the crook of his arm.

"Two of you sleepin' real tight." Stella smiled as she looked up from her final stitches, her heart swelling at the sight of her two men together.

"What you makin' there?" William stepped closer. From a distance he could see a swath of white cotton dotted with symbols and shapes in myriad colors. A stack of small cotton squares in all the shades of the rainbow sat layered in a neat pile beside Stella: "Ain't that your favorite quilt?" He was so distracted by the realization that she'd taken apart her cherished blanket, he didn't notice the map she'd spent all night stitching.

Stella placed a palm on top of the stack of cotton squares,

her fingers gently caressing the yellow one that had been cut from Miss Emilienne's favorite frock. "I don't think the ladies will mind," she responded softly. "They created it with love, just as I did when I made this for you." Stella lifted her most recent handiwork so William could see.

"What's that?" He squinted his eyes. It was too large to be a handkerchief, yet too small to be another swaddling cloth for Wade.

As he held the baby close, William peered down at the embroidered cloth, amazed and overwhelmed once he understood what Stella had created. She'd taken his rough, crude drawing on a brittle piece of paper, and transformed it into a durable guide. The old woman's house was marked with a large blue X, and from there a simple running stitch depicted the dirt path toward the main road, the ensuing right hand turn at the red barn, and then the yellow-colored house on the sugarcane plantation. His finger reached to trace the tiny stitches that lead to the general store. In the center of the small building she'd placed a dark black cross.

"'It's not a church,' I remember you tellin' me," she said. "But the name of the place," she made sure she had recalled just right.

"Cross's General Store," he confirmed, impressed by Stella's sharp memory. She'd listened to his every word, unlike those men who'd ridiculed him.

"You didn't mention the name of the town to me though. Thinkin' that's essential 'cause if you get there and go backward from the store, that's the way to get to him."

"Iberia," he informed her, still studying the map. He would never forget the name.

She repeated it, sounding out the letters. "Maybe I can stitch that on there somewhere. Then you can show it to a Union man, and maybe they'll undertake the trip to find him. Get your flute back, too."

She didn't say what was in her heart. She didn't want William to go on the journey himself. Stella didn't want to risk him ever leaving again.

60

The third military hospital they visited the following day brought no sign of Jacob. Lily scanned the battered faces of war-torn soldiers, confined to bed after bed. She learned to move quickly past the men with ginger or blond hair, only studying more closely those with dark hair or bandages covering their heads. But still, her efforts proved futile.

"It is as I expected," Eliza stated afterward. "Without a letter or some other specific information telling you exactly where he is, it's an impossible quest, Lily."

But Lily would not give up hope. At least, not yet.

The following day, Eliza needed to stay home to cook so the girls and Samuel's midday meals would be prepared for the next few days.

On Tuesday, the two women set off again, this time venturing farther west to the old Baxter plantation that had been converted into a Union hospital.

After a long morning of travel, their wagon pulled through the peeling iron gates. Tall poplar trees, their branches naked of leaves, lined the gravel drive. To the side of the Palladian-style facade, a casket maker stood with an apron over his dark suit, gesturing instructions to several young men cutting and shaving wooden planks intended for coffins.

A matron greeted Lily on the front steps. "Are you here for a loved one?" she inquired gently.

"I'm searching for my husband," Lily began. "I don't actually know if he's here. His name is Jacob Kling, a musician in the 163rd Infantry. I know his regiment has been in Mississippi as well as Louisiana. Port Hudson, Port Gibson... Baton Rouge..." she rambled on what she remembered from his letters.

"That's a rather broad area," the nurse demurred. "Many of our men have been lucky enough to send word to their families, often through a letter written by one of our sisters, providing details about their arrival here. We are always grateful when a relative then arrives to help with their care, or arrange for their transport home." She folded her hands in front of her, her face engraved in a well-practiced expression of compassion and sympathy. "But, without that prior notice, I'm afraid simply proceeding from one hospital to the next seldom provides the kind of information or happy reunion you seek."

"I can certainly appreciate that, particularly as my recent efforts have indeed failed to yield the results I had hoped." Lily stared at the ground before lifting her gaze to meet the nurse's. "But I could not stay home and do nothing if my husband were hurt somewhere."

"I do understand, truly. That is why my fellow nurses and

I have all come to this place. We, too, could not stay home and do nothing with so many Union men needing care." She signaled for Lily to follow her inside. "Come with me, ma'am. The name Jacob Kling doesn't sound familiar, but we have many soldiers here whom we haven't yet identified. You're more than welcome to take a look around."

In the mansion's vast rooms, the walls painted shades of gray and gold, the former antebellum splendor was replaced with the sick and wounded. In the enormous parlor, dozens of beds were packed side by side. Wooden pulleys for men in traction crowded the space. On the mahogany furniture, basins of bloody water waited to be cleared.

"We have more rooms upstairs," the matron informed Lily. "Several are being used for surgery, and others are where some of the amputees are recovering." She looked down at the watch pinned to her breast. "I'm sorry, I must leave you for now." She touched Lily's arm. "Please don't go upstairs unless you find a nurse to accompany you. The surgeons cannot be interrupted. And, of course, the severely wounded must be approached with great care."

She took a few steps before turning back to face Lily. "I wish you luck, my dear, whatever you may find here."

Lily walked through the rows of metal beds, glancing at each face as she searched for Jacob. Her stomach twisted as her eyes fell upon so many battered spirits, so many bodies she knew would never fully heal.

But yet again, she saw no evidence of Jacob.

She eventually caught sight of the matron again. This time the nurse's smock was streaked with fresh blood, and a dark red fingerprint stained the top of her starched white cap.

"Might I be able to look in the rooms upstairs?"

"Yes," the matron answered softly. "But please, prepare yourself. What you'll see will not be easy for you."

Lily followed her up the dark walnut-colored stairs, passing by two enormous oil portraits of the estate's steely-eyed ancestors. Men and women who looked like they were passing judgment on those who had taken possession of their house and their family heirlooms.

The nurse opened the first door and Lily saw straightaway, past the bloodstained stump, the flash of the patient's red hair. "He is not my husband," she announced quickly as the matron nodded and shut the door behind them.

In the second room, the smell of cauterized flesh seemed to still linger in the air. Lily nearly gagged as she stepped inside. Aside from the missing arm, his shoulder bandaged tightly around the fresh wound, the young man's face was also wrapped in layers of white gauze. Lily forced herself to draw closer to ensure it wasn't Jacob.

"It's not him," she whispered.

The last room they entered, Lily's heartbeat escalated as soon as the nurse opened the door. The flash of black curly hair. The same nose and cupid bow's mouth. The slender build and long fingers that fanned out against the white linen.

"Jacob?" His name flew from her mouth like a bird flying from its cage. She hurled herself to the side of the bed, looking past where his left leg had been cut off.

She heard a faint whimper escape from his lips, a low murmur. But as her hand reached to grip his, the young man's eyelids lifted and Lily was greeted not by the shade of green, but rather dark brown.

"Mary?" the soldier's voice was faint, still groggy from morphine. His grip tightened around Lily's fingers.

"Shhh," she whispered, as she held back tears, her heart sinking again in her chest. She didn't say another word until he fell back to sleep.

On the way back to Satartia, Lily was quiet.

"No luck, then?" Eliza had asked Lily as she climbed next to her on the driver's seat.

Lily shook her head and turned so her sister-in-law wouldn't see the tears falling. She had really believed she'd found Jacob in the last room, and now the reality that she might never locate him was setting in.

Eliza's sharp profile and straight posture was like a knife's blade as she steered them back toward Satartia. Lily adjusted the ribbon of her bonnet and pulled her cape closer as the sky grew darker and the wind kicked up. She closed her eyes, replaying over and over again the sight of that young man with the black curls, his lids opening only to reveal his dark irises. And the pain of that memory sliced through her as much as the onset of the driving cold and rain.

"Mama, Hortensia burned the pies." Clementine's voice greeted them as soon as they removed their wet garments.

"Hush," Eliza scolded her. "Your aunt and I have been out all day, and your sister was only trying to warm up dinner."

Lily stepped into the parlor, tired and weary from yet another hopeless day of searching. Inside the dimly lit room, her eyes fell upon Samuel, fast asleep in his wheelchair, in his favorite spot by the window. One of Clementine's rag dolls and a miniature tea set were strewn across the carpet.

"You've been watching your papa all day, then?" Lily asked the younger girl when she returned.

"He sure doesn't do much," Clementine confessed. "He takes a swig of his medicine and he sleeps most of the afternoon." She pointed to a tiny glass vial on the sideboard.

Lily walked over to it and read the label. Morphine.

"Mama tells him he can only have it when the pain's real bad, but I think he likes to sleep more when me and Hortensia are supposed to take care of him. He says it makes him less of a *nuisance* to us girls, whatever that means."

Lily scanned the parlor, the tears at the edge of the curtains, the port wine stains on the carpet. The Union army might have ravaged the house, but the more insidious wounds festered, invisible from view.

An hour later, after Samuel had roused, the five of them sat down for supper. The burnt mince pie had been delicately scraped clean by Eliza, but aside from that the meal was glaringly sparse. A chipped porcelain bowl with a few salted boiled potatoes was passed around and nothing more.

"I'm sorry you haven't been able to find him," Samuel said, his speech still a little slurred from his long day of sleeping. "But I'm not sure there are any other Union hospitals around these parts."

Lily nodded. "Yes, I suspect I have likely exhausted every possibility around here."

Samuel rubbed his eyes. "After my nap, I thought about the next steps you could take. You might consider heading toward New Orleans. I think General Banks's headquarters could potentially have some information about Jacob's regiment. You did say it might be stationed in Louisiana."

"You will need to go through New Orleans anyway to get back to New York," Eliza added, barely hiding her eagerness to have her household to herself again.

Lily's eyes fell to her plate. "That sounds like as good a plan as any at this point, I suppose. But how will I even get back to New Orleans if no local driver will take me?"

"Don't worry about that, dear Lily." Eliza's voice was emphatic. "I'm sure lots of men will be happy to get paid to take a Yankee out of town."

61

Stella had been eyeing the dark circle on the ceiling all morning. The rain had been constant over the past week, and the leaky roof had only gotten worse. Only in the past few hours had the skies cleared and the sun broken through for the first time in what seemed like forever.

"My hand's feelin' better," William said as he lifted the metal pail from the center of the room where the water had accumulated. "I thought maybe I'd go on the roof and see if I could patch up that leak."

"Don't want you hurtin' yourself," Stella cautioned. "I was thinkin' maybe Ammanee could ask Benjamin to take a look at it next time he was in town. He's mighty handy, and he's been sneakin' over to Janie's house for a visit when she's out, now that Ammanee's taken to sleepin' over there." She smiled, happy her sister was, at long last, getting some of the joy and affection she deserved.

"You don't think I'm man enough?" he laughed.

"I think you plenty manful, but your hands used to holdin' that flute of yours, not a hammer or nails."

His eyes twinkled at Stella's playfulness. "You forgettin' I was in the army. So now I'm handy, too. Get me a ladder and I'll go up and fix it," he insisted. "Probably don't need much except a spare shingle and some tar."

"Don't have a ladder, but I think Mama does. I'll go over there now and check. You stay here with Wade."

"I guess I get off easy for now," he said, planting a kiss atop the little boy's head. "But let me know if it's too heavy, and I'll come over and fetch it. Don't need Benjamin's help. Can do it myself. I sure enough did a lot tougher things back in Port Hudson."

Stella walked down Rampart Street, breathing in the brisk February air. The rain had left the large magnolia trees with a coating of frost on their leaves. Miss Hyacinth's rhododendron bush curled like a tight fist from the cold.

"Mama?" Stella knocked on the blue door of Janie's home. When she received no answer, she let herself inside.

Janie was slowly making her way to greet her. "Sorry, child, I was gettin' your sister a cup of tea. She not feelin' too well today."

Stella put down her basket. "What's wrong, Mama? Her stomach actin' up?"

"No, it's not that. A cough. A little fever. She think she came down with somethin' when she went over to that contraband camp in Algiers to deliver some food." Janie's disapproval was palpable. "Your sister's got a big ol' heart, but she's always forgettin' that she also need to take care of herself."

"Well, that's Ammanee, always has been," Stella said as she reached for the tea. "Let me bring this to her. I only came by to see if you had a ladder Willie could use, but that can wait." She took the warm mug, inhaling the medicinal herbs that Janie had steeped.

"Tell her to drink it all up," Janie reminded her. "You know my medicine is more powerful than anything you can get from a doctor."

Stella nodded. Both she and Ammanee knew that all too well.

Stella found her sister tucked into the small wooden bed they'd shared as children.

"Brought you something for your cough," she said as she handed the steaming brew to Ammanee.

"Mama's been making me tinctures all mornin'." Ammanee forced a smile, but Stella could see how poorly her sister was feeling. Her skin was tinged gray, and little beads of perspiration glistened beneath the rim of her tignon. "Just hoping she don't give me no wolfsbane."

"This smells like dried chrysanthemum to me, so you're safe," Stella teased as she lifted Ammanee's head slightly off the pillow and helped her to take a few sips. "What's ailin' you? Tell me."

"It's just a little cold, that's all," Ammanee tried to brush it off. "I went down to Algiers with some of the Union crew to deliver supplies to the contraband camp there. Things real awful over in those parts. Runaways…no shoes. Some of 'em don't even got no shirts. Freedom real enticin' until you're hungry and shivering in the cold."

"You always doin' too much, sister."

Ammanee blew on the tea and shrugged. "Just doin' what the Lord tells me is right. And some of us born to do for others, whether we want to or not. There were some women and children there, too…couldn't sleep thinkin' 'bout them sufferin' any more than they already have."

Stella knew her sister's whole life had been spent serving and helping others, and now she only wanted Ammanee to allow herself to be cared for in the way she deserved. She gripped her hand. "You gonna need to rest now, get better soon. Wade wants to see his auntie, and Benjamin wants—"

"He wants me to be his gal, get married and have a baby, too." Ammanee's eyes sparkled through the fever. "You right. I need to get better real quick so I'm ready for the next time he comes," she laughed weakly. "Now, let me be so I can rest. And I heard what you said to Mama about the ladder. Go home and tell Willie Mama has one out back. He can take it. No one will miss it."

62

Lily settled into the worn-down coach her sister-in-law had arranged for her. She was not looking forward to the long and arduous trip to New Orleans. The adrenaline that had fueled her journey south had evaporated amongst all the death and decay she'd witnessed since her arrival. Now a terrible sense of hopelessness weighed on her.

For the entirety of the trip down, she kept her eyes glued to the window. She had not wanted to miss a single sight, and she felt obligated to bear witness to all that had happened on these battlefields and beyond. But now all Lily could manage was to shut her eyes.

The last few days had gutted her. How naive she had been sitting in Adeline Levi's Brooklyn parlor, trading gossip with the rest of the women in the Sanitary Commission. As they stitched their quilts and rolled yards of bandages, they'd erroneously believed they were making a significant contribution to the war effort. But it was all playacting compared to what those brave nurses on the front were achieving! Everything she'd done over the past three years now felt like it had been executed from the sidelines.

Even her abolitionist work seemed fraudulent now. What was the use in protesting and writing anti-slavery speeches, when the real bravery was shown by those who worked the underground channels to bring runaway slaves up North to actual freedom? Lily's head rattled against the peeling interior of the coach. Its dank smell and rickety undercarriage only worsened her despondence.

When they reached the city of Brookhaven, midway between Satartia and New Orleans, the driver went to secure two rooms for the night in a local boardinghouse. "Now, don't open your mouth," he reminded Lily in his thick Southern drawl. "We don't need no trouble. And remember, no one in Mississippi is going to offer up lodging to a Yank, even if she is a *lady* like yourself."

They entered the mustard-colored Victorian home, its boardinghouse sign displayed outside the parlor window. Lily stayed a few steps behind the driver as he arranged for separate rooms for their stay.

The owner of the house, a pale-eyed woman with blond hair, made small talk with him. "Union troops come and gone through here last year. That brute Colonel Grierson ordered his Yank cavalry to burn down nearly every building around. Then he told 'em to rip up the railroad. Just lucky they didn't torch down my home, too. Got two babes to care for, and their father out fightin' somewhere in Tennessee."

"Murderin' Bluebellies," Lily's driver muttered as he handed over the bills she'd given him in advance.

"Ain't that the truth," the woman snorted. "You say you

two headin' down to New Orleans? Real shame the journey takes twice as long now. It used to be a straight shot from our li'l railway station down to the big city. Real good for business back in the day."

Lily nodded demurely. She, too, would have preferred to travel by train.

"Y'all must be tired," the woman noted, handing over two heavy brass keys.

"Now, breakfast will be modest, mind you." She smiled over at Lily. "Just a few eggs and some hard rolls. No bacon or mash."

"Understood, and thank you kindly, ma'am," the driver answered and then passed Lily the key to her room.

When they reached the first-floor landing, she informed him that she had no intention of staying long enough for them to eat a morning meal there.

63

"Don't fool yourself that this is a safe city, just because it's controlled by Blue Coats," the coachman warned as he counted up his final payment later the next day. "Lots of thieving and whoring in these parts. New Orleans is a wicked place."

"I'll be sure to keep my guard up," Lily replied, as she instructed the porter to carry her trunk into the inn for the night.

The small hotel in the Garden District, with its fragrant sweet olive bushes flanking the porch, hardly seemed like a place of ill repute. She had been advised by Samuel to find her lodging in that part of town, as it was close enough to make inquiries at the Union headquarters and also convenient to where she'd eventually need to book her passage home.

That evening, in the privacy of her room, Lily shed her travel clothes. She folded the bodice, skirt, chemise and petticoat, and placed them on the bedchamber's chair. It felt good to finally be in her own skin, free from the weight of cotton and wool, as she sponged off her neck and shoulders, her breasts and under her arms, with the water she poured into the porcelain basin.

There was a time when she used to put flowers in her bathwater before she slipped beneath the eiderdown with Jacob, the feathered quilt luxuriant on their naked limbs. She longed for those early days when they were first wed. The sensation of being entwined with another, as tightly as two silk ribbons. She never dared tell him, but she loved how he made her body awaken under his fingertips. Sometimes it embarrassed her, it burst out so loud. Under his caress, her body was an instrument that came alive only for him, and she longed for it now more than ever.

The war had forced her to adopt a steel-hard shell. That softness of a young bride seemed so far away now as she gazed in the mirror, brushing out the coils in her hair. Lily slipped into her nightdress and slid into the heavy wooden bed, bringing the sheets up to her chest.

Tomorrow, she'd put on her bravest face and head over to the Union headquarters. She wouldn't leave for home until she unturned every possible stone. Lily closed her eyes and remembered the last time she was under crisp white sheets with Jacob. She dreamt that she was not alone in the bed.

64

The steps to the Union army's main office had yet to be swept of their brown leaves. Lily pulled up the hem of her skirt and walked inside. The large granite building, which had been used as the customhouse and post office before the war, was now bustling with Yankee men.

"How can I help you, ma'am?" An officer in a pristine navy blue uniform asked from behind a reception desk.

What a relief she felt gazing upon a bright-eyed Union officer after seeing so many wounded and dying back in Mississippi. "Yes, I've traveled from New York, in search of my husband, Private Jacob Kling. He mustered in as a musician with the New York 163rd Regiment, Company K," she said. "I have lost contact with him and I'm concerned he might be wounded or worse…"

The young man nodded. "Please wait here," he instructed. "I'll see if my superior officer might be able to help you."

He returned with an older gentleman in dark blue threads,

slightly balding with gray muttonchops meticulously groomed down the length of his pink face.

"Ma'am, how might we be of assistance? You have traveled a long way, I've been told."

"I am searching for my husband. He is in the New York 163rd Regiment," she began again.

"I am afraid we are not able to search for specific soldiers," the officer informed her.

"Please, sir. I've spent the last week combing through all the field hospitals in proximity to Vicksburg. I am desperate." She couldn't let this last chance at information slip away. "I'm beseeching you to look at your records. Your office might have some further information, at least regarding his regiment. Perhaps they have passed along lists of the wounded, or the missing?" She paused and sucked in her breath. "Or the dead."

A sympathetic expression swept across the Union officer's face. "I certainly commend your efforts, coming all the way down here. But we have no lists of this kind, I'm afraid. You must understand the magnitude of the situation. We're in the middle of the largest war in our history. Countless men are wounded or killed each and every day. Any list along those lines would contain the names of thousands and thousands of men." He shook his head. "Not only would that be overwhelming. Quite frankly, it would be impossible."

"I understand," Lily sighed. "But surely there must be some sort of documentation, if they were left in a hospital or buried somewhere?"

"Ma'am, the only records that we keep are when roll call is made each day, if a soldier is reported present or absent. If he's not able to answer, we can assume, he's dead or wounded. Or a deserter."

Lily's eyes fell. Samuel had been right all along, searching for Jacob was like looking for a needle in a haystack.

"I apologize I can't be of more help," he added. "You are not the first wife to come here and ask. Nor, I'm afraid, will you be the last."

Her search had come to a fruitless end. She had failed to find Jacob. Just as her father had warned, it would be impossible for her to learn anything more. The only choice left was to return to New York, where she would have to wait to see if eventually a letter—either from Jacob or someone else finally informing her of his fate—might arrive.

The air in New Orleans was thick and pungent. The smells of horse manure on the streets and the plumes of smoke coming off the riverboats filled the air. Lily headed toward her hotel in the Garden District to inquire how to purchase a steamship ticket for the journey home.

Around her Southern women in their hoop skirts and frayed silk bonnets went about their business, some with a young slave who carried a basket of provisions. The only men she noticed were either too old, too young or too broken to serve in the Reb army.

As she approached Jackson Avenue, she spotted several children spilling out from a garden. Three girls in white smocks threw jacks on the sidewalk. Two of them had their dark hair pulled into tight braids. The other was a redhead, with freckles, and her white dress was splattered with mud.

"Stop it, Rivkah!" One of the girls snatched the ball away from the other's hand. "You're not playing fair!"

The child's name caught Lily's attention. It was a Jewish one.

She stopped and looked up at the name outside the gates. "The Association for the Relief of Jewish Widows and War Orphans" was neatly engraved in gold letters on a black plaque.

A strong tide of emotions washed over her. She couldn't

help but think of what had happened to the poor children at the Colored Orphan Asylum.

"Rivkah!" The third child also scolded the girl for not abiding by the rules.

From behind the gate, a young Black man was planting spring bulbs. He looked over at the girls and laughed. "Now, Miss Rivkah," he admonished, "you better behave before Miss Hollander comes out and gives you a talkin'-to about not sharin'."

The flame-haired girl regretfully handed back the ball to the other child. As the man returned to his work in the garden, he began singing to himself. "*I'm in love with a girl with a heart of fire, she whom I adore. With her copper hair and white, bright smile...*"

Lily froze in her tracks, unable to believe her ears. The man's song was exactly the one Jacob had written for her; it was as if he himself were there singing it for her.

Lily willed herself to walk through the gates and approach the young man. "Excuse me," she asked tentatively. "May I ask, where did you learn that song?"

"'Girl of Fire'?" he laughed again. "Me and my brothers in the Corps d'Afrique sang that song on our way to Port Hudson. Man named Willie taught it to us."

"Willie?" Lily could hardly contain herself.

"Yes, ma'am. Finest musician I ever heard. Could play any tune. From da classical stuff to a praise song. I just saw him the other day. He was out getting some stuff for patchin' a leak." He brushed off the dirt from his hands and stood up. "I've had that song in my head ever since seein' him again."

Willie had to be the musician Jacob had written about so often, the great friend he had made. If anyone knew of Jacob's whereabouts, it had to be him. She forced herself to take a breath before asking what she knew was her final opportunity to learn anything about her husband. "By any chance, do you know where I can find Willie?"

"Indeed, I do, ma'am. He tol' me he livin' over there by Rampart Street, near St. Anthony of Padua Church."

Her heart was racing inside her chest. "Rampart Street. Is that close to here?"

He was about to suggest she go inside and ask Miss Hollander to sketch her out a map. But Lily hadn't stayed long enough for him to duck in. She'd already flagged down a coach and left.

65

The carriage let her off in front of St. Anthony of Padua. Its stucco archways looked like they needed an extra coat of paint, but the heavy central door was mercifully unlocked.

Lily hadn't been inside a church for some time. The last time she could recall was for the wedding of one of her school friends and she'd also taken a tour with some of the women from the Sanitary Commission of the new St. Patrick's Cathedral on Fifth Avenue, before the war began and they stopped construction on it. She didn't frequent religious sanctuaries often. The last time she'd gone to synagogue was for the High Holidays at Temple Emanu-El, where she'd sat quietly next to her father and looked longingly at the women who had been her classmates and now had babies in their bellies and their husbands safely beside them.

She pulled open the door of St. Anthony's and stepped inside, a musky smell assaulting her nostrils. A young Black girl was on her knees scrubbing the floor, the pail of soapy water sloshing not far from a stand of flickering votive candles.

Lily walked deeper into the church, toward the altar with its carved crucifix of Jesus, a faint trickle of painted blood dripping from the wound in his side. In the past, the sight had always unnerved her, but Lily now gazed upon it and saw a young man in terrible pain who was sacrificed too soon. His anguish resonated within her on a more human level, one that transcended religion.

"May I help you?" A man in dark clerical robes approached her. "Are you here for Confession?"

"No," Lily answered. "I'm hoping someone might be able to help me. I'm trying to find a musician by the name of Willie. I've been told he lives nearby."

"Ahh—I assume you are not a local of our fair city," the priest responded, having noted her accent.

"I left New York nearly two weeks ago in search of my husband, a soldier. I believe he served with someone who lives near Rampart Street."

"Rampart?" His voice revealed his surprise.

"Yes. Supposedly he's a flutist," she said. "Like my husband, a skilled musician."

"I don't know of anyone who fits that description. It's mostly women living in the cottages on that street."

"But I was told there was a musician named Willie living mere blocks away from here," she insisted, not ready to give up.

"I'm sorry, ma'am," the priest said, excusing himself. "I must prepare my sermon for tomorrow. I only thought you were here for the Confessional."

As Lily began to make her way toward the door, her heart sank, knowing she had reached yet another dead end. The only other option was to knock on every door asking if anyone knew of a man named William. She prepared to start yet another search.

Just as she was about to exit, she felt her skirt being tugged by a small, gentle hand.

"Ma'am?" the girl in the apron asked politely.

Lily turned around. "Yes, my child?"

The little girl's eyes met Lily's, and she visibly softened upon hearing the sound of a Northern accent. "I heard what you was talkin' 'bout with dat man," she whispered. "I might be able to help you."

Lily followed the little girl down Rampart Street, watching as she navigated every pothole, her apron strings bobbing up and down in the back. She made a sharp turn right, proudly directing Lily toward one of the last houses on the row.

"It's this one," she indicated, pointing to Stella's door. "Miss Ammanee—she got me my job at the church—her sister live here. Her beau named Willie, he came home just last month." She looked up at Lily triumphantly. "No one pays much attention when they're talkin' in front of me, but I'm always listenin'."

"Thank you for trusting me with this. It seems not everyone around here is willing to be as helpful to an outsider." Lily smiled. "I think that priest was holding something back."

"Yo' from the North. I know you bring no harm."

Lily stood rigid at the porch step, her two fists balled in nervous anticipation, and also fear that she might be confronting another dead end.

"Just go on and knock," the child urged. "Like my mama tells me all the time, sometimes you just gotta be brave."

66

Stella had been up most of the night, nursing Wade and worrying about Ammanee's fever. The sudden knock at the door immediately put her on edge, for she feared it might be Janie telling her that her sister's health had grown worse.

Instead, she found a stranger. A redhead with paper-white skin stood peering out at her beneath her bonnet's brim.

Stella's face blanched. She had never met Frye's wife, but could she have come looking for her, or even worse, for William or Wade? In spite of his service, Willie had no free papers. And Wade was the son of a slave.

Her protective instincts immediately rushed through her veins and she cupped Wade's head in her free hand, drawing him closer as if to shield him. A paralyzing fear coursed through her, as this female stranger gazed at her and her baby.

Before the woman had a chance to open her mouth, Annie,

the little girl that Ammanee knew from church, poked out from behind the lady's skirt. "Miss Stella, this woman from up North. She lookin' for Willie," the child announced. With that, the girl darted away, her brown legs flashing as she ran back to the church.

"I am searching for my husband," the woman started to explain. "His name is Jacob Kling and I believe—"

"Jacob?" Stella's eyes widened at the name. "Please, ma'am," she urged Lily. "Please come inside."

The two women stood in the center of the parlor, staring at each other as though somehow they knew each other from the stories their men had shared.

Stella took in the tall, rather gangly-looking Lily, her dress smudged with a bit of dirt on her skirt, her boots scuffed from travel and her copper hair peeking from beneath her bonnet. These imperfections in Lily's appearance made Stella feel less embarrassed by the messy state of her home. A pile of Wade's clean nappies lay unfolded on the kitchen table. She'd left sassafras leaves boiling in the kitchen for a broth intended for Ammanee, and its anisette-like fragrance permeated the house.

"I'm sorry for the state of things. I wasn't expecting anyone," Stella apologized.

Lily was still in shock that she had finally reached a destination where she was not only welcomed, but that seemed to have a verifiable connection to Jacob. She looked at Stella—her beautiful child nestled against her, her warm brown eyes framed by the pale yellow cloth wrapped around her head—and her heart broke open.

"You have no idea how little any of that matters to me," she sobbed. "I'm still struggling to believe how I have been led to this place, to you, to your William."

"Let me go get him," Stella said. "He's outside fixin' something. These last few weeks since he been back, he's had to start usin' his hands in a whole new way."

Willie quickly followed Stella from the garden into the living room, where a White woman had just taken off her silk hat, a few tendrils of red hair falling out slightly from the center of her bun.

As Lily turned to face this man she'd read about so fondly in Jacob's letters, her green eyes teared up with emotion. "William," she uttered his name solemnly, like a benediction.

He did not answer her directly at first. Instead, he turned to Stella and whispered, "Go get the map."

William shared the story of what happened to Teddy and Jacob that fateful Christmas morning in vivid detail. As she watched this woman learn what had happened to her husband, Stella's heart ached anew.

When William got to the point of making his map, Lily's eyes grew wide. "You made a map of how to get back to him?"

His eyes fell to the cloth folded in his hands. "I did it first on paper, but my Stella, she then made it even better with her stitchin'," he said, then offered it to Lily so she could see how Stella had preserved the route through needle and thread.

In between her shaking hands, Lily gazed at the map. The careful black running stitches of the path, the red barn and yellow house markers toward what appeared to be a church marked with a cross. On the bottom the word I B Y R E E A was sewn.

"This will lead me back to him." Her voice broke with emotion.

"I will need to come with you though," William insisted. He did not see Stella's eyes dart up at him like arrows. "You see dat map must be read a certain way. The cross don't mark a church or anything like dat, but Cross's General Store in Iberia." He pointed to Stella's letters sewn on the cloth. He spoke more rapidly as the plan he'd been making to get back to Jacob now seemed likely to come to fruition sooner with Lily's help.

"I couldn't ask you to come," Lily said. "It's far too dangerous. You've already endured so much, and you have your family to protect here," she said, looking over at Stella. "And I'm sure I could make sense of what Stella has indicated with her careful hand stitching."

William inched forward on his chair, his dark eyes growing serious. "Ma'am, I'm aware it's dangerous. I know the risk returnin' to hostile territory, 'specially as a Black man travelin' with a White woman." He stopped. "But we got but one shot to get 'im back. We can't leave nothin' to chance." William's eyes lifted and fell upon Stella, silently beseeching her to understand his predicament.

But Stella would not now offer him her blessing. Leaving her once again was one thing. But leaving their son, too, she would never approve that.

She had felt a respect for Lily when she came into her home, but now she hated her. Hated that she was taking her man away and bringing him back into danger. Her mind traveled to an even darker place, to a thought she knew she couldn't possibly say aloud. With Jacob left in the wilderness somewhere, with a woman who William said wasn't right in her mind... Was Jacob, at this point, even alive?

"I'll arrange for a coach and pick you up tomorrow," Lily told him. As many times as she stressed that William should not come with her, he insisted it was the only option. "But I will keep the map for now. So I may study it."

"Yes," he said. "Please, take it with you."

But she had no intention of showing up the next morning. As much as she wanted to keep her word to Willie, who had done so much for Jacob, she felt bound by an even deeper covenant that existed woman to woman: you do no harm.

67

Stella felt a wash of relief come over her when Lily failed to appear the next morning at the pre-arranged time. She hated to see William pacing in the parlor, his eyes peeled to the window, hoping Jacob's wife would return as she promised. But the woman had given her a gift by not taking him back into the wilderness.

"She's not coming, is she?" William asked.

Stella remained quiet. She was well aware that anything she said would not be enough.

"No, she gone, and we got no idea if that map gonna make any sense to her." He pressed his thumbs to his forehead. "And she don't even know I left my flute there, either."

"If she gets Jacob, he won't leave your instrument behind." That much Stella could say for sure.

He sat down and put his head in his hands. "I understand

you didn't want me to go, Stella. But livin' with the knowledge I left him there... Right after I left Teddy under nothing but a pile of oak leaves and spruce needles." His voice broke. "It's like now I've let them both down."

Stella pulled over a chair and sat beside him, taking his hand in hers. "This Lily did right by me. Keepin' you safe while she go gets her husband. She's a White woman. No one gonna be tryin' to hurt her, like they would you—*like they already did.* You wanna put your neck out there when there's a chance some Reb gonna string you up from a tree? Or some Union man gonna accuse you of desertin' like the last time?" She held his fingers tight. "Lily know you safest here with me. And I like her a whole lot more now that she sees that. She not just takin'. She gets you're precious to me. And to your son."

William nodded reluctantly. "Just hope she can find her way with the map."

"Miss Hyacinth once told me my maps are lucky." She smiled. "I have a feelin' that Lily's got her wits about her. We sendin' her off as good as we can."

For as long as she could remember, Stella was the beneficiary of either her mother's or Ammanee's fine cooking. But now, with her beloved sister ill, Stella found herself behind the stove for the first time, as Janie nursed Ammanee. She knew how to make tinctures and certainly simple meals like grits or dirty rice, but not how to prepare the more sustaining vittles that she hoped would give Ammanee her strength back. She needed to remember what herbs and vegetables her sister had used from the garden to make broth whenever Stella was feeling unwell, particularly during her pregnancy.

The other women on the street pitched in, too, now that Ammanee couldn't bring food back from work. Miss Emilienne brought some groats and Miss Hyacinth a jar of manuka honey that she swore would make Ammanee well again.

One day Benjamin arrived at Janie's cottage, carrying a canvas sack with five chicken bones inside. He handed them over to Janie. "Thought the marrow would be good for her," he told her.

"I'll do it, Mama," Stella offered as she took the sack and brought it over to the hearth to boil. She had watched Ammanee do this for her in the weeks just after Wade's birth, when Stella was so tired she could hardly pull herself out of a chair. *No one missin' the bones*, her sister said when she'd come home with them after work.

"Where she restin'?" Benjamin asked. Stella could see the deep lines of worry on his face. "I know I'm not s'posed to do anythin' but run my errands in town and then turn straight back home, but I had to see her." He looked over at Janie, hoping she didn't mind him arriving unannounced.

"She's in the back. We keepin' her quarantined because I don't know if it's typhoid fever or somethin' else. She's in bad shape." Her voice was flinty and staccato. Stella recognized the tenor, for it was the one her mother used whenever she was trying to steel herself for a storm.

"I gotta go see her, ma'am. Just want her to know I came…"

Janie lowered her eyes. "Stella goin' bring her some more herb tea. Tried to tell her to go home and stop risking herself, but she won't. You go in with her, but don't stay too long."

Stella guided Benjamin into the dim room. Ammanee's small face looked even smaller now; her black eyes resembled two sunken stones.

"Ami," he called out to her. It was a name Stella knew only the two of them had used, back when they were children together on the plantation.

Ammanee didn't answer, but Stella noticed her eyes flicker at the sight of him.

"I missin' you real bad. Brough' yo' mama something to make your blood strong," he said as he brought her fingertips up to his lips and kissed them tenderly.

"Thank you," she mustered.

"I'm goin' leave your tea by the bed." Stella walked it over, and a thin feather of steam lifted off its surface. "I'll give you two some time by yourselves," she said. "But not too long. We need to get your fever down and get you well again."

68

As much as she knew his stewardship would have helped her, Lily only hoped William would understand why she could not possibly have taken him along. His responsibilities now lay with keeping Stella and their new baby safe, and she would never forgive herself if something happened to him. Her conscience had left her with no other choice. She hoped he would forgive her and not see her actions as a betrayal, but rather—in the spirit of the immense gratitude she felt for him—a release from any further obligation he might believe he had.

William had already done so much, far more than most anyone else would have. The map he'd drawn crystalized his intentions to get back to Jacob, and Stella's careful needlework had ensured its longevity. It was a gift the young couple had bequeathed to her, and she only prayed her arrival in Iberia wouldn't be too late.

Lily wished she knew how to steer a horse and buggy the way Eliza could. Without that skill and without a man like William, she'd been forced to hire yet another driver to take her from New Orleans to Iberia. Weeks before, she had protested when her father insisted she take an extra hundred dollars with her on top of what she'd allocated for the trip. *Give in to at least this request, daughter,* he'd said as he closed her fist around the crisp notes. *It will help me to rest easier knowing you have extra funds with you, should you ever need them.*

Leaning forward, Lily spotted Cross's General Store, the neat black letters of its sign making it unmistakable. She informed the driver that he needed to find a path off the main road. She showed him the map.

"I never saw a map like that before." The coachman could hardly contain his bemusement, but he understood it well enough to find the place.

Before long they had passed the lemon-colored manse on the sugarcane plantation, and he was drawing his reins to stop in front of the farm with the red barn and sheep.

Lily looked down at the embroidered stitches that had guided her this far and remembered William's instructions: *Once we get to the store, we need the buggy to take us as close as we can to the edge of the woods. Even if Jacob's leg is good and braced, he'll still only be able to cover a short distance.* "You can let me out here, and just wait," she instructed. "I'm going to walk the rest."

The hem of her dark skirt trailed across the earth. Despite the early-afternoon hour, the trees cast heavy shadows on her path. Lily tried to summon all of her strength. So much had happened to get her to this point, and she only prayed that she could bring Jacob safely home.

She continued down the path until she saw the house that William had described, the roughly built structure with the tin roof and the shed in the backyard. As she approached, she was sure she saw the back of Jacob from afar. He teetered a bit, relying on a heavy tree branch that served as a makeshift crutch to support himself.

She started toward him as quickly as her legs could take her. She even called out his name.

Just as Jacob turned to see her, an old woman came out from the porch step. No taller than a sapling, her wild gray hair falling over her breasts. Even from where Lily stood, she could see the metallic reflection of a gun.

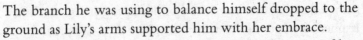

"What ya doing on my land?" she barked.

Realizing that Lily was not in fact an apparition, but his wife actually standing there in the flesh, Jacob lifted his free arm in the woman's direction.

"Mama, it's safe," he told her firmly. "She's my wife."

Lily, already aware of the woman's delusion, remained frozen in her tracks.

"Your wife?" Her voice was hoarse.

"I told you, I had to get back to her as soon as my ankle was healed. But it looks like she come for me first."

The old woman looked over at Jacob, and then at Lily.

"You both best come inside then," she said, shaking her head. The pistol tapped at her nightdress as she walked barefoot back into the house.

Only then did Lily rush forward and fall into Jacob's arms.

The branch he was using to balance himself dropped to the ground as Lily's arms supported him with her embrace.

He had forgotten the smell of her hair, the taste of her

mouth. Now his senses awakened as he inhaled her deeply into his lungs.

"How can this be?" Jacob asked between their kisses. He still struggled to believe she had found him.

"I have a carriage waiting. Just up the bend. I'll help you make it there." She bent down and gave him his makeshift crutch.

"I can't leave without getting something from inside first," he told her. "Lily, just follow my lead." He steadied himself. "This woman believes I'm her wounded son. I'm going to need you to play along, so we can get out of here without any harm."

Inside the cabin, the rafters black from soot, a feral smell greeted Lily. The woman was hunched over a stovepipe adjusting the fire with a long iron poker, her gun rested beside her feet.

"Mama," Jacob uttered the term so gently it sounded genuine to Lily's ears. "My wife's come round, surprised us with a visit. Told you that I had to get back to my girl once my ankle was all better, didn't I?"

The woman's fingers reached for her pistol. She stood up straight, her fragile silhouette visible beneath the coarse white linen of her nightdress. "You not leavin' me, are you?" The gun wobbled in her shaky hand.

Jacob lifted his hand, motioning for her to put the weapon down. "No need to point the gun," he said in a steady voice. "We gotta get back to our own home now, Mama." He made his words lilt like a Southerner. "You braced my ankle. Nursed me through my fever. Took real good care of me." He paused, then reached out to take hold of her blue-mottled hand. "I'm a real lucky son…"

"You comin' back though." She lowered the pistol.

"I'll come again, next Christmas," he promised.

Jacob's eyes directed Lily toward the silver flute on the long wooden table, signaling her to take it. Then the two of them made their way slowly toward the door.

"I wasn't sure we were going to make it out of there." Lily breathed a sigh of relief once they were a few yards from the house.

"I took the bullets out of the chamber while she was sleeping as soon as I was well enough to stand. I don't think I would have been as calm otherwise."

"I should have known you'd keep your wits about you, even in those conditions," Lily remarked as she helped Jacob make his way up the path.

"I knew William wouldn't have left the flute unless he thought he was coming back," Jacob said as he labored to hobble up the dirt road.

"It was his intention," she assured.

When they finally reached the coach, Lily and the coachman helped pull Jacob inside.

Only then, with him nestled beside her, did Lily show Jacob the careful and deliberately stitched map.

69

Ammanee's fever would not abate, despite Janie and Stella taking turns to wrap her in sheets soaked in cold water.

"We gotta get her more help. Perhaps even see if Charity Hospital will help her." Janie's voice revealed her fear for the first time in Stella's memory. "I'm scared it's more than just a fever. She got a spotty rash this morning on her chest."

"Mama, she good and comfortable here. I always hearin' that our kinda folk who go into a hospital rarely come out again."

"She don't got yellow fever. Her eyes not yellow."

"Still, we can't leave her for some strangers to take care of her."

Janie knotted her hands. "You gotta go home to William and the baby. We don't know what she have, damn contraband camp with all its diseases flyin' around. Yo' sister sufferin' now, and it tearin' me inside."

Stella touched her mother's arm. "You doin' a good job. We gonna get her well again, Mama."

Janie looked up. "Well, one thing fo' sure, you need to go home to William and the baby. Don't want to put you in any further harm than I might already have."

"But I gotta help, Mama."

Janie shook her head no. "Go home to your family. I'm taking care of my girl."

The house was in disarray when Stella returned to the smell of soiled nappies. Wade was crying, and she could hear William attempting to soothe him with song.

In the bedroom, she found William clasping Wade around the waist, his diaper soaked through.

"We run clear out of clean cloths, Stella, and I didn't know what to do. He been cryin' all day."

Stella's maternal instinct flared and she rushed over to her baby. The possibility that she might have brought Ammanee's fever home, and got Wade sick, sent pangs of fear through her.

"He feels cool, thank the Lord," she appraised, as she pressed a palm against his tiny forehead.

Just for safe measure, she then also touched William's brow.

"You, too," she said and breathed a sigh of relief at its coolness before taking Wade from his arms.

"Mama thinks I shouldn't be comin' round there until Ammanee's fever breaks. She not sure what's ailin' her, but typhoid been goin' round those camps."

"We better hope it's not yellow fever," William said as he watched in awe as Stella easily managed to settle Wade and unfasten his heavy diaper, his skin happy for the balm of fresh air.

"No, Mama said her eyes showin' no sign of yellow, and after a week of fever, she figured you'd see that by now. She thinkin' Ammanee musta' picked up somethin' bad at the contraband camp when she went to bring 'em some food."

William shook his head. "Whole lot of mess over there. Everybody runnin' to find somethin' betta, but it's all nothing but a dead end." In the past two days, he'd been feeling particularly disheartened. Even with Louisiana in the process of passing a new state constitution that would abolish slavery, and the tide of war clearly going the Union's way, his prospects for supporting his new family still seemed slim.

"Yes," she agreed. "I guess now I understand why Benjamin told Ammanee he didn't want to run. Maybe he saw what those camps were really like, and realized tillin' the land for Missus Percy was better."

Wade's leg kicked back and forth as he rolled a little on his back, giggling.

"I hate to use this, but got no choice, I guess," she muttered as she lifted his bottom and took the embroidered swaddling cloth and wrapped it around him.

William's eyes fell upon the border of cowrie shells that now rimmed his son's chubby thighs, and felt a calm reclaim him. Stella was incredibly resourceful, always managing to find a solution even in his most challenging hour. Seeing the trim of shells and the flash of blue thread around his son, he couldn't help but think back to his own mother.

She don' made the ceiling the color of the sky when you were born, son, Ol' Abraham had told him. *She give ya a shield, she trap dose haints up dere so you be safe*, he'd said as he placed the hand-carved fife beside him.

William looked up at the bedroom ceiling as Stella rocked Wade in her arms, her lips pressed to his tiny ear. The first thing he would do when he got himself a job was buy paint for the wooden planks above where he, Stella and their baby now lay, in the palest shade of blue.

Stella was pacing the parlor, rocking Wade, when the sound of carriage wheels pulled up outside her cottage. Through the veil of the curtains, she saw the back of a tall woman and the unmistakable red hair peeking out from underneath her bonnet. As the woman alighted, Stella saw the coachman assisting a fragile-looking young man.

"William!" she called out. "Come quick!"

She was just about to tug him to the window when they heard a knock at the door.

"Go ahead and answer it," she said, beaming. "It's more than alright."

William saw Jacob standing there, a large branch keeping him upright. Almost like an apparition, his friend was wearing the same coat he'd worn on that fateful Christmas day. His trousers were torn and stained with dark blood by the ankle, the material frayed where his ankle had probably been braced for over a month.

But it was the flash of silver by Jacob's side that blinded him. "I think you forgot this, my friend."

Jacob handed over William's flute.

The sensation of the cold metal pulsed through William.

Jacob hobbled over to embrace him with his one free hand, and the two women observed each of their men bloom back to life a little more.

70

Stella never thought she'd welcome another White man into her cottage after years of suffering the degradations of Frye. But a strange, unexpected joy swept over her as she ushered Jacob and Lily inside.

"The map worked!" Stella cried ebulliently. This was the first evidence she'd had that her stitches had enabled someone to safely reach their destination. She lifted baby Wade into the air and did a little dance. "Yo' daddy, he made it so." She kissed the little boy on both cheeks and he gurgled in delight.

"You have helped us so much!" Lily exclaimed, her face flushed with such happiness that together, they'd all succeeded in bringing back Jacob. "We are forever indebted to you both."

"Please," William insisted, as he lifted his flute and blew a few happy notes to punctuate his joy. "Come sit down. You must be tired from the trip."

Stella handed Wade to William. "Hold 'im so I can fetch somethin' for our guests to drink."

Jacob and Stella sat down on the wooden chairs. The fatigue they both felt had finally lifted. The elation of the reunion had revived them.

"I hope this is to yo' liking," Stella offered warmly as she brought them two cups of mint tea. "Wish I had somethin' to sweeten it fo' you, but we got no sugar with the war still on."

Lily took the cup in her hands and savored the light aroma. "It's perfect. Thank you."

Stella settled down and retook Wade into her arms. "Thank you for bringin' his flute back. I know Willie was missin' it more than he was willin' to admit."

"We brought you something, too, Stella." Jacob reached into his breast pocket and pulled out a folded piece of paper. "I promised William back in Port Hudson that I'd deliver this to you one day."

Stella took the dirt-smudged sheet and opened it. It was a letter—the first she had ever received.

Stella glanced at the sentences, written in a careful, neat hand.

Stella,
Where are you on this dark night? Have you gone into the garden to look at the stars, the white moon? We're separated now, but we both are beneath the same tarp...

She read the words, sounding them out in her head. Some she struggled to discern, but she could read enough to understand the emotion and meaning behind them.

My heart beats hard when I think of you. I wanna fall into your dark eyes and find comfort there. I wanna believe that when I left

you on your own, I did the right thing and that no harm will come
your way...

She set the paper on her lap, tears brimming on the surface of her eyes.

"He wanted me to write down what was in his heart. I carried it the whole time next to mine. A promise to a friend must always be kept," Jacob insisted.

William looked over to Stella. "Couldn't write it myself, *ma' dere*, but the words are mine." Their fingers entwined tightly. "World still has some good people," William announced as he allowed the warmth that floated through the room to penetrate deep into his bones.

"The war has taken so much," Lily added. "But today is a joyful day."

"Yes, it sure is," Stella agreed.

"We need to get back to the hotel and clean ourselves up. Get some new clothes for Jacob for our trip back up North."

Jacob's eyes darted over to William. "Yes. But before we leave, I wanted to mention an idea I had." He paused to catch his breath, his body still aching from the walk out of the woods to the coach. "Lily and I've been talking about her father and his music business. Just thinking he may have some opportunity up North that you might be interested in."

71

"We ain't movin' up North," Stella informed William. "Got my mama and sister here. I'm not leavin' them behind."

"Well, they can come with us. Jacob said his father-in-law got a good business. Says he sure I could get a job sellin' some of their sheet music during the day, and maybe he know some places for me to perform at night. Ain't nothin' here for me, Stella," he pleaded for her to understand. "Down here, I'm just an ex-slave not yet freed. Plus everyone is gonna say I deserted, 'cause I didn't muster out properly. How am I gonna take care of you and Wade like you deserve?"

She reached to touch his cheek, but he pulled away.

"I'm a man, Stella. Can't just stay here loafin' round the house all day, scared every time someone come to the door."

Her hand dropped to her side, her eyes fell, wounded.

"And I got dreams for us…real ones," William stressed.

"We all got dreams!" she shot back. "But isn't it enough we have each other now? Got no mas' chasing either of us. We got a baby, a roof over our heads."

"But for how long?" His voice was impatient. William knew he was revealing a new side to her, one that had grown inside him like a tempest. "Insurrections happenin' all the time round here. Rebs taking revenge on innocent Black men and their families. Just the other day when I went to get some supplies to patch the roof, I heard whispers about a free man who got his house burned to the ground. Men come on horses holding torches, and no one did a damn thing."

"Rampart Street's different," she insisted. "The women here, we all take care of our own."

William swallowed his words. Didn't she see? He was the only man left.

Stella hated this unrest between them. There was no hollering, no exchange of nasty words. But the silence somehow felt worse, the distance between them seemed greater than when they'd been apart. Wade, too, appeared to sense the discord. When Stella held him, he reached out for William. And when William took him in his arms, the child's hands stretched out for his mother's.

"Us fightin' not good for the baby," Stella finally interjected the next day in the kitchen. "We gotta work this out."

William tugged his hair in obvious frustration. "You and Wade are my life, Stella. I'm just tryin' to better myself so I can better you all, too. Not enough for me anymore to just not be a slave. Trying to build something for our future."

"I've been up all night, tossin'. I can say yes to leavin'—if Ammanee and Janie also come with us." She stepped closer, so Wade was now between them. "But we not gonna be broken up by any choice of mine alone." Stella would not talk about the journey North any further. "You can discuss it with Jacob," she stated plainly. "I'm gonna focus on gettin' Ammanee well, even if Mama don't let me near her."

That afternoon, Stella met Janie outside her home. "She's in bad shape," her mother confided. "Fever won't leave her. She seein' things in the room that aren't there. And her stomach crampin' real bad." Janie took a deep breath. "She been askin' for you all night."

"Let me see her, Mama. I'll be careful."

Janie, visibly exhausted, nodded her head. "Maybe seein' you the one thing that can help her now."

She opened the blue door to the cottage and the two women stepped inside. Stella held her breath, as the closed quarters reeked of staleness and illness, not the fragrance of shea butter and sage that had always defined her mother's self-care.

She walked to the small room at the back where Ammanee and she had spent countless hours together in their youth. Where they'd slept and laughed, and where her sister had first shown her how to communicate her feelings through a needle and thread.

"Ammanee?" Stella whispered as she crossed the threshold.

Her sister, thin as a reed now, her face glistening with perspiration, stirred at the sound of her name. "I'm here," Stella said as she reached for her hand, her sisterly love overpowering the danger of contagion.

Ammanee drifted in and out of consciousness during the hour they spent together. Stella was unsure if her sister could hear her, but she spoke in her softest voice, telling her of the beautiful things that were soon to come to them all.

"Got some good news," she shared. "We might all gonna be takin' a journey together sometime soon."

Ammanee's eyelids fluttered open.

"We'll be gettin' a place so we can all be together. We gonna cook together, sew together." She tried to paint a picture of their joint future. "And we gonna raise our babies together."

"The Lord is good." Ammanee's voice was hoarse. "Benjamin and I are gonna have a baby, aren't we?" She was crying. "Little one all our own, just like your Wade."

"Yes, that's right." Stella's fingers folded tighter over hers.

"I'm tired," Ammanee said as she closed her eyes. "But I hear my baby laughing. She here in the room with me."

"She's waitin' for you to get better so she can be born."

Stella let go of Ammanee's hand, patting it before she left. "You rest now, sister. I'll visit again tomorrow."

When she returned home, Wade was propped up in his basket and William was playing his flute to the baby's delight.

"He likes the spirituals my mama loved," William gushed. "And he got some rhythm of his own. He squealin' to the notes, Stella, I swear it!"

She swooped over and picked him up and kissed him on both cheeks. Hearing Ammanee speak of her deepest wishes made Stella realize she had to appreciate all the gifts she'd already been given.

"My little man goin' be a musician like his daddy?" She bounced him in her arms.

William gazed at the two of them and smiled. "I have somethin' to tell you. Jacob and Lily stopped by while you were out."

Stella stopped dancing and raised an eyebrow. "You talk about making the trip?"

"Yes," he confirmed. "I told 'em you'd only go if Ammanee

and Janie come, too. So they said they'd buy four tickets on the steamboat. But I told 'em I'm paying 'em back as soon as I get my first pay up there."

"I think we need one more though," Stella admitted. A wave of discomfort washed over her because she had failed to think of it before.

"Ammanee's not leaving New Orleans without Benjamin."

72

Five tickets rested on the kitchen table for steamboat passage to Chicago for the following week.

"Jacob said we can exchange them if your sister isn't well enough to travel then."

Stella glanced over at the billets. "I hope you told 'em I wasn't makin' any promises just yet. Haven't even mentioned it to Janie. She's so preoccupied with takin' care of Ammanee."

William nodded. "Go visit your sister. We don't have much to pack if we go. My flute. A bag with our clothes, and nappies for Wade." His excitement was obvious, his mind already on the journey North with his friend.

Stella didn't answer. Their few belongings might seem weightless in William's eyes, but they were everything to her. The sum of their lives.

Benjamin was in Ammanee's room when Stella walked in with gingerroot tea.

"Ami," she overheard him whispering to her. "You gotta get better. I'se nearly free," he informed her. "Mistress gonna give us our own shack to live in while I farm the land."

Ammanee suddenly shot up in bed. "She's here, don't you see her, Benjamin? Our baby girl, Mina!" Her hair was wild and matted, but her voice was suddenly strong and clear as a bell.

"Shhh." Stella rushed over to her sister's side, placing the steaming brew on the nightstand. "Lay back down." She took her handkerchief and wiped Ammanee's brow. "That's right, Mina is here. She wants you to get stronger so you can hold her."

Ammanee groaned and then started to weep. "My stomach hurt so bad."

Her whimpering felt like needles pricking Stella's insides. She tried to settle Ammanee as she pulled the sheet up to her chin. "Let's think of somethin' nice to make you feel better."

Benjamin pulled out a memory of his own to soothe her. "Ami, remember when we was children, how we used to hide by the marsh and you'd braid seagrass into two little crowns, one for me and one for you? So we could be king and queen of the paddy?"

"Yes," Ammanee answered softly. Her lucidity had returned for a moment.

"Will you make another one for me soon, Ami? Will you?" He bent his head down, his forehead tipping against her hollow stomach as though in prayer.

"Mmm," Ammanee managed to respond. Though it was so faint, Stella still heard it clearly.

She stepped closer to wipe her sister's brow again. Only then did she notice that Ammanee's wide brown eyes were frozen. Like two shining stones, they did not blink.

73

"I felt her spirit leave the room." Stella fell into William's arms. Her sobbing was relentless.

He held her in his arms, his chin resting on her head. The sound of her grief—an almost animal-like howl—stirred something long buried inside of him, bringing William back to his childhood. It gutted him to again hear a woman he loved in so much pain.

"She was seein' things, the baby she always wanted." Stella balled her fist and pressed it hard against William's chest. "At least Benjamin was there with her at the end," she said, shuddering. "But still. It's just so unfair."

William brought her to the bedroom and laid her down. "I'm gonna feed Wade some rice water," he said. "You get some sleep. Nothing else we can do for anyone tonight. Ammanee's spirit flying toward heaven on her own now," he reassured her. "No faster angel's wings than hers."

His words brought her little peace, though she did allow herself to be slipped beneath the cotton sheet. She wished she had the quilt that had always brought her comfort. Those rainbow squares that, without fail, felt like an embrace.

"William?" she called out to him before he reached for the door. "Can you get me something before you leave?"

"Anything, *ma' dere*."

"Go into the bottom drawer of the wooden chest. There are some squares of colored cotton stacked in two rows."

"Yes…" he said.

"Fetch the pine-colored one for me," she asked.

Moments later, he returned with the verdant-colored cloth.

"This one's from Ammanee's apron." Stella sat up and brought the fabric to her face, inhaling the material as if it still contained her sister's scent. "She was always tellin' me green was the color of hope."

"It is," he agreed. "You have so many pieces of her still, not just that bit of cloth." William tapped his heart with two fingers.

Stella curled back into the bed, falling asleep with the green cotton between her palms.

74

They would have to bury her in a cemetery for the enslaved. As Louisiana had not yet made Ammanee free, the quiet resting place of St. Anthony of Padua's was forbidden to her.

The women of Rampart Street collected whatever money they could spare for a modest funeral.

"Let me offer something to help," Lily had said. But Stella refused more of her charity. "Thank you, but we take care of our own down here. But I would like to ask you for one thing," she said.

"Yes, anything. Without you and William I would never have Jacob back. I'm forever in your debt."

"Could you go to the store and buy me some thread?"

Stella knew that it was an odd request, but that was all she needed to prepare for Ammanee's departure. When Lily returned with a basket of colorful threads, Stella accepted the gift graciously, although she chose not to explain what it was for and Lily was sensitive enough not to ask.

"We hope you will still consider coming with us," Lily said as she stepped over to her carriage.

Again, Stella chose not to commit to anything. The grief was still fresh and raw.

But as Lily's carriage drew away, Stella felt a new strength come over her. She heard Ammanee's laugh, and saw her flash of bright white smile. Stella drew it into her like a breath.

She went into the bedroom where Wade was sleeping tightly and opened the top drawer of the pine chest, retrieving her needle cushion and a pair of shears. Stella placed them in her sewing basket with the new spools of thread and then bent down to the last drawer, where she took out the multi-hued squares of cloth from her cherished coverlet and its larger canvas backing.

Over the next few hours, she worked quietly and diligently, restitching the pieces of fabric back together and restoring the quilt as it once was—except for one missing piece. She cut off a square from the bottom of the dark blue skirt she was wearing and replaced it where the one from Ammanee's deep green apron would have gone. That small piece of her sister, she would keep for herself.

Ammanee was buried the following afternoon, in a simple pine box that Benjamin and some of the other men on the plantation made themselves. As William played a soft melody on his flute, Stella held her mother's hand, steadying her as Ammanee's shrouded body was lowered into the ground.

Only those who loved her most knew that inside the casket, Ammanee was wrapped in the quilt made by the women of Rampart Street. A final embrace that transcended words. A coverlet that now had a piece of Stella and her heart stitched into it.

75

As much as she tried to persuade Janie to go North, her mother would not relent. "My life's here," she protested. "What's an old woman like me gonna do in a strange big city?"

"You still have plenty of living to do. And I'll worry about you, Mama."

"You got a baby now, and a man who loves you. You got a lot of livin' to do on your own," she said. "I'll take some of your furniture though." She forced a laugh after so much crying. "At least I'd get something good from that bastard Frye." Her pink-rimmed eyes brightened when Stella handed her Wade. "Benjamin promised he'll look out for me. Says I'm gonna be his mama now that he be freed soon." She gripped Stella's hand. "Don't you worry, my baby girl. I'm gonna manage just fine. Like I always have."

"I scared to go someplace new. Never known any other life but here," Stella confided.

"Can't tell you it's gonna be easy. Can't tell you it's gonna turn out just the way you planned it. But at least it's the start of somethin' new, chile. And that's more than most of us ever get. A new beginning."

William brought Stella's furniture and all their pots and pans over to Janie, who had gone with so little for so long.

"Thank you," she cried as she embraced Stella, William and Wade one last time.

The next morning, their satchels filled with spare clothes and some provisions for Wade, but otherwise carrying almost nothing but a square of green fabric and a silver flute, they arrived outside the waiting room of the steamship company.

Over Wade's fussing, Stella could barely hear the words that now escaped Lily's lips. Yet she found herself full of hope. She saw William and Jacob embrace as friends. And she felt the warmth of Lily's hand.

★ ★ ★ ★ ★

AUTHORS' NOTE

The idea behind *The Thread Collectors* has been in our hearts for many years, but in the early summer of 2020, as the world wrestled with growing awareness of racialized violence and inequality, we decided to harness our creative energy to find beauty in that darkness. The novel is loosely inspired by our own backgrounds and is born from our decades-long friendship as a Black woman and Jewish woman, each proud of their heritage. We wanted to explore the Civil War experience through two underrepresented lenses and illuminate the important and often overlooked tragedies of this era. But we also wanted to show how ingenuity and creativity can bridge cultural divides and create power for the seemingly powerless.

Approximately 2.75 million soldiers fought in the American Civil War, and the devastation and heartache that it brought in its wake altered the country forever. The death toll would exceed over 618,000, making it the deadliest war in American history.

The first seeds of inspiration were planted in 2012 by Ric Burns's riveting documentary *Death and the Civil War*, which focused on much of the historical research of Drew Gilpin Faust's nonfiction book *The Republic of Suffering: Death and the American Civil War*. After seeing that film, we were both struck by the revelation that Civil War soldiers sometimes made maps to mark the burial sites of their compatriots. We were also tremendously affected by the footage of the Black soldiers who had enlisted to fight against slavery, but found themselves digging ditches to bury the fallen White soldiers.

Impressively, 180,000 Black men enlisted to fight in the Civil War. This number represents close to 10% of the Union Army. Just enlisting required great hardship and risk for Black men. We realized we could write an impactful novel about a Black soldier who creates a map during one of our nation's darkest times and the relationships that it leads him to. Placing William in the battle of Port Hudson was critical, for it gave us the opportunity to highlight this important historical milestone. Many people believe that the 54th Massachusetts Volunteer Regiment was the first military unit of Black troops to fight valiantly in the Civil War, as it was famously played out in the movie *Glory*, but in fact, the Louisiana Native Guard fought at Port Hudson—and were massacred—weeks earlier. The Louisiana Native Guard included Black line officers (such as Captain André Cailloux, who appears in our novel), even after General Nathaniel P. Banks, Commander of the Department of the Gulf, began a systematic campaign to purge all the Black line officers from Union regiments. Reflecting the diversity and complexity of being "colored" in Louisiana at the time, in the Louisiana Native Guard, free men of color fought alongside fugitive enslaved men who had turned to the Union Army for a chance at dignity and freedom.

At the time of the Civil War, the Jewish population in the US was only .05%, and their experience was unique for many reasons. While there is not yet an exact accounting of how many Jewish soldiers fought in the Civil War, it has been approximated by scholars to have been close to 8,000 men. Many of these soldiers were immigrants who fled religious persecution from Germany and Hungary, only to find themselves confronted by antisemitism, distrust and language barriers in the US.

While fascinated by these pieces of history, we both knew that to create something truly special, we also needed to turn to our own family trees. Alyson grew up hearing from her grandmother about two great-great-great-uncles who fought on opposing sides of the Civil War. Jacob Kling, who fought on the Union side, enlisted in the 31st Regiment of New York as a musician. In stark contrast, his older brother, who years earlier had moved to the South and founded a mercantile emporium, enlisted in the 29th Regiment of Mississippi. During the war, with its close proximity to the Vicksburg battle, General Grant's army actually took possession of the family residence in Satartia, Mississippi (the Kling house is presently preserved as a historic homestead). As a child, Alyson heard countless stories from her grandmother about how the brothers' philosophical and moral divide irrevocably split the family up forever.

Shaunna wanted to examine the diverging fates of African Americans within a single family. The character of Stella is partially inspired by her great-great-great-aunt Janie, a Black woman who managed to become a financially independent landowner while her relatives struggled to find economic stability. Her father's side of the family ultimately came to own a sugarcane farm carved out of a plantation. She and her siblings own that farm to this day. Through the characters of

Stella (who is of White and Black parentage) and her half sister, Ammanee, Shaunna wanted to delve into how skin color and, in the case of William, musical talent afforded opportunities to some that would remain wholly unavailable to others.

We could not have written this book without the assistance of so many incredible individuals who shared their knowledge and expertise with us. A special thank you to Professor Barbara Fields for sharing historical resources, Michael Pinsker, Ranger Marvin at Port Hudson, Heather Green at The Historic New Orleans Collection, Eliza Kolander and Adrienne Rusher at the Shappell Manuscript Foundation for their knowledge and recommended reading for us to learn more about the Jewish experience in the Civil War, and for the medical guidance of Karen Scott. Kitty Green and Seretha Tuttle for sharing Gullah history and their culture with us, as well as Dr. Kara Olidge, Executive Director of Amistad Research Center, Phillip Cuningham, Head of Research Services of Amistad Research Center, Debra Mayfield, for advice on antebellum history and Dr. Stella Pinkney Jones, Stella Jones Gallery, for knowledge on African American handicraft and culture.

We are grateful to our early readers, Denver Edwards, Charlotte Gordon, Stephen Gordon, Jardine Libaire, Lynda Loigman, M.J. Rose, Robbin Siegal, Michelle Sowa, Allison Von Vange, and the attention to detail and fact-checking done by our copy editor, Gina Macedo. A special and heartfelt thank you to our agent, Sally Wofford-Girand, whose early belief in this book and tenacity to support our desire to create something powerful and with artistic integrity has meant the world to us. And finally, we so appreciate Melanie Fried, our editor who sought to ensure our book read with intention, clarity, and energy and saw an early vision for a book from just a few sample pages, and the entire team at Graydon House, including our publicists, Leah Morse and Justine Sha, and marketing manager, Pamela Osti, for their enthusiasm and support.

THE
THREAD
COLLECTORS

SHAUNNA J. EDWARDS
&
ALYSON RICHMAN

Reader's Guide

GRAYDON
HOUSE

1. We typically think of sewing as an activity that repairs damaged cloth or, in the case of embroidery, beautifies it. What does sewing mean for Stella? How is it different for Lily?

2. The authors have capitalized both Black and White in the novel. Did you notice this? Did you ever ponder why White is not traditionally capitalized, but Black is? How has this change affected how you perceive descriptions of race in the written word?

3. William's musical skills allow him more freedom than other enslaved men, which eventually leads to his relationship with Stella and his escape. However, his uniqueness does not shield him from the horrors that befall the Black soldiers at Port Hudson. For members of marginalized groups, what impact does individual talent have (or not have) in improving one's circumstances?

4. Jacob and William find themselves forging a strong friendship against the backdrop of war, despite coming from completely different backgrounds. What do you think

draws them together? How does music and outsidership play into this novel? Is there an unusual friendship that you have forged?

5. What surprised you the most in *The Thread Collectors*? Were you aware of some of the historical events that take place? For example, the Louisiana Guards' participation in the Battle of Port Hudson or the burning of the Colored Orphan Asylum in New York City?

6. At Port Hudson, the Black soldiers sing "Amazing Grace," a hymn originally written by John Newton, an 18th-century slave trader. While he underwent a spiritual conversion, he continued in the slave trade for some time. Can you separate the present beauty of art from the past sins of the artist? Can you think of modern examples of this dilemma?

7. The sisterhood between Stella and Ammanee plays an important role in the novel. How does the unequal nature of the sisters' circumstances affect their relationship? How does the relationship change over the course of the story?

8. Tilly, Janie and Stella all make sacrifices in the name of motherhood. Were you surprised by any of their choices?

9. Love is communicated in many ways in this novel—humming by Tilly, sewing by Stella, quilting and writing by Lily. Are some ways more effective than others? How do you communicate love?